Dottie
Hope

"Story"

The Devil On Chardonnay

Ed Baldwin

Ed Baldwin

ALSO BY ED BALDWIN

Bookman

Boyd Chailland series

The Other Pilot

CHARACTERS

JACQUES – Viral researcher
HENRI – Banker and Jacques' lover

CAPT. BOYD CHAILLAND – Air Force pilot
EIGHT BALL – Boyd's dog
MAJOR GENERAL BOB FERGUSON – Director, Counter Proliferation Task Force
ANGELA KELLY – Air Force nurse

RAYBON CLIVE—Pilot, Mombasa Marine Tours
DAVANN GOODMAN – Co-pilot, Mombasa Marine Tours
MARIAM AJAK – Davann Goodman's fiancé
OYAY AJAK – Mariam's uncle

COL. JOE SMITH – Army pathologist
MOSBY, aka LYMON BYXBE – Owner of BioVet Tech
PAMELA PRESCOTT – FBI agent, lawyer
MACDONNALD WILDE – Paroled felon
KHALID – Businessman in Qatar
COOPER JORDAN – President, Planters National Bank

MICHELLE MEILLAND – European merchant banker
WOLF GOEBEL – Michelle Meilland's bodyguard
CHARLES MEILLAND – Michelle's grandfather, owner of *Chardonnay*
NEVILLE ST. JAMES – Captain of *Chardonnay*
CANDIDO MENDES – Azorean sailor on *Chardonnay*
CONSTATINE COELHO – Azorean smuggler and pirate
COL FERREIRA – Portuguese Chief of Security at Lajes Field
CAPT ANGEJA – Portuguese search and rescue pilot

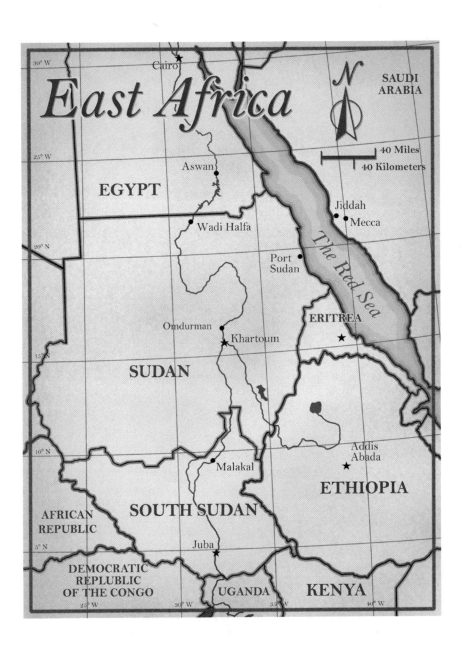

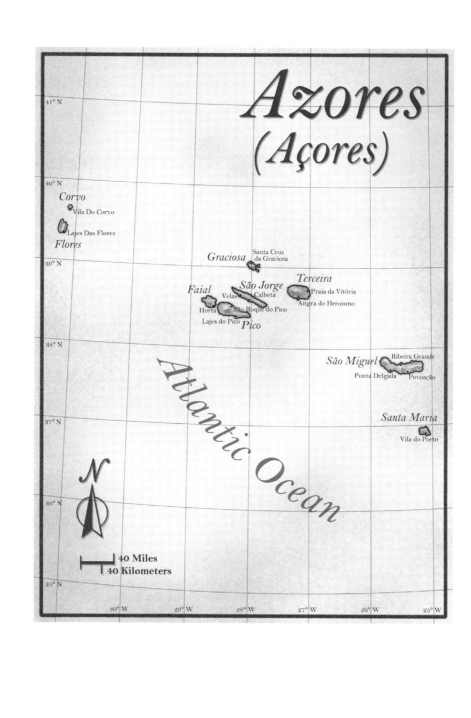

CHAPTER ONE
DEMOCRATIC REPUBLIC OF THE CONGO

Blood was everywhere. It oozed from cuts and dripped from noses, and even fell like tears from saddened eyes. The shiny black skin of these farmers, recently prosperous and now mostly dead, was blazoned with blotches and tiny red spots.

Fifteen years of working with laboratory animals at the Pasteur Institute in Paris had not prepared Jacques for the emotional impact of applying a tourniquet to the arm of a pregnant woman as she begged for water, drawing tube after tube of blood until the vein collapsed and then moving on to the next hut, leaving her to die.

Sweat ran down his sides and he fought for breath through the filter of the biological-hazard suit he wore. He'd worn these suits before, but it had never felt this close. He carefully put the filled vacuum tubes into compartments in a Styrofoam container, making sure no blood touched the outside of the tubes. He would be the one who would handle them later, without the suit.

"Jacques! Allons!"

Jacques turned toward the muffled call. Willi, his assistant, stood with his bloody hands held out awkwardly at his sides, his half-filled box at his feet.

"Non!" Jacques yelled through the suit. He pointed at the box and then the next hut.

Willi stood for a moment, then pulled the box into the dark interior of a plywood shack.

Waiting in the hotel in Kinshasa, Democratic Republic of the Congo, for nearly two years had not been easy. Jacques had recruited Willi more for companionship than technical help. The big German's easy smile and long-winded stories in the bar had helped pass the time as the streets were taken over by roaming bandits periodically making travel outside the hotel unsafe. The hotel housed a pleasant enough international community of mining and oil-field engineers, diamond buyers, embassy personnel, aid workers and advisers.

Ironically, it was one of the country's incessant civil wars that allowed Jacques to finally beat the World Health Organization to an outbreak of a rare filovirus. Rwandan soldiers had again entered the republic from the east, this time to challenge the Democratic Forces for the Liberation of Rwanda (FDLR), a Hutu army bent on repeating the Rwandan massacre of the Tutsi, and had gotten into it with the Congolese Army; a three-way fight that lit up the eastern third of the country. Chaos reigned, and most of the international organizations stopped all travel to wait it out. Rumor on the streets in Kinshasa told of an outbreak of hemorrhagic fever on the Lulua River downstream from Kananga in the Kasai Occidental district, midway between the capital and combat in the east. Jacques and Willi chartered a plane and flew to Kananga.

"Batarde!" Willi yelled as he crashed backwards through the wall of a hut, pulled by a naked man with blood streaming from his mouth and nose clinging to his waist. Willi beat at the man's head and arms until his hold loosened and he fell away.

"Okay," Jacques said, shaking his head and motioning for Willi to follow him. He carried his second box toward a waiting pickup.

Willi quickly followed and, now a paragon of efficiency, loaded all the boxes into the bed of the battered Toyota.

A wedding feast had brought Ebola out of the forest. Not content with chicken or pig, the villagers had wanted something special: monkey. The hunters shot a big male, and the skinning and gutting had been a communal affair. The illness spread so quickly that the first villagers to die were left unburied, rotting in the sun.

Jacques' truck bounced along a rutted trail through the jungle for a mile before breaking out into a clearing where loggers had cut gigantic, centuries-old iroko trees for export as African teak. Other trees had been cut up for charcoal, leaving an atrium in the forest.

Hauling the teak out of the jungle to the sawmill at Kananga required the loggers to build a better road than the rutted one Jacques had just driven, so the going from here back to a waiting plane would be easier.

Jacques and Willi jumped out of the truck and retrieved their boxes, loading them into a crate taken from the back of a Land Rover parked next to one of the huge stumps. Stepping away, they opened their biohazard suits, being careful not to touch the outside surface with their exposed limbs.

"My suit tore when I fell through that building," Willi said in French, holding up his left arm while standing in the legs of the suit.

"The skin is not broken," Jacques said reassuringly as he looked at the bare arm. He stepped out of his suit and tossed it into the back of the Toyota.

"That was horrible back there," Willi said as he pulled his left leg out of the suit and bent over to remove the right leg. "Why would anyone want the Ebola virus? It is the devil himself."

Jacques quickly pulled a small automatic pistol from the pocket of his bush pants and brought it close to Willi's head. The slight crack of the report was scarcely noticeable in the vastness of the forest.

Willi crumpled to the ground, blood flowing from a small hole behind his ear.

Jacques grabbed Willi's shoulders and dragged him to the side of the Toyota, propping him against the rear wheel. He crouched behind the truck and pointed the pistol at the gas tank beneath it. He fired one shot, then stood and sealed the crate holding the vials of blood and dragged it to the Rover. With some difficulty, he loaded it into the back. He started the Rover and left it running with the front door open while he rummaged around in a satchel in the back seat and pulled out a hand grenade. He walked casually back to the Toyota, tossing the grenade from hand to hand like a juggler.

Using a handkerchief to prevent his fingers from being soiled, Jacques opened Willi's mouth and inserted the grenade. Blood was still trickling from the bullet hole in the dying man's head, running in dark rivulets down his neck to soak into his shirt, wet from shoulder to waist.

"Goodbye, Willi," Jacques said and sat back on his heels for a moment, looking into the lifeless eyes staring out of half-open lids. He fought back the tightness in his throat. Then he pulled the pin on the grenade and sprang up, covering the hundred feet to the Rover with the speed of a track star.

When the grenade exploded, obliterating Willi's head and igniting the gasoline vapor, Jacques' Rover was fishtailing down the logging road headed for Kananga.

It wasn't the 50,000 Euros, Willi's share of the payment for Ebola, it was his unreliability that caused Jacques to decide to eliminate him. The episode in the village was just the beginning. The hard part of the bargain lay ahead. The deal was to capture Ebola, replicate and purify it, and leave no trail.

CHAPTER TWO
POINSETT BOMBING RANGE

The flash was obscured by the roof of the Chevy van, and smoke flew out of both windows.

"Shack," the range officer said immediately.

Boyd Chailland looked back over his left shoulder to see his practice bomb hit and grunted against five G's as his F-16 Falcon pulled out of its dive. He snapped a left turn and throttled back, level at 2,000 feet.

"Anyone want to press?" he asked over the radio.

As usual there was a dollar riding on each event in the dive bombing mission: low level, high level, and pops. One bomb per pass, two passes per event, three events: three bucks. Like dollar Nassau in golf. A press means double or nothing on the last hole, or in this case, bomb.

"Negative," his wingman said, followed by two clicks of static as the other two pilots keyed their microphones but said nothing.

Leading a four-ship flight on the Poinsett Range near Sumter in South Carolina, Boyd flicked the second turn in the square they flew around the impact zone and saw the new lieutenant miss his first pop by a hundred yards. After the third turn, Boyd pushed the throttle forward into afterburner and pulled back on the stick, feeling the G's pushing him into the seat as the Falcon shot upward. He glanced into the impact area and located the target; the flat black van was still smoking from his last direct hit. Still headed west, he glanced at the altimeter and at 5,000 feet squared the wings east and west and pulled the nose over, pointing now to the south and the target.

"Biker 1 in hot," he said over the radio, announcing his intention to the range officer to drop a bomb on this pass. Upside down and craning his neck backward, Boyd again located the van. He pulled the nose beyond horizontal into a 60 degree dive at the edge of the trees a half-mile north of the truck and rotated his Falcon so that he was upright as he began his dive.

Now looking through his heads-up display, he could see the van, an attitude indicator superimposed on the crosshairs of the targeting device, and a "pipper" indicating the spot where the computer had calculated the bomb would land if it were dropped now. Moving his aircraft, he brought the "pipper" below and slightly to the right of the van, now growing in the viewfinder, and used the attitude indicator to make sure his wings were square to the target so when he pulled out he'd go up and not sideways. When he was 500 feet above the drop point, he moved the aircraft so the "pipper' was on the van. He could see the holes from previous hits.

Practice bombs, about the size of a man's arm and made of cast iron, weigh about 25 pounds. They contain a detonator and a small amount of black powder produce a flash and some smoke when they hit so the range officer can score the drop.

At 1,500 feet, Boyd pressed the green button on the stick in his right hand and pulled the nose up. He grunted as he strained against the G-force and rotated the wings counterclockwise so he could look over his shoulder and see his bomb hit.

"Shack," the range officer said again.

With four shacks out of six drops, Boyd had won this wager going away. He pulled back on the throttle to slow down as he headed east and watched his wingman at the top of his pop maneuver. The wingman corrected a shallow dive as he descended, dropped his bomb and pulled up.

"Twenty-four," the range officer called out a moment later.

Boyd looked up and behind his wingman to see the lieutenant at the top of his pop maneuver, struggling to get his aircraft pointed south while bringing his nose through horizontal to a dive. He was halfway to the drop altitude before he thought to bring his wings around so he could pull out after he dropped. He dropped below the thousand-foot minimum altitude, and the bomb disappeared into the trees, 200 yards from the impact zone.

"Foul!" The range officer said ominously.

Boyd made a mental note to take the kid out in the D model the next week and teach him to drop bombs before he hurt someone. The poor performance of the new pilot had taken some of the fun out of the mission. He was already thinking of a way to skip out after the debrief so he wouldn't have to listen to the kid make excuses for missing the whole damn drop zone with his final bomb.

It had been fun rat-racing single file down the Wateree River to the Congaree River just above the treetops, zipping across Lake Marion and east to the Santee River and then out over the Atlantic. They'd entered the Military Operations Area and gone supersonic just for grins before climbing to 30,000 feet and doing rejoins and formation flying. Boyd would rather have done air combat maneuvers, but the two new pilots needed some basic work before going up against a captain with 2,000 hours flying, including six years in the F-16. After expending most of their fuel and with their 12 minutes of range time only 20 minutes away, Boyd had waggled his wings to signal "rejoin." He headed west, throttling back to save fuel.

It was time to head home, debrief and hit the club on a Friday night. In his younger days that would have been the highlight of the week; drinking and raising hell with the other fighter jocks. Now, that wasn't enough. Boyd wanted something else to happen later, something dark. Something he didn't understand.

"Biker 1 to Shaw approach control," Boyd said, initiating the sequence to get his formation permission to land at Shaw Air Force Base, just 10 miles away between Sumter and Columbia, South Carolina. He felt more excitement now than he had during the dive bombing. He was sure now he would slip away from the festivities at the club.

For the past couple of months, he'd thrown himself into running and working out, with free-weight sessions lasting an hour most nights. He'd concentrated on a rotation of presses and curls, exhausting each muscle group to avoid looking into places within himself that he didn't like to see. It wasn't just the woman in Colorado. He missed her, but he missed something else more.

Landing within a minute of the estimated landing time filed in his mission plan, Boyd turned off the firing mechanism beneath his ejection seat and opened the canopy as he turned off the runway. Steering with his feet he placed both elbows on the sides of the aircraft and pulled into the slot indicated by the ground crew, who would inspect the aircraft for damage and armed bombs that hadn't dropped. They put chocks under the wheels and a safety tag on the 20 mm cannon. He opened his visor and dropped one side of his oxygen mask as he looked over at the three other aircraft pulling into position beside him.

The shimmering heat of a South Carolina July afternoon added to the heat from the four jet engines, and the feeling of sweat evaporating from his damp flight suit reminded Boyd he must be thirsty. He pulled his water flask out of the G-suit pocket on his left calf and had a long drink.

The cool water reminded him of a warm night in Texas the summer before. He remembered drinking out of a gallon jug like a parched desert traveler and looking into the laughing green eyes of a pretty girl with long hair. Under the endless, starry Texas sky, they'd planned the adventure that changed their lives. After water had slaked his body's thirst, the inner man had demanded beer, and they had finished a six-pack of ice cold, silvery cans.

Boyd wondered whether a couple of longnecks would bring back that feeling.

"No," he said aloud and sighed. Longnecks would not bring back that feeling. He turned to look down at the other aircraft, watching to see that the tires were properly chocked and that the crews were looking for damage, making sure the guns were safe and hitting each checkpoint. He looked back over his shoulder to see whether the next flight was on time and ready to assume the positions his flight occupied.

****

"Shit hot, Boyd. Shit hot." The squadron commander slapped Boyd on the shoulder as he stepped behind the bar in the pilot's lounge in their squadron building to grab a cold beer, the day's bomb scores in hand.

Boyd smiled, tipped his beer bottle and took a sip. He turned in the swivel seat at the end of the bar and scanned the room, watching the dozen guys excitedly reliving their day. He tried to look like he was caught up in the camaraderie. As soon as others began to head over to the Officer's Lounge at the all-ranks club, Boyd left.

CHAPTER THREE
BONE'S CLUB

Bone's Club was back in the bottomland, 200 yards from the gravel road and two miles from the highway bridge crossing the Great Pee Dee River. Spanish moss hung from a live oak whose branches shaded the parking lot from the sun during the day and a lone mercury vapor light at night. Behind the club, the Great Pee Dee slid past silent and dark. Cypress trees marched out from the shore, thinning as the river grew deeper.

Moths circled the light and spiraled down to the gravel to recover and try again. The club was made of concrete blocks with tiny windows up high; an ancient window air conditioner rattled against the heat and humidity. The door was open. The rich baritone voice of an old country and Western favorite spilled out into the night.

Boyd cut the engine of his pickup, newer but otherwise identical to the half-dozen others already in the lot. He wore running shoes, jeans and a black T-shirt. As he crossed the gravel to the door, he felt alive and engaged. The feeling wasn't there yet, but it was close.

Standing in the door, eyes adjusting to the light, he saw the room as the people in the room saw him. Tall, broad-shouldered and lean, he'd been there before, just looking, scouting it out. It was perfect. He crossed the room, passing the pool table where the big guy, Crank, stood with a cue, poised for a shot but staring at Boyd.

"Bud longneck," Boyd said as he sat at the bar and turned to see Crank take his shot. Bone opened the bottle and set it on the counter. His dress shirt seemed out of place with the clientele and with his own greasy black hair and long sideburns. The khaki work pants were clean, pressed and held up by a tooled black leather belt. He wore Wellington boots. He took Boyd's money and returned with change from the mechanical cash register with the ornate metalwork of a bygone day.

Crank was clearly proud of his break. He looked at Boyd and smirked, then walked around the table for his next shot, stretching the front of his huge bib overalls with his considerable girth. Like statues, the others sat, leaned or stood, watching Boyd. The next shot went in, and Crank flashed Boyd a grin, his teeth were punctuated by bits of tobacco from the wad of chew under his lower lip. He spit into a coffee can under the table and took a third shot; stretching the length of the table, he revealed a thinning, dirty-blond crown. Boyd took a long sip of beer and turned to make small talk with Bone.

When he felt the brush from behind, he knew it was time. Boyd stiffened and saw Bone move away. This was a club for regulars. Strangers were an event, and the highway being two miles away wasn't an accident. Boyd understood Bone's formal attire now. It was sort of official, like a referee. It was designed to keep things from getting out of hand. Someone could get killed.

"Oh. Sorry," Bobby said, acting surprised.

They weren't going to start with the big guy. Bobby was a bit under six feet and chunky. Of the six guys there, he looked to be the fourth-toughest. They were going to give someone else a chance to kick some ass before the big guy stepped in to finish it.

Boyd stood. They all stood. He stepped away from the bar, not wanting to get pinned there. Crank grinned, obviously feeling as good as Boyd felt.

Bobby telegraphed the punch a millennium before he threw it. First, he squeezed up his face in a grimace, then shifted his weight to his right foot and feinted with his left hand while drawing back his right. When he shifted to the left foot the punch came straight in. Boyd's head retreated ahead of it, allowing it to just graze his jaw. He took two steps back to be in the center of the room.

Bobby was right with him, off-balance but coming with the right again, thinking Boyd was in full retreat. Boyd slipped to his right, and the punch bounced off the side of his head. The left was right behind it and hit Boyd square on the forehead.

Something clicked. The feeling was there. With the punch, the adrenaline kicked in at last. The rush was better than a climax. Bobby's momentum carried him into Boyd and he grabbed for a bear hug. Boyd pushed him back and, when Bobby flailed a windmill right, Boyd flicked a left jab into his fat, wild-eyed face. The solid contact with bone felt wonderful. The right cross smashed Bobby's cheekbone and he went down on his butt, dazed.

"Pickin' on Bobby!" someone shouted.

The next two came at once. He slipped a right under another windmill punch and dropped the smaller one, but the other landed a solid punch that spun Boyd's head around and staggered him back. He grabbed the guy by the shirt and pulled him close, enduring some body punches and savoring the free-flowing high. Pushing forward to the center of the room, he trapped the man's hands between their bodies and pounded his face with a half-dozen fast jabs from close range, turning it into a pulpy mess. He dropped him and stood alone. Crank still had the pool cue as he strode across the space between them, tobacco-stained teeth bared in a gleeful, childlike grin.

****

The pressure on his chest was not painful, just there. Then there was the beep-beep of a Road Runner cartoon, punctuated by whistles and insane laughter, followed by a wet kiss, sloppy, all over his face, and warm. It smelled like bacon.

The headache came when he opened his eyes. Sitting on his chest were two children. The 3-year-old, nude, flicked the channel changer between two cartoons while his 2-year-old brother, in a wet diaper, ate a piece of bacon and wrestled for control of the changer. The dog, a hound mix, licked Boyd's face while Boyd lay on a black Naugahyde couch beneath the front picture window of a 14-foot-wide mobile home. Seeing his pants on the floor by the television, Boyd raised up to see blood on his boxer shorts, his only remaining garment.

"Oh. You're alive," a female voice came from behind him. He turned to see a woman in a faded cotton night-gown frying bacon in the kitchen. She was in her mid-to-late 20s, and her breasts jiggled freely as she scraped the frying pan to remove the bacon. Her long hair, shoulder length the night before, was tied in a simple knot behind her head. He remembered her as the waitress at the bar at the hotel in Sumter. He'd pulled those pink panties down sometime in a vague, misty past.

"When did I … uh," he said, thickly. His mouth tasted worse than the dog's.

"Oh, you showed up about 12. You came in here with a busted lip and a powerful need." She laughed and shook her head, breaking an egg into the bacon grease.

She looked fresh and happy. Obviously not affected by whatever had made Boyd so ill, she moved quickly and efficiently around the kitchen.

"Did we, uh …"

"We sure did, baby," she said with a smile, turning to face him. "You were great, till you got into that moonshine jar Billy Ray left over there. You better stick to fightin' and lovin' and leave the drinkin' to Billy Ray."

"Who's Billy Ray?"

"My husband. Ex-husband, really. The divorce is final sometime next month. He lives with his mother. You like your eggs runny?"

An officer and a gentleman, he thought, as he surveyed the scene he had created. An open door across the living room showed a king-size bed with rumpled sheets. His jaw was simply sore, but his right hand was swollen and purple behind the little finger. The nude boy walked down the hall to the bedrooms in the back. The other one dug into a plate of grits and sugar with a side of bacon his mother had just placed on the floor in front of him. The dog looked alert for an opening on the bacon.

"This is Billy Ray's weekend with the kids. I need to take them over to his mother's before 9. Then we can get back to business."

"Why 9?" he asked, just to say something. He didn't feel like what she was planning.

"That's when he usually comes to get 'em. Last thing I need is to have you and Billy Ray trying to see who can throw who out that picture window first."

She laughed again and looked at him, shaking her head in disbelief. "Don't know why I always get the ones with demons."

A South Carolina Saturday morning, he thought, looking for his socks, feeling miserable and ashamed.

CHAPTER FOUR
THE MISSION

"Chailland! Wing Commander wants you in his office right now," the squadron operations officer said, hanging up the desk phone in the office he shared with Boyd. Boyd was just coming out of the men's room where he'd been running cold water on his hand, hoping to minimize the swelling.

"What'd I do now?" Boyd asked, trying to sound cheerful, but feeling no pleasure in the nagging worry that Crank might still be comatose.

When Boyd walked into the wing commander's office, the secretary smiled and motioned him toward the open door. He crossed the expanse of carpet smartly and was about to snap to attention and report when the brigadier general stood and spoke first.

"Come in, Boyd. Have a seat." He motioned toward a chair to the side and sat back in his chair, looking across the shining, nearly empty desktop.

Boyd took the seat and looked down at the general's desk to see his own personnel file there, open to his photo. The general, taller than Boyd but much thinner, was dressed in a flight suit, the stars on his shoulders clearly setting him apart from the average jock. He was relaxed, calm, almost mellow. He looked back down at the record he'd been reading.

"I was awakened at 5 this morning by a call that a major general was inbound from Andrews and due to land at 0800. Not having heard about the visit beforehand, I assumed I was to be fired and replaced." He smiled and leaned back in his chair, enjoying his tale. "Then, about 7, he radioed the command post that his visit was classified and he wanted no DV greeting, just a crew bus to bring him here for a meeting with me at 8:30, and with you at 9." Brigadier General Charles "Dunk" Wells looked at Boyd, waiting for a response.

"General Ferguson?" Boyd asked, knowing it could be no one else.

"Old friends? From another base perhaps?" Wells wanted to know who this guy was.

"No, sir," Boyd said, straight-faced. He couldn't tell, and he didn't want to make his boss mad.

"Well, I thought this might be something interesting, so I had Ginny pull your personnel file. You are an extraordinary fellow. I hadn't heard that before. You have an Air Force Cross, awarded last year. The citation says it was for valor of the highest order during peacetime, and the aircraft and location are classified."

"Yes, sir."

"I've never seen that before. I've seen classified locations, never a classified aircraft. Your flight record shows only T-37, T-38 and F-16. Did you fly anything else?"

"Yes, sir." In his mind Boyd remembered the jolt and fire as the cannon shells hit the engine of the restored P-51 Mustang, and then the silence as he pushed the nose into a dive and, dead stick, began to gain on the attacker who'd assumed he was dead.

"I won't ask. It must be some story. Apparently they want you to do it again, whatever it was. The general is waiting in the office across the hall. He said he wanted a few minutes with you and then lunch. He's due to leave at 1400."

The feeling was back. Ferguson was an admirer, but no friend. Boyd had a deal with Ferguson: Keep his mouth shut about what he knew and what he'd done the summer before, in exchange for a full three-year tour flying Falcons at Shaw followed by an assignment to Fighter Weapons School as faculty. He didn't want or need anything funny with the promotions board, though they'd offered that. They had a fast track outlined that would have him with stars before he was 40, but Boyd had turned them down because it was mostly schools and Pentagon assignments. Boyd wanted to fly. He'd not expected to ever see Ferguson again.

"Yes, sir," Boyd said, standing, then smiled at the general and added, "As soon as they say it's OK, I'll be glad to tell you all about it." He knew they never would and that the details of one of the century's most unusual adventures would be known only to him and a few other participants. He also knew that day in Texas had spawned the demon that had made him go to Bone's Place.

He crossed the hall and opened the door.

"Boyd. Good to see you."

Ferguson, dressed in a flight suit with two stars on the epaulets, told the lie with a warm sincere smile. He rose from the couch in the vice commander's office and shook Boyd's hand. In his other hand was a manila envelope filled with papers. Boyd closed the door behind him, trying to hide the wince of pain from the general's firm grip on his recent boxer's fracture.

"You've probably figured out that I'm here to offer you a job. It's a temporary duty assignment, actually, for 180 days. Afterward, you'll come back here and finish out your tour as we agreed."

"I thought this secret, behind-closed-doors stuff was over," Boyd said, sitting without being asked.

"The government is being run in accordance with the Constitution, if that's what you're asking about. As far as this assignment is concerned, we need somebody who can think on his feet. Someone who can take care of himself, keep quiet, and – "

" – who doesn't have a family." Boyd finished the sentence, cutting off the general who seemed about to make a speech.

"Yeah. That's part of it, too. This is an uncertain world we live in."

"I'll take it." Boyd said, feeling alive at the prospect of action.

"I thought you would. Your orders are already here."

"What if I'd declined?"

Ferguson smiled knowingly and said, "Boyd, you're a shooter, a born shooter. You need to be out in front. Out where the action starts. We planners and schemers need guys like you when the balloon goes up."

"Is the balloon going up?"

"No. This is not a war. This is something else."

Ferguson moved behind the vice commander's desk and emptied the manila envelope, motioning for Boyd to follow and take the seat at the side. "I've got a new job. I'm the director of the Counter-Proliferation Task Force. We deal with weapons of mass destruction."

"Nukes?"

"Nukes, chemical, biological. Whenever one of the intelligence-gathering agencies comes across someone trying to buy, build or deploy such a weapon, they turn the case over to us. We've got the experts, and we're empowered to act, if necessary."

"Act?"

"It's a task force; elements of all the services, the complete range of capabilities, from intelligence-gathering to deployment to kinetic response."

"And I'm in the kinetic-response end of it?" Boyd asked, knowing it would be something else.

Ferguson chuckled. "Well, you sure brought the kinetic response last time, and at a time and a place nobody could have foreseen it would be needed. Like then, we don't know what we've got here, so we're going to put a shooter in charge from the get-go."

"Prudent."

"In January, the World Health Organization called us with the report of an outbreak of a rare disease that's so dangerous our bio-warfare people don't even like to talk about it," Ferguson said as he dumped the contents of the manila envelope onto the desk. He picked up several 8X10 glossy photographs. "This guy, in the top picture there, died of it in less than three days."

"Humph. I don't want to go there."

"No." Ferguson said, leaning over and pulling reading glasses out of his flight suit pocket. "Look at the next picture."

"Same guy, from a different angle," Boyd said, seeing a nude black man with blotches and spots all over him and blood dripping from his nose and mouth. Then he added, "Still dead."

"See that trickle of blood from his arm, the place where they take blood in a lab? Then, see the footprint there? Looks like a moon boot? The WHO guys said someone in protective gear left 20 people dead in this village in the Democratic Republic of the Congo after drawing a lot of blood. See these other pictures?"

Ferguson took the other photographs and spread them on the desk, pointing out more moon-boot prints and other bodies.

"So?" "Boyd asked, stumped as to why they would want him for something like this.

"No one needs that virus for worthy purposes. Having it is like having a dozen nuclear weapons. Our bio people tell us there's no way to even transport it safely, much less work with it in anything but the most sophisticated Level 4 containment lab. Someone is playing with Pandora's Box."

"Tell me where they are, and I'll drop a Mark 82 into their jock strap," Boyd said, leaning back, no longer looking at the gruesome pictures. He chuckled at the thought of a five hundred pound bomb in some guy's jockstrap.

Ferguson didn't laugh.

"Day before yesterday, someone sent a distress signal from a previously uninhabited island in the Seychelles. It said, 'We are dying of a filovirus infection. Quarantine this place. We have made a terrible mistake.' The Seychelles sent a patrol plane. Both of the buildings on the island were in flames, there were no signs of life."

Boyd looked darkly at Ferguson, beginning to see what his role might be.

"You'll be completely protected in a biohazard suit," the general said. "They say it's cumbersome, but not really uncomfortable. The rest of the team, for now, is an Army pathologist, one of the world's experts, but we don't know what he might find, or find and not recognize. We need somebody there who can, well, do something if it's needed."

"Why not send a Navy ship?"

"It's the middle of the Indian Ocean, and the ships we have there are busy chasing pirates off Somalia."

Boyd searched Ferguson's face intently. He was being strung along here.

Ferguson looked up and caught Boyd's gaze. "Uh, and they don't want that on one of their ships."

"Same with the Air Force I'll bet."

"Yes."

"So, two expendables go to this place and look around."

"Pretty much, yes. Gather some samples. Do autopsies if there are any bodies."

"That would be the Army guy's role."

"Yes."

"Then what?"

Ferguson paused, looked away, taking his time in answering. "We want you to go to Diego Garcia for a few weeks, uh ..."

Long pause.

"It's a ... a kind of a hospital."

"Quarantine?"

"Yes," Ferguson said quickly, seemingly relieved not to have had to say that.

"If the Navy doesn't want 'that' on one of their ships, and the Air Force doesn't want 'that' on one of their planes, how do I get from the middle of the Indian Ocean to Diego Garcia?"

"We're working on a contract flight."

"Yes, we seem to contract out the real shit jobs. Does the contractor know 'that' is going to be on his aircraft?"

"Ah, that would be your job, to explain all that, and to plan the mission."

Boyd laughed, his head dropped back and he looked up at the ceiling, shoulders shaking. He was oblivious to the stern look he was getting from Ferguson. The laugh went on for three or four breaths before he stopped, still smiling, and looked again at Ferguson.

"I'll bet I wasn't the first guy to get a chance to go on this adventure."

"It just came up yesterday. You're the first."

"OK. So, I go to the Seychelles, babysit an Army pathologist looking for bodies, pack 'em up in bags or something, then fly to Diego, hope I don't get sick, and then what?"

"Take what you find and figure out who's trying to do what. You'll be in charge of the team. Contact me for whatever you need, but operate independently."

"When do I leave?"

"Fourteen hundred. I'll fly you back to D.C. in my C-21. We have you on a flight to Mombasa in the morning."

"Oh, and what is this thing I'm looking for?"

"Ebola."

CHAPTER FIVE
PACKING UP

Eight Ball emerged from beneath the porch as Boyd pulled up in a cloud of dust and jumped out of the truck. The big black Lab's tail hit the wooden steps solidly three times as he stood expectantly, waiting for Boyd to offer his hand.

"Goin' on a trip, big guy. Clyde Carlisle is gonna drop by every couple days. He may move in next week if he can dump his lease. I told him about the covey we've been watching behind the bean field." Boyd talked as he would to a roommate. He knelt, rubbed the big Lab's ears. He was sure Eight Ball understood. Boyd climbed the steps and opened the rusted screen door, sorting the keys on his ring and finding the house key.

"You're gonna like Clyde," Boyd said, Eight Ball following as he rushed into the bedroom and pulled out his desert camo travel bag. "He's the guy we went fishing with over on Lake Marion. You saw a duck and jumped out. Nearly swamped us. Gonna have to learn not to do

The Devil On Chardonnay

that, or we won't get invited back." He packed quickly and light.

The landlord had apologized for the bare wooden floor of the old house and had offered to put down some tile or carpet if Boyd would pay another 10 bucks a month in rent. The gray, worn wood reminded Boyd of a little house from long ago, and he'd elected to buy some throw rugs.

A car drove up in front. Eight Ball ran to the door, tail wagging in anticipation of meeting yet another new friend. Clyde Carlisle, dressed in a flight suit with bronze oak leaves on the epaulets, bounded up the steps.

"Secret mission! Damn, Boyd, you get all the luck," Clyde said as Boyd opened the screen. He knelt and rubbed the dog's ears, then entered the house and began looking around. "This'll work great. I think I can get moved in right away."

"Let me show you where that covey is," Boyd said, packed already and dropping his bag at the door. He walked back into the kitchen and pointed out the window. "They're usually around that brush pile on the other side of those beans back there. Eight Ball knows how to find 'em. We've been keeping our distance. They've still got chicks now."

"I'll give 'em some space."

"Food's in there," Boyd said, pointing to the dog food in the pantry. They settled the rent and utilities in the time it took Boyd to walk through the front room and down the

40

steps with his bag. He paused at the truck to rub Eight Ball's ears again, waved at Clyde and left.

****

Boyd parked his truck in the lot across the street from the squadron building, lugged his bag through the double doors to the desk where the flights were posted and gave the keys to the airman behind the desk.

"Major Carlisle will come by sometime this afternoon to pick up the truck. My locker key is on there, too. I'm leaving my helmet and G-suit. Keep those dirtbags out of there," he said with a nod toward his friends. Several of the other pilots had gathered, knowing he was leaving and curious about where to.

"Can't be much of a TDY if you won't need your gear," said the lieutenant, who'd now have to learn the pop maneuver from someone else.

"We'll see," Boyd said, shaking hands all around and heading out the doors in the back leading to the flight line. He could see the general's C-21 parked out among the F-16s. He waved jauntily, entirely consistent with his mood as he carried his one bag out to the plane.

The unknown was a challenge he was willing to take. The last time he'd solved a mystery, it was out of honor to a fallen flier. He'd been unwilling to drop the trail until he knew where it led. Today, he was going to do it to feed something started then, something that was no longer satisfied with supersonic aircraft and practicing for war. There must be others like him, needing to be out on the edge of their own strength, stamina and guile. Most would draw their pay from terrorist, underworld or hostile government sources. This thought gave him a pleasant anticipatory buzz. When the ass kicking started, there'd be no reason to hold back.

CHAPTER SIX
MOMBASA, KENYA

"Shark! Big one! On the right side of the aircraft," Rabon Clive said over the intercom, trying to inject some excitement into his voice. There were always sharks circling along the outer reef of the Mombasa Marine Park, but today he had half a dozen actual customers paying to see them.

Four middle-age German tourists and an old English couple rushed to the right side of the ancient Grumman Albatross.

"We'll circle, get a better look." He pulled the yoke back and the plane rose quickly, throwing his passengers back toward their seats. They grabbed any available hand hold as the Albatross banked a full circle. "Out the left this time." He swooped down along the waves, deliberately hitting a couple to send spray back along the side of the aircraft.

The hour tour up, Raybon pulled the Albatross's nose up and lumbered south toward the harbor at Mombasa, Kenya. "Mombasa Marine Tours" was painted in big red letters on the side of the old aircraft. Several customers lined up at the lavatory door, airsick from circling over the shark. Rabun took that as a sign they'd gotten their money's worth. He turned up Tudor Creek and flew by the center of Kenya's seaport city to the marina beyond and landed on the bay, then moored the seaplane in the harbor and took a launch back to the yacht club dock. He had a visitor. A young man dressed in khakis was leaning against the locked door of his office above the yacht club. He looked like CIA.

Raybon helped his co-pilot out of the launch and handed him his cane while watching the man in the door watch him. He wanted nothing to do with the CIA. He got angry, angrier than usual, walking up the dock.

"The embassy said you were Air Force," the man said with a big smile, still leaning against the locked door as Raybon climbed the steps to his office. Several steps behind was his co-pilot, a black man laboriously climbing the steps by crouching on his left leg and swinging a rigid right hip to the next higher step then pushing himself upright with the cane.

"Retired." Raybon said, not smiling. He opened the door.

"Boyd Chailland, captain, U.S. Air Force." Boyd extended a hand and Raybon took it, searching Boyd's face for signs he was being set up for something.

"Raybon Clive, captain, U.S. Air Force, retired," he said, still standing at the door as his co-pilot caught up. "Davann Goodman, staff sergeant, United States Marine Corps, retired, my co-pilot." They shook hands and Davann flopped down on an old leather couch by the window and made a call on his cell phone.

"Interesting plane you've got there," Boyd said, standing at the still open door and looking down into the bay below. "Not many Albatrosses left in the world."

"Just a few dozen," Raybon said, closing the door behind Goodman. "And with good reason. Burns gas like a bitch."

"Well, I'd like to talk about some contract work," Boyd said, turning into the room and looking about.

"It ain't cheap," Raybon said. He'd dealt with the U.S. government before and didn't like the experience.

"Can we talk here?"

Raybon thought about the new telephone that had just been installed, and then remembered the tax collector dropping by for his monthly baksheesh the week before, and asking questions about rumors he'd heard that alcohol was being smuggled in Rabon's aircraft. The man knew very well Raybon smuggled alcohol, that was the whole reason to have the seaplane, and the whole reason the tax collector was there taking his monthly bribe. Something was up. Maybe it was just a way to ratchet up the bribe, maybe somebody else wanted in on the rum running racket, maybe. Kenya is a Muslim country, and Mombasa is a mostly Arab town. Muslims are touchy about alcohol, and Arabs live in a world of bribes, treachery and deception. Any trouble, and Raybon would be the first to feel it.

"Want a beer?" Without waiting for an answer, Raybon opened a refrigerator and got out three Tuskers, the local brew. He tossed one to Davann on the couch and walked out onto the deck overlooking the bay and leaned on his elbows looking down at the boats. "I'm not flying anybody into the upper Nile Valley," he said as Boyd closed the door behind him and stepped to the rail.

"OK," Boyd said, blandly.

"The new CIA station chief blew her cover two months ago, the first week she was in Nairobi. Everyone in Kenya knows who she is now, and she showed up here last month, in broad daylight wanting me to fly some 'operatives' into the upper Nile."

"Touchy business."

"Very. Davann and I are hangin' by a thread here. Anything the local boss doesn't like, and we'd be gone. They only tolerate us here to appear to have a tourist industry. Pretty place. Dangerous as hell."

"Like I said, I'm Air Force, not CIA."

"The Air Force has planes."

"Not like yours."

"What do you want?"

"It would take you away for a few weeks, maybe longer."

Raybon thought that over for awhile. He was sick of scraping by, living on the edge of the world, depending on a worn-out old airplane and a very tenuous smuggling business while watching Arabs plotting the second coming of the Caliphate, which would include Kenya, and not him.

"I'm still listening," he said.

"And, I need to leave the day after tomorrow."

****

The big chip on Raybon's shoulder began slowly to slip off with the lubrication of a couple more Tusker beers and Boyd's brief tale of having dropped practice bombs in South Carolina only two days before, and his nearly nonstop flight to Kenya via London's Heathrow. They were rejoined by Davann and walked downstairs to the bar at the Mombasa Yacht Club.

"I flew the 'handsome, high performance Lockheed C-130 Hercules,' " Raybon said proudly, reciting the pilots' somewhat lengthy description of their aircraft.

"Nearly as old as the Albatross," Boyd observed.

"Not really. The only thing that old is the original design. The last C-130 I flew was the H model. It was built in the late '90s."

"Special ops?"

"Yeah, MC-130 H, Combat Talon."

"Bet you've got some tales."

Davann broke a big smile as the waitress, an attractive young woman with shiny black skin, brought another tray of frosty mugs to the table.

Raybon nodded in the affirmative, took his beer and said nothing. The MC-130 is designed to insert, supply and extract special operations combat troops – black ops. He'd taken an oath to keep his tales to himself, and he was going to. He didn't need to beat his chest in front of this fighter jock. There was an awkward silence.

"So, how'd you wind up here, in Kenya?"

Another half pint of Tusker slid down Raybon's throat. After a moment, he belched and took another generous sip. Davann was whispering in the waitress's ear, and they both giggled at some private joke. Raybon leaned back in his chair and lifted his leg up to table level and pulled his pants leg up.

"No pilot seats for one legged pilots," he said, revealing an ornately carved wooden leg.

"Oh," Boyd said.

"Me and Davann, with our limited employment oppor-
tunities, bought that old Albatross a couple years ago from
an old Navy pilot who'd been running rum along the coast
for 20 years."

"So, now you fly tourists around."

"Not really, we're still runnin' rum," he said as he turned
toward Davann and they both laughed. "No money in tourists. Hell, hardly any tourists," they laughed again. Their
beers were gone.

"Davann, you learn to fly in the Marines?" Boyd asked.

"Naw," Davann responded, looking at Raybon. "My
mentor's sittin' right here."

"We both got shot at Camp Bastion in Helmand Prov-
ince, just up the mountain from Kandahar. I was flying a
resupply mission out of Qatar. It was a blizzard. Snow so
thick you couldn't see 10 feet. We were scheduled in with
some food and ammunition, and the C-130 can land anywhere, anytime, so we came in on instruments. Problem
was, it had snowed so much the usual security had broken
down, and a Taliban sapper team got through the wire and
was waiting at the end of the runway. They couldn't see us,
but they could hear us coming. As we passed, not 50 feet
over their heads, they let fly with RPGs, and one hit the nose
of the aircraft. It killed my co-pilot and took off my leg and
blew out the instrument panel. I pushed the nose down,

and we hit the runway hard, slid off and mired in the mud. The aircraft caught fire. The flight engineer pulled me out of the seat and down the stairs and threw me out into the snow. The Taliban followed the skid marks firing in our general direction as they came. The flight engineer and two loadmasters opened up with M-16s from the door of the aircraft to slow 'em down. I crawled away in the snow and tried to stop the blood spurting from my stump. I should have had a tourniquet, but didn't."

"I heard about that crash, not much detail in the news."

"They didn't want the Taliban to know how effective they'd been," Raybon said, starting in on another Tusker. "Just as I was about gone, 50-cal slugs started snapping over my head and a Humvee came plowing through the snow. There was Davann, standing in the back blazing away with the MA 2."

"Ma Deuce to the rescue," Davann said, holding up his beer and tapping mugs with Raybon. "Taliban hate that 50 cal."

"The bad guys dropped back, and Davann jumps down and runs over to me, puts his tourniquet on my leg, cinches it tight, and drags me back to the Humvee. Then the rag-heads shoot Davann in the butt."

"Blew my fuckin' ass off," Davann said, indignant.

"Even with his ass blown off, he pulled me into the back of the Humvee and got back on the 50 cal, standing on his good leg while the rest of the crew piled in and the driver hit the gas in reverse. Next thing I knew, me and Davann were in the back of a C-17 headed to Germany."

"That was three days," Davann interjected. "I don't remember nothin', either."

"Then it was surgery and then more surgery, and then another C-17 ride across the Atlantic. We asked them to keep us together, so we ended up at the National Naval Medical Center at Bethesda. I got a new state-of-the-art bionic leg, and Davann got a titanium ass."

"I got no ass. What I got is a titanium hip with a ceramic cup where the ass bone used to be," Davann said.

"That didn't look like a state of the art bionic leg to me," Boyd said, pointing at Raybon's leg.

"The wooden one is my party leg." They all laughed. "Anyway, we go through the whole rehab process, then the medical boards, and finally they cashier us out and there we are standing on the street, no job, no prospects, just the VA. So, I gave Davann the only thing I had to give the man who saved my life. I taught him to fly."

CHAPTER SEVEN
IS IT OUT NOW?

The door opened a crack and the light from the hall fell across the little girl, still asleep after three hours. He crept in and stood quietly, observing. Her respirations were fast, shallow. He put his hand gently on her forehead; burning with fever. He retreated and opened the door a bit for more light. Her left arm was thrown across her chest, and on the forearm was an irregular blotch that hadn't been there three hours before. He moved closer and took her wrist to find her pulse.

"No!" Her eyes popped open as soon as he touched her, and she withdrew the arm as if she'd been pinched.

Her eyes were bloodshot red; hemorrhagic, the worst he'd seen.

"No!" She screamed again, and retreated to the head of the bed, her eyes focused on something behind him, something he didn't see.

He reached out to calm her and touched her arm again.

"Aeeyii!" She screamed, louder and rolled to the side. As she did, her bowels released and she fouled the bed.

"Lien! It's me, Daddy." He smelled blood as he pulled the sheet back.

"Gurupph!" She vomited blood in a thick stream over the side of the bed.

He pulled her shoulder to bring her back into the center of the bed and she vomited again, straight up. His arm was covered in warm, hot, bright red blood.

"Lien!"

The child stiffened, her legs straightened out and her toes pointed. She turned her gaze upward and to the right and the rapid respirations stopped. Her arms stiffened and her fists clenched at her sides as she was wracked by a strong grand mal convulsion.

"No!" He awoke with a start and, still in the dream, tried to stand. He rolled off the pallet of medical equipment he'd been sleeping on and fell 5 feet into the web seating at the side of the aircraft. "No! Lien!" He rolled off the web seat onto the floor and struggled there to rise between the seat and the pallet. Consciousness returned and he stood, and then sat back on the seat.

Col. Joe Smith, director of Medical Product Development at the U.S. Army Medical Research Institute of Infectious Diseases (USAMRIID), shaking and drenched with sweat, looked around the cargo bay of the Air Force KC-135 aircraft to see whether any of the crew had seen his loss of control. The boom operator and loadmaster were asleep on web seats near the front of the aircraft, and nobody was visible up the steps to the cockpit. He stood and moved his torso gingerly. Nothing broken. Damned Ambien. He'd taken a 10 mg tablet and climbed to the top of the pallet to be near the heat vents at the top of the cargo bay as they'd crossed the Alps after stopping for gas at Ramstein, Germany. The old tankers are notoriously cold on long flights. The Ambien had worn off, and he'd had a rebound bad dream. It's in the product literature, he told himself.

The image of his 3-year-old daughter Lien returned. He knew she was safe back in Maryland with his wife and her big brother. He'd kissed her goodbye not 48 hours before, but the tightness in his chest remained.

He hadn't wanted to go on this mission, yet he'd been on Ebola's trail his whole career and was determined to find a way to stop it before he retired. He'd been a pathology resident at Walter Reed when an outbreak occurred in a Reston, Va., monkey lab. For a few weeks, they thought the mysterious scourge of the Congo basin might get out into the nation's capital, but it turned out to be a much less dangerous new strain, a mutation. The wild strain popped up in Kikwit, Zaire, in 1995, and he'd been sent there by the

Army as a hotshot young pathologist and viral researcher. He'd seen more than 50 cases of Ebola there. It was the wild strain from the jungle, and 92 percent fatal. It stopped only after it killed nearly everyone exposed to it.

Joe Smith made his way forward and got some coffee from the kitchenette beneath the cockpit. The plane, a modified Boeing 707, can carry 200,000 pounds of fuel, and/or six pallets of cargo. Built for long, grueling missions, it has a boom at the rear for delivering fuel to other aircraft in flight, two bunks in the cockpit, a flush toilet, and a kitchen comparable to that found on airliners. On either side of the cargo bay are 65 nylon web seats, folded up now, as Smith was the only passenger. He walked by his two pallets strapped to the floor of the cargo bay to the rear of the aircraft and climbed down into the boom operator's station where he could lie on his stomach and look straight down through the refueling station.

"It's down there," he said to himself, watching the dark jungle of the Congo basin slide slowly by, 35,000 feet below. He'd seen the western parts of it during several visits, but the northeastern corner, where South Sudan, the Central African Republic and the Democratic Republic of the Congo come together near the headwaters of the White Nile is the deepest, darkest, most inaccessible part of it, and the likely home base of the world's most dangerous virus. He ticked off the known outbreaks since Ebola was first described in 1976; Juba, Sudan, Yambuku, Congo, Nzara, Sudan, Gabon, Gulu, Uganda, Kikwit, Congo and several recent outbreaks in the Kasai Occidental District in the Congo. They all made a circle around that jungle down there.

It was a mystery. If Ebola killed people so fast that epidemics burned out before they could spread to the greater population, and if it did the same thing to the monkeys that infected the people, then where did the monkeys get it? A virus dies when its host dies. So where did this virus live between outbreaks? And how long has this game been going on? Just because medical science "discovers" a disease doesn't mean it's new. Has Ebola been living in that jungle down there for millennia, breaking out every few years to wipe out primates – monkeys and people – that get too close and then retreating back into some cave or animal reservoir? What's it protecting? What's it waiting for? Is it out now?

CHAPTER EIGHT
THE ISLAND

The corpse sat on the rocks, looking out to sea with vacant eye sockets. The gulls had eaten his eyes, lips and ears, leaving a skeletal, phantomlike grin. Bird droppings smattered on his blue shirt.

"Suppose that's the guy who radioed the alarm?" Boyd asked, his voice muffled by the protective suit. "Told the world to stay away and then came out here to see if anybody would come?"

Joe mumbled something Boyd couldn't hear as he bent over and cut the buttons off of the shirt with surgical scissors. He pulled open the shirt to expose the chest. Blood had run down from his face and dried in the blond chest hairs, protected from the gulls. There were dark blotches, two or three inches across, on his chest and abdomen.

"That's purpura," Joe said, straightening up and looking over at Boyd, balanced on an outcropping of black lava.

The surf was gently breaking a few yards out. Safely in the distance bobbed the Grumman Albatross, anchored in 100 feet of water off a charted but unnamed island in the Seychelles Islands in the Indian Ocean, 700 miles east of Mombasa.

"Did Ebola do that?"

"Yeah. It comes from a defect in coagulation in the small blood vessels," Joe replied. "It does a lot of other things, too. We'll do an autopsy. Let's carry him up by the house and look around first. We can post him after lunch."

Boyd chuckled at the morbid humor as they rolled the dead man onto a plastic tarp, rolled him up and carried him to the remains of a burned house 50 yards up the hill. They'd already decided their time on the island would be limited to how long they could go without food or water. Taking off the biohazard suits this close to an obvious Ebola outbreak would contaminate them. If that occurred, they had instructions from Joe's boss at USAM-RIID to camp out on the island for three weeks; the pallets they'd unloaded at Mombasa contained equipment and supplies for that.

The island was barely a hundred acres, devoid of all vegetation except for a few scraggly weeds. Formed by a volcanic eruption a century before, globs of puddinglike lava had flowed from a cone in the center of the island into the sea.

This was the last place Boyd wanted to camp out for three weeks. He was going to stay in that suit no matter what.

Dropping off the body, they crisscrossed the island like two bird dogs looking for a scent, alert for any sign of who'd been here and what they'd done.

Boyd climbed the volcanic cone, a pile of lava 60 feet high in the center of the island, and scanned for anything they'd missed. It was the loneliest place he'd ever been, nothing in sight in any direction, and it had taken them four hours of flying over empty ocean to get here. The breakers outlined an underwater lava presence much larger than the actual island, at least 2 miles in diameter. This was really a vent in the middle of a caldera, or crater, of a volcano rising a mile above the surrounding floor of the Indian Ocean. A fit place to tinker with a virus that could scrub the planet of human life, Boyd thought as he looked down into the hole in the cone. He couldn't see the bottom.

There were three buildings and a makeshift privy on the island. The main building, about the size of an average ranch house, was in the middle of the widest part of the island and protected from the prevailing winds by the cone. Behind it was a small generator house. On the other end of the island, exposed to the wind and just above high tide had been a small building of just a few hundred square feet. Like the main house, it was twisted rubble.

Approaching the main house, Boyd pulled back a panel of twisted metal roof, exposing the ash of the building's wooden structure and a few metal appliances. The first section was a kitchen with camp stove, chest-type freezer and small refrigerator. Plastic water pipe began as a melted blob a few feet away and snaked up the hill to a large plastic bladder filled with rainwater collected from plastic sheeting staked to the nearby hillside. The refrigerator held bottles of French and German wine and Dutch beer along with some badly spoiled sausage and German mustard. The freezer had ready-made frozen food, spoiled, but protected from the fire. The labels were all in French. Various pots and kitchen utensils were scattered about. Joe joined him and they pulled back another roofing panel.

At first Boyd thought the body was a piece of furniture, a pillow perhaps, black and red. Joe walked right to it and brushed off a light coating of ash.

"A male," Joe said, pointing to the crusted remains of genitalia.

The charred body lay stiffly on its back, stubs of arms and legs pointing in four directions. The pelvis was attached to an intact thorax by an intact spine. The intestines had boiled out of the abdominal cavity and lay, thoroughly cooked, to one side. The charred head had detached from the neck and lay with its chin up and its forehead next to the floor, staring back at the door with vacant sockets.

Boyd was grateful smell didn't penetrate into the suit, but he remembered enough about burned bodies from a plane crash the year before to become nauseous anyway. He walked through the laboratory, which was filled with microscopes, computers, centrifuges and incubators, one larger than the freezer in the kitchen. In one corner, the remains of two biohazard suits were piled, their bright silver external covers scorched but not melted.

"I'm going up here," Boyd said, gagging as he climbed over the next panel of roofing to get out of the building. Choking back his lunch, he headed back to a smaller building about 40 yards away. Approaching, Boyd thought it looked like the outhouse he and his father had used until he was 9, but when he got there he found a perfectly good 8,000 kilowatt gasoline generator housed in a wood frame building with cheap plastic siding and no roof.

"Odd," he said to himself, seeing that the siding covering the structure was untouched by the fire at the main house. Instead, the inside of the little building was scorched, though not enough to stop the generator from running until it had run out of fuel. He looked up at the nails that had held the slanted roof beam in place. They pointed skyward.

Ten yards behind the building lay the scorched, twisted metal roof. The wooden frame blown off with the metal roof was entirely burned away, even the ashes were scattered by the wind.

"Blew the roof off," Boyd said to himself, looking back at the little house. Boyd turned over the metal roof, hoping he wouldn't find another body. Instead, duct taped to the roof, he found a melted plastic device with solid state electronics – a cell phone. He cut the duct tape away and put the cell phone in a specimen bag and into a cargo pocket on his thigh. Returning to the generator house, he reconstructed in his mind that the cell phone had been taped behind the main roof beam at the lower back of the house, out of sight. It had triggered an explosive device, probably incendiary. Instead of setting the building on fire, as had probably happened in the other two buildings, the explosion was confined to a smaller space and had blown the roof off, leaving it to burn furiously a few feet away.

"Primate cages," Joe said solemnly as they stood looking at the remains of the third building.

Two dozen wire cages were scattered about under the metal roof. Five of them contained cooked monkeys. This building had been smaller and of lighter construction, so the fire hadn't been as hot. The monkeys presented a grotesque array of singed, charred and contorted creatures, confined to contemplate their fate as the building had burned.

Things must have heated up pretty quick, Boyd thought, as he easily found two of the cell phones concealed in the remnants of electrical junction boxes near the center of the building. Someone got double-crossed here.

"Look here! Incredible!" Joe said, beckoning toward a scorched bundle at the corner of the building. "Two monkeys out of a cage and wrapped in paper, probably died before the fire. I can't believe these guys were so careless. They violated every principle of maintaining laboratory animals. To just leave dead primates wrapped for disposal not 6 feet from the rest of the population is cruel, criminal and highly dangerous. Maybe they didn't know what they were dealing with," he added, shaking his head and stooping again to turn over one of the creatures and look into the bloated face of a dead monkey.

If there had been any doubt about why Joe was needed on this mission it was dispelled in the next half hour. He laid all the monkeys out in a row in front of the building, opened his equipment container and arranged syringes and specimen containers by each body. Then he went quickly down the line attaching a fresh 4-inch-long needle to each syringe and probing the chest of each monkey to draw blood directly from the heart. Ignoring Boyd, Joe next produced some large wide-mouth jars and filled them from a gallon jug of formalin, placing one at the head of each monkey. He plugged a small recorder into his biohazard suit and attached it to his chest, then approached the first monkey and opened his instruments. Grabbing a scalpel he made a sweeping circumferential cut around the forehead of the monkey, peeling the scalp back from the front. Next, he produced a battery-operated hand saw and sawed the top of the skull off in the same plane. When he reached in and cut the spinal cord with a scalpel and removed the brain with one hand, Boyd vomited into his suit.

"Monkey Number One is a pigtailed Macaque that appears to have died of natural causes before the fire. The brain shows numerous petechial hemorrhages over the cortex. Upon slicing ..." Joe continued dictating as he worked. Using a cutting board and large knife, he sliced the brain like a loaf of bread. Seeing something that interested him, he cut a small square out with the knife and dropped it into the formalin. Still retching, Boyd retreated to the generator house to look for more clues.

Savoring the sheer misery of living with vomit inside his helmet, Boyd coughed and spit to try to clear the air passage and get his lunch to drop down inside the suit itself. He walked around aimlessly, unable to concentrate, until finally it dried and he could breathe again. While wandering around, Boyd encountered a marshy area where water had accumulated in a depression in the lava. It was only a few inches deep and was mostly filled with green slime and a few scraggly cattails clinging to life at the edges. He took a picture.

Boyd returned to the monkey house to find Joe tidying up. He packed the seven specimen jars and the vials of blood into a box and closed the lid, securing it with a seal. He produced a gallon of diesel fuel from his equipment box and dowsed the dissected remains, now piled unceremoniously in a heap. The flames shot 10 feet into the air, and black smoke billowed.

"Now for our fellow scientists," Joe said, dragging his equipment back toward the main house. Boyd rushed over to help. Soon the labeled jars were at the head of each man and the recorder was turned on. Blood was drawn in the same fashion as with the monkeys, and Boyd was astonished to see fresh appearing liquid blood flow into the syringe from the charred corpse.

"The first human is thoroughly charred, the skull is separated from the spine and the extremities are mere stubs ..." Boyd circled the autopsy site, eyes on the Albatross, bobbing in the waves, wishing he were there.

"Need you to take some pictures here," Joe said. "I've got stuff all over my hands. Get the back of this guy's head."

With that, Joe picked up the skull that had separated from the charred body. The back of the skull was open and the inside was empty. Joe held it with one hand and pointed with the other. Retching quietly, Boyd took the pictures, and then walked away, hoping for some fresh air.

When Boyd heard the electric saw start up again he retreated to the ocean and the rocky outcropping where the first man had communed with the gulls for a week before they'd found him.

Sitting on the rock, looking out over the Indian Ocean, Boyd thought about the blond man. When he came here to sit, he must have known he was dying. The buildings were probably burning, meaning his partner, companion, co-worker, friend, whoever, was already dead. He may have been angry that their mission, whatever it was, had turned out so badly. Did they fail? Had there been someone else here?

"Nobody would die that way," Boyd said, standing, looking around his feet at the rocks. No rational man would just sit there and look out at the sea and die. He'd have something to say to someone. He'd write a letter or note.

"Hey, Boyd!"

Boyd stood and looked up to see Joe waving.

"Got something here. Need you to have a look." Joe was pointing down at the bodies.

Reluctantly, Boyd returned. The charred body's chest had been opened with the saw and the heart and lungs were remarkably fresh appearing.

"Get the camera. This guy's been shot," Joe said, pointing to the heart, which had a small hole in one side. "I think the bullet is still in there." He knelt back down and was kneading the heart with both hands. "Can't feel well enough with these damn gloves. Need a picture of the hole there, and there's another one in the spine."

Busy with the camera, Boyd's nausea passed. He didn't even mind when Joe cut the lungs from the trachea and lifted them out. He took additional photos with Joe passing a metal probe through the hole in the heart back to the two holes in the back.

"One gunshot enters the pleural cavity through the body of T-5, passes beneath the tracheal bifurcation and penetrates the descending aorta and the left ventricle. The bullet is within the cavity of the ventricle. The other entrance wound is through the sixth rib, 3 centimeters left of the body of T-6, and passes through the left lung. The exit is not in the chest wall; presumably it exited through the abdominal wall, which is burned away. The pleural space has an estimated 1000 ml of blood."

Joe droned on about bone fragments and missing tissue while Boyd kept right up with the camera as the autopsy proceeded into the abdominal cavity.

"I gotta pee," Joe said, standing right in the middle of removing a kidney.

"Let it fly," Boyd said, laughing.

"You gone yet?" Joe asked suspiciously, as if Boyd would spread the tale if he did and Boyd didn't.

"It just feels warm for awhile. Hell, I've had a face mask full of vomit for an hour. Wet pants are nothing compared to that."

Joe stretched, took a couple steps toward the Albatross and stood looking at it for a minute, then returned to work, shaking his head.

Soon the organs were sliced, pieces put into the jar and the rest returned to the body cavity. Boyd held open the body bag and Joe lifted the body into it, then poured a gallon of formalin over it and zipped it up.

Unwrapping the other man, the one from the rocks by the sea, Joe rolled him on his back and went through his pockets.

"Uh oh," He said, his hand deep in the man's right front pocket. He pulled out a .32-caliber automatic pistol. "Looks like there may have been some friction here on the island."

"Murder weapon?"

"Probably so. That looked like a .32-cal bullet I got out of the heart," Joe said, looking at the pistol. "Walked up behind his buddy and shot him in the back."

Joe cleared a bullet from the chamber of the pistol and dropped the pistol and the bullet into a plastic bag and dropped that into a cargo pocket on his leg. He leaned back to the man and checked his other pockets, retrieving a wallet and some keys, which he bagged. He began dictating again.

"The second man is a blond Caucasian of medium build approximately 35 years old ..." He ran his scissors up the legs of the man's trousers to the waist and pulled them away. "Ah, what's this," he said, turning off the recorder. He pulled a small notebook out of the red bikini briefs the man wore.

"I knew it!" Boyd exclaimed triumphantly. "He had to leave a note. That's going to tell us what happened here."

He reached down and retrieved the notebook and opened it excitedly.

"Shit. It's in French."

CHAPTER NINE
LAST WILL AND TESTAMENT

Henri,

I am dying. The irony is that I've accomplished one of the most complete technical achievements in history, and through the perfidy of my employer, am reduced to recording it in a simple laboratory notebook in pencil, just like Pasteur before me. All the rest of the documentation has been destroyed by the fire. Greed blinded me to the risk, and when I was out maneuvered by this virus, there was no way to escape. Cooperate with the authorities. Mosby must be stopped. Give them this letter. You've broken no laws and are entitled to the money. Enjoy it and remember our dreams.

My last thought will be of you.

Jacques

To the World:

Mosby is a middle-age American, slender and bald, who said he was trying to produce a vaccine for Ebola. I don't know why. He paid me to wait in the Congo for two years for an outbreak of Ebola. When I found it, I collected it and brought it here. I isolated the virus in monkey tissue culture and reproduced a small quantity of live, freeze-dried virus. I gave that to him in February. I produced more, and separated pure RNA from the protein coat. I prepared a vaccine by splicing a segment of the RNA he had identified with a plasmid he provided.

The project to test immune response to the vaccine is what has gone wrong. We vaccinated 10 Macaques and then exposed them to Ebola. Several got sick, and one died. We brought in 10 more and vaccinated them, and some of them got sick when we exposed them, but none died. When we brought in the third group, monkeys started getting sick before we vaccinated or exposed any of them. One of the previous monkeys must have had a subclinical infection. All the fresh monkeys got sick and eight of them died. Then Franz and I got sick. The vaccinated monkeys are all still alive.

If evil can be personified in a submicroscopic particle, Ebola is it. It is primitive and constantly mutating. I saw it become dormant to await a fresh group of monkeys, and then jump from Macaques to humans before the illness was recognized. Mosby spent $2 million to secretly acquire viable virus, purified RNA, and a vaccine. He knows exactly what he has.

CHAPTER TEN
THE ALBATROSS

Raybon Clive dove nude into the Indian Ocean and savored the cool water on a warm day. He let the dive take him deep, then kicked to return to the surface with a surge of power using his specially adapted flipper prosthesis and a dive flipper on his good leg. He broke the surface like a swordfish and splashed on his side. He'd been a competitive swimmer in college and mentioned that to the VA therapist during his rehab. They'd made him a special flipper attachment for his prosthetic leg. Now he turned on the speed, freestyle, and swam the length of the Albatross, turned and swam back with the backstroke, then butterfly, then breast stroke.

Watching from the cargo door, Davann held their "shark gun," a bolt action .30-caliber rifle with a 7-power scope loaded with hollow-point, 180-grain bullets. Their AR-15 assault rifle would throw out lead faster, but it was high velocity and only .223-caliber. The shark gun's bullet would explode on impact, blowing a volleyball sized hole in the fin of shark. That would teach even the largest great white a lesson.

Raybon swam in leisurely circles admiring the Albatross, now owned by the United States of America for the second time.

"A toast! To the United States Air Force," he'd proposed two nights before at the Yacht Club, standing and holding up one of the three shots of bourbon he'd ordered. They'd been drinking beer throughout the early evening as Boyd explained his mission and what their part would be. Boyd had been honest about the danger. Raybon didn't care, and he knew Davann didn't care, and he knew Davann wouldn't let an Air Force toast stand without toasting the Marine Corps, and then Raybon was going to toast the Army, then the Navy and then the Coast Guard. He was eager to be a part of the action again, but first he was going to negotiate the terms.

CHAPTER ELEVEN
FORT BELVOIR, VIRGINIA

"Let's just go right to the data," General Ferguson said, impatient as ever. Joe Smith set up his laptop on the conference table and hooked it into the flat screen TV in a crowded office conference room of the US Strategic Command's Center for Combating Weapons of Mass Destruction at Fort Belvoir in suburban Virginia, less than 20 miles from the Pentagon. A handful of other officers found seats. Boyd and Joe had driven down from Fort Detrick, Maryland, where they had debriefed with USAMRIID and spent their first weekend back from Diego Garcia, rested and apparently free from any contagion.

"They were here," Boyd said, pointing as a map of the Indian Ocean came up on the screen. He described the buildings and the island.

"How long do you think they were there on the island?" Ferguson asked.

"Four months."

"Based on what data do you make that assumption?"

"The amount of shit in the privy, sir," Boyd responded with a straight face.

A wave of suppressed laughter crossed the room. Ferguson smiled faintly, and then cut it off. "Colonel Smith, what do you have?"

"There were two men on the island, and seven monkeys, all dead." With that, Joe opened the first picture of the charred skull with Joe's finger pointing out the gaping defect where the steam from the boiling brain had blown out the back of the head. The ghastly picture filled the 60-inch flat-screen on the wall.

"The crispy critter was gravely ill with Ebola but died of two gunshot wounds to the back," as he showed the open chest with the bullet hole in the heart.

Ferguson sat up a little straighter, as if he hadn't expected such a graphic report.

"The purpura is clearly seen here on the liver," Joe went on. "And spleen," and changed again. "This electron photomicrograph shows filovirus in liver tissue taken at autopsy. Cultures of blood were positive, and radioimmunoassay showed an immune response to filovirus." He closed the file and opened another. After years of lecturing to medical students, using material much duller than this, Joe was a master at arranging slides to document and highlight his monotone lectures.

"The bullets were .32-caliber, and the ballistics matched perfectly the French MAB .32-caliber automatic found in the pants of the second subject." He showed a picture of Jacques and the automatic beside his right front pants pocket.

"Judging from the angle of the entry and exit wounds, the assailant stood behind the victim while he was seated and fired two shots, the same number missing from the magazine. Death was within two minutes, though incapacitation would have been immediate. The fire came later."

"Was there any sign that anyone else was on the island, either then or before?" asked one of the officers at the other end of the conference table.

"No sign of anyone else. Two plates, two cups, two sleeping bags. Of course, there could have been someone else at some time in the past. The buildings were over a year old," Boyd answered.

"The other individual provided us with the interesting narrative you have read," Joe returned to the slides. The picture showed Jacques, now nude, supine on the ground, his long skinned penis draped across his lower abdomen and pointing to a small tattoo of a leopard on his hip. The laboratory notebook was just beyond, open to the handwritten notes. Joe went on to show the internal organs and describe the positive cultures and immune response to

Ebola. He ended the section with the brain, exposed by the electric saw and exhibiting "typical petechial and subependymal hemorrhages."

When the bloated monkey, chest and brain exposed, appeared, Ferguson excused himself and went to the bathroom down the hall. Boyd and Joe exchanged smiles.

A strong friendship had begun when they took off their biohazard suits and stood there in urine soaked undershorts, feeling dirty and exhausted. Boyd stripped off nude and walked to the edge of the rocks and jumped into the ocean. Joe followed, and when Raybon got there with the Zodiac, they were splashing about like kids. They'd landed with half a ton of equipment, and were leaving nude with two body bags and a sealed box no bigger than a briefcase. The rest burned brightly on the island. Raybon and Davann, napping all day, now preflighted the Albatross, and they were off on a seven-hour flight to Diego Garcia and three weeks of drinking beer and fishing while checking each day for a rash to develop; a rash that would signal the end of their days.

Feguson returned. "So, what made that man's face so grotesque?" he asked, as if he'd not been puking in the bathroom for 10 minutes. The monkey picture was still on the screen.

"Gulls, sir."

"What?"

"Seagulls, sir. They pecked his eyes out. Ate his lips, sir. He was sitting there on the beach for nearly a week," Boyd responded, respectfully but fighting to maintain a straight face.

Joe said, blandly, "The clinical information is pretty standard from here on, sir. We can skip the next six monkeys and go right to the equipment, if you like."

"Ah, good idea. Yes. Can't get bogged down here. Press on."

"This is a tissue incubator," Joe said, closing the monkey file and opening another, the first picture of which showed a burned stainless steel cabinet that looked like a small refrigerator. "They used it to grow Ebola in a cell culture, probably monkey kidney, as that's common and they had a full supply of monkeys." He changed to a picture of charred plastic and metal box, about 3 feet square.

"This isolation chamber is really too small for their purposes, but they apparently used it to make inoculations and to work with cultures. They isolated the virus in this centrifuge."

Joe changed slides rapidly now.

"And freeze dried it in this. This is an ultracentrifuge, which will separate RNA from the protein cover of the viral cell."

"Wait, why would they do that?" Ferguson asked, recovered from the monkey pictures and back to his job as a general officer, stopping the show and asking questions.

Joe frowned, stopped changing pictures, and looked at Ferguson. "That's what's bothering me. What did Mosby want with RNA? I can think of a couple of harebrained ways he might use it for a vaccine. I get sweaty when I think about some of the other things he might do with it."

"Like what?"

"He could start cutting it up into segments and trying to splice them into something else to see what each segment does. He might have the idea that some feature of Ebola, if separated from the rest of it, might be worth something. Very, very dangerous thing to do. Especially if he isn't any better at it than these two clowns were at what they did. He could end up putting Ebola's worst trait into some common virus, like herpes, and letting it get out."

"Herpes?" Ferguson asked, quizzical look on his face.

"In addition to a cold sore, you'd get purpura and hemorrhages like we saw on Jacques there," Joe responded, pointing to the flat-screen.

Ferguson frowned, then added, "OK, go on. What next?"

"This next slide shows the back of the centrifuge where the manufacturer puts a plate telling which model it is and where it was made. You can see there, it's been ground off. Everything was like that. They knew going in they were going to leave the equipment, and they didn't want it traced."

"How much is all that worth?"

"Two hundred thousand dollars, maybe a little less. Some of it was old."

"Not state of the art?"

"No, but adequate." He paused, waiting for more questions. "OK, that's what I have. Boyd, you're up."

He closed his files and opened Boyd's.

Boyd went through a brief summary of the interesting volcanic birth of the island only a hundred years before and showed some slides of the cone and the lava flow to the sea. Then the generator house came up.

"See those nails bent up. A slow explosive, like gunpowder or dynamite, would have built up pressure slower and blown the building apart. Plastique is hot and fast. It acts as an incendiary when it's not contained, and a very fast explosive when it is." He flicked through the sequence of the roof, summarizing a week's work with some army bomb experts while on Diego. "The detonator was an electronic blasting cap, initiated by a satellite phone. Someone simply called a number and blew the place up. That had been built into it from the beginning, and Jacques and Franz probably didn't know it. Jacques shot Franz to stop him from sending the distress signal and then had a change of heart and radioed the warning about Ebola. Someone in Victoria heard it and made the call to blow everything up. By then, Jacques was outside. Seeing the place go up, he retrieved the notebook and wrote the note, then went down to the beach to die. At least, that's what I think happened."

Boyd stopped, waiting for comment.

"So, we have someone who knows viruses, vaccines, RNA, and explosives, and isn't afraid to kill a few people to get what he wants. Now he has it," Ferguson said. "What will he do with it?"

"Actually, we know more than that," Joe replied, no dry humor, and he had those wrinkles that Boyd had first noticed on Diego when they'd talked about Ebola. "He's well financed. He knows the world community of infectious-disease experts well enough to recruit a journeyman researcher like Jacques. He's been patient, waiting two years for Ebola to surface again in the Congo. What worries me the most is the effort he's made to keep the secret. If his researcher hadn't panicked and broadcast the news to the entire world, Jacques and Franz would still be dead on that island, but nobody would know it except him. He could burn the buildings and the next storm would wash or blow everything away."

"A vaccine for Ebola would be worth a lot," an officer interjected.

"Yes, millions," Joe responded. "If you were a research company trying to turn a buck on a vaccine, your profit would come when you announced your discovery and sold your idea to a large pharmaceutical company to bring to market. Or, you could sell stock at this point. Secrecy only helps if others are on the same trail. But nobody wants anything to do with Ebola, so this guy is on the trail alone, yet secrecy is still his top priority."

"So, he's not going to sell a vaccine," the officer responded.

"Not to the general public. Someone else wants it, and is paying for it. That brings us to the dark side of the business we're all in: biologic warfare. Virtually every dictator taken down in the Arab Spring uprisings had a biological ace up his sleeve. Saddam Hussein used it against the Kurds between Operation Desert Storm and Operation Iraqi Freedom, and it eroded his prestige in the world so he didn't use it again. Mubarak had some that he didn't use. Khadafy had some that he didn't use. Assad had some that he didn't use. Using a biological weapon destroys whatever reputation a government has, so it's pretty much a last-ditch option, and not a good one."

"Are we jumping to a conclusion that this vaccine is to be used in biological warfare?" Ferguson asked.

"That's the only use for a secret vaccine that I can think of. With something as dangerous as Ebola, you wouldn't need a sophisticated delivery system to spread it, so it could look accidental. If it looks accidental, the strongest disincentive to using a biological weapon is taken away. The second disincentive to using bioweapons is that your own people can get the illness, which is removed if you have a vaccine. If it's a secret vaccine, now you could quell an uprising or occupy territory and it just looks like your soldiers are foolhardy, fastidious hand-washers going into a natural outbreak of a dangerous disease."

"And your reputation remains intact," the officer in the back finished the sentence.

"Exactly. And if the world finally figures out you have the vaccine, you can claim you cooked it up in response to the natural outbreak and retain your reputation – enhance it, actually, as you'd have an ace nobody else had. A secret vaccine to Ebola would be better than a nuclear arsenal."

"If it worked," Ferguson said darkly.

"It worked on some of the monkeys, but not all, so he's not done yet," Joe said. "And that's really the big danger here. He has more work to do, and he's playing with something that's been hiding in that Congo jungle for a long time. There is a lot about Ebola we don't know. Jacques' note stated the virus went dormant after the first two groups of monkeys. That's a pretty big assumption from the data he had but, if he's right, Ebola is more dangerous than we ever thought. We need to heed Jacques' warning."

"Back to clients, for a moment," the officer in the back interjected. "We ought to keep that open, list as many possibilities as we can. If we assume it's a government and it isn't, we might miss the chance to find him."

"Good point," Ferguson said, turning to look back at the rest of the room.

"One thing that came up while we were in quarantine in Diego," Boyd said. "Raybon Clive and Davann Goodman, the two disabled veterans we contracted to fly us in and out of the island, have been in Mombasa for a couple of years. They said the jihadists are thick there, and they all see themselves as holy warriors bent on returning the whole planet to righteous rule under the Prophet's law. Imagine what a boost it would give them if they were immune to Ebola and the infidel was not."

Ferguson shook his head and sighed.

"What about an attempt at worldwide extortion, a doomsday weapon so terrible it will bring the world to its knees unless we send someone all the gold in Fort Knox. That's the plot in most of the James Bond movies."

"That makes a better plot for a movie than it does in real life," Joe said. "How would you spend the money? You'd have to have some way to hide and then spend a huge amount of cash. Money laundering is a clandestine, intricate business.

"Still, we'll put that on the list." Joe said, writing on a legal pad.

They added some more possibilities over the next 10 minutes, and then Ferguson rose to close it out.

"Governments, terrorists, criminals. It looks like anyone would like to get their hands on some Ebola vaccine, so we'll have our work cut out for us. Homeland Security has alerted the air-freight companies and the post office to watch for anything that looks like a biological specimen. The CDC is going to start spot checking all the companies licensed to do any kind of biological work, but that's a slow process with no guarantee of success. Boyd, go over to the Secret Service office and get your Special Agent status reactivated, then go to France and talk to Jacques' boyfriend, Henri. The embassy has already contacted him and told him his buddy is dead and that we want to talk in more detail before releasing the body. He should cooperate."

Joe said, "The notebook is gas sterilized. It's harmless now. The body will be transported back to France in a sealed casket when you give the word." He opened his briefcase and tossed the bloodstained notebook onto the table.

CHAPTER TWELVE
PARIS

"Jacques spoke English. I didn't say he preferred it," Henri said impatiently.

Things had started amicably enough. Henri spoke perfect English, so Boyd had arrived alone, dropped off by the military attaché from the embassy. Henri had welcomed him into the small apartment with stiff formality. Henri was bulky but moved with the grace of an athlete. He was dressed in tight jeans and a black turtleneck shirt that seemed to accentuate the spread of his midsection. Boyd apologized for the delay in returning Jacques' body and assured him that precautions were necessary as the disease Jacques was working with was so dangerous. Henri knew that already. Boyd had then asked why Jacques had written the note in French – a major blunder, as the French are very proud of their language.

"I'm sorry," Boyd responded to Henri's flash of anger. "I'm working on this case and I'm not really a trained interviewer. I'll just give you the notebook so you can read the message and then you tell me what you think I need to know."

Boyd opened his briefcase and handed the notebook to Henri.

Wiping his eyes as he read, Henri was absorbed for several minutes as he read and re-read the note. Then he put the notebook on the table between them and walked to a window looking out on a tree-shaded street in front of his home and stood there.

Boyd tried to imagine Jacques, as he was before the gulls got to his eyes and lips, here with Henri. How did that tattoo of the leopard fit into this overstuffed apartment with the modern art on the walls and the soft, muscular man sobbing at the window? Did Henri know Jacques had murdered two assistants –Willi in the village where he first captured Ebola, and Franz on the island? Was Jacques' relationship with Henri spousal, business or revolutionary? It seemed spousal and, probably, business. Boyd was leaving the third possibility open until he heard more from Henri.

Giving Henri some space, Boyd excused himself and went into the bathroom. Taking his time washing his hands he looked into the mirror and began to think about his own life. Certainly, there was nothing there to hold up as an example to young lovers. There was a woman in Colorado whom he'd asked to share his life. It never occurred to him that she might ask him to give up flying. She wouldn't even consider leaving her tenured faculty position to take something in South Carolina so he could go back on active duty and have a better chance at getting into the next war in the first wave. When they recognized that neither would give up the one thing the other required, their interest waned. They still rang each other's bells, but it was no longer music. He hadn't even called to let her know when he'd left Shaw for Africa.

"I have some pictures," Henri said as Boyd re-entered the room. "The letters he wrote from Africa, some things we bought together, like that painting over there. And this," and he laid the notebook back on the table between them. His eyes were red but dry.

"So, he'd been gone for a while?"

"Two years. He was a researcher at the Pasteur Institute. Jacques was working on a vaccine for some disease in swine and was invited to present part of his work at an Institute symposium on new vaccines. He's not a full scientist, he never completed his thesis, but he was very good and always worked with the top scientists. At the end of the day, an American approached him and complimented him on his work. Jacques thought he was going to make a pass and was about to brush him off when he asked if Jacques would consider a job offer."

"Mosby?"

"Yes. The man, Mosby, said Jacques would have to move to Africa for a year, maybe more. When Jacques expressed interest, Mosby made him pledge secrecy until they could meet again."

"And, did they?"

"No. Mosby called the next day and offered Jacques three times his salary at the Institute plus expenses and a bonus if he was successful."

"Never met him again?"

"Never. The money was wired into our account at the bank every month. While Jacques was in Africa, he lived entirely off his expense account. He came home for a few days every two months."

"What was the job? Did Jacques know what he would be doing?"

"Oh, yes. It was clear from the beginning what he'd be doing. He was to move to Kinshasa and wait for an outbreak of Ebola. If he got there before the authorities and was able to get some blood without being detected, or traced, he would get a bonus of 500,000 Euros."

"What's that in dollars?"

"Six hundred forty six thousand at today's exchange rate," Henri said without hesitation.

"That was fast."

"Sir, I'm a banker," Henri said with a modest shrug.

"Did Mosby pay up?"

"Yes he did. Then he offered another 500,000 if Jacques could isolate the virus from the blood. He had Jacques travel to Victoria, Seychelles, from Kinshasa. From there a mysterious charter boat captain met him in the hotel bar, mentioned Mosby's name and the next day he sailed out to the island. Everything was already there."

"There was another man on the island," Boyd said, pausing to try to be as tactful as possible.

"Franz."

"Yes."

"His assistant, a friend from the Institute. Jacques hired him to speed up the work."

"And one in Kinshasa."

"Willi. They were lovers," Henri said darkly.

"Did you ever go out there, to the Seychelles?"

"Yes. Jacques isolated the virus quickly, in a few weeks. Then he separated RNA and freeze dried both. Then he had to infect monkeys with it and bring slides of monkey tissue along to prove it was Ebola. A boat picked him up and took him back to Victoria. Mosby called him at the hotel and told him to wait a month, so I came out."

"Why wait a month?"

"To see if he got sick. Jacques thought Mosby was staying nearby, watching. Mosby was very careful and very patient. He called the hotel every two weeks. Coffee?"

"Yes, thanks," Boyd said, contemplating that Henri was involved in this from the beginning. "Then what?"

"Mosby wanted Jacques to take some of the RNA, cut it up and splice part of it into something else and try it as a vaccine. He offered a million Euros for that. That was much harder to do, so Jacques hired Franz to go out there and help him."

"That's when trouble started?"

"Yes, he was there for a few months and then I got a call from your embassy that he'd been killed."

"Did he get the first two bonuses, a million Euros?"

"Yes. It came by electronic transfer just like the monthly expense money."

"Any way to know where it came from?"

A grin crossed Henri's face as he poured boiling water into a shiny glass vacuum-filter coffeemaker.

"I was wondering when we'd get to that. The money came through Citicorp in New York City. I talk to someone there every day in my job at the bank. My contact there knew where it was coming from. I just casually asked one day and he told me. The money originated from the Planters National Bank in Charleston, South Carolina."

CHAPTER THIRTEEN
PAMELA PRESCOTT

"Boyd, we've got an FBI agent on the way down. She just called from the airport. Could you guys clean up just a bit and, check in the bathroom, she might need to, ah, whatever." Ferguson rushed into the office from the Pentagon, speaking as he tossed his briefcase onto his desk.

"Right, boss," one of the officers said as they began stuffing donut bags and pizza boxes into the wastebaskets in the meeting room.

"She has a law degree, and the Director's office said she was the best they have at finding money that people want to hide," Ferguson said, picking up coffee cups and taking them to the sink in the corner. Boyd had never seen him do that.

The front door opened and they hurried as conversation indicated a visitor at the reception desk.

"Miss Prescott," the receptionist opened the door.

All eyes were on the door. All activity stopped.

"Smells like a fraternity house." Pamela Prescott stood there smiling. Her brown hair was braided into a business-like bun and she wore an expensively tailored business suit. She carried a small, discrete briefcase.

"Ah, Miss Prescott. Thank you so much for coming," Ferguson said, wiping his hands and rushing to meet her. "I was on my way to meet you, and the Joint Staff went into special session and called me. Please forgive me for asking you to take a taxi."

"It's quite alright, general. I was flattered by the appreciative glances of yet another Nigerian taxi driver." She set her briefcase down and surveyed the room.

Introductions were made. Joe and two other lieutenant colonels were in uniform. Boyd was not because his hair was now longer and not within standards. Pamela was "read in" to their project, meaning that she knew what was involved and acknowledged that it was classified and signed a statement as such.

"We were here all weekend," Ferguson said, sitting after collecting the security paperwork and nodding at the food packaging stuffed into the wastebaskets. "We're on a short schedule, and we've hit a dead end. Boyd and Joe have just come back from East Africa with some very disturbing findings. Joe, could you show Miss Prescott what we're up against?"

Joe plugged in his computer and activated the flat-screen on the wall. He gave a slight wink at Boyd as the first picture came up. It was the picture the World Health Organization had sent them. Joe's dry commentary quickly told the story of Ebola, the frantic radio transmission and the fire, and their visit to the island.

"I've seen autopsies before, gentlemen," Pamela said icily as the picture of the charred skull was replaced by the open chest and the bullet holes. Her initial irritation at having to endure what she thought was a boyish prank dissolved into interest as the show continued. She nodded her appreciation of the situation as Boyd related the events in Paris with Henri.

"The Director's office sent me the files on the Planters National Bank. I went over them on the plane. Pretty straightforward stuff," she said, opening her briefcase. "Could you load this for me?" She handed Joe a flash drive.

"Planters National is a small regional bank with a dozen branches in South Carolina and Georgia. Total assets last year were $2.2 billion."

"A billion dollars? That's small?" Boyd broke in.

Joe, too, looked curious.

Pamela furrowed her brow and looked at Boyd, then Joe and Ferguson. She seemed to be weighing a sarcastic response, then lay the remote control on her briefcase.

"You guys are not, uh, familiar with the banking industry, I take it. Shall I start with something a bit more basic?"

"A billion dollars seems to be quite a lot of money," Ferguson said. "You might characterize this bank in comparison with other regional banks and go on from there. If we need any remedial work we can get it later."

Even a mediocre general can control a meeting, Boyd thought.

"Yes, well, the bank is a small player in the Southeast, maybe 20th. By contrast, Bank of America, headquartered in Charlotte, has $2 trillion in total assets, third in the nation."

Looking around at the room she added, "Assets include all their deposits. That isn't all their money. Planters National is traded on the NASDAQ Stock Exchange, so they're also overseen by the Securities and Exchange Commission. Directors own 20 percent of the stock, which is a lot for a bank holding company of their size. Their last audit was squeaky clean, and their profit and loss statement corresponds well with the shareholder's report."

She paused. They all stared blankly at the screen.

"You're wondering how we get them to tell us where that money came from," she said, putting the remote control back on the desk.

"Yes, that's why we called on the FBI," Ferguson retorted.

"It's not that easy. They're just a bank – a well capitalized, honestly run, regional bank. There are no signs of fraud, though this is just a preliminary report. If you have some indication, we could begin a full scale audit. The question of whether the bank is involved in those cash transfers as an agent or as a principal cannot be answered from information available publicly."

"Can't we just subpoena their records?" Joe asked.

"Sure, we can go to the U.S. Attorney and show him our information, and he could ask for their records. You'd get 10 gigabytes of data. Then what?"

The officers had a pretty good idea who might have to sort through that 10 gigabytes of data. They were silent.

"So?" Ferguson, as usual, jumped right in.

"That means it's their business," she snapped. "What a bank is, and who owns it, and who makes how much from it, is public. Individual services for a client are not. We can ask them, of course. If they are in a mood to cooperate with the government, they can tell us. If they even know. A wire transfer of less than a million dollars, and now almost half a year ago, is going to be like a needle in a haystack, even for a small bank like this."

"A customer list might be enough," Joe said. "I'd recognize any major viral research or pharmaceutical companies."

"They've broken no laws?"

"Murder, times two. At least," Boyd said.

"Murder is not a crime a bank can commit. A customer list goes into the area of their proprietary interest. We'd have to show the U.S. Attorney that a crime has been or is being committed."

Pamela sat back, seeming confident the next step would take this investigation into someone else's arena, leaving her to either play a peripheral role or bow out altogether.

"Miss Prescott, this is a matter of national security," Ferguson said. "I explained that to the Director. We need to get to who sent that money, and we need to do it now, and we need to do it without them knowing we're looking. Now, how can we do that?"

Ferguson had pulled the general officer's favorite trick; they must learn it charm school right after their promotion is announced. Challenge. Push. Break down the façade, then skewer the responsible officer in front of their peers. Humiliate. Create a reputation that makes people wet their pants at the mere thought of not having a complete answer. It didn't work with Pamela Prescott.

"You can't force them to tell you their private business unless there is some evidence a crime has been committed. You can ask!"

The rising crescendo of anger left the room in silence as her final word reverberated. Not content to leave it at that she stood and faced the general.

"You guys have me in here on some sort of half-baked scheme that has nothing to do with bank fraud, which is my field. You should just go down to Charleston and ask the banker who sent that money to Paris. If he knows, and isn't involved, he'll tell you. Why would a bank be into something this weird anyway? You don't need me."

She held her ground, standing at the head of the conference room table red-faced and glaring at Ferguson.

Boyd suppressed a grin as he stole a glance at Joe. It was fun to watch someone take on a general. Being only a captain, he'd never seen that before. He noticed that Pamela was a robust girl, and the top button on the worsted wool suit she wore was under some tension, like the middle button on a man's sport coat when the belly gets out of hand.

Ferguson stood, his height immediately dominating.

"No need to get excited here Miss Prescott. Perhaps we've all had enough today. I have to go back to the Pentagon. Let's break for today and we'll pick this back up tomorrow."

He didn't wait for an answer. He walked to the door, opened it, turned and added, "Right after lunch."

When the door closed the silence lasted a full minute. Each seemed to be listening to be sure he was gone.

"Well," Joe said, packing up, smiling. "See you guys tomorrow."

"Two years in Oklahoma," Pamela erupted, as she threw the remaining papers and her flash drive into the briefcase and slammed it shut. "The heart of the ignorance belt. Bad food, bad hotels, hot in the summer, cold in the winter, and I catch the slickest thief in the 10th Federal Reserve District." She slammed her chair back under the table. "I get home and the telephone rings. Ah, I think, someone calling me with a word of thanks, an 'attagirl.' "

The officers sat in awe. The force of her anger animated her features, giving an intensity of feeling to what had seemed a mask when she first arrived.

"But no! Your general, living up to the worst of the military stereotypes, a pea-brained martinet, somehow gets my number and gets me sent to Washington in August. Great!"

She scanned the room as if she expected one of the surprised officers to respond.

"How about a drink?" Boyd asked.

"Yes."

CHAPTER FOURTEEN
BLACK OPS, OFF THE BOOKS

"Double Jack Daniel's, on the rocks, water by," Pamela said, not waiting for the waitress to speak, slamming her briefcase into the booth in the bar atop the Sheraton hotel overlooking the runways at Reagan National Airport.

"Bud. Longneck if you have one," Boyd said, amused at her anger and her coping mechanisms.

"That man, the sheer arrogance," she said as she slid her briefcase to the back. "The most intensely unpleasant person I've ever met. Who does he think he is?"

"My boss," Boyd said quietly, sliding in across from her. He looked out at an American 737 on final, approaching from the east, appreciating its controlled descent to touch down with a burst of smoke as all the tires hit the runway at the middle of the dense white stripes. "Navy landing," he added, nodding at the plane.

She looked up, surprised at seeing an airport so close.

"Navy guys have to land on aircraft carriers, so they train to hit the approach end of the runway with authority. They can't afford to have the ground effect float them along for a hundred yards. They'd drop off the carrier deck. Air Force guys glide a plane down soft; Navy guys hit the runway."

"You're a pilot?"

Their drinks arrived. Pamela took a gulp of her bourbon, then seemed to remember he was there, and nodded in his direction, "Cheers." Then she took another drink. Her eyes were restlessly searching the room as if something evil might come through the door.

"Cheers," he responded and took a pull on his longneck. "I fly the F-16."

"Is that one of those little planes?" She took another gulp. The double bourbon was now mostly ice.

"Single engine fighter."

"One of those fast ones, like the Hell's Angels fly?"

"It's the Blue Angels, the Navy exhibition team. The Air Force exhibition team is the Thunderbirds."

"How fast?" She motioned for the waitress.

"Fast." He took a draw on his beer, still mostly full. "I could come up the river here, at sea level, about 900, and it'd break out all these windows." He nodded out the floor to ceiling windows overlooking the Potomac River just on the other side of the Reagan National runway. "If I went up to 35,000 feet, I could make 1,500, and just make a loud noise."

"Another Jack," she told the waitress. "And a bud." Then, turning to Boyd she added, "This round's mine."

"So, does the FBI usually investigate banks?"

"No. This sleazeball in Oklahoma turned up when the bank examiners did the books at a bank he controlled. Then the IRS caught him cheating on his taxes, and the Securities and Exchange Commission caught him selling unlicensed securities."

"They had him, why did they need you?"

"They didn't have him, couldn't pin it on him. They couldn't find the irrefutable trail of money leading to him. He was living like a king on the money, trying to spend it all before they sent him away," she said, beginning to relax.

The rage was slipping away and now her eyes were mostly on Boyd. She leaned forward on the table, intent, conspiratorial. "They needed someone to get into his business, to find out how he did it."

"How did you get him?" Boyd asked, enjoying the transformation.

"Follow the money. That's what I do best."

"Did you go undercover?"

She paused.

He waited.

"Sort of." She took a sip. "He had an accomplice, a guy who worked at his bank. He was the bag man for all this, the enabler. I got him. He ratted out the big guy to save his skin."

A long pause as she looked into the ice in her glass, thoughts elsewhere.

Boyd nodded, silent, watching the agent remember. He finished his first beer and took a sip of the second.

"In a case like that, someone always has a record of where the money went. You just have to find out who it is, and make them give it to you."

Boyd nodded, but didn't say anything.

"I tricked him," she said quietly, looking back into her drink. "It was a lawyer's trick. He had been very careful to act only in his capacity at the bank, taking orders from the bank president and board. But, in prosecuting a conspiracy, you only have to show he knew the details of the illegal activity. He revealed to me he knew the location of an off-the-books property, and that tied him to the whole thing."

"We don't have time for anything very elaborate. Someone has Pandora's Box open and we need to find out who it is."

"There are constitutional safeguards in this country that protect private citizens from their own government going on a fishing expedition through their financial records.

We could, pretty quick, get the depositor list from Planter's National. We could then pick likely candidates to be involved and subpoena their records. Depending on how many wire transfers they've done in the past year, we could probably find who sent the money to Paris."

"Why didn't you tell us that this afternoon?"

"General Ferguson was so busy trying to control everything. You don't need me. If the bank would cooperate, you can get what you need from them."

"What if they're involved?"

"Then you have to go to court."

"Two years."

"At least."

She twirled her drink again, then finished it and looked up.

"Your general and the Director seem to have already come to the conclusion that the only way to get the information you need is to resort to dirty tricks, and that's why they sent for me." She paused, looked out the window, then back at her drink. "Shit!"

"Not your field?"

"Apparently, it is my field. I'm becoming the 'go to' girl for barely legal, shady, undercover work." She paused again. "Look, I cleared that case in Oklahoma by betraying a man who thought I was his friend. His involvement was peripheral to the real fraud, and now he's a convicted felon and can never work in banking or the securities business again."

"But, he was a crook."

"Yeah."

Boyd laughed.

"It's not funny," she said, looking morose.

"That's 'Black Ops' off the books, the same thing I do."

She furrowed her brow, as if she didn't follow his terminology.

"We call secret operations Black Ops, and we have a whole command that does that kind of stuff. But, when they want to do something barely legal, shady, undercover, something that might involve some ass-kicking, they call on me. I'm someone nobody knows, and nobody would miss if I didn't come back."

"'Black Ops' ... off the books," she smiled, thinking about it. "Maybe we could have some cards printed up. I fit the same profile." She thought some more. "Damn, those bastards ..." She didn't finish.

Three hours passed. Pamela Prescott had two more Jack Daniel's doubles, and Boyd kept up with longnecks. He told her about his previous adventure; including the classified part, and she did the same. They had dinner, and she sketched for him where the legal boundaries were that had to be honored to get the U.S. Attorney to do any kind of takedown, and how they might stand on one side of them and reach across to get information – way across. A plan emerged, but they'd need some specialized help. She knew just the person.

There was a pause, each looking out at the night and the Reagan National runway lights, contemplating the next adventure in their lives.

"What do you do when you want to shoot your gun?" She asked, elbows on the table, eyes on Boyd, a sweet, innocent look on her face.

****

Pamela's breasts spilled out of her bra as she opened the clasp in back. Boyd stood against the bathroom door in his room in that same hotel, watching as she kicked off her shoes, dropped her wool jacket on the dresser, removed her blouse, and now turned, bare breasted, flushed.

He removed his shirt, stretched languidly and began removing his khakis. Pamela unzipped her skirt, allowing it to fall to the floor. She attempted to remove her panties and pantyhose all in one motion, but they caught at her knees and she fell sideways to the floor, struggling to pull one leg out.

"Cool move, Pam," she said thickly, pulling herself upright and hopping to the bed.

Her breasts jiggled as she kicked her feet to free them from the pantyhose. Still unable to free herself, she pivoted on her buttocks and pointed her feet toward Boyd on the bed behind her, barely able to contain a laugh.

"You didn't leave your socks on did you?" Pamela asked as he pulled her pantyhose off, pivoting her buttocks back to lengthwise on the bed so she could see his feet. "Nothin' worse than doin' it with a man who won't get naked."

Her intoxication was ever more evident as she fell backwards onto the pillow and stared at the ceiling for a moment before rising on one elbow to look at Boyd, now stretched out beside her.

Boyd was troubled by being here in government-provided quarters, naked with a co-worker. Pamela's breasts straddled his face as she rolled sideways toward him. The warmth, and her intake of breath as he began exploring them with his face, redirected his thoughts. The buttocks that had seemed too large for the wool dress now seemed to be ideal, the curves providing a fascinating landscape for his roving palms.

"When I'm drunk, I like to drive," came Pamela's voice from above him somewhere as she rolled off of him and sat on the bed. "But, I'm not sittin' on that thing without a rubber."

Boyd got up. When he returned from the bathroom she was seated on the side of the bed.

"Let me," she said, taking the condom from him and fumbling with the package.

He stood patiently while Pamela rolled it on, and then made room for him to lie beside her.

"Black Ops, off the books," she said with a laugh, throwing a leg over him and rising to sit astride.

CHAPTER FIFTEEN
MacDonnald Wilde

"In these days when Congress watches everything the military does, do you suppose Ferguson and the FBI director have any anxiety about springing a bank robber from Leavenworth and then sending a Lear Jet to fly him here?" Boyd asked Pam as they waited by a staff car parked in front of Base Operations at Andrews Air Force Base.

"He's not really a bank robber. He was convicted of conspiracy to commit securities fraud and perjury," Pamela said absently, eyes on the empty sky at the end of the runway. The Command Post had radioed that the C-21 was on final.

"Interesting idea, using a crook to catch a crook," Boyd said.

"Donn has unique abilities. If that banker in Charleston knows anything, Donn Wilde will find it."

"We could wrap this thing up pretty quick."

"Your part, yes."

"Big difference from my last job. Fractured my skull, broke three ribs and collapsed a vertebra."

"Kicked some ass, too, didn't you?"

Boyd smiled.

"I need to straighten out what happened last week," she took her eyes off the end of the runway and looked across to the Air National Guard Base across it, not looking at Boyd. "Sometimes I drink too much, way too much. I do things. I get slutty."

"I should have stopped," Boyd said, remembering her breasts spilling out of her bra.

"Please, let's just work together. Maybe when this is over, we could try again."

Now she looked at him.

"Deal. Just business," Boyd said, briefly locking eyes, then turning back to the south. "Uh, plane's here."

The landing lights of the C-21 could be seen in the distance.

****

"High card, double or nothing?"

The man, in his middle 30s and his hands cuffed in front of him, spread a deck of cards out on the suitcases stacked in the narrow isle of the aircraft as Boyd climbed the steps.

"No way, you already got my per diem," the aging federal marshal said, shaking his head. He wore Western boots and a tooled leather belt.

"Was luck. Could've gone the other way. You dealt half the hands."

The younger man was dressed in jeans and a golf shirt sporting the logo of a golf club in Oklahoma. He wore expensive loafers.

You must be Donn Wilde," Boyd said, offering his hand, and then pulling it back when he saw the cuffs.

"That's right, and delighted to be here to serve my country," he said, his bright eyes and smile lighting up the passenger compartment.

The marshal opened a briefcase and removed papers, arranging them on the makeshift table.

"Pamela, you bitch," Donn said gaily, as Pamela climbed the steps.

"Donn, you criminal," she grinned, unable to resist his smile.

"Strange way to greet the person who got you out of the pen and could send you back just by refusing to sign this paper," the marshal reminded Donn soberly.

"Naw. Pammie and I go way back. What is it now, Pam, couple, three years?"

Donn seemed relaxed and in control, as if this were his plane and Boyd and Pamela were coming to pick him up from a routine business trip.

"You can sure have him, ma'am. Just sign these papers. You gonna want to keep him in cuffs?" The marshal offered Pam a pen, pointing to the custody papers.

"I think Capt. Chailland can control Mr. Wilde," she said, signing. The marshal unlocked the cuffs. Donn rubbed his wrists, stood up and stretched his shoulders.

"Well, Mr. Wilde, it's been a pleasant trip. I want to wish you luck, but the next time I fly with you, we ain't playin' no cards, OK?"

The marshal laughed, his oversize belly bouncing like Santa Claus. He gathered his bag and briefcase and climbed down the steps, heading for the passenger terminal a few yards away, as if he'd done this before.

"Is that where they keep the president's plane?" Donn asked jauntily, looking around as they walked out to the staff car. He pointed at a large hangar in the distance.

"Probably," Boyd said, not knowing whether that was true or whether it was classified.

"What does his seat look like?"

"His seat?" Boyd asked, opening the trunk and dropping Donn's slender bag in.

"Yeah, where the president sits. He flies all over the world, travels with all the heavy hitters. He's the top guy. What does his seat look like? Is it some special made thing with controls and knobs all over it, or is it plush so he can sleep in the air?"

Boyd shrugged, started the car. Donn got in back, still talking.

"Pamela, thanks. You know I didn't mean that back there. We're old friends."

Then, turning to Boyd, "She put me in there, you know. She's the one who finally caught me."

"I just followed the money, Donn. It led right to you."

Boyd could see Donn's face in the mirror, it hardened as he looked at Pam, who had turned in the seat with her last lighthearted comment.

"I went down because I took a date to Buck Wayne's penthouse, Pam. You never caught me with anything but knowledge."

"Well, you're out now," she said, turning back to the front.

"Indeed. And now we're on the same team," Donn said, bright again.

"That could be a mixed blessing," Pam said without turning.

CHAPTER SIXTEEN
THE PLAN

The hotel room was spotless. Sunlight streamed through the open drapes. A lively sonata played from the classical music channel on the hotel's entertainment feed. Boyd, returning to the room he shared with Donn, had just finished a run down the road to the Pentagon, across the south parking lot to the George Washington Freeway, up the path along the Potomac to the Memorial Bridge and across to the Lincoln Memorial. He was hot and sweaty

"Boyd," Donn exclaimed as he stepped out of the bathroom. He was adjusting a Windsor knot on a beautiful silk tie. He wore a lustrous white cotton broadcloth shirt with long collar points and generous cuffs.

"A Gen. Ferguson called and wants us all down at the office in an hour. Better hurry. But get some coffee first. It's excellent."

He slipped on the jacket of a chalk-stripe, double-breasted wool suit and poured from a silver coffee service that sat on the table, steam rising from the pot.

"Where'd you get that?" Boyd asked, staring at the transformation.

"It's off the rack, but it'll do until I can have something made."

"I've just been gone two hours. You didn't have that in that little bag you brought in last night?"

"No. When you buy a $1,500 suit and tell them you're in a hurry, you can get the pants done in 20 minutes."

"How did you buy a $1,500 suit?

"With money," Donn said. "You gonna take a shower?"

He handed Boyd a cup of coffee.

Boyd accepted the cup from the resplendent Wilde, who was obviously enjoying Boyd's confusion. He took it into the bathroom and stripped off his wet clothes and ran some water. He took a sip. It was rich and delicious. He'd lived at the hotel for a week and hadn't tasted their coffee.

****

Donn had seen the slides and paced the room as he spoke.

"So the problem, Gen. Ferguson, is that your only clue to the identity of the individual or organization hiring those unfortunate laboratory workers we saw the remains of is a wire transfer from a bank in South Carolina."

Ferguson, Smith, Prescott and Chailland were seated, drinking coffee in the late morning.

"Correct. Agent Prescott tells us you have a special knack for gaining the confidence of business people. We can give you a week to find out what we need to know. If you haven't gotten it by then, we rely on the FBI and the U.S. Attorney in South Carolina."

"I appreciate Miss Prescott's recommendation. My lawyer assures me the parole is complete and final and as soon as I have completed this, uh, project, I am a free man."

"Yes, Donn. You'll be free as soon as I sign a letter releasing you from probationary custody," Pam said.

"What about expenses?" Donn asked.

Boyd thought about the suit.

"No problem. Just fill out an expense voucher," Ferguson said.

"I may need some leeway here. Bankers travel in different circles than military officers. The usual government rules on lodging and dining may become, ah, restrictive."

"I have a special account. Itemize your expenses and I can authorize payment off the usual government per diem system," Ferguson answered.

Boyd nudged Pam and mouthed the words, "Off the books."

She smiled.

"OK, we have a deal then," Donn said, smiling his most winning smile. He walked the length of the room, turned and looked at the audience.

"Planters National Bank in Charleston is involved with the people who are bankrolling this operation. Wire transfers are an insider's tool, done by bankers for trusted customers."

Ferguson nodded, happy to hear some positive talk for a change.

"It's probably a smaller company, so some of the money might have been borrowed. Small companies have to sell their bankers on their projects in order to get the money to do them. That's where the money is in banking. Making small companies grow is the business of banking. So, that banker knows who sent the money, and he probably knows why."

"What if somebody just came in and wanted to wire the money?" Joe asked.

"The bank would require them to open an account, fill it with a cashier's check from another bank, and that would be verified by at least a call to the customer's other bank. It would take days, and they'd have to give positive ID. In a transaction of this size, the bank president would become involved, or at least know about it. It would be somewhat of a curiosity. By using Citicorp in New York, the senders were trying to achieve anonymity. It was a pretty safe assumption for someone with an already established relationship with a regional bank. Citicorp handles millions of dollars in wire transfers every day. This would have been small potatoes."

"Except another banker's squeeze was involved," Boyd broke in, laughing.

"The smart monkey doesn't monkey with another monkey's monkey," Donn said quickly.

Pamela looked confused.

"So, how do we find out who it is?" Ferguson asked, brow furrowed.

"We use the only bait that really gets a banker's attention: money."

"How much money?" Ferguson glared.

"Oh, a hundred million dollars should be enough."

"My special account doesn't hold quite that much," Ferguson laughed.

Boyd was surprised Ferguson was taking this as well as he was. He was usually a humorless man. He'd been a lot more relaxed since he and Donn had chatted amicably for a few minutes while waiting for Joe Smith to drive in from Maryland. By the time Joe had arrived, Donn was showing the general a golf grip he'd learned from a pro at a pro-am golf tournament in Tulsa two years before.

"I need to make some calls, find out a few things about the area there in South Carolina," Donn said. "I can have a detailed plan tomorrow. In the meantime, Pamela, I need to have you set up a call to the president of the Federal Reserve Bank in Kansas City, and, Gen. Ferguson, we need to install a new outside phone line into the office of the president of First Bank in Tulsa, and get some printing done. Also, Capt. Chailland, Agent Prescott and I are going to need new wardrobes and some jewelry. We can't go down there looking like FBI agents."

The man had style, Boyd thought. Ferguson was busy writing down the tasks he'd received from Wilde. He spent the next few minutes clarifying but not quibbling.

Donn waited less than 10 seconds after Ferguson left to pick up the telephone and dial their hotel from the DTRA Command Center.

"Concierge," he paused, waiting. "Pammie, what kind of food do you like?"

Pam glared at him, mood clearly foul again.

"Yes, Macdonnald Wilde, here. We're guests at your hotel. I'll be entertaining some friends tonight. Aside from the fine restaurant you have there in the hotel, what is the happening place in D.C.? Ah, yes, I've heard of it. Also, is there a limousine service you rely on?"

"No! Donn, we're not even started yet," Pam exclaimed, rising but not moving for the telephone.

"Ask them to send by a limo at eight, and, could you call up … why yes, that would be delightful. Five. Thank you so much."

Donn smiled benevolently at Pam, now seated again. "Training, Pam, training." He began putting papers into his briefcase.

"I assume the good doctor has a wife?" Donn asked, looking at Joe, who smiled and nodded in the affirmative. "You would be doing your country a great service if you could bring her to this address around half past eight."

Joe took the slip of paper, packed his briefcase and left.

"Now, before we have cocktails, Lesson One in the game of business. Sometimes it's necessary to project, ah, a certain image. Maybe that image is a bit ambitious for you at just this moment, but is well within where you expect to be, soon."

Donn began pacing again.

"Devise an identity that is so close to your own, you don't have to lie very often. Pam, you're going to be our corporate attorney and bean counter. Don't smile. Ask technical questions. We don't know these people yet. Show a little leg, but don't be a bimbo."

Pam glowered.

"Boyd, you'll be an Air Force jock who got out and became a securities salesman. Laugh a lot. Tell war stories. If someone asks you a question you don't know how to answer, tell them you're new to the securities business.

"As for tonight, the Smiths will be our clients. Just follow my lead."

****

"Wait for the doorman, Boyd," Donn said as he restrained Boyd from opening the door as their stretch limo pulled up in front of the Chateau Michael.

The doorman opened the door and stepped back. Boyd got out and offered to help Pamela. Loosened considerably by all four of the little Jack Daniel's bottles in the courtesy bar in her room at the hotel, she smiled pleasantly as she took his arm.

"Thank you," Donn said, addressing the doorman, pausing to look around the parking lot and at the few bystanders before striding purposefully into the restaurant. He approached the maître d'.

"I'm MacDonnald Wilde. The hotel called."

"Ah, yes. I am Anthony. Your table is ready, sir."

"Anthony, my driver will be outside. Could you send out a sandwich, some coffee? Whatever he wants."

"Of course."

"We'll be meeting Dr. Smith, a larger man than I, about the size of my associate here, reddish hair, balding. He'll have his wife. I haven't met her."

"She's Chinese," Boyd offered.

"Ah, perfect. We certainly want them to feel welcome."

He smiled at Anthony.

Boyd watched Donn work the room. While he talked with the maître d', no one passed or saw anything but Donn. He was polite, forceful but not loud, upbeat, enjoying himself, bringing out the best in those there to help him. He walked slowly, confidently, to their table, looking around the room, attracting attention in his fine-looking suit, smiling. Boyd felt the eyes, too. It was an entrance.

When the Smiths arrived they were brought to the table by the maître d'. Donn met them halfway, shaking Joe's hand and introducing himself to Joe's petite wife. The waiter popped the champagne cork as they took their seats.

Mrs. Smith looked bewildered. Pamela offered her glass first to the waiter, a gay smile on her flushed face.

They had a sumptuous meal with appetizers, soup, spectacular entrees and flaming deserts. Donn had an animated discussion with the wine steward, finally letting him choose a white and a red for the occasion. Throughout the evening, Donn kept up the pace with stories of oil deals in Oklahoma, outrageous golf outings, and down-home tales of hunting and fishing expeditions and colorful characters he'd met. Their table's periodic explosions of laughter had the room politely craning their way to hear the stories.

Pam had rushed down to the Crystal City Mall to buy some high heels for the evening. At the end of dinner, as they were leaving, she tripped on a step and broke off one of the heels. With a broken heel she continued walking toward the door, too drunk to notice. Boyd rushed to her aid, stopped her, reached down to slip off both of her shoes and helped her quickly out to the car. Donn followed with the Smiths, thanking the staff, slipping bills into discretely offered hands, promising to be back soon.

CHAPTER SEVENTEEN
DOHA, QATAR

Khalid was aware of the bulletproof doors and windows as his Pakistani driver eased the Mercedes slowly down Al Ashat Street in Doha, Qatar, stopping in front of the main entrance to the Gold Souk. Emerging onto the sidewalk, Khalid stood to his full 6 feet 2 inches and squared his shoulders, well aware all eyes were on him. He wore the traditional Qatari white robe, or thoub, with a carefully ironed, folded square cloth covering his head, held in place with a black double coil. Looking to the uninitiated like any other of the thousands of men wearing traditional garb in Doha, he was, in his own estimation, unique. His ghutra, or headdress was folded just so – like no other. The street was filled with men rushing about in all manner of dress, but there were no traditional white robes in sight. That, and the smell of garbage from a dumpster in the alley across the street, reminded Khalid that he was in the rough part of town and surrounded by foreigners, servants and infidels.

"Wait here," he said quietly to his driver, surveying the scene. He strode across the broken sidewalk and up the three steps to the main entrance. A man lounging there leaped to open the door for him. "*Shokran*," he said to the man as he breezed by into the interior, his robes flaring as they trailed behind him.

The Gold Souk has been at this location for more than a century, since Doha was the center of the pearl trade. As oil replaced pearls as the economic engine of prosperity and gold became important in cementing familial relationships in the newly rich Bedouin nation, Pakistani and Persian traders moved in and dominated the marketplace. Qatari tribesmen concerned themselves with other matters. The pearls now come from Japan, and the gold and precious gems are from everywhere.

Gold bracelets and trinkets of all types twinkled from dozens of showcase windows as Khalid passed the larger, more ornate windows, turned quickly down a side hall and slipped into a small shop.

"Welcome, my friend!" A man in white robes with a small white skullcap rose from behind a jeweler's workbench and rushed around the counter to greet Khalid.

"Salam, Hamid." They exchanged the traditional kisses, which are really just a close juxtaposition of the face used in greeting. Trust is assessed and built with proximity.

A younger man came in from a small room in the back with a small pot of tea and two cups and put them on the gem counter in the center of the shop. He brought two seats, then pulled the blinds to the windows on the hallway in front, and left by the front entrance, locking the door behind him. Hamid brought a blue velvet drape and put it over the counter, then dropped some diamonds from an envelope he was holding onto the counter. He turned on the jeweler's light, and the two men huddled over the diamonds.

"If it is God's will, our shipment will be ready soon," Hamid said.

"Allah be praised," Khalid said.

"My friend in the diamond business is ready for his reward."

"Insha'Allah. But what does he offer for proof of the special nature of this gem?"

"The Americans went to the island where our product was produced, and they are trying to follow him. He is being very careful. He was going to ship our product by air freight, but that is impossible now. It will come by sea."

"Here?"

"No. He will keep it in the Atlantic Ocean for now. He suggests you test it."

"Yes, we have a plan to do that."

"First, he must have 5 million Euros."

CHAPTER EIGHTEEN
CHEROKEE TRUST FUND

"Mr. Cooper Jordan, please. This is Nadine Spears, special assistant to Mr. MacDonnald Wilde with First Bank, Tulsa, Oklahoma." Pamela's feminist ire was riled, but her voice was pure Oklahoma gentility.

"Is he on?" Donn asked, anxiously.

Pam shook her head, and then nodded, handing the phone to Donn.

"Mr. Jordan, Donn Wilde. How is the weather in sunny Charleston today?" Donn boomed out his greeting as if he were sitting at a big desk overlooking the skyline in Tulsa instead of a rented, windowless office in the DTRA Command Center in suburban Virginia.

"Why, it's warm here, too. My reason for asking, Mr. Jordan, is that I'm going to be down your way tomorrow, and I need to impose on your hospitality, if I may."

He paused, smiling, effervescent.

"How true that is, Mr. Jordan. Banking is not the gentleman's business it once was, and it's a damn shame." He paused again, laughing. "The city of Charleston maintains an account at your bank, sir. Tomorrow we're going to wire $400,000 into it for some bonds they're offering. We need to complete the transaction tomorrow, as the subscription period ends on September first. We've arranged to have the city treasurer pose for some promotional pictures, you know, signing the bonds, shaking hands. We were wondering if you had a meeting room, something discrete, tasteful, that we could use for about half an hour."

Donn leaned back, putting his feet on the table.

"Yes, sir, it's trust money. We've started a fund to manage money for trusts for our bank and some smaller regional banks here in Oklahoma. Charleston's 5 3/4, 30-year tax exempt is highly attractive this month. The pictures are to kick off a promo, to show how we cross the continent to find our customers the best deals."

He paused, listening.

"I'm afraid we can't get in until late in the day. Perhaps we could finish by 4. Why, yes, we'll be there overnight, at the Omni. Certainly, let's have a drink. Yes, sir, look forward to meeting you."

Donn hung up, shot a fist into the air and hooted, "Hot damn!"

Boyd looked down at his shiny new business card, which read, Cherokee Trust Funds, Boyd Chailland, account executive. He chuckled. While they were driving to the printers, Donn had challenged him to come up with a name that might appeal to Oklahoma residents. He thought of his roommate at the Academy from Cherokee, Okla., and how proud he was of the Indian tradition. When he suggested it, Donn thought for a moment, opened the Wall Street Journal that seemed always by his side, checked the mutual fund section to see if there was already one by that name and then said it was perfect.

"It sounds familiar," Donn said later, looking down at his own card, which identified him as fund manager. "People will think they've heard of it."

"Is there really a First Bank?" Boyd asked, looking at their logo beneath Cherokee Funds.

"Yes."

"Is it OK to just use their logo on a business card like this?"

"No. Illegal as hell," Pam said. "Hope they don't find out."

CHAPTER NINETEEN
CHARLESTON

Just wearing the Rolex gave Boyd a different feeling. Heavy on his wrist, it was a constant reminder of the $10,000 Pamela had said it had cost the drug dealer who had run afoul of the U.S. Department of Justice. He tipped up the green bottle of imported beer and looked out on Charleston Harbor. A large, rusty freighter moved slowly past, headed toward the Atlantic. Looking back up the river he could see others ships loading and unloading.

"I had no idea. Charleston seems to be quite the place, exportwise," said Donn, standing with Cooper Jordan and looking out the full-length window on the fifth story of the Planters National Bank Building.

"We're very proud of our community, Mr. Wilde. And its prospects," Cooper Jordan said, sipping bourbon. His words drew slowly out, as if carefully considered and individually crafted. Their bond-buying completed, Boyd,

Donn and Pamela had been invited into Jordan's office for "a late afternoon libation."

"Sir, the smell of profit is heavy in the air," Donn announced, sipping his scotch, rattling the ice in a crystal glass.

"Well, indeed, there is opportunity here," Jordan said pleasantly.

Pamela was occupied with two younger suits talking about interest-rate fluctuations. Two bourbons had her pretty much in stride, and she was animated and convincing as the lawyer and accountant she really was. The smart satin blouse she wore allowed an interested observer to realize how each of her breasts had a center of gravity some distance out from her chest wall, and how each tiny movement of her torso caused a reverberating counter-movement of the breast, leveraged by that distance. Both of these young bankers seemed to be interested observers.

Boyd moved to the corner, where the window allowed a view back toward the Battery, the original settlement where pre-Civil War homes still stood. The bright pastel homes, contrasting with the dark green of the massive live oaks dripping with Spanish moss, made for an appealing view. He didn't need to imagine the horse-drawn carriages of old, they were still there, bearing tourists and outnumbering cars on a sleepy Friday afternoon.

"The banker's dilemma in Oklahoma, Cooper, is what to do with all that oil money," Donn said. "The debacle of just a few years ago was our attempt to invest it all back in the state, but there's just so much there that will return a profit. You can only build so many shopping malls and office buildings."

Donn was pacing now, gearing up for the pitch.

Boyd moved from the window, wanting to see how Donn pulled this off. If something didn't happen in the next 10 minutes, they'd wear out their welcome and have to either ask or subpoena to find out anything. Pam also sensed the moment had arrived. She handed her glass to one of the suits and smiled for a refill. When he turned, she stopped talking to the other and looked at Donn. The room was silent.

"First Bank was siphoning off the capital to New York, investing it from there, and collecting the fees from there. We were just a branch. We saw an opportunity. We formed the Cherokee Trust Funds to have something for our customers we could manage locally. It was an 'in your face' move to the big boys in New York that appealed to our customers. It's been successful beyond our wildest expectations."

Jordan nodded politely. There was no sign of interest beyond that.

"The bond fund is pretty easy to manage. We can buy bonds through a broker to place the $20 million we have there. The equity fund is more problematic. We're under some pressure to put money into something we've researched. We need to show our customers, mostly smal-town banks and small pension plans, that we're heavy hitters out there in the world of emerging business giants."

Donn walked to the bar, splashed some Glenlivet into his glass and turned.

"We need to place $56 million into equities before the end of October. Half of that must be in small and emerging companies."

Cooper Jordan's eyebrows went up, just a couple millimeters. A slight man, he would have seemed frail had he not had a strong baritone voice. He nodded, and said in that voice, "Sounds like you've got some money burnin' a hole in your jeans, Mr. Wilde."

"Indeed I do, Mr. Jordan. Indeed I do."

Donn took a contemplative sip of his scotch.

****

"Is that it?" Pamela exploded, after they were safely out on the street, walking the two blocks back to their hotel.

"Pammie, Pammie. We just got into town this morning," Donn exclaimed, huge jaunty smile on his face.

"I don't see how that's going to justify, to my superiors, springing you from prison and financing an expensive trip down here. We have nothing."

"Pam, look up. Which window is Jordan's?"

Pam looked up, noting the executive suite five floors up.

"We'll drive back in two hours. The light will be on. It's Friday night. He'll be working. You'll see."

"How can you be so sure? And, what if he is?"

"He's gonna call the Federal Reserve in Kansas City as soon as he can, because it's still 3:30 there. They'll tell him First Bank in Tulsa is solid as Fort Knox, which it is. They don't know me from Adam, which they don't."

Donn turned the corner toward their hotel, almost running down an older couple in his excitement.

"Next, he'll have his secretary call First Bank in Tulsa. He won't use the number on the card I gave him. He'll either use the ABA list he has, or have her call information. He'll get the president's office. When he mentions my name, or Cherokee Trust Funds, they're agreed to profess knowledge but refer him to a vice president in charge of trust services. That's the extra line we had installed there last week. It goes to your buddy at the regional FBI office. What's his name?"

"Thacker. Alvin Thacker, dullest bean counter since Bartleby," Pamela said, beginning see how it all might fit together.

"Right! And he'll tell him about the $56 million we have to spend, and about how I'm a rising young fund manager and you're our legal eagle, and Chailland is a stud who has all the female trust officers in Oklahoma beating the bushes for more money to put into the Cherokee Trust Funds."

****

"Mr. Wilde, ah hope ah didn't wake you."

Donn was doing a Cooper Jordan imitation for Boyd in the coffee shop on Saturday morning, drawing out the vowels, dropping consonants from the ends of some words. He was gloating that his plan had worked exactly as he'd predicted so far.

"This is Cooper Jordan," Donn continued, perfecting the dialogue. "If you gentlemen, and Ms. Prescott, would be stayin' in Charleston through the weekend, Mrs. Jordan and I would be honored to have you to our home for dinnah on Sunday evenin'."

Boyd chuckled, noting that the Charleston accent was not that different from the Oklahoma dialect Donn tried to suppress when he was in high-roller mode.

"I told him we were so charmed, that's the word I used, charmed, that we have delayed our flight back until next week."

"Looks like we're on track, then," Boyd commented, turning to look out into the lobby. "Any sign of Pam?"

"She needs some more rest."

****

The air was heavy and sweet, scented with the fragrance of gardenia, Noisette and Bourbon roses lovingly selected and maintained by the wealthy owners of the restored Battery homes. Giant oaks, live and river varieties, crossed their branches over the street to shade it from the waning rays of an August sun. The two matched draft horses smelled of leather and sweat, an honest scent and not unpleasant.

When Donn learned that Cooper Jordan lived in the Battery, he'd insisted they take a carriage to dinner. He and Pamela sat together facing the front and talking about bankers they knew in Oklahoma. Boyd faced the rear trying to block out the cars and telephone poles to see how the city might have looked in those heady days of 1860, when the residents thought they could actually defeat the Northern states in a war of secession.

To the west, visible through occasional breaks in the trees, a dark cloud mass emitted an occasional rumble. As they drew up in front of the address they'd been given, a breeze blew through the uppermost limbs of a giant oak across the street.

Jordan's home was what the Charlestonians call a single house, built lengthwise on one side of the lot, leaving ample room for the sea breezes to blow through the neighborhood. He met them at the wrought iron gate as they were dismounting from the carriage.

"Mr. Wilde, Ms Prescott, Mr. Chailland. Amalie and I are delighted you could join us for dinner. I hope your carriage ride was up to your expectations."

They climbed steps to a long porch that extended the full length of the house, and from which they could view the immaculately maintained garden, complete with a tinkling fountain. A stately woman with faintly African features and cinnamon skin met them at the door.

"I'm Amalie Jordan. Cooper tells me you're quite smitten with our city."

Though narrow, the rooms were spacious because of their high ceilings and length. The crystal, oriental carpets and early American antiques indicated their hosts were definitely the "heavy hitters" Donn so loved to talk about. With drinks in hand, they toured the garden and heard the history and lore of the area that had been home to Jordan's family for 200 years. The temperature dropped noticeably as the breeze intensified.

Dinner was served on a massive dining room table beneath a portrait of Cooper Jordan's great-great-grandmother, a French countess. Boyd wondered whether some of Amalie's ancestors might have been in the area that long also, though perhaps not as socially prominent in the early years.

"Certainly, Mr. Jordan, your bank seems poised to profit from the coming boom in exports from this area. We would like to consider it in our quest for equities."

Donn stood by the fireplace, gazing up at the countess from two centuries ago, holding a brandy snifter in one hand and a lit cigar in the other.

"Why, Mr. Wilde, we'd be delighted to have you as minority shareholders in our bank."

As Cooper Jordan's resonant, syrupy, response floated through the cigar smoke, a bright flash was followed 3 seconds later by a sharp clap of thunder that reverberated back from clouds stacking up over the Battery and Charleston Harbor. The wind was stirring the largest of the trees in the yard.

"I was wondering, sir," Donn said, turning back to face Jordan. "If you had any leads on emerging companies in this area. In addition to the usual carefully researched purchases we plan to make for the long term, we have a need to, well, take a flyer. We need something in the technology sector, something that might have a prospect for some excitement in the near term."

"I could introduce you to some of our medium-to-large clients. These would be companies that have some growth potential. There are several technology companies here that we are proud of, very proud." Jordan nodded, took a long puff off his cigar, and blew the smoke into the center of the room.

The air was heavy, palpable through the blue haze of cigar smoke that had driven Pamela and Amalie to tour the library and Amalie's collection of linen and lace. A deep rumble from north of town was followed by a flicker and dimming of the lights. The silence stretched for more than a minute as Donn and Cooper puffed on their cigars, eyes locked. Boyd chewed on his, letting the smoke curl up, smelling the rich tobacco scent of his own private cloud accumulating round his head. Another flash was followed instantly by a clap of thunder that rattled the windows.

Cooper Jordan's reverie seemed to break with the thunder, and he walked to the French doors separating the dining room from the foyer and closed them. He refilled his brandy snifter, held it up to the light and swirled it, deeply inhaled the fragrant fumes, and smiled at Donn, eyelids nearly closed, and asked, "Can we speak confidentially?"

"Of course, Cooper," Donn said, a look of pleasant anticipation on his face.

"There is one company, thinly traded, hardly known outside of the region, with poor earnings for a decade."

Donn moved closer as Jordan's words were barely a whisper. The rain was hard now, pounding the windows on the north side and gurgling down the drain from the roof.

"An old friend has toiled in the fields of biomedical research for 20 years, always just behind the latest discovery. Now he's found something."

Boyd could feel his heart pounding in his chest. It was more than the nicotine. The rain was a roar now, falling straight down, running off the roof in a cascade that hit the sidewalk with a crash and echoed off the stone walls of the nearby buildings.

"What I'm about to tell you must remain in this room. Even if you decide not to participate, I must have your word never to speak of it."

Boyd and Donn nodded heads only a foot apart now. Another flash lit the room momentarily, followed by a clap of thunder, this time from the east over Charleston Harbor.

"This company has found a new virus. They've used it to pioneer a breakthrough in vaccine technology."

The rain seemed to acquire a rhythm, like drums beating in the distance. Boyd saw the blotches and hemorrhages on the African farmers in his mind, and heard the cries of sick children. Drums were warning of spreading danger. He was certain now: Ebola was here, on the coast of South Carolina.

"The company is BioVet Tech," Jordan said in a whisper.

CHAPTER TWENTY
CENTERS FOR DISEASE CONTROL, ATLANTA

"Joe, what's the Army been doing with this stuff?"

Joe Smith was taken aback. The question came from an old friend, Dr. Dale Casperson, director of the Division of Preparedness and Emerging Infections at the Centers for Disease Control and Prevention in Atlanta. Joe had just come from the airport with the final microscope slides from the autopsies done on the island to supplement the first batch of viral isolate he'd sent 10 days before. Although USAMRIID has extensive research capability, CDC is better equipped and better staffed and, on something this hot, they work together.

"What do you mean?" Joe was annoyed. Dale had insisted on seeing him as soon as he got to town, and his carry-on bag was in the hall. Dale hadn't even asked about his flight or shaken his hand. That was rude.

"Steve, close the door," Dale said to Dr. Steve Ng, another viral researcher who had picked Joe up at the airport.

"Those samples you sent last week ..."

"Yeah?" Joe was getting angry.

"How'd you get those?"

"I told you the whole story. They're from the island."

"When you got back from the island, what did you do?"

"Isolated the virus, grew it out, freeze dried it, and sent it to you."

"You didn't infect any living animals?"

"No, didn't have time."

"Well, don't," Casperson was beginning to relax, but he was still tense.

"We won't, but what's the big concern?"

"Those two isolates, they're different from the isolates from the Lulua River where Jacques collected his initial samples."

"You've got the RNA sequence already?"

"This morning. Put it through our new Roche 454 sequencing platform. We compared the island isolates to the Lulua River isolates, and then both of them to the samples you brought back from the Kikwit outbreak in 1996. The Lulua River isolates show some random variance from Kikwit, about what you'd expect in a simple RNA virus in nearly 20 years. The samples from the island show all those same mutations, so that confirms they came from the Lulua River, but they've evolved just in the time they were on the island, about six months."

"Hmm," Joe wrinkled his brow. "Evolved or altered?"

"The changes look random, no long sequences different. It's like there was acceleration in the natural mutation process. We think Jacques heated it up too hot when he freeze dried it and that caused a lot of random changes. We just wanted to make sure you guys didn't mess with it."

Joe began to sweat. He well knew there were some deep-seated and rarely discussed suspicions held by some researchers at the CDC about the Army and their research efforts at USAMRIID. Armies of the world have tinkered with biologic warfare since the Plague of Justinian swept out of Central Asia and crippled the army of the Eastern Roman Empire in AD 541, leading to the collapse of the Byzantine civilization. Researchers today are unable to tell whether it was an early strain of *Yersinia pestis,* the same bubonic plague germ that swept through Europe in the 14th century, or something else. Whatever it was, it came out of the Arabian Desert.

"Did I send you the equipment list from the island?" Joe reached into his briefcase for a folder. "They had some pretty basic stuff. They were equipped to do some simple splicing."

"I got the list. I agree. Jacques couldn't have done that, not knowingly."

"We certainly didn't. We've never had that capability." Joe's sweat began to be more noticeable, and he was embarrassed by it. This was a sensitive issue, not because the Army was trying to hide something, but because their actual capabilities had eroded so much over the past decade that they really couldn't do much of anything. They had been able to replicate the virus, but that was about the limit of what they could do. The CDC is where the expertise is. Don't tell that to Congress, though. The magnitude of USAMRI-ID's appropriations indicates Congress thinks they're funding two state-of-the-art facilities.

"Tell me again, Joe. Where did the two samples come from?" Don was still in inquisitor mode.

"The one marked R42A was from one of the monkeys already dead before the fire. It probably died two weeks before we got there. The R42B sample was from Jacques, the guy from the Pasteur Institute. We have other samples, from several more monkeys and from Franz."

"We want to have a look at every one. We may be able to pinpoint at which point the mutations occurred. It will take a year to work through what those changes might have done to Ebola, if anything. But, that's not the big news. Read again that segment from Jacques' note."

Joe retrieved a copy of the note Jacques had written before he died. He read the whole thing, ending with: "I saw it defeat the macaque's immune system in two passes, become dormant to await a fresh group of monkeys, and then jump from macaques to humans before the illness was recognized. Mosby spent $2 million to secretly acquire viable virus, purified RNA, and a vaccine. He knows exactly what he has."

Casperson said, "First, it looks like Jacques did make an effective vaccine. Ironic in view of his careless technical style and his complete misunderstanding of what happened on that island."

He stood and went to the window.

"Jacques must have been sick when he wrote that note. It doesn't make sense: 'defeating immune systems in two passes, laying dormant, jumping to people from Macaques.' That's just odd. But that's a perfect scenario for something much worse – a vector."

"Oh, that's right." Joe Smith's heart leaped to his throat; he should have seen that.

"It could have been fleas. They could have fed on the monkeys that were sick but got well because the vaccine gave them a head start on Ebola. Then the fleas, bellies full of Ebola virus, jumped across the building to the new monkeys, and they got sick before they could be vaccinated."

"I don't know of any hemorrhagic fever that uses fleas as a vector."

"There's always a first."

"What flea?"

"We'll have to get some vet guys in here and start look-ing at fleas. Surely monkeys have fleas. Most warm blooded animals do."

"I don't know of any virus that uses a flea as a vector," Joe said, mind reeling with the consequences of the world's most lethal virus suddenly becoming able to move from ani-mal to animal with the help of a vector. Fleas may seem slow and plodding, but they're very effective vectors. Typhus and bubonic plague are transmitted by fleas. Troubling as all this was about vectors, Joe felt something else. Something they'd missed.

"Oh, shit."

"What?" Casperson turned from the window.

"You didn't see all the pictures we brought back. Boyd Chailland took a bunch of pictures just walking around. There's water on that island, a marsh."

"Ooh. Mosquitos."

CHAPTER TWENTY ONE
BADGES

Cooper Jordan breezed into his office just after 8 on Monday morning, stopping suddenly when he encountered Pamela Prescott and Boyd Chailland standing by his secretary's desk.

"Why, Ms. Prescott and Mr. Chailland, I thought you were on your way back to Oklahoma. I hope there isn't a problem."

"We have some new business." Pam said, smiling.

"Oh?" He looked toward his secretary, as if to question what the schedule looked like. He knew he had an appointment in 10 minutes and was weary of these Oklahoma people.

"Yes."

"Well, perhaps, uh," he looked down at his secretary's desk at his schedule. A twinge of anxiety emerged, but Cooper wanted these two out of his office.

"Now," she said, smile frozen on her face.

"Yes," he said, allowing impatience to replace his usual Southern gentility. He entered his office and stood in the center of the room, hoping he could handle this quickly and not willing to sit and exchange small talk. There wasn't any.

"FBI," Pam said, showing her badge.

"Secret Service," Boyd said, showing his.

"What?" Cooper's heart was suddenly in his throat.

"Have a seat," she said, and remained standing when he sat.

"Donn Wilde was bait. Last night, you engaged in a conspiracy to commit securities fraud – insider trading. I'm pretty sure we can audit your accounts and find that you own securities in BioVet Tech that aren't registered with the SEC. That's a felony. You were offering Donn an opportunity to buy stocks on insider information, hoping the price would spike and you could get out of the hole you're in. Mr. Chailland is investigating the electronic transfer of funds overseas for illegal purposes – money laundering, also a felony."

"But you've entrapped me!" His mind began churning, trying to remember his lawyer's name to drop. Maybe stop this assault.

"Yes, we have," Pam said, softening her tone. "We want your cooperation. We want to know everything you know about BioVet Tech."

Cooper Jordan's mind reeled. Curiously, he was reminded of a television show where he'd seen two police officers play "good cop/bad cop" with a suspect to get him to reveal information. If Pam was playing good cop, he didn't want to even think about Boyd Chailland as the bad cop.

"… and we want to know it now, this morning. This is a matter of national security, and you're going to sit in that chair and not make any telephone calls until we find out what we came here to find," she continued.

****

Weeds poked up through the asphalt parking lot, and a stray dog that had been loitering around the dumpsters in back hurried into the woods as Boyd's car rolled to a stop that afternoon. The BioVet Tech sign, built into a berm in front of the building, still looked new. The grass needed mowing. The last of the half-dozen cars parked there during the afternoon left just before 6, and Boyd, dressed in running shorts and a faded T-shirt, pulled in a few minutes later.

Going through his routine stretch beside the car, he watched for any sign of security. There was none. Jogging slowly, he looped behind the building, getting a quick look at the trash area before getting to the county road just off the highway between Goose Creek and Monck's Corner, a few miles north of Charleston. Forty minutes later, he returned, sweating like any jogger. He paused behind the building and tested the doors, looked into the dumpsters and jotted down the serial numbers of several pieces of equipment set out for the trash company to haul off.

CHAPTER TWENTY TWO
A Taco Truck

"A taco truck?" Gen. Ferguson exploded.

"Yes, sir," Boyd responded. "A complete bust. The money wired to Paris to pay off Jacques came from Island Enterprises LLC, an offshore company headquartered in the Cayman Islands with an account in Charleston. As I said, their only asset visible to Planters National Bank is a taco truck leased to a Salvadoran family that operates it on the Battery in the summer. It's closed now that the tourist season is over."

"Any connection to that vaccine company you're watching?"

"None," Boyd said, cringing at the rage he was feeling over the telephone. They'd burned up a pile of cash making like big-shot bankers and now they had zilch. To make it worse, they'd brought in teams from the CDC, FEMA and Homeland Security. Federal agents occupied an entire floor of the Omni, with more on the way. He was calling Ferguson on the secure line they'd had installed since expanding their investigation. They'd been having daily meetings with the U.S. Attorney, presenting him with what they thought was sufficient information to get a warrant to search Bio-Vet Tech. He was unconvinced. The CDC was insisting on some kind of immediate takedown in the name of national security, and FEMA and Homeland Security were in agreement. The Justice Department was insisting that the CDC and South Carolina had authority to inspect BioVet Tech any time they wanted under existing statute. It was a stand-off.

"Wrap it up. Leave it to the bureaucrats. File a final report."

"Yes, sir."

CHAPTER TWENTY THREE
CHARDONNAY

The white of her sails was visible from Cooper Jordan's office two hours before the sleek cruising yacht *Chardonnay* furled them in front of the Battery and motored smoothly up the Ashley River to the Charleston Yacht Club. Locals and tourists alike stared at the tall masts and rakish profile of this graceful ship. Unlike anything built in the past century, *Chardonnay's* open deck and long bowsprit epitomized elegance and adventure, rare in this day when sailing vessels bulge with enlarged cabins to accommodate comfort at the expense of speed and simplicity.

A woman stood on the foredeck, barefoot, clad only in the briefest of shorts and a longbrimmed baseball cap. She scanned Charleston through binoculars as Charleston scanned her ship. Between Fort Sumter and the Battery, when the flotilla of gawking tourists discovered that the tall slender individual in the cap was female and began taking pictures, she went below. Boyd watched *Chardonnay* approach through a long tripod-mounted telescope in the office of the president of Planters National Bank.

"She made the crossing in only 10 days!" Jordan had exclaimed when the yacht club called the night before with the news that *Chardonnay* had radioed from a hundred miles out of the mouth of Charleston Harbor. "Even the big motor yachts don't do it any faster than that."

No work had gotten done in the office of the president since the sail first appeared on the horizon at 9 a.m. Boyd, Pamela, Donn, Cooper, his secretary and various other bank employees checking in every few minutes watched the approach of the yacht. At first, Boyd didn't understand what the big deal was. It was just a boat. Then the size and uniqueness of the ship became evident.

"*Chardonnay* is 118 feet long, her mast is 129 feet tall, she is all wood, constructed in 1909," Cooper recited proudly, as if speaking of a granddaughter.

"Impressive," Donn said, taking his turn at the telescope. Boyd thought he might be talking about the woman and not the boat.

With Cooper Jordan's cooperation, they had maintained their banker identities for a few more days as the federal agencies continued their wrangling over at the Omni. The stakeouts of BioVet Tech had produced nothing.

"The provenance is even more interesting," Cooper Jordan broke in to take yet another gaze at the spectacle sailing into Charleston Harbor. "*Chardonnay* is owned by the grandson of the founder of Meilland Freres, one of the oldest and most prestigious of the European merchant banks, and the lady you see there is his granddaughter. They are the aristocrats of the banking industry."

"Aristocrats or predators?" Pam said darkly.

"Hah! A student of banking history. Yes, Meilland Freres has been at the center of European political turmoil for 150 years. In Europe, the merchant banks have been the only source of capital. They bring new stock offerings to the public, underwrite bonds, both corporate and government. It was the merchant bankers who enabled expansion, financed wars, massive projects like the Suez Canal, and even propped up governments during times of panic and crisis. As the providers of capital, they've been at the center of whatever happens in government, science and industry," Cooper responded, stepping back from the telescope.

"And, they've fed upon the losers," Pamela said, taking his spot to look at *Chardonnay*.

"Yes, fortunes are made and lost, and the merchant bankers handle the transition."

"It was more than that," Pam said, stepping back and letting Cooper's secretary have a look. "When the French

Revolution began the process of making commoners of royalty, and they had to sell off their estates to pay the taxes, it was the Rothschilds, and the Warburgs, the Lazards, and the Meillands who handled the financing. Then, as wars coalesced the small duchies and kingdoms of the Middle Ages into modern Germany, France, Austria and Italy, the losers cashed out with the merchant bankers."

"Pam, you're a socialist. You should love that," Donn said with a laugh.

Boyd was in awe of her passion. When Pam got started, it was something to behold.

"The merchant bankers helped the strong devour the weak. Then they licked the plate," she said in disgust. But, she couldn't stop.

"They financed Bismarck when he jumped into World War I to expand Germany's borders. They were at the table, urging appeasement with Hitler, when Chamberlain gave away Czechoslovakia. Jews, gypsies, blacks and liberals of all types fled Hitler, and the bankers bought their property for a fraction of its value. After the war, it was the merchant bankers who handled the aid payments from America to rebuild Europe, taking their cut as always. The Glass-Steagall Act was enacted to ensure the U.S. never has permanent insiders, upper class bankers, like the Meillands."

"Isn't the president of Citicorp like a Meilland? Boyd asked, remembering Pamela's rage at Ferguson when she had first met him. Elitism seemed to spark a special hatred.

"No. He's appointed by a board of directors, and they are elected by shareholders. When they feel inclined, they replace him," she exclaimed, as if the replacement would be accomplished with a beheading. "And his son does not step into the job."

She sulked now, point made.

"There's some gossip," Cooper Jordan said cheerfully.

"There always is," Pamela responded, rancor dissipating.

"It seems Mademoiselle Meilland has been involved in a series of intrigues of the heart."

His smooth, deep voice drew out the vowels, the result added emphasis to each part of the sentence.

"A count and his wife, the countess, had an actual duel with pistols in the casino at Monte Carlo. The rumor was that they were both in love with Mademoiselle Meilland."

They all laughed.

"Who won the duel?" Boyd asked.

"They were both terrible shots." Jordan responded slowly, as if savoring each syllable. "A croupier lost part of an ear. Several cut glass mirrors were broken, and a chandelier was destroyed. The royals were unscathed physically, though they must have suffered whispers and snickers for some time afterward."

"What's she doing here?" the secretary asked.

"She's come to buy Sand Island, and she's been invited to a party in her honor at the yacht club tonight. It should be quite the affair. You should come. The elusive Lymon Byxbe should be there," Jordan said, turning to face Boyd with a wry tilt of his head.

"Lymon Byxbe?" Boyd asked.

"Lymon is the chief researcher and majority shareholder of BioVet Tech."

****

A soaking rain was falling as Boyd arrived at the Yacht Club, parking two blocks away and sprinting past the lines of cars trying to get the ladies close to the door to save their hastily coifed hair. Inside, chaos reigned. The 119-foot yacht was a splinter compared with the USS Yorktown, a World War II aircraft carrier permanently anchored in the Cooper River on the other side of the Battery, yet here were scores of people gussied up for a party called in just the past 24 hours to celebrate its arrival.

"Oh, Boyd, thank God you're here!" Amalie Jordan exclaimed, grabbing his arm as he entered. "Cooper is back in the kitchen arguing over shrimp and liquor, and the club president is late as always. *Chardonnay* has radioed a request for the covered launch to pick up Mademoiselle Meilland, and I've no one to send with the driver. Would you be a dear and take some umbrellas and go along, to help her?"

"I can handle that," Boyd responded.

Amalie thrust two umbrellas into his hand and indicated a young black man dressed in rain gear waiting by the door. He followed the man out into the rain, through the yacht basin with a hundred or more closed up sailboats and fishing boats, out to the dock where the motor launch was tied.

Chardonnay loomed much larger than he'd expected when he had watched her approach that sunny morning. Now in the rainy, early evening gloom, her bowsprit pointed upriver like the tusk of some ancient sea creature. Lighted by floodlights on deck, the two masts brushed the clouds.

The launch maneuvered toward steps lowered from the deck a few feet above them. Boyd felt inadequate holding two flimsy umbrellas with swells raising and lowering his launch three feet at a time and rain falling straight down so hard the noise drowned out all sound but the gurgle of the launch in neutral.

"Permission to come aboard!" Boyd called out, remembering something about the proper way to board a naval vessel in port.

His voice was lost in the rain. He looked to the launch driver who stared blankly back. Repeating his request, louder, he closed one of the umbrellas and stepped onto the bottom step. The flimsy stairs, little more than a ladder, swayed with his weight and he was afraid they would break. As he looked down into the dark, oily water below, a shadow passed.

The light gray parasol had tassels hanging from the sides and flowers embroidered on the top. It appeared all the smaller because it was held in the grip of a massive hand, protruding over the stairs and attached to an equally impressive arm. Boyd heard a female voice speaking rapidly in French and then, quickly, pink high-heel shoes were on the steps above him, leading to fine shapely legs that disappeared beneath a short white skirt. Tearing his eyes from their natural tendency to follow the legs into the dark, Boyd looked up, above the skirt, to see a straight back with squared shoulders and blond hair done tightly in a braid. The rain brought down her scent, and Boyd was smitten before he even saw the face of Michelle Meilland.

He stepped back into the boat and held up his larger umbrella for her. She backed quickly down the stairs, trying to keep her head in the small sheltered space created by the parasol held by the large man still on the deck above her. Reaching the last step she turned to face Boyd and hesitated just a moment before leaving the parasol and ducking under his umbrella.

"Thank you. You are Monsieur Jordan?" She asked breathlessly, straightening her clothing as she stepped under the cover of the launch and finally standing to look up only slightly into Boyd's wide-eyed, speechless face.

"Uh. No. I'm Boyd Chailland. Cooper Jordan is back at the club, arguing over shrimp."

"A crisis already. I hope it's not on my account."

"Well, no. Cooper wanted to meet you. I mean, we all wanted to meet you." This was going badly, he thought.

"I'm Michelle Meilland, Mr. Chailland. Are you French? You have a French name."

"A long time ago. Will there be anyone else?" He asked, looking back up the steps.

"Yes." She looked back up the steps. "Wolf. We are waiting."

Bareheaded and nearly soaked, Wolf descended the stairs quickly. His tanned calves seemed to squeeze into shoes too small to support a man so large. He turned on the last step and glided into the shelter of the launch, his wet shirt stretched over pectorals. His tiny puckered nipples seemed afterthoughts, hiding from the cold rain under a bulging mass of muscle. He offered his meaty hand.

"I'm Wolf Goebel."

"Boyd Chailland." Boyd took the hand, not afraid of a strong grip.

When he looked into Goebel's eyes for the first time, Boyd was surprised. Square Nordic face, blond hair and blue eyes, thick neck and squared trapezii, Wolf outweighed Boyd by 30 pounds, though he lacked an inch or two in reaching Boyd's height. Instantly, he knew Wolf to be one of those he'd expected to meet on this mission. The surprise was in how quickly he knew it: Wolf had killed.

Wolf knew just as quickly. The smile seemed genuine, but he was wary. He kept himself between Boyd and the woman. The launch started, and they swung out into the channel and back toward the Yacht Club.

Keeping the two large umbrellas overlapped, Boyd and Wolf kept Michelle Meilland dry, getting soaked themselves as they hurried up the wooden dock to the brief awning at the back door of the Yacht Club. The door swung open as they arrived, and Donn and Cooper Jordan rushed out, eager to help, now that the job was done. Shaking off the water, Boyd and Wolf stepped under the awning; their combined bulk shadowed the others from the mercury vapor light overhead. Brief introductions, and then the door was opened again and they entered. The room, noisy with the conversations of a hundred people, became silent in an instant.

Cooper Jordan maneuvered himself to be on Mme. Meilland's left, and he took her arm as if he had assisted her across the quarter mile of rain-swept sea to this spot. His baritone voice, seemingly out of place in such a frail, mousey little man, boomed out a formal introduction in French.

"Please, I am Mikki. Please call me Mikki. Michelle is so formal. My grandfather calls me Michelle, my friends know only Mikki."

She pronounced Mikki with equal emphasis on each syllable, which gives more weight to the second than is usual in South Carolina pronunciation, which would draw out the first and clip off the second.

Boyd chuckled to hear dozens quietly repeating, "Mikki," with the emphasis on the second sound. Every eye was locked on her as she wiped her face and then ankles with the proffered towel. Boyd and Wolf dripped unnoticed.

Her pink shoes accented faint pink edging on the cuffs, collar and lapels of the white linen suit. The simplicity of expensive linen carefully padded in the shoulders and snug around the buttocks, then fuller just slightly as the skirt ended midthigh, assured even the casual observer that this costume was made for, indeed was crafted on, this woman and no other.

As she held out her hand to the first of a forming line of well-wishers, her diamond earrings captured the light in a dozen twinkling ways. They were simple, yet none who met her failed to look at them for a moment at least.

"Mme. Meilland, I understand you have met professor Lymon Byxbe, our esteemed scientist and industrialist." Cooper Jordan had placed Byxbe at the head of Charleston society for the introductions.

Both men beamed under the charismatic charm of Mme. Meilland. Boyd craned to see. Byxbe was bald, thin, middle-age. He fit Jacques' description of Mosby.

CHAPTER TWENTY FOUR
OYAY AJAK

Davann Goodman leaned on his cane for balance as he stood at the foot of the bed mating vigorously with the African girl he'd met at the Mombasa Yacht Club. His war injuries impaired ambulation but not copulation, and he was pursuing that with a single-minded enthusiasm. The rounded perfection of Mariam Ajak's freely offered posterior had driven Davann to carelessness, and he hadn't noticed when the door downstairs squeaked open or the passage of several large bodies up the stairs.

Completing the act, Davann dropped his cane to the floor and collapsed on the bed with Mariam. She covered herself, then rose and walked to the toilet and closed the door. Several minutes passed and Davann went to sleep.

"Sir!" A deep melodious voice broke the silence.

Davann woke to see three large black men at the foot of his bed. In an instant, he was the Marine again, mind racing. He hadn't seen any guns, good, as his was in his pants behind the intruders. He rolled to the side of the bed and pulled the survival knife he always kept strapped to his ankle, an ace in the hole when everything else fails. The window, and a three story drop to the street, was behind him. He calculated his chances.

"Sir, I am Oyay Ajak, Mariam's uncle. We mean you no harm. Greetings."

The man was huge; tall, wide, thick, with shining black skin and wire-rim glasses. He wore a khaki bush jacket, and the two men with him, equally large and younger, wore work pants and T-shirts.

Davann cowered between the bed and the wall, backing further into the corner. There was no way he could jump up on the bed and leap out of the window, that fused hip just wasn't the tool for that trick. Still, no guns. What was that about greetings?

"Davann! Uncle Oyay is my father's brother, and your friend." Standing in the door to the toilet, dressed, Mariam spoke perfect English. He'd been surprised at first, thinking all these Africans spoke Swahili or Arabic or some strange dialect he'd never master. But, English is the official language in South Sudan, and Mariam, from Juba, had studied it since grade school.

Did they do shotgun weddings in Sudan? Davann relaxed a little. At least it wasn't a kidnapping, a common tool of Arabs for vengeance or ransom. These were not Arabs.

"Sir, I apologize for entering your home this way, but you're being watched. It was the only way to speak to you alone."

The man had a civilized look to him, much more so than his two companions who looked like laborers from the street.

Davann had had his share of girlfriends and had been on friendly terms with a few brothers, and an uncle or two. His homeys didn't talk much about marriage; this would be quite the twist. Then he noticed that he was naked and everyone else in the room was dressed. The two muscle guys seemed to have a slight smirk. He grabbed the sheet.

"You won't need this," Mariam said as she removed his M9 from his trousers and laid it on the table, and then brought the trousers across the room. She knelt in front of him and held them for him to step into. He leaned against the wall while he zipped up and fastened his belt. She retrieved his cane.

"I must get a message to your president." Oyay Ajak said, seated at Davann's kitchen table sipping tea hurriedly prepared by Mariam. His two bodyguards slumped in chairs, also drinking tea. Davann had coffee.

"Why tell me?"

"You are CIA."

"Me? No."

"Yes. We've watched you. You fly American agents with equipment. You smuggle people in and out of Kenya. You have contacts with others in Zanzibar and Ethiopia."

"It's just contract work. They pay, we fly."

"How about Colonel Smith and Captain Chailland. You flew them with their equipment into the Congo Basin and were gone for two months. That was no ordinary contract flight."

"We didn't fly them into the Congo Basin. We flew them ..."

Davann paused. This was well into classified activities, and the whole Indian Ocean trip was best left out of this talk.

"... someplace else, well away from here."

"Your Arab hosts believe you are CIA. They watch everything you do."

"I believe that. But they're wasting their time."

Actually, the Arabs weren't wasting their time. After selling the Albatross back to the United States, relieving Raybun and Davann of their airplane mortgage payment and insurance, operating the Albatross was now quite cheap. Their contract called for six months of payments, and those were still coming in just like any government entitlement check. They had enjoyed their foray into the Indian Ocean and their quarantine on Diego Garcia drinking beer and fishing. Raybon planned to negotiate an extension of the contract to allow the CIA or any other government agency to hire them out for whatever clandestine activity might be needed. It was fun.

"We need to get a message to Mr. Obama."

"Don't you have an ambassador?"

"He stays in Nairobi. If it comes from you, he will listen."

Davann was stumped. Oyay was educated, cultured, yet naïve. Davann felt himself to be buried so deeply beneath the rubble of human activity as to be inconsequential. Yet here was this request to get a message to the president of the United States. He wrinkled his brow, confused, unable to respond.

"Mariam says you are a good man, an important man."

That hit a nerve. Mariam was more than just a woman of his acquaintance. She had a sense of dignity and self-worth that set her apart from other young women he'd known. His grandmother was a woman of dignity. A Memphis school-teacher, she'd allowed no profanity or foolishness in her presence. Now an arthritic old woman, she still dressed every day in a carefully ironed dress and heels as if she were in front of her high school English class. He was both attracted to her and afraid of her sometimes-harsh principles.

As a young man, he'd pursued the easy girls and shirked his grandmother's rigid rules of scholarship, and he'd gotten into trouble. The Marines offered a quick exit, one that earned an appreciative nod from the other tough guys in his South Memphis neighborhood. At Parris Island the drill instructor must have taken notes during one of his grandmother's English classes. It was all about respect – respect for self, respect for the Corps. There is no more rigid code of honor than in the Marine Corps, and Davann was a Marine.

Davann may have been guilty of overstating some of his exploits in an attempt to impress Mariam. She didn't topple the moment he expressed an interest in her, unlike most of the women he'd known. Mariam had been courted.

"What's the message?"

"Do you know our country?" Oyay relaxed a bit and reached into a briefcase by his side, extracting a map. He placed this on the table between them.

"Mariam has talked about South Sudan," Davann responded.

"We're a new nation, but Sudan is an old one, composed of two very different peoples. The north is desert," he said, gesturing toward the map and the tan expanse of Sudan. "The Arabs have lived there since antiquity. Here," he said, pointing to South Sudan, "is forest, and swamp, and grazing lands. Tribes from the mountains and the Congo Basin moved onto the plains long ago. We are herders."

He straightened the map and pushed it closer to Davann. His thick, wide finger punched down on Khartoum, the capital of Sudan.

"These are Muslim. We are Christian, or worship our ancestors. These are Arabs." The finger punched back at Khartoum. "We are African," the finger punched at Juba.

"Mariam has told me about the fighting."

Oyay waved his hand as if to dismiss the concept of fighting.

"We have won our independence, and with the help of the United States, and others, have the weapons to keep it."

"But, there's still fighting."

"Yes," Oyay responded casually. "Tribes steal livestock and women. It's the way of the desert. You hear about this tribe or that tribe breaking out, making threats. It's nothing new. We know these people."

"They want your oil. That's what the news says," Davann said, already beginning to dismiss this as tribal maneuvering for more help.

"No. It's not about oil. It's never been about oil. The Arabs have plenty of oil, and the dribble that we produce isn't of any interest to them. It's water."

Oyay's finger came down again on the map, again at Khartoum.

"The Nile! The Blue Nile comes from Ethiopia, here," he traced his finger from the mountains of Ethiopia down to Khartoum and on toward Cairo. "The White Nile is bigger, and it comes from here," the finger stabbed down south of South Sudan onto the mountains of Uganda, Rwanda and the Congo. "Our birthright! Our gift from God! We have been blessed with the water. Water for our animals, water for our crops, water for our forests!"

Oyay stood now, towering over Davann, eyes bulging, sweat popping out in beads on his forehead.

"The White Nile flows here, into the Sudd wetlands, our breadbasket, our pasture, the foundation of our civilization! They have a plan, the Jonglei Canal Project, to drain the Sudd and divert our water to Cairo!"

"Oh?" Davann said politely, wondering whether he could get on Mariam again this afternoon if he was cordial to her uncle. "But, there's something new?" There must, after all be some purpose to this visit.

"Yes." Oyay punched a finger down on the border between Sudan and South Sudan.

"Here. Men we have not seen before – Bedouin, Palestinian, Iraqi, Turk, Saudi, Omani, Pakistani, Afghan. We killed some. Then we captured some. They are jihadists, and they talked of a new offensive: the Wind of Allah. It will be a new weapon, and they, the jihadists, will sweep across us in triumph. They are very confident, and some of our fighters, superstitious people, are beginning to worry."

"We saw some of that in Afghanistan. They pump those guys up with all sorts of tales to get them to go on suicide missions. How would you like to travel a thousand miles down into the worst desert in the world to fight dudes you'd never seen?"

"No, it's more than that. They are expecting something unusual."

"So they say."

Oyay reached into the briefcase again.

"They have these."

He brought out a picture of a truck speeding through a desert town, stacked four high with crates of live monkeys.

CHAPTER TWENTY FIVE
AN INVITATION

Michelle Meilland swept off the elevator on the executive floor of Planters National Bank, entourage in tow, like the principal of a major European merchant bank, which she was. Cooper Jordan had met her at the street and given her a brief tour of his bank. Now they were heading to his office to execute papers designating Planters National Bank and Meilland Freres as correspondent banks, empowering each to transact business for the other in their respective locations. This had all been hurriedly arranged a day after her grand arrival in Charleston.

Cameras from WCBD, WCIV and WCSC, the network affiliates in Charleston, had caught the entry downstairs and were clamoring off the other elevator to set up for the signing in Jordan's office. The reporter for the Charleston Post and Courier was already snapping photos. This was news because of the perception, planted by Cooper Jordan, that a correspondent agreement with a European merchant bank meant Charleston was the up and coming U.S. East Coast port. Boyd thought it might have other implications.

"… and representing First Bank of Oklahoma City, in Charleston for this momentous occasion, is Mr. MacDonnald Wilde."

Boyd's head snapped around as he heard an enterprising TV reporter begin an interview. The reporter had hurriedly set up his camera while his competition was idling during the final preparation of the papers. There was Donn Wilde facing the camera in full regalia, with his banker's suit and beaming smile in front of the floor to ceiling window overlooking Charleston Harbor.

"Thank you, Ray," Wilde said to the reporter as he beamed into the camera. "It's such a pleasure to be here in fair Charleston and to be a part of this historic occasion as Planters National Bank bursts onto the scene of world commerce. As the people of Charleston know, ships from here take goods to the four corners of the world and bring back the bounty of other lands and nations to enrich the lives of Charlestonians."

Boyd marveled at how a man who had been in prison only a week before could be pontificating on television on a subject he knew next to nothing about. That he pulled it off so well, delighting the young reporter who had thought to quickly set up to catch this interesting looking character, made Boyd wonder how many other local experts were slinging bullshit.

"Boyd?" Mikki approached him from behind, the signing over and the reporters leaving.

From her lips, his name came out as a single syllable, like a bubble bursting.

Boyd turned to face her, the magnetism causing him to stop. She leaned close, and her fragrance drew him in. The eyes were luminous, laughing. Whatever she wanted from him, he was game.

"Could we ride back to *Chardonnay*? Neville St. James, my captain, has taken our car to the market."

"Mais oui, mademoiselle," he replied, in terrible high school French.

****

Capt. St. James was supervising the loading of boxes of food from the trunk of a Chrysler Town Car onto a dolly to cart it down to the launch. Two swarthy crewmen, remarkably alike enough to have been twins, or at least brothers, were busy lifting the cases of mineral water, canned food, beer and dried provisions. *Chardonnay* was riding high in the Ashley River where she had dropped anchor the night before.

"May I see your boat?" Boyd asked.

"Of course," Mikki answered.

"It's a ship, mate. A boat is that little dingy there." Neville's Scottish brogue was pleasing, even though clearly annoyed by Boyd's lack of respect for his vessel. His reddish hair was speckled with gray, and his ruddy face was freckled and peeled from years in the weather. His only acknowledgement of the warmth of the mid-September afternoon was to pull up the sleeves of his wool sweater.

Boyd grabbed a case of tomato sauce and added a case of beer onto it and turned toward the launch. Wolf ignored the seamen and the load and walked with Mikki, empty-handed, behind Boyd.

Chardonnay had a sense of simplicity and elegance that made her as compelling as her owner. Polished brass, carefully varnished teak and spotless glass were the only surfaces other than the deck. Putting down his load, Boyd walked to the front, the deck rough and warm on his bare feet. He stared at the long bowsprit.

"You are a sailor?" Mikki was trailing behind him, carrying her shoes, full skirt gently wafting in the breeze.

"No. I'm a securities salesman. I used to be a pilot."

"*Chardonnay* is a very old ship. Her keel was laid in 1909, and she has been in my family since then. My grandfather sailed her around the world when he was a young man, and my father was born on her on a channel crossing to England."

"That must be some story," Boyd exclaimed, looking up from the bow.

"Perhaps some other time. The story is not entirely pleasant," she said, passing him and stepping out onto the bow, balancing, looking down through the net beneath the bowsprit.

Boyd thought she looked like a child, standing there with her shoes in one hand, intent on her balancing.

"The bowsprit is what you notice. They don't put those on ships any longer. With modern materials, sails no longer need to extend beyond the deck. Yet, we can put up three jibs. The power is ... I wish you could feel the power." She seemed wistful.

Was it a question, he wondered. "Yes. I'd like that."

"We're leaving the day after tomorrow," she said sadly.

"Why so soon?"

"This is a holiday, really. I have business in Europe in two weeks. I must be back."

"Does someone have to go out there when the ship is underway?" Boyd asked, stepping up onto the railing as it met the bowsprit and pointing to the end of it about 30 feet in front of the ship. It was clearly made to traverse, as the top was flat and the net was there to catch someone who might fall from it.

"Of course. We set the jib. That's a small sail that attaches to the mainmast there, and bowsprit. It adds a great deal of power and is easy to rig. Two can attach at the end, and one here," she said, indicating the forestay.

Boyd's eyes followed the steel cable from its attachment at the bow upward to its attachment two-thirds of the way up the mainmast, towering more than a hundred feet above them.

"Does anybody go up there?"

"Not often. The mainsail is self-furling. There is an electric … how do you say it? Engine?"

"Motor?"

"Exactly. An electric motor pulls the sails up. We go up only if they jam. We can furl them in a storm and not even have to leave the pilot house."

"Where's that?" Boyd looked back along the largely bare deck.

Behind the mainmast, which was well forward, was a waist-high storage box for sails 6 feet long. Behind that was a large air intake that looked like the mouth of some great horn. It was set on another waist-high, polished teak structure. Louvered windows allowed some sunlight into the compartment below, and the modest extension gave someone below additional headroom. Farther aft were several other extensions with louvered glass and vents, but they were modest in comparison with other ships he'd seen pictures of. Most of the sailboats in the yacht basin had sacrificed virtually all of their deck to have additional room below.

"In bad weather, we put up canvas around the wheel. Also, we can set the autopilot."

"Like a plane? Just set it and it takes you where you want?"

"No, it just keeps a heading," she responded as they walked aft, toward the ship's stern.

The tallest structure was chest-high and located midway between the masts. It had small rails on its top, indicating a likely place to catch some sun, though the highly polished teak would discourage putting any furniture there. Through louvered windows, Boyd could see down into an elegant saloon, with an oriental carpet and more polished teak and brass. Aft, double doors opened onto stairs descending into the saloon, through a small radio and instrument room. Mikki paused as she stopped to look down.

"That is called the doghouse," she said gaily. "We can enclose this area in canvas when there is weather."

She pointed to the area aft of the wheel, which was just aft of the smaller mast.

"So, this is a schooner?" Boyd asked, looking at the two towering masts.

"No. A schooner has the smaller mast in front of the mainmast. This is a ketch, with the smaller mast just in front of the wheel, which is over the rudder. A yawl would have the smaller mast back further, behind the wheel."

"What do you call the smaller mast?" Boyd asked, looking up the smaller mast, 60 feet above them.

"The mizzenmast. Its sail is the mizzen – the mainmast has the mainsail, and the jib is rigged from the mainmast to the bowsprit."

"This must be something to behold with all the sail out on a windy day," Boyd said, aching to see it.

"If it were truly windy, we wouldn't put them all out. With 20 knots, we could, and it is beautiful."

She smiled, apparently at his enthusiastic interest in *Chardonnay*.

Wolf emerged from the doghouse carrying three open Michelobs, his suit replaced by cotton shorts, no shirt. His chest and arms were huge, outlandish in their excess. His abdomen was ridged with muscle and flat as a board. His thighs were large by normal standards but small when viewed with the massive pectorals. Obviously a very serious weight lifter, Boyd thought, and no stranger to steroids.

"Want a beer?" he asked, holding up the two in his left hand.

Taking a beer, Boyd waited for Mikki to take a tentative sip, then let the first third of his slide down in one cool gulp. He felt the cold all the way to the bottom and was glad they didn't drink beer from cans.

"I have some additional business up the coast tomorrow," Mikki said, looking across Charleston Harbor. "There is an island for sale. You can come along if you like. Bring your friends. We will leave at eight."

CHAPTER TWENTY SIX
JAHAZI COFFEE HOUSE

"Aarif, kind of you to come," Raybon said, rising to welcome his guest at a small coffee house in the old-town section of Mombasa.

"Hello, my friend." An older man in the traditional white robe of Arab dress approached. He wore a wound scarf on his head like a turban. He sat cross-legged at a low table in the dark rear of the shop. A waitress brought a steaming pot of tea as he sat.

"The sunrise was beautiful today," Raybon said as he poured tea for his guest.

"A gift from Allah."

"Allah be praised."

They each took a sip of tea and looked around at the nearly empty shop and out to the busy street.

"Our business has not been good this month," Raybon began.

"My friends are not so interested in our product now. We are being watched closely by the government."

"Have my visitors upset your friends?"

"Visitors always raise the question of loyalty."

"Who do you think my visitors are?"

"CIA," the man said matter-of-factly.

"Some were. Captain Chailland and Colonel Smith were from the United States Air Force. I took them to an island in the Seychelles for a scientific investigation."

"My friends think you took them to the Congo."

"Why do they think that? Did they not see the equipment? There was a boat, tents, scientific instruments."

"They think you were recruiting tribes from the mountains to fight the Janjaweed."

"I've heard some disturbing news, something I don't understand," Raybon said, looking into his host's eyes.

"Oh?" Aarif returned the look.

"A friend, coming back from Juba, has told me of an army forming north of there."

"Yes. The Sudan is a dangerous place," he said warily.

"It is not the Janjaweed, herders fighting for their land, or the Army of Sudan on the border. It is jihadists from many lands."

"Jihadists in Sudan?" Aarif stroked his chin, brow furrowed.

"Yes, old friend. Why would jihadists be in Sudan?"

"It is forbidden for Muslims to have two Emirs in this world, as it causes confusion and conflict. Jihadists fight to unify Islam."

185

"There are several leaders in Muslim nations who call themselves Emir."

"That is forbidden." Aarif took another sip. "It is true, but it is forbidden."

"So jihadists are supposed to unify all Muslims?"

"It is written that every Muslim man must struggle, which is what jihad means, toward self-improvement and to defeat the enemies of Islam and unify all Muslims under one Emir."

"But what has South Sudan to do with unifying all Muslims? There are no Emirs there."

"I am a simple trader from Oman. What am I to know of these things?" Aarif was becoming reticent.

"You have been very generous with me, old friend. I appreciate knowing you. Should I leave Mombasa? Am I not welcome here?"

"It is written that the infidel can be tolerated and given a chance to recognize the wisdom and follow the Prophet, if it is the will of Allah."

"Allah be praised."

"You have been a friend, Raybon. It is dangerous for you here, but you can stay. If I hear of any plans against you, I will call at once. And I don't know why jihadists are in Sudan."

CHAPTER TWENTY SEVEN
SAND ISLAND

Neville St. James raised the mainsail as they passed Fort Sumter, the wind snapped the canvass taut, and *Chardonnay* surged. With just the mizzen and the first jib, she'd seemed sedate, wallowing along while motor cruisers skimmed past. Now that the mainsail was up, it felt as though there were a visceral force in the teak and brass. Boyd gripped the railing over the doghouse and ran his hand along the smooth top. It was power. Not the vibration an engine can give, this was more spiritual, more thrilling.

"You feel it?" Mikki smiled at him.

Boyd couldn't suppress the grin, like a child experiencing something wonderful for the first time. Donn and Pamela also were holding on to part of the ship, and grinning. Wolf smirked, drained his beer and dropped the bottle into a plastic bag attached to the mizzenmast. Neville St. James stood by the wheel. Bare-headed, he squinted back toward Charleston and took a deep breath.

Chardonnay hit a small wave and spray flew from the bow, a few droplets carrying back over the deck. The wind pushed, and *Chardonnay* seemed to push back, creaking as the canvas and rope adjusted to the increased force. There was a sensation of riding the swells now as the speed increased.

"Beautiful wind," Mikki said, looking back at Charleston. "We had wind like this all the way across the Atlantic. Steady, from the south."

"This is the time of year for the big blows," Neville commented from the wheel as they neared the widening exit from the harbor.

They turned north, and the mizzen and main sails were allowed to rotate to starboard to catch the wind. Neville directed the Portuguese crewmen to let the sails out, and one of them climbed out the bowsprit and attached the end of a jib while the other climbed a third of the way up the mainmast to attach the other end. They were making *Chardonnay's* maximum speed of 12 knots. The passing scenery included a beautiful sky, other boats, waves, birds and the bluing Atlantic.

Boyd shook off the warm comfort of the morning and refocused on the job at hand. Their mission had been to find Ebola, and they had not. They'd followed the trail of money to Charleston and lost it. Someone was laughing at them. Was it Lymon Byxbe? Had Ebola ever been at Bio-Vet Tech? If they kicked the door down, would they find anything at all? He was afraid not. Whoever sent money to Paris knew what they were doing. That taco truck was a sign that this wasn't just about money. Someone was playing games.

Mikki emerged from the doghouse wearing the same shorts and long-brim baseball cap Boyd had seen through the telescope from Cooper Jordan's office. Her compact, low-slung breasts were thoroughly tanned and almost unobtrusive on her long torso. The virginal nipples bespoke that, although she was nearly through her reproductive years, she had not borne children.

Through manners or instinct, Boyd looked quickly away from Mikki. Wolf and Neville were watching Pamela and Donn stare at the breasts. Mikki carried a tray of glasses and a bottle of white wine, but her eyes scanned the whole group. The Portuguese seaman turned aft and busied himself with coiling some rope.

"Vouvray is such a good morning wine. Would you like some?" She placed a towel on the shining teak atop the doghouse and put the tray on it.

Donn and Pamela approached Mikki, taking a glass, eyes flicking from wine to breasts to face. Mikki poured, smiling blandly. Pamela had worn shorts and a white golf shirt, the pattern on her bikini was visible beneath it. Donn sported his big flowered Hawaiian shirt and shorts. Boyd wore tennis shorts and a white knit shirt.

"We have planned to reach the island at high tide, noon. Neville is afraid of shoals. We are making good time, no?" She looked back at Neville at the wheel. He nodded.

"Which island is it?" Donn asked, looking out over the bow again.

"Sand Island. I've been interested in finding a private island. There are none available in the Mediterranean. The Adriatic has some, but life is uncertain there."

Boyd knew Sand Island well. It was a teardrop-shape island just west of the Military Operations Area off the Atlantic coast. It was known for the spit of sand extending from its pointed southern tip that varied in length with the tide. He'd briefed dozens of missions, always pointing it out as a landmark at the edge of the MOA. He'd assumed it was a part of the nearby Francis Marion National Park and Seashore.

The Isle of Palms was sliding past a mile west. The crowded shoreline seemed tacky with its tiny, multicolor houses, an easy commute from downtown Charleston. There was hardly any beach.

"You haven't been below," Mikki said, pouring the last of the wine into her own glass after giving Wolf a top off. Their eyes met briefly.

She removed the tray and towel and led the way through the double doors into the doghouse. Wolf walked aft. Boyd lingered until last, and then followed down the slightly curving stairs. The chart room was just a wide pause in the passage below deck filled with radar screens, depth, weather, and navigation instruments, books and charts.

Boyd saw a chart laid out on the map table that showed the coast of South Carolina and a plastic overlay with a course charted to Sand Island. It looked much like the flight plans he prepared when he planned a mission.

The light shining through the skylight forward of the doghouse lit the interior of a small but lavish dining and sitting room as the stairs circled from aft forward. The heavy table to one side was large enough to feed a dozen. Across the expanse of oriental carpet, accented by shining brass lights hanging from the ceiling, there was an additional table with chairs and a velvet settee at least 10 feet long. Fresh flowers and a fruit bowl adorned the wet bar at the end of the room. A narrow galley filled a hall beyond.

"The crew's quarters are aft of the mast. A guest stateroom is there," Mikki said, pointing to a small, discreet door adjacent to the wet bar. Opening it, she revealed a nicely appointed room with a settee and a double bed.

"You may use the toilet there."

She walked back to the stairs they'd just used and pointed to another closed door.

"Wolf is there."

Opening double doors behind the stairs she walked into a spacious room lit by another skylight with a settee on one side and a double bed on the other. A large beveled glass mirror dominated the forward wall. One sidewall was a bookcase, the other had a small dressing table and closet.

"I sleep here."

She turned to face her guests, peering behind her into her private space, then closed the doors.

"*Chardonnay* is a sailor's ship, built to sail fast and far," Mikki said, ending the tour.

****

"Ten meters!" Mikki yelled back to Neville at the wheel.

She was sitting on the chart table watching the depth gauge. Wolf stood at the bow, watching for logs or debris. Pamela and Donn were stationed on either side. Sand Island lay nearly a mile away, yet Neville's caution had the sails furled and the diesel idling them along at only a couple of knots.

"She draws 12 feet," Neville said to Boyd, standing by with a long pole in case some debris was spotted. "Your

Eastern coast is a ship's graveyard of shoals, shifting constantly."

"Why 12 feet? We surely didn't go 12 feet down those stairs," Boyd asked, understanding the intensity of the captain's anxiety, even with 30 feet of water beneath his hull and the ability to back up at a moment's notice.

Boyd knew well how it felt to fly an aircraft worth thirty-five million bucks and belonging to someone else. He'd seen guys crack one up by some once-in-a-zillion-odds accident and never be allowed to fly again.

"Keel. We have a lead weighted keel six feet below the hull. We need it to balance the sail. A stiff wind would blow her over. With the keel, the force of the wind is transmitted into forward motion. It's where the power comes from."

Neville St. James held up one hand and motioned at it with the other to represent the wind. The first hand went forward.

"We don't want to run onto a sandbar, with a dropping tide, we'd be here for a week."

"Fifteen meters!"

"This island she wants, it's just a sandbar. One big blow, and she'd be gone," Neville said quietly. "This whole area here is shifting sand. *Chardonnay* is for deep water."

Five hundred yards from shore, Neville dropped anchor in 12 meters of water. Sand Island rose from a long bar south of Cape Romain. It was one of the barrier islands that protect the Santee River estuary from the open sea. Boyd knew well the miles of salt marsh punctuated occasionally by wooded hillocks that lay inland. Sand Island was no more than a wooded hillock farther out, surrounded by water instead of marsh grass.

Wolf and Boyd lowered the Searider, a large inflatable launch with rigid bottom and outboard motor. Mikki donned a T-shirt and shoes and led her guests down the ladder. Wolf followed, lugging a cooler filled with beer and sandwiches for lunch. Soon they were bouncing over the swells, spray flying as she opened up the 40-horsepower outboard. They selected a landing spot on the northern shore.

"The agent said it is offered by the heirs of one of your richest families," Mikki said, jumping out of the stern in thigh deep water.

Wolf jumped out of the front and began pulling the launch onto the brief beach tangled with brush and driftwood. Donn and Pamela hesitated getting their feet wet. Boyd, taking the lead from Mikki, slid over the side and waded in, pushing the boat.

It may have been just a sandbar, but the trees on Sand Island had been there for three hundred years. Live oaks with trunks 12 feet thick and branches spreading 90 feet, parallel to the ground, do not spring up in one man's lifetime. Palmetto palms grew thick in the sand near the shore but gave way in the interior to huge oaks, poplars and gum trees. It was quiet and cool.

A circular charred area just off the beach surrounded by oyster shells, ketchup bottles and beer cans suggested trespassers used the island.

Wolf was tense. His bulk clearly didn't lend itself to stepping over logs or around brush and vines. He'd already scratched his leg on a thorn and a thin line of blood was visible on his calf. He walked as if there was nothing like this in his native Austria, or on the French Riviera where he lived. He seemed to expect a wild beast to leap out of the forest at any moment.

Boyd and Eight Ball walked woods in the midlands of South Carolina almost daily. He knew each tree and bush here but hadn't seen anything this old outside the gardens of the plantations along the Cooper River north of Charleston.

"Private islands are hard to come by in Oklahoma. I tried to buy a town once," Donn said, walking through the brush to the interior.

"A town?" Mikki asked.

"Yep. Skunk Wells, Oklahoma. The oil fields around there dried up, and cattle prices were down. The local bank went bust, and I offered them a package deal. Bank, town square, town hall, the whole deal for two million bucks. I was going to put in a golf course and sell lots."

Near the center of the island, Boyd came upon an ancient magnolia, its thick trunk nearly obscured by the drooping of its lower limbs. Midway up, on the very outermost tip of a long branch, was a rare late season bloom, pure white in the darkness of the forest.

"Here, hold this," Boyd said impulsively, digging into his pocket for the small knife he carried. He handed it to Pam.

Pam took the knife and looked at it for a moment and then looked dumbly at the tree.

Boyd ran at the tree and leaped at the trunk, planting one foot as high as he could while grasping a branch and pulling himself smoothly upward, pausing momentarily with his torso across the branch before throwing a leg across it and standing. Now 10 feet from the ground with his head six feet higher into the foliage, he repeated the process and disappeared.

"I'll pull the branch down," Boyd's voice came from within the tree.

From her pose, it was evident Pam had no idea what he was trying to do.

He walked out on a large branch, holding a smaller one above it. When he got near the end, both of them now sagging, he pulled himself up on the smaller branch and it bent near to the ground. On the end of that branch was a pristine white flower 8 inches across.

"Cut it with the knife," he said, hanging from the branch. "But don't touch the flower."

Pam cut the branch several nodes above the flower. The others gathered to look at it while Boyd dropped to sit on the branch on which he'd been standing. He sat there for a moment and then grabbed a lower branch and swung down another level, dropping to the ground and rolling in the soft earth. He walked to Pam and took back his knife and the flower. The fragrance, as always, took him back to early summer nights at home in southern Missouri, cicadas buzzing in the big oak and the fragrance crossing the road from the magnolia in the neighbor's yard. He trimmed the excess leaves from the stem and handed it to Mikki.

"You climbed the tree just to get a flower?" Wolf asked.

"It's a magnolia. It blooms mainly in the spring, but for special occasions will sometimes produce one this late. This tree has been popping these out for a hundred years or more. It'd be a shame not to look at one up close."

"It's beautiful," Mikki said, smelling it. "Thank you."

They walked south, taking turns carrying the cooler.

"So, are you going to buy it?" Boyd was walking with Mikki.

"Perhaps. The price is high. I want it." She looked around, then back at the magnolia. "There is a feeling here."

Boyd nodded without speaking, looking back at the woods they had just traversed. A cloud passed overhead and obscured the sun. In shadow, the forest changed.

"Primordial. Do you know the word?" Mikki asked. "It is primordium in Latin. The English word must be the same."

She turned to look at Spanish moss drooping from the limbs of a live oak, its massive trunk somehow supporting limbs larger in girth than a man and drooping to the ground only many feet from the trunk.

"Primordial. Yes, that's the word."

"You belong here. You seem …"

"I fit in?" Boyd laughed. "I'm a primordial man?"

"Not so bad in a troubled, dangerous world," she said simply, and then walked, watching the others in silence as they walked through the trees.

"My cousin has heirs and will own the bank when my grandfather dies. He is younger, but male. I am preparing to leave the bank at the end of this year."

She paused and leaned against the trunk of a fallen tree, her intense blue eyes focused on Boyd now. He felt the attraction.

"It's a fine island."

Boyd glanced into the eyes, still on him. In his mind, he replayed the grand entrance of *Chardonnay* into Charleston Harbor, the Yacht Club party, the hurriedly arranged meeting with Byxbe, and now the island and impending trip back to Europe. This wealthy sophisticate didn't leave the playgrounds of the Riviera to buy Sand Island or to hear a pitch by Lymon Byxbe on a new vaccination process.

"Do you own part of your bank?" she asked, shifting her buttocks further back onto the trunk of the fallen tree.

"No. I'm just a hired man, a securities salesman." Boyd smiled, looking away to the east.

He felt her gaze, searching. This lady was smart. He tried to blank his mind. When he couldn't, he tried to think salesman thoughts. Failing again, he imagined Mikki's bare breasts, not too hard considering he'd had ample time to study them that morning. He didn't know whether people could really know what another was thinking, but he knew he could spot a liar. Could Mikki?

The troupe converged at the southern tip of the island and walked out onto a clean sand beach that stretched 200 yards farther south before disappearing in a point beneath the blue water. To the west, several miles away, lay the mainland and the beginning of salt grass and tidal creeks that went well inland. Bull Island, a large wooded island was just visible to the south. The expanse of the large bay their small island sat in gave them a sense of isolation. *Chardonnay* sparkled in the bright midday sun, riding high and proud at anchor a half-mile east.

"It's lunchtime," Donn announced, lugging the cooler out onto the beach and opening it. They gathered, sorting through for their choice of French mineral water, beer or a bottle of Absolute vodka. Boyd took a beer, kicked his shoes off and walked alone to the spit of beach at the end, using the serenity to mull over his problem. At the end, he stood in ankle-deep water and looked back over the 200 yards of sand that separated him from his companions. He imagined the blotches on the dead farmers, saw Jacques sitting on the beach and heard the drums. Ebola was the adversary here, and a pattern was becoming evident.

He recalled Joe Smith's bad dreams while they'd been quarantined at Diego Garcia. Joe always thought of Ebola as a thing, a united force, not a zillion individual creatures. It broke out of the jungle by playing to the basest impulses in humans. The actual illness was secondary, just a means of reproduction. Ebola wasn't going to be back in Charleston in a freezer controlled by a couple of businessmen desperate to unload worthless stock. Follow the pattern. Ebola had jumped to another vector. If he wanted Ebola now, he would need to be out there, on *Chardonnay*, bound for Europe.

CHAPTER TWENTY EIGHT
SKINNY DIP

Boyd pulled off his shirt as he walked back down the spit of land. With the shirt behind his back he pitted his triceps one against the other, then put his fists together in front of his chest and maximally contracted his pectorals, then twisted to each side and flexed his lats. In the two minutes it took to casually walk back to the group he had engorged his upper torso as effectively as if he'd done a dozen bench presses. He walked to where Mikki stood by the cooler and reached in for a beer, popping the top and gazing at the sky. As he posed, he let the whole bottle gurgle into his throat before casually dropping it to the sand.

"It's not like we have to be anywhere this afternoon," Boyd said. "This is as pretty a section of beach as there is in America. I propose we enjoy having it all to ourselves."

The sound of the change in the pocket of Boyd's shorts hitting the ground caused four heads, turned momentarily to look at the beach he'd just praised, to snap around. He stood there nude like Adonis, soaking up admiring glances, then took a quick step toward Pamela.

"Come on Pammie! Let's go swimming."

Boyd picked her up and accelerated into the surf, easily hoisting her weight onto his shoulder. The waves tripped him and he dived forward, throwing a loudly protesting Pamela, as they splashed into the sea.

****

Holding the bow several points east of due south, Boyd steered *Chardonnay,* feeling her spirit in the wheel. The wind had shifted to the southwest, and they had to close-haul out to sea to get back to Charleston. Hitting a swell now, the spray blew back onto the deck with some regularity and was a refreshment when it did.

"Mikki was a wee lass when I first shipped out on *Chardonnay,*" Neville said, returning to the deck from the doghouse where he'd gone to light his pipe. The sun was warm still, but low in the west. Boyd had chosen the fading sun and *Chardonnay's* wheel to cocktails and laughter below. The others were having a grand time reliving the afternoon and tending to Pamela's sunburn.

"Her family big sailors?"

"*Chardonnay* belongs to Mikki's grandfather. He inherited her as a young man and sailed her long and fast. Quite a man."

"You the captain all that time?"

"No. I was the mechanic. You had to have a full-time mechanic in those days. Diesels weren't as reliable as they are now. We prefer to use pure sail, but get in a bad blow and you'd better have the diesel."

"You must have seen a lot," Boyd said, looking around, alert for traffic now that Charleston Harbor was in sight.

"Aye, that," Neville said, puffing, looking east at the horizon. Several minutes passed.

"Mikki seems spirited. Is that just from being rich?"

"It's in the blood." Neville said, puffing again.

Then, lowering his voice, he said, "Lad, they are a fierce clan."

"Fierce?"

"Aye."

"Fierce?"

Neville didn't answer. He walked forward to stand alone on the bow, looking at the distant lights of Charleston.

****

"I won't go! That son of a bitch said I had a big butt!" Pamela exclaimed the next morning just after dawn, glowering at Donn.

They had anchored *Chardonnay* at the Yacht Club just after 9 and stayed below listening to Neville tell sea stories.

203

It had been exotic places, big blows and pirates. Donn joined in with stories of elk camp in Colorado and snake hunting in Oklahoma until after midnight.

"I said she had a big sunburn," Donn said, laughing. He'd spent the night in his own room and was already packed. Mikki had spent a lot of time sitting with Donn, and now Pam was jealous, hung over and badly sunburned.

"Agent Prescott, you will go, and you will continue in your undercover role or see disciplinary action from your supervisor, which right now is me," Boyd said, sounding too much like Ferguson.

He'd spent an hour with Ferguson on the phone already this morning and heard the tale of jihadists in Sudan that Davann had gotten, and Raybon's failure to find out any more from his Arab friend. The CIA was reaching out now to covert agents around the world. What was "the Wind of Allah?"

"My butt hurts," Pamela said, throwing her suitcase on the bed. She was clad in a chaste terrycloth robe provided by the hotel. On the beach, she'd pulled steadily on the Absolut, her inhibitions dropping away like Salome's veils, until finally she had traipsed nude down the spit of sand like a well-fed wood nymph. This time it was Wolf and Mikki whose eyes kept flicking back to the goodies. After lunch,

Pam fell asleep, face down on the sand, her pale, muscular buttocks taking on a reddish glow.

Sitting cross-legged on the bench beside Donn that night, Mikki had laughed to the point of tears after hearing of his pitch to the residents of Skunk Wells, Okla. Taking shares in his corporation instead of money for their town was the smart move, he'd told them, because soon scores of free-spending millionaires from Tulsa and Oklahoma City would buy second homes there to retreat to "the sylvan splendor" of their community on weekends. The citizens had wised up at the last minute, and several had actually worn guns into town the day they advised him to leave.

"Pistols? Like the Old West?" She had laughed incredulously.

"Matched Colt 44s! Another guy had a Winchester 94 model. I got the message all right," Donn laughed, as Mikki sat close, her fragrance renewed after a quick shower.

"We leave tomorrow for Europe. Will you come?" Mikki had finally asked. "It will take two weeks. I must leave at Lisbon and fly to Luxembourg. You may return from there or go on to Cannes. We will stop in Bermuda and the Azores."

Pamela, who'd brightened their afternoon with her so freely shared charms, was by the evening again glassy-eyed, having sobered up in the early evening to find the vodka and finish it. Donn basked in Mikki's attention as he interspersed his stories with Neville's.

Boyd sat shirtless in the heat of the cabin. Wolf, shirtless also, had provided some kind of Swiss sunburn balm for Pamela to apply to her rosy breasts before covering them with a wet T-shirt to ease the pain. Now he sat next to her glowering at Donn and Mikki.

"You will have to share the guest room. With three, it should be interesting. No?" Mikki said with a gay smile.

"We can sleep in shifts," Boyd had volunteered, delighted that their escapades had made them seem an essential part of the crossing back to Europe. Only passing entertainment for a rich girl tired of her musclebound lover, true, but on board for the next leg.

Now that Pamela was packing, Donn returned to his room and found some Alka Seltzer, which he dropped into a hotel glass of water and offered it to her.

"Thanks. I wish you guys would stop me when I get over the line like yesterday." Pam said, coming out of the bathroom where she had hurriedly dressed. She gulped down the Alka Seltzer and made a face.

"You did great," Boyd said. "Wolf couldn't keep his eyes off you all day. Did you find out anything?"

Boyd swung her filled suitcase out onto the waiting bellman's cart in the hall.

"The two seamen are from an island called Faial in the Azores. Mikki said she plans to give them a couple of days there before going on. There's a sailors bar there, Peter's, supposedly quite the place for transatlantic sailors. She may be meeting someone there. She said she had to be there by the 20th."

"Very good, Pam. When did you get that?"

"On the beach, while you three big men were playing in the waves like kids."

"Anything from your end?" Boyd asked Donn, pushing the cart toward the elevator.

"She's a stock manipulator. Said she'd just as soon let her cousin manage the real estate and banking business. She likes action."

"Well, she likes action of a nonfinancial nature, too," Boyd said as they waited for the elevator. "Don't get too caught up in the fun."

CHAPTER TWENTY NINE
THE ATLANTIC

"That's the sea breeze, laddie. Wait 'til we get into the Atlantic. You'll see. We'll have the wind. She rides the wind!" Neville seemed glad to be gone from Charleston. They had hurriedly taken on more provisions with the addition of three guests to feed and entertain, and had set sail by 8.

"We must be 10 miles from shore, I can't see the land," Boyd said, turning to look back at Charleston. As far as he was concerned, this was the open Atlantic. They were headed northeast, with the east wind crossing to starboard.

"This is coastal water. See, it's brown," Neville said. "That breeze, it rushes from the sea, which is cool, toward land, which warms up early in the day and sends the air over it higher. In two hours, we'll be in the open sea."

The captain walked forward into the doghouse to light his pipe and look at some charts.

Boyd sipped his coffee and enjoyed the feel of *Chardonnay* through the wheel as he stayed on the course of zero six five, designated by the captain. One of the Portuguese seamen had begun sanding a teak railing nearby. Donn and Pamela were leaning out over the railing of the bow, laughing. Wolf and Mikki were below, checking inventory in the storeroom.

"We've got a blow, lads. In the south," Neville said, returning from the doghouse a half hour later, addressing Boyd and the Portuguese sailor.

Candido Mendes stepped over to see the paper the captain held in his hand. He was a short man with narrow shoulders and hips, black hair and a bushy mustache. His deeply tanned skin was wrinkled and leathery, indicating years at sea.

The paper was a weather fax of the southern North Atlantic. The East Coast of the United States was visible on the western edge of the map, with open ocean in the center. A spiral of clouds was evident west of the Cape Verde islands, off Africa on the eastern edge of the map.

"Is that a hurricane?" Boyd asked, seeing the familiar pattern of the clouds.

"No, the winds are only 50 knots or so. Not well organized enough to call a hurricane, but more than we want to be near," Neville said, still looking at the FAX.

"Not a place to be sailin'," Mendes said in perfect, unaccented English.

"You sound American," Boyd said.

"I am. I grew up in Fall River, Massachusetts," the dark-skinned man answered.

Everything about him looked European – the clothing, the hair, the mannerisms. He smiled at Boyd.

"There are a lot of Azoreans in America. I left Faial when I was 10, when my father moved here to work on his brother's fishing boat. When I got my seaman's card, I worked tuna boats for a while."

Neville, running a pipe cleaner down the stem of his momentarily cold pipe, said, "The Portuguese, and especially the Azorean Portuguese, are consummate sailors. Candido and his cousin have been with *Chardonnay* for 20 years."

"So, do you live in Fall River?"

"No. I moved back to Faial. My wife wasn't happy. Her family is all on Faial and Pico, the next island. You'll see it. It's beautiful there."

As if suddenly realizing his reason for mixing with the guests was the fax, now examined, he smiled and moved away.

"So, is this a problem? Looks like that storm is about 3,000 miles away," Boyd said, returning to the fax.

"The northeast trade winds blow to the west below 30 degrees latitude. This storm should track well south of us. We'll be north, above 30 degrees to catch the prevailing westerlies back to Europe."

Neville tapped the map above Bermuda and well north of their present position.

The wind died over the next hour, and noon found them wallowing in an oily smooth sea with minimal swells. Sensing the loss of power, Mikki came up from the doghouse, looking at the NavStar GPS printout of their position.

"Are we far enough north for the westerlies?" she asked Neville from the doghouse.

"Aye. Should pick it up here, may have to wait."

"We'll give it two hours. Start the diesel then if we don't get wind." She turned and went down the stairs.

There was no doubt who ran this ship.

Before long, a wisp of breeze blew out of the west. Neville nodded to Candido, who needed no further instructions. He quickly rigged a jib from the mainmast to the tip of the bowsprit. Meanwhile, Neville allowed the mainsail and mizzen some slack as the wind from the southwest caught them, pushing them across the deck to the port side. *Chardonnay's* sails tightened and she leaned to port and began to move northeast.

****

Dawn lit the eastern horizon with a red glow as Wolf climbed the steps carrying a tray of hard rolls, liver sausage, white cheese, butter and jelly, and two steaming cups of coffee.

"In Switzerland, we have a big breakfast," he announced, obviously in a fine humor and looking forward to his eight hours of watch.

Boyd had volunteered to pull the first night shift. Wolf had turned in early the night before to be ready for the morning relief. *Chardonnay* had scarcely needed the auto-pilot to keep her at zero eight zero course through the night. The steady west wind had been most dependable. Boyd had charted the course hourly, logging 109 miles during his shift.

Freed by the autopilot from having to stay by the wheel, Boyd had spent the night walking the deck, watching the stars and doing some calisthenics. Though liver sausage wasn't his idea of breakfast, he tried some in the spirit of Wolf's good humor, later adding jelly to ease it down.

"Neville wanted us to stay on zero eight zero, but looks like we'll have to change a few degrees to the east or we'll miss Bermuda," Boyd said, showing Wolf his record of their course during the night.

Wolf added two slices of cheese to the liver sausage on a generously buttered roll and looked over Boyd's shoulder, nodding. He took a big bite, nodded some more, and stepped back onto the deck. He scanned the horizon in all directions while chewing his first bite.

"Neville is eating. He'll change the course when he comes up," Wolf said, breathing deeply as he smelled his coffee, and then washed down the first bite with a big gulp.

Boyd finished his coffee watching the sun rise out of the Atlantic and then went below.

Mikki sat on the bench behind the table in the saloon, drinking coffee and looking at another weather fax. She nodded but didn't speak.

"Guess my compatriots are still in the rack," Boyd said, looking toward the closed door to the guest stateroom. He was tired and wanted to sleep.

"Take any bed," Mikki said, sliding out and trotting up the steps. Halfway up she began to speak to Wolf in French.

Neville shrugged, smeared some jelly on a roll and stood to refill his coffee from the pot on the bar. He went above. Boyd found some cereal and milk and sat looking at the fax. The storm didn't look as dense as it had the night before and was tracking due west, just as Neville had predicted. It was no threat. He heard a shower start in the guest room.

Pamela emerged, hair up in a towel, wearing the robe she had charged to her room at the Omni in Charleston.

"Hey, it's a fine day. You guys sleep OK? I tried to avoid all the bumps," Boyd said cheerfully.

"I slept fine. Don't know about Casanova. He bunked with our hostess." Pamela entered the galley and opened the refrigerator, taking out some eggs.

Mikki came down the stairs, crossed the saloon and refilled her cup.

"Want an omelet?" Pam asked, bright, unaffected.

Boyd quickly stepped into the bedroom, hoping to avoid the confrontation that seemed inevitable.

"Yes! Eggs for breakfast. I am fond of them," Mikki said, ignoring Boyd as he closed the door.

CHAPTER THIRTY
MIKKI

The fight may have come as a complete surprise to Boyd, but Mikki had known it would happen since that rainy night in Charleston when he'd held the umbrella for her. Before, actually, for she'd brought Wolf to her bed the first night out of Cannes with the expectation that in America, a delicious conflict might arise.

She had enjoyed watching Wolf's confidence build until there was hope that he'd become more than just the bodyguard, hired by a cautious old man to watch his precious granddaughter.

Mikki had been able to claim the hearts of handsome, wealthy men since she was 12. It was so predictable as to be without pleasure. The thrill was when someone risked something for her. As a teen, it was older men as they risked disgrace and the retribution of her grandfather by slipping into her room or trysting with her in all manner of semi-public places. Being caught *in flagrante delicto* produced an especially intense pleasure.

Later, as an adult, with her own residence and the freedom to travel as she pleased, scandal, divorce and ruin followed in her wake across the capitals of Europe. Her mere presence in a resort created a ripple of anticipation among the cognoscenti, as they speculated about who it would be this time – lured, trapped, exposed.

Conflict bred danger, and danger fed the insecurities of a doting old man. He hired bodyguards to protect her from the consequences of scandal. Bodyguards introduced Mikki to a new game. Now the stakes could be more than just divorce or disgrace. Now the stakes could be death. The exquisite intensity of sex with a man who had just risked death in combat over her took Mikki's pleasure to a whole new level of intensity. The fights so far had been stopped before death occurred. The playgrounds of the wealthy are always well policed. But, on *Chardonnay,* in the middle of the Atlantic, with only a geriatric captain and two smallish seamen to step in in the name of authority, there would be no stopping a fight between two big men, men who knew danger, men who liked the feeling death left when it passed close by.

There was another element now, too. Life without struggle is boring. The plan her grandfather had hatched had seemed, at first, just a way to settle some old scores and to consolidate their control over a business she didn't understand. Then, somehow, it became clear. They were going to destabilize equatorial Africa and, in the chaos, seize control of the diamond business. The power to change the course of world history had sharpened Mikki's senses, given her a new energy and increased her need for the kind of fun her guests could provide.

Mikki loaded the gun by inviting the Americans for the crossing back to Europe. She cocked the hammer when she took Donn to bed, displacing Wolf. She pulled the trigger in international waters 200 miles west of Bermuda, an hour before dawn.

"I couldn't sleep."

Donn had had the late watch the night after Boyd had taken his turn. He turned with a start.

"Oh. Better put on some clothes."

"No."

CHAPTER THIRTY ONE
THE FIGHT

"Wolf! No!"

The scream woke Boyd. The thud on the deck above started the adrenalin flow. He leaped from the bed he had shared with Pamela, curled in a blanket at the opposite end. Fully dressed already by the agreement that allowed him to sleep in the guest suite instead of on the couch in the saloon, he took the stairs two at a time. It was still dark, and the scene on deck was illuminated by a full moon.

"Stop!" Mikki, nude, flapped ineffectually on Wolf's huge shoulders while he hammered and tore at a limp Donn Wilde like a dog killing a rat. Donn was clinging to life on the starboard railing. In another moment was going to release his hold and be gone over the side.

Charging forward, Boyd ducked under a flailing Mikki and grabbed Wolf's legs, pulling them forward. Wolf fell backward onto Mikki who screamed in pain. Donn rolled off of the railing onto the deck. Blood flowed freely from his nose, and his upper lip was open on the left side, teeth in disarray showing through the gap. Jumping to his feet, Boyd found himself forward of the mainmast, with his back to a furled and jacketed jib, and the bowsprit.

Wolf regained his feet quickly and kicked Mikki away. He faced Boyd. In the week Boyd had known Wolf, he'd faced him in his imagination a dozen times. Wolf was past his prime by five years. He was 40 pounds overweight and had taken steroids to build those huge arms and shoulders. Though impressive, the price paid for them was loss of flexibility. Boyd had noticed when Wolf walked he carried his elbows slightly bent, and he could barely reach above his head.

Though his abdomen was ridged with muscle, it was thick. His legs, neglected by a fitness routine focused only on the more fashionable upper body, were too small to carry a large frame with power. The way to beat Wolf was to stay at a distance and beat his snarling face to a pulp with a longer reach. The way to lose was to get caught close by those overdeveloped arms and crushed. Wolf charged.

Trapped, Boyd put everything into a straight right aimed at Wolf's chin. Wolf slipped it to a glancing blow and his momentum carried him onto Boyd on top of the sail. As the arms closed around him, Boyd hooked a leg around and over Wolf's and pushed Wolf's head and body toward the mainmast. Twisting, they fell onto the deck with Boyd on top. He flexed his knee and butted it repeatedly into Wolf's groin. Wolf screamed in rage and pain and released him. They rolled apart.

Circling, Boyd was able to flick out a half dozen jabs smacking Wolf in the face. It felt good. Wolf began to block them, learning Boyd's style quickly. Then he ducked under one, and an uppercut lifted Boyd off his feet and caught his tongue between his teeth. Blood cascaded down the front of Boyd's chest. Infuriated, Boyd stepped back when most men would have run or attacked.

Wolf crouched. Breathing hard, he came in swinging. Boyd endured some more shots to the face to concentrate on body blows. Wolf was very solid. They were ineffective.

Boyd backed quickly to get out of the clinch. They reached midship as Candido Mendes came up the crew's ladder in the rear. Wolf risked a roundhouse right and received a crushing two punch combination counter that sent blood spraying across the deck to the cowering Mikki. That slowed him down momentarily, and a right cross staggered him. A mighty body blow, delivered without restraint and with no resistance by the stunned bodyguard, took his wind. He dropped to the deck on his knees.

The glint of steel in the moonlight would have been missed by a man rushing in for the kill, made primitive by adrenalin or vulnerable by hatred. Boyd saw it. Saw it flick from the boot and prepare to gut the attacker. Saw it as a coolly premeditated intent to kill.

"You son of a bitch!" Boyd roared as he led with his foot, smashing the knife and the wrist that held it onto the deck. Now, he was mad, madder than he'd ever been in all the fights he'd had. Now he felt the rage that would have made him vulnerable to the blade a moment before.

This was battlefield rage. It transcended the fear and excitement of the usual bar fight. This is what had driven the men of the Dark Ages with broadswords and axes to pound at an opponent until he weakened, and then hew and bash until brains and limbs covered the field. This rage demanded satisfaction.

Eyes blazing, Boyd crouched and swung at Wolf, trying to rise, holding his broken right arm with the left. He quickly jerked backward but caught the next blow straight on the chin. He staggered backward toward the side, and Boyd grabbed him by the throat and groin, lifted him to chest height and threw him over the rail.

Wolf disappeared into the darkness without a sound. *Chardonnay* hit a swell and there was a rush as foam and spray flew from the bow.

Boyd found a life preserver which he threw over the side, running aft, looking into the black water for Wolf. At the stern, he dove in.

CHAPTER THIRTY TWO
THE PENTAGON

The telephone in Joe Smith's bedroom at Fort Detrick rang at 0446 hours.

Joe answered it sleepily, looking at the clock, rubbing his mostly bald head.

"Joe, wake up. Joe, it's Bob Ferguson, General Ferguson at the Pentagon."

"Uh. Yes, sir."

"You awake?"

"Yes, sir."

"Good. I just got word we're on the schedule to brief the tank at 0930 hours this morning."

"Yes sir. What's the tank?"

"That's the conference room where the Joint Chiefs of Staff meet."

****

Called from a small waiting room, they were ushered into a luxurious but small conference room in the depths of the Pentagon. Joe couldn't have found his way there again if he'd had a map. There were only a dozen people in the room, and they all had stars, except for Joe, and one colonel who acted as the moderator.

"We have Major General Ferguson of the USSTRATCOM Center for Combating Weapons of Mass Destruction regarding a new biological threat."

The colonel stepped back allowing Ferguson to take the podium.

"Sirs, the World Health Organization notified us in January of an outbreak of filovirus in the Democratic Republic of the Congo. Fifty people died. A viral researcher on leave from the Pasteur Institute in Paris got to the outbreak before the authorities and collected blood containing live virus. Subsequent events have shown that researcher isolated a rare virus, Ebola, and replicated it. He died on a remote island in the Indian Ocean while testing a vaccine on live monkeys. We traced the money paid to the researcher to Charleston, South Carolina, and believe a Dr. Lymon Byxbe and his company, BioVet Tech Corporation, are involved, though we don't have hard evidence linking them with the money or the virus. Based on information collected on that island by Colonel Joe Smith, USAMRIID's resident expert on Ebola, the CDC in Atlanta felt strongly we might be facing a dangerous outbreak here in the United States and recommended an immediate seizure of the property and quarantine of the contents. That was done yesterday and was reported by the local television stations in Charleston last night. BioVet Tech was essentially empty. Nothing was found that could immediately be identified as virus or vaccine, though the CDC took a lot of samples and is evaluating them. Dr. Byxbe was gone also."

They sat like stones, no facial expressions, no questions, no notes taken. They dealt with "might, maybe, and possible" every day.

Joe had brought all his slides and submitted them to the staff an hour ago to be scanned and uploaded in case he needed them for questions. He hoped there wouldn't be any. He had downed three cups of coffee rushing down from Frederick, Md., and now he needed to pee.

"We believe a European bank, Meilland Freres, based in Luxembourg, was the source of the money, and a principal of that bank left Charleston four days ago in a sailing yacht bound for Europe. She met with Dr. Byxbe the night before she left Charleston. She may have the virus or the vaccine. We have an undercover team on board that yacht. It will be in Bermuda tomorrow."

"You don't really have anything at this point," a skeptical Chief of Staff of the Army said. "I heard 'we think' quite a bit in your statement."

"Yes, sir, that is true," Ferguson admitted.

"Is it that easy to just whip up a vaccine?" the Chief of Naval Operations asked, then added, "You hear about that taking years. Would it work?"

Ferguson looked at Joe. "Gentlemen, Colonel Joe Smith, USAMRIID." He stepped back from the podium.

"Safely, in this period of time, with the equipment they had on that island, no," Joe said, standing. "But it is beginning to look like the researcher had extreme confidence in his ability. He tried a simple technique, and his preliminary notes indicate it did work. We think he stripped the protein coat off the virus, attached some of it to a messenger RNA segment that could take that bit of protein into living cells and force those cells to manufacture some more of that same protein. When released into the bloodstream of a living primate, the primate would recognize that protein as foreign and begin to produce antibodies to it. With his preliminary success, it would still take years of study in tissue culture, monkeys and, finally, humans before it could be called a vaccine."

"Sounds like a crackpot on a wild goose chase," another flag officer added.

"Yes, sir, as far as the vaccine is concerned," Joe said. "But, I saw firsthand on that island what Ebola can do if it gets loose, and someone has a bunch of it."

"Someone has already spent more than $5 million on this project," Ferguson said, returning to the podium to stand by Joe. "It's like plutonium. You can make a bomb with it if you know how, or you can poison a bunch of people if you can't make a bomb."

Joe waited a few seconds and, when there were no more questions, returned to his seat. Ferguson said, "The State Department has notified the government of Bermuda, and they will board the vessel with a customs inspection, a very detailed customs inspection. The Justice Department tells me we have enough evidence to seize the ship and any cargo on board if they find anything."

CHAPTER THIRTY THREE
BERMUDA

The Jewish exile from Israel/Judah began in 597 BC, when Nebuchadnezzar sacked the First Temple and scattered the Jews. The Second Temple was sacked by the Romans in AD 70 and, again, the Jews were scattered. And finally in AD 135, the Roman Emperor Hadrian plowed the city under and changed the name to Syria Palestine and forbade Jews to live there. Scattered to the four corners of the world, the Jews became permanent outsiders wherever they lived. Prevented from the usual occupations and aided by their stubborn insularity, they became money lenders and merchants in diamonds and gold. Always at the mercy of the mob, Jews perfected the hiding and transfer of wealth across borders and around the world.

****

The customs inspector approached *Chardonnay* in a launch with two armed police officers and a dog trained to detect drugs and explosives. He'd been warned that contraband of a biologic nature might be on board and was notified by the captain that a medical emergency necessitated that several people be transported to the hospital. Warily, he climbed the steps to the deck where he encountered a large man with a swollen, puffy face and both arms in slings, and another man horribly disfigured with gaping facial lacerations and missing teeth.

Mikki leaned against the rail as the customs inspector carefully searched Wolf, Donn, Pamela and Boyd before allowing them to board the launch and head to the hospital. She remained calm, aloof, as the crew was searched and took another launch to the Harbor Master's office to make their report on the incident that had occurred in international waters.

Chardonnay looked like a rich man's toy, a sailing cruiser in classic form. In reality, *Chardonnay* had been conceived, designed and built from the keel up to smuggle gold, diamonds, currency, antiquities, art and people. She had hidden and transferred the fortunes of desperate and dishonest people for more than a century. Even with his dog, this customs inspector wasn't going to find what Mikki was carrying for her grandfather. She'd played this game before, and though it wasn't as much fun as other games she played, she was good at it.

"Sir, did you wish to inspect?" She asked innocently, holding up a ring of keys.

From bow to stern he opened every drawer, went through every suitcase, and tapped walls and floors looking for secret compartments. His dog sniffed everywhere, eventually growing bored and taking a nap while the inspector opened bottles and jars. Nothing.

But, Ebola was there. Hidden in a compartment in the keel beneath the diesel engine, it was secure, secure as the diamonds her great-grandfather had smuggled from Africa to defy the diamond cartel; the gold, art and currency as Jews fled the Third Reich; she had transported radios for the resistance; spies for the Allies; antiquities leaving Russia after the fall of the Soviet Union; and lately, currency leaving China. There is always a need to move wealth on the sly.

CHAPTER THIRTY FOUR
DARK WATER

Boyd had hit the water off-balance and the blow to his side and the cold of the water disoriented him. Still underwater, he opened his eyes and swiveled his head a complete turn before seeing the glow of the moon in the foam left by the ship's passing. He kicked in that direction and broke the surface. Gasping for breath from the cold and exertion, he looked about. *Chardonnay* was already 100 yards away and only the top half of her mast was visible in the swells of the open Atlantic. He heard the engine start.

The enormity of his risk in jumping in to save Wolf now became evident. Dark closed in like velvet as a swell blocked the moon. There was no sound.

A swell lifted Boyd and a beacon flashed only a dozen feet away. He swam toward it. Candido had thrown a flag float over just as Boyd had hit the water. It actuated immediately and its strobe and 10-foot-high flag gave a comforting center of activity to approach. A life jacket was attached.

"Wolf!" Boyd shouted into the vastness of the North Atlantic.

There was no response.

The next swell lifted Boyd and quickly he scanned 180 degrees behind him. With the next swell he scanned toward the moon. The third swell he looked back again, and this time he saw a smaller beacon several dozen yards away. It was the self-actuating beacon on the life jacket Boyd had thrown to Wolf.

Donning the life vest attached to the flag float, Boyd swam awkwardly toward the other beacon. As he approached he could see Wolf's head bobbing, barely above the water.

"Boyd?" The wheezing desperation in Wolf's voice dispelled any lingering doubts that he might try to even the score out here in the water. He had found the jacket but had been unable to get it on.

"Hey, man. I lost it back there," Boyd said apologetically as he slipped Wolf's broken right arm into the jacket. Wolf cried out in pain as he attempted to lift the other arm and slide the jacket onto his back. There was a resistance in the left shoulder he'd not felt with the right. Persisting in spite of the discomfort to Wolf, he got it on and fastened in front.

"Danke," Wolf said weakly.

Sails furled, *Chardonnay* approached from the north under diesel power. Candido was rigged in a life jacket with a lifeline. Neville was at the wheel. Mikki and Pamela held extra jackets. Donn was not in sight. As the ship pulled closer, she turned into the wind, toward the west, and the engine changed to a higher idle speed as Neville shifted to neutral.

Boyd grabbed the thrown line and attached it to his waist, then looped it around Wolf, who could barely keep his head out of the water. They were pulled slowly toward the stern and the transom boarding platform there.

Chardonnay wasn't easy to remount from open water. Even on this calm night, 4-foot swells raised her to what seemed an awesome height to those helpless in the sea. Boyd failed in his first attempt to lift Wolf onto the transom. Dropping then, it nearly pushed both of them below the surface. Boyd waited for the next one and pushed Wolf onto the transom at the low point of the cycle and it lifted him effortlessly from the water. Shivering, the big man was helped by the swarthy Portuguese onto the deck. Boyd climbed up unaided.

Neville St. James wore a shoulder holster with a 9 millimeter automatic securely snapped into it. He engaged the engine and *Chardonnay* began to move again as Boyd passed by, carrying the flag beacon and life jackets.

"Stay forward for now," Neville said quietly. "We don't need n'more trouble."

Candido and his cousin Manuel also wore sidearms.

Glancing back from the door of the doghouse, Boyd appreciated the logic in the design of the ship. The crew's section, the aft third, included the wheel, engine room, a separate entrance to their quarters and the galley. Uncertainty can arise at sea, especially with Mikki Meilland on board. Neville was right to take charge.

Donn lay on the settee with ice in a wet towel on his mouth. He lay still, but his eyes followed Wolf. Mikki and Pamela pulled the dining table away from the bench seat. Wolf sat, grimacing in pain, dripping wet. A dinner fork deformity of his right wrist was obvious as he supported it at waist level with his left hand. He nodded to his left shoulder as Boyd descended the stairs.

"It's dislocated," Wolf said plaintively, looking pitiful there in his helpless bulk. "I hit the water holding the other arm, it went back, over my head."

He grimaced again, remembering the pain.

"Neville!" Mikki called, and Boyd could see the little girl, scared, calling for the big strong captain who had always been there to make the world safe for her.

Neville appeared at the top of the stairs. He stooped and looked into the saloon, but didn't descend. He said nothing.

"Wolf's shoulder is dislocated. Can you put it back?"

"No, Mikki. I'll be stayin' up here for now. Your friends need to stay down there while we straighten things out."

The prospect of the two big guys having a go at each other, or maybe one of the crew, was clearly motivating a high degree of caution.

"Someone!" Wolf looked around the room, pale, shivering, miserable.

Nobody moved.

"I can do it." A muffled voice came from the bloody towel over Donn's mouth. He sat up. "Lie back. Pam, hold the other arm for him."

Wolf lay supine as Pam took over the support of the broken right forearm.

Dropping the towel, Donn revealed a hideously lacerated, swollen mouth. He stood painfully upright and stepped across the room, his pale torso showing the round purple bruises of body blows.

"Hold my hand and relax," he said, as he knelt beside Wolf.

He clasped his fingers with Wolf's left hand, and the two sat quietly, holding each other's gaze. Donn placed his right hand gently behind the huge shoulder as he held Wolf's left hand motionless. Wolf had no choice but to trust.

"My roommate in, ah, college, used to dislocate his shoulder all the time," Donn said, slowly bringing Wolf's hand off his abdomen where he'd held it rigidly since releasing the right arm to Pamela.

"Are you going to pull it?" Wolf asked, sounding afraid.

"No. I'm just going to move your hand slowly out. The shoulder should go back in."

For five minutes they were nearly motionless, the ever so slow elevation of Wolf's hand was like motion on a Ouija board. Silence was broken only by the occasional rush as *Chardonnay* hit a small swell and threw spray over the moonlit Atlantic.

Boyd wrestled a new demon. Rage had left him shaking, even now, dry and in warm clothes. Raging, brute hatred had driven him like a berserk machine. He'd not been in control. Now, sitting here in awe of what had happened to him, he realized a bigger evil had set it up. Just to watch.

Mikki sat with her back to the corner of the settee, eyes bright. Boyd forced himself to look back at Wolf and Donn. The shoulder reduced with an audible snap as the muscles, stretched painfully by the dislocation, pulled the humeral head back into the socket.

****

"Africa is where the new fortunes will be made," Mikki said earnestly, drawing an outline of the Dark Continent on a napkin.

Behind her, the masts of sailboats bobbed in the anchorage of the Yacht Club in Bermuda.

Boyd nodded, feigning disinterest. He'd been unaware, until the past two days, of the range of inducements a female could use to attract a male. He'd resisted smiles, glances, sighs, brushes, glimpses of body parts, everything but a verbal invitation to join Mikki in her cabin. Now, with the others gone to take Wolf and Donn to the doctor, he'd allowed them to be alone for the first time, and she was all business.

"Why do you care?" He was genuinely interested in why a wealthy woman, already possessing a fortune, would want to work for more.

"Meilland Freres will belong to my cousin. I will not be a part of it when my grandfather dies. He is very old. I want to have my own bank."

"In Africa?"

"No, of course not. Meilland Freres has handled the affairs of businesses in Africa for many companies. The principals do not live in Africa."

Boyd let his eyes flick behind Mikki to see the ships at anchor and the yachtsmen carrying their provisions aboard on little carts.

"Gold, oil, minerals and diamonds lay openly available in Africa. They are mined by the laborers, refined in the industrial centers and exported to the world market. All the financial arrangements are made in Europe. Africa has made Luxembourg rich," she said, apparently annoyed at his lack of interest.

"Gold?" His eyes were back on Mikki.

"Yes, of course. Cash is needed to buy the ore, pay the miners and extract the gold. Profits must be retained in liquid form to buy gold coming from the small producers in Africa. The price could drop. That would be disastrous."

His interest seemed to increase the rate of her speech. He wrinkled his brow.

"Europeans have the monopoly in gold, diamonds, copper and other minerals," she continued. "They contract with the governments of South Africa, the Democratic Republic of the Congo, Angola, Mozambique, Kenya and Namibia to buy minerals produced there. Governments keep the penalty high for those attempting to buy outside the system. Our bank handles huge amounts of rands and Mozambican meticals, Congolese francs, Namibian dollars and Angolan kwanzas, as well as fund transfers of dollars and pounds. The cash is to buy from the small producers and to bribe the government officials."

Boyd nodded, but expressed no further interest.

She lowered her lids and said softly, "I will need a strong man to help me. I will take my inheritance this year. My grandfather wants me to start another Meilland bank. I will have clients in Africa."

She looked up, then asked, "Will you join me?"

"Why me? You know nothing about me."

"You are honest. You are strong. That is what I need. I have accountants who add the figures."

"What about Wolf?"

"Wolf is a dear friend," she said, as if he had just died. Then she added, "He works for my grandfather."

"You seem to be lovers with Donn. He's my boss. That could be a problem."

"I have many lovers. Donn is a dear friend. It would not be a problem if you worked at my bank."

"I'm not so sure working at banks is my field. A lot of this numbers stuff is dull," Boyd said, eyes scanning the horizon for the sails of yachts that might have been a few hours behind theirs.

"That is not what I would wish for you to do. Do you remember our talk on the island we visited?" She was smiling now, with a conspiratorial glint. "The primordium?"

"Yes."

"Africa is dark and primordial. There are dangers there. The risks make the rewards greater for the winners."

"With modern mining techniques and equipment, and political stabilization, the risks should be less than before," he said off-handedly.

"There are some factors that may give us an advantage. You Americans call it an edge. Things might not be as stable as some would wish."

"Oh?" Boyd asked innocently.

"Some businessmen have grown old and fat. Their heirs are lazy."

"Does any of this have to do with your trip to the states?" Boyd asked, deciding on a whim to try for better information. Instantly he saw it was a mistake.

"I've wanted to cross the Atlantic. It was the only time *Chardonnay* was available. I have no interest in anything there."

Annoyed, she stubbed out her cigarette and left the table.

****

"She was naked when she came on deck," Donn said, slurring the words through his newly stitched mouth. He shook his head in disbelief.

"You've surely seen your share of naked women, including her," Boyd said, teasing Donn now that it was clear he was going to recover and keep virtually all his teeth.

"It was my watch, midnight 'til dawn. I was aft, watching the bubbles come up in the wake. I turned around and she was there. She looked like a ghost in the moonlight. I 'bout jumped over the rail."

Their beers arrived. Boyd drained the last sip of his first and pushed the empty wine glass Mikki had used toward the waiter. She had just caught a cab in front of the bar in Hamilton, Bermuda, going to the hospital to arrange for Wolf to be admitted overnight for the reduction of his fractured arm under general anesthesia. Pamela and Neville had remained with Wolf.

"She said she couldn't sleep. She wanted to do it, right there on the deck. I said I had the watch, couldn't we wait. She purred and rubbed around just like a cat, you know, when they want something."

"Yeah," Boyd responded warily, amused, yet realizing he was seeing something that had far bigger implications. She'd been hanging around him for two days since the fight.

"She wanted to go up to the bow, to that bowsprit."

"Yeah?"

"She looked like one of those carved naked ladies on old ships, hanging out over the water." He laughed, and the pain cut him short.

"So, there you were …"

"I guess a lot of guys have fantasized about doing something like that, with the ship rising and falling, splashing through the waves. It was weird."

"That's when Wolf came up?"

"Yeah, and was he mad."

"He thought she was his honey. Didn't she tell you that?"

"She said he was just the help, not to take him seriously."

"She forgot to make that point with Wolf."

"I can see that so clearly now," Donn said, pausing to look at his beer. Then he asked softly, "Why did you jump in to save him?"

Boyd could see the dark water and the surprise on Wolf's face as he hit it and sank out of sight. In a moment, the sum of 35 years of hopes and strivings and labors sank into the North Atlantic. The knife had only been a prudent man's effort to have a last chance in a tough world where losers were just that – losers.

"That was me in the water," Boyd said simply.

CHAPTER THIRTY FIVE
JAHAZI COFFEE HOUSE

Raybon scanned the street carefully, walking past the coffeehouse to a street vendor and stopping suddenly to see whether he were being followed. The heat of a midday sun beat down, and there were few on the street. He crossed the street and ducked into the coffeehouse. Aarif, his Arab friend and business partner was already there, at the table in the back they had occupied only two weeks before.

"Greetings old friend," Aarif said, standing to accept the obligatory facial touching of friends and close associates. They sat and tea appeared immediately. The waitress, a young black woman, placed napkins at each place and a tray with a steaming teapot in the center of the table. There was a thick envelope beneath Raybon's napkin.

"That was a refreshing rain yesterday," Aarif said. "My garden enjoyed it."

"Allah be praised," Raybon said as Aarif poured his tea. "Your garden is the finest in town."

"You are kind. My humble efforts have been blessed with success. Allah be praised."

They sat in silence for several minutes, watching the street.

"Our business has recovered."

"I've discouraged troublesome visitors as a sign to your friends."

"They have noticed."

Raybon had landed on Mtwapa Creek the night before and unloaded 50 cases of Scotch whisky into a barge. Aarif paid him for the booze, but he never touched it, or the money that Raybon received. The money always was handed to him by someone else.

"I have asked some friends about jihadists in Sudan. It seems that they are there, quite a few of them. They are there to fight over a swamp." Aarif frowned as he said this.

"A swamp?" Raybon recalled that Oyay had told Davann that the Arabs wanted to drain a swamp to divert the White Nile to Egypt.

"Yes. The Al Sud swamp in South Sudan. It is the homeland of several African tribes."

"Is that part of jihad?" Raybon was pushing Aarif into a corner, philosophically.

Aarif didn't answer. He sipped his tea and looked out at the street. Several minutes passed.

"Islam is based on the same forgiving scriptures you Christians follow. We call you followers of the Prophet Jesus, peace be upon him, Ahl-Al-Kitab, People of the Book. It is written that Muslims must respect what is their neighbor's, especially if the neighbor is a fellow Muslim or Ahl-Al-Kitab. The tribes who have lived on the Al Sud since the time of the Prophet Muhammad, blessings and the peace of Allah be upon him, are followers of the Prophet Jesus, peace be upon him. Taking their land is an act of thievery and forbidden by the Holy Qur'an."

"Then why are jihadists there?"

"Some Muslims take a very narrow view of the Holy Qur'an." Aarif was squirming a bit now, uncomfortable. "They label as kafir anyone who doesn't agree with their narrow definition of Islam. Once labeled kafir, or nonbeliever, a person can be persecuted by any good Muslim. We moderate Muslims label as kafir only those who refuse to accept the dominion and authority of Allah, the one true God."

"So, by stealing the land from the tribes in South Sudan these jihadists are violating the principles in the Holy Qur'an."

"They are."

"What do they plan to do with the water?"

"There are two possible answers, old friend, and it troubles me to bring this to you, but I must."

"You are a good friend, and a loyal follower of the Prophet, peace be upon him," Raybon said by way of encouragement.

"Many believe that the last time all of Islam was unified under one imam was the Fatimid Caliphate from the 10th through the 12th centuries, and Cairo was the center. That was the Islamic Golden Age, when we led the world in science and art and literature. Restoring the caliphate to Cairo is the goal of all jihadists. They will need the water for the resurgence of Islamic civilization."

Raybon nodded but didn't speak. He waited; it was coming.

"There is land along the Nile in Egypt, dry, barren land. With water, it could become a paradise for agriculture. Some are buying this land to profit when the water comes."

"Land speculators! They're using jihadists to take land so speculators can profit?" Raybon checked himself, seeing the pain his outburst produced in his friend.

"It is a sad day, if that is true." Aarif looked glumly down at his tea.

CHAPTER THIRTY SIX
THE STORM

"There's a blow turnin' ta chase us, laddies. A high over Florida, and a storm north of Puerto Rico. We may be in for some excitement," Neville said as he brought a weather fax down from the doghouse and spread it out on the table.

All hands, save Candido on deck, were finishing their breakfast, two days out of Bermuda.

The map showed a tight spiral with winds in the 65-knot range stalled 200 miles from San Juan. *Chardonnay* was 400 miles east of Bermuda heading east at 12 knots.

"How far is that?" Mikki asked, wrinkling her brow.

"It's 600 miles from here," Neville answered.

"That's a long way, and we're headed away from it," Pam said. She seemed more anxious than the rest.

"Aye, but it can move a lot faster than we can. We still have 1,500 miles to go to Faial," Neville answered, taking a long drink of his coffee and placing the cup in the sink in the galley.

"Should we turn back?" Pam asked.

"We couldn't make 10 knots against this wind. It'd take three days to get back to Bermuda, we might sail right into it. It's best to head east as fast as possible."

Lounging on the deck through the day, Boyd noticed a steady deterioration in the weather as well as in the mood of the crew. High clouds appeared, then thickened, and the day grew darker. They watched the satellite weather feed of the Bermuda radar. By noon, it was clear the high over Florida was moving east and would push the storm north and east. By 4 p.m., the barometer began to drop, and the seas were dark with swells 4 to 6 feet. Fortunately, the wind was just right, 10 degrees south of west, for them to make maximum speed. All sail was out.

Chardonnay leaped through the water, spray flying well back onto the deck as she slid down the building swells to buck up the next one.

"Wear the lifejacket at all times, even in your bunk. When on deck, everyone must have a safety harness attached to the mizzen or mainmast, or along the life rail at the sides."

Neville had called an all-hands meeting in the saloon and was laying down the law.

"We have four of these radio beacons. If we go down, or someone is swept overboard, they can be lifesavers. We'll keep one here, the rest should be with someone on deck."

Wolf looked very bad. His right arm was in a fiberglass cast from his fingertips to his shoulder, and his left arm was strapped to his chest. Mikki and Pam took turns feeding him.

****

Thrilled by the towering waves and steady rush of the wind, Boyd remained on deck as evening came. Neville had the wheel. Candido and Manuel had shortened the mainsail and mizzen by half in the steady, 25-knot wind, stowed the jib they had used early in the day, and were below eating. Donn was seasick. Wolf was in bed. Mikki came on deck.

"The power of the storm. I love the power," she said, attaching her lifeline next to Boyd's and Neville's by the wheel. She looked up at Boyd from within the hood of her rain gear, and he saw a little girl on an adventure.

"The front hatch is open!" Mikki called out as she peered around the mainmast. She cupped her hands around her mouth to be heard. They all peered forward in the gathering gloom.

"I'll turn on the lights," Neville called out. Turning, he found the control panel and turned on the outside lights. The hatch over the storeroom in the forward compartment was open.

"Candido can close it," Neville said quickly.

"I can go," Boyd said. Never having seen the hatch open, he had no idea how to close it.

"I will go. Candido is entitled to eat his meal in peace. I have the line," Mikki said, already moving forward.

Boyd looked at Neville, who shrugged. After all, it was her ship.

Carefully, Mikki unhooked the carabiner, just like the one Boyd had used rappelling at the Academy, and attached it to the nylon-covered steel cable rigged atop the railing around the sides of *Chardonnay*. She made her way forward, carefully holding the rail as she moved the carabiner over the cable. At the bow, she bent to close the hatch, still attached to the rail by her safety line. The spray obscured her, even with the lights, and she appeared as just a yellow blob 75 feet away.

The wave was a giant, 20 feet of towering gloom, and its bulk seemed to stop *Chardonnay* in a trough. Night was complete in a moment as the fading light was blocked by water on all sides. In the instant before it hit, Boyd looked up and felt he was in a deep hole. Black water covered the bow, and swept all the way back to the skylight over the saloon, behind the mainmast. The crash was as a locomotive passing, and the splash to the rear knocked Neville and Boyd down into the cockpit, which filled with water.

Chardonnay had met such waves before and came through this one, too. In a moment, she was on the crest, high and strong, with a fading sun still in the west.

But Mikki was gone.

"Mikki!" Both men yelled simultaneously. Boyd grabbed the flag beacon that had saved his hide when he'd foolishly jumped in to save Wolf and threw it overboard. Neville did the same with a life preserver behind the wheel. *Chardonnay* slid down into a trough and it got dark again.

Boyd was looking forward to see whether Mikki's lifeline was still attached to the railing when the next wave rolled over the bow. This time, the sea seemed to rise and flood over the bow, instead of crashing in a huge monster wave. The rise brought Mikki, tethered still to the railing but trolling along in the water beside the ship, back into view for just a moment.

"Close the hatch!" Neville yelled, agitated.

Boyd wondered why he was worried about the hatch when *Chardonnay's* owner was drowning. Then he saw water from the second, smaller wave wash in a solid wall down the stairs into the saloon. He rushed forward and saw Candido and Manuel struggling in knee-deep water below, lights flickering. Many more of those waves through the open door and *Chardonnay* would sink. He disconnected his carabiner and pulled the door closed and slammed down the hatch over the top, then turned to the starboard side and attached to the railing, sliding forward. Looking down he sensed it getting dark again.

The third wave brought Mikki up into view again, limp. Boyd grabbed her line and the wave hit, knocking him down along the railing. The splash roared back along the deck and upended Neville again. *Chardonnay* rode through the wave and crested again. Candido and Manuel burst onto the deck.

Still holding Mikki's line, Boyd pulled her up to the railing. Candido's strong hands went under her arms and steadied her. Boyd reached down to grab her legs and pull her over the rail. A wave washed back and they fell into the rail, Mikki draped across it before finally falling onto the deck. Boyd picked her up. Candido checked quickly forward. Seeing no impending wave, he disconnected their carabiners, and Boyd made for the doghouse.

Rushing down the steps, Boyd's first impression was that she was dead. He laid her on the table and ripped apart the yellow rain gear that had wrapped her into an inert bundle. Her face was blue, especially around the mouth, and her yellow hair was plastered to her head, making her look more frail and defeated. Mikki made no effort to breathe.

Boyd shook her briefly. No response. He bent to her mouth, pinched her nose, covered her lips with his, and exhaled into her. The air returned when he broke contact with her lips. He repeated it three more times. She was very cold. His hand found her throat, and the carotid pulse attested to the beating of her heart. Cradling her head with his right arm, his lips covered hers again and he exhaled deeply. She coughed, and he tasted sea water. She moved.

The expensive oriental carpet was squishy wet, but the knee-deep water had drained into the bilge. The lights flickered as another huge wave bashed the upper deck, and water could be heard hitting the top and sides of the dog-house, but the hatch held, watertight.

Pam grabbed Mikki's rain pants and yanked them down, exposing a wet sweat suit beneath. Mikki inhaled deeply and coughed again. Boyd stepped back, awed. His breath had restored a life. He promised God a more regular attention to the Sabbath. The emotion he felt paralyzed him from further action.

"She's hypothermic," Pam said, taking charge. "Get her into the bedroom, and we can dry her off. She's breathing."

Boyd picked Mikki up and carried her forward into her cabin. She moved in his arms and coughed again.

"Turn on that heater over there," Pam, right behind him, ordered as he put Mikki down. He turned to see an electric space heater in the corner and stooped to turn it on.

Pam stripped Mikki with swift efficiency. The wet clothes flew into the saloon as Mikki was roughly rolled over and slapped on the back, Pam holding her around the waist. Mikki coughed and spit. Her thin buttocks were pulled against Pam's life jacket as Pam shook Mikki's torso and pounded her back. Mikki responded by struggling and freeing herself, coughing and spitting the whole time.

Mikki rolled out of Pam's grasp and turned to sit, bewilderment on her face. She coughed some more and her color improved. Neville came into the room and, finding Mikki nude and in capable hands and improving, retreated to the deck.

"Get some towels. In there," Pam turned from Mikki and pointed with her head toward Mikki's bathroom.

Boyd found a stack of large, thick, cotton towels and returned. He sat on the bed across from Pam and followed her lead drying a now sobbing Mikki. *Chardonnay* hit another wave with a shudder that threw them off balance, and the crash reverberated back along the deck above them.

"I was drowned," Mikki said, looking at Boyd wide-eyed. "I saw my mother."

Boyd remembered the soft, cool lips.

"She held her arms out to me. I was falling ..."

Pam snatched the wet towel Boyd had been circling in one spot on Mikki's back and replaced it with a dry one in front. She continued fluffing Mikki's hair. Boyd dried her small, puckered breasts, and moved to abdomen and thighs. He kept his eyes on hers as he dried her legs.

"Your breath was warm, it drew me back. I saw a great light, then it was dark again. I felt your arms around me." Mikki's eyes never left Boyd's. Her teeth began to chatter.

Pam wrapped a wool blanket around Mikki, then stepped to the cabinet by the door and brought back a decanter of brandy. She sloshed some into a heavy crystal glass and handed it to Boyd.

"Get that down her," she said sternly, standing now, surveying the situation, the brandy decanter still in her hand.

Boyd's mind swirled with awe and confusion as he put the glass to Mikki's lips, which were now quite pink.

"Get her under the covers. Stay with her. Keep her warm," Pam said, handing Boyd another crystal glass and retreating out the door. She closed it solidly.

Boyd stood and removed his rain gear and lifejacket, dropping it into a wet pile in the corner. He sat down, and Mikki's arms were around his neck.

"I'm so cold. Please hold me." Her little girl voice, the memory of the soft lips and the helpless exhaling of their breath made him want to.

"Here, have some of this first."

Boyd helped her with the brandy and she finished it, making a face as she retreated into a ball back under the wool blanket.

Boyd tugged to turn down the bed. Mikki rolled over, then back into the now open bedding. Boyd dropped his wet jeans, slipped off his shirt and socks and was beside her.

"You're so warm," she said, her nude body, still quite chilly, covered him.

Mikki's lips were warm now, and flavored by the brandy. Passion more powerful than any he could remember gripped Boyd, and he rolled Mikki to her back. Lips locked together, they shared breath in a reliving of the rescue. *Chardonnay* crested a swell and was flung into a trough. Wind howled, and shouts on deck bespoke sailors working to adjust sail in the mounting storm.

Arousal, passion, and climax merged into one exquisite plane for Boyd, and he was no longer aware of the storm.

CHAPTER THIRTY SEVEN
16 SEPTEMBER

"The USS Kearsarge departed Norfolk Naval Base yesterday. It has Harriers, Super Cobra gunships, the MV-22 Osprey and 1,800 Marines on board. With the Kearsarge, we could take the whole Azores, if your ship ever gets there," Navy Capt. Curtis Lestrange said proudly.

He was standing in the DTRA Operations Center briefing Ferguson and his staff, now enlarged by Marine and Navy officers.

"You raise a point," Ferguson said. "I talked with Captain Chailland when they were in Bermuda on 10 September, and a storm passed through there right after that. We don't know where they are. I put in a request to the National Reconnaissance Office to find that ship, but they said it would take too much satellite time and might not find anything. Finding a ship at sea can be really hard." He paused. "I guess you Navy guys already knew that."

"Yes, sir. There are drones on board the Kearsage. They can fan out with drones and the Osprey and the helicopters and cover a pretty wide swath of ocean. They'll be at Bermuda tomorrow night, 17 September, and on 21 September they'll be 200 miles south of the Azores. They can loiter in the Azores for three days, then they need to move through the Straits of Gibraltar into the Med on the 27th."

"We don't know how this is going to play out. What do you have after that?"

"Well, sir, the Nimitz is coming back to Norfolk from a deployment," Lestrange said, looking at a computer print-out in his hand. "They'll pass south of the Azores on 30 September, but they can't loiter. They need to be in Norfolk on 5 October."

"I don't think we need the Nimitz. That would be a bit much for our mission."

There was a chuckle through the room.

"OK. State Department, what have you got?"

A casually dressed young staffer from the State Department stood and replaced Lestrange at the head of the room.

"Sir, we have notified the Portuguese that *Chardonnay* may be carrying biologic materials bound for Africa. We also explained that the ship was searched in Bermuda and nothing was found but that our team believes it is there.

258

They would prefer we try to get the material off the ship while it's in port rather than try to board it at sea. They do have a Portuguese frigate in their port at San Miguel."

"OK."

"They want to know exactly when it will get there and which port we expect it to enter."

"Where's Faial?"

"That's one of the islands, sir. It's popular with transatlantic sailors, and the port is named Horta."

"Ok, guys. When will *Chardonnay* get to Horta?" He turned to his staff.

"We figure they left Hamilton, Bermuda, on the morning of 11 September. Their top speed is 12 knots, but most cruising sailboats don't achieve that because it takes so much time to rig the sails, so figure 10 knots per hour for a day. That storm hit on 12 September, and the usual procedure would be to turn into the wind, furl the sails and use the diesel to ride out the storm. We figure that took 12 September and then 13 September to recover the lost time. They have about 1,800 miles of ocean to cover. Most sailors shut down at night and chug along on the diesel, making 8 knots, say average 10 for the 24 hours if they're really diligent sailors. They'd make Horta in about 7 days – 21 September."

"OK. Tell the Portuguese to start looking for them on 19 September."

CHAPTER THIRTY EIGHT
17 SEPTEMBER

A fish exploded from the wake to grab the shiny plastic lure and nearly tore the rod from Boyd's hands. He quickly recovered and set the hook with a mighty, torso twisting yank.

"Eno pa'. Grande atum!" Candido shouted, reeling in his line to make room for Boyd to play his fish.

Diving, the fish caught up with *Chardonnay* and began to go beneath her. Boyd resisted, and the surf rod he held bent nearly double, line singing out of the reel.

Candido had awakened Boyd before dawn with the exciting news that the sonar depth finder had suddenly gone from near infinity to only 30 meters. They'd arrived on the Princess Alice Banks, a rich and unspoiled fishing paradise near Faial. The water, made shallow by the volcanic activity that formed the Azores, allows the bottom feeders to live close to the surface where the sunlight causes the lower life forms to thrive. It was the higher life forms Candido and Boyd were after this day.

Tiring from the constant pull of the rod and the 10 knots *Chardonnay* was making in the light breeze, the fish was brought alongside where Manuel gaffed it and brought it aboard.

"Wow. That's a beauty. What's an atum?" Boyd asked, admiring his catch.

The bullet-shape fish had a beautiful silver-blue luster, with a mouth filled with teeth and a powerful forked tail. Clearly, this fish made its living in the open sea, swallowing smaller fish.

"Yes! Very good fish," Candido said, laughing at Boyd's enthusiasm. "It's a tuna."

They'd caught fish all morning, but none as worthy as this one. Candido and Manuel seemed to know just when to set the hook and how to keep the fish on the line. Boyd had lost several fish before landing this one. They quickly flicked the 6-inch silver Rapalas back in while Manuel emptied the rest of the ice in the ice maker into a large Coleman cooler and laid Boyd's catch in with their half-dozen smaller fish.

"Land ho! Hey, we're there." Barefoot and tan, his sculpted hair beginning to go shaggy, Donn jumped down from the doghouse where he'd been watching the horizon and descended the stairs with his news.

Pico, dominated by the 7,000-foot cone of an extinct volcano in its center, was visible on this clear day 75 miles away. Its pointed top poked through a layer of clouds that lay like a laurel around its midsection. The base of the island was a smudge beneath the clouds.

Candido and Manuel chattered in Azorean Portuguese as they crowded Donn for a turn with the binoculars. Each man laughed when he saw their home island, Faial, in the foreground shadow of Pico.

Neville's only acknowledgement of the landfall was the plume of pipe smoke circling his head and streaming behind them like a contrail. He'd been at the wheel all morning, checking the GPS reading with every relighting of his pipe and watching his crew catch fish.

The storm hand chased them across the North Atlantic. They had left Hamilton, Bermuda, on the afternoon of 10 September to try to outrun it. With steadily increasing winds from the west, *Chardonnay* had made unprecedented speed and distance before tropical storm Norbert nearly caught them 500 miles east of Bermuda. Neville had made the decision to press ahead, risking disaster if the storm overran them, as the extreme winds would push *Chardonnay's* bow into the waves, sinking her.

But just at the last moment, when the barometer began to drop precipitously and they were all crowded around the satellite feed of the Bermuda radar watching the storm move east, the storm drifted north. It spit them out toward the Azores and dissipated in the cold North Atlantic between Bermuda and the Grand Banks of Newfoundland. Within a day, the sky was blue and the breeze was warm.

The Azores are nine volcanic islands 900 miles due west of Lisbon, Portugal. The prevailing westerly winds that bore *Chardonnay* across the Atlantic have brought sailors back to Europe from the New World since men have gone out into the ocean in boats. Thus, the Azorean Portuguese are renowned sailors. Yachtsmen making a transatlantic crossing use the prevailing winds for transport, and after a week or more at sea from Bermuda are happy to pull into the first island they encounter: Faial.

Faial's port city, Horta, boasts a spacious leeward harbor tucked under a daunting cliff. Pico, the volcano, dominates the island of Pico, located across a protected 4-mile-wide channel from Faial.

Five hours after Donn first sighted Pico, they pulled into the harbor at Horta. The yacht basin sports docking facilities for scores of cruising yachts in the 30- to 40-foot range, and dozens in the 60-foot range, but they were mostly vacant. Smart yachtsmen had called the season over and headed to the mainland. The experience of the past week was a lesson the crew of *Chardonnay* would never forget about September on the North Atlantic.

Chardonnay, at 119 feet, was regal as she furled her sails and passed under the cliff at the entrance to the harbor. The crew felt the eyes of the entire port on them as their ship, a one of a kind, a queen of the high seas, had taken the challenge of the North Atlantic and succeeded.

Mikki emerged from her stateroom transformed. She wore a neatly pressed khaki safari jacket and slacks with calf-skin leather boots. Her makeup was in place, and Boyd could smell the fragrance he hadn't noticed since that first night in Charleston.

"Boyd, would you go with me into Horta? I have some business," Mikki said, pleasantly. "We can take Candido and Manuel with us. When we return this afternoon, the rest of you can go ashore."

A short, well-fed Portuguese Harbor Master reviewed their papers and took a modest anchorage fee. Their business was conducted in Portuguese, in which Mikki was fluent. Boyd wondered how. Within five minutes they were back out into the bright sun.

"Peter's Bar is right over there. I need to go there before we return to *Chardonnay.*"

Mikki was cool.

Odd, Boyd thought. Their night of passion was just that, a one-nighter.

The sidewalk was a mosaic of small black and white paving stones. They crossed a small park, climbed steps to the main street along the harbor, and made for a bar in the center of the block. "Café Sport" was carved into a wooden scroll hung across the front of the building, and wooden whales hung over each of the two doors. The bottom floor of the three-story building was painted blue, the only non-white building on the block, and the wooden shutters on all the windows gave it a Cape Cod look.

Boyd and Mikki ducked as they stepped down into the darker interior.

"Mikki!" The bartender called out.

"Jose! Como vai?"

The small man came around the bar and hugged her, then called into the kitchen.

"This is Jose Enrique Azevedo," Mikki said, waiting with Boyd. "And his father, also Jose Enrique."

An older man, also small, came from the kitchen and hugged her.

"Jose the elder was a boy when my grandfather sailed *Chardonnay* through here in the '40s. My father caught a world's record swordfish off the Princess Alice Banks in 1970, the year I was born."

Boyd shook hands with the two men, who were beaming at Mikki's arrival. The small bar seemed dark because of the rich, wood-paneled walls, festooned with the flags from dozens of yachts. A large carved eagle with outstretched wings and flags in its talons hung over the bar. The half-dozen customers seemed to be locals, and they ignored the visitors. Aromas, both garlicky and greasy, wafted from the kitchen.

Boyd listened with interest to Mikki's tales of her childhood on *Chardonnay* and at Horta. As she laughed and talked with the Azevedos, the years seemed to drop away. They lapsed back into Portuguese, and Boyd walked over to the bar to get a beer.

Another bartender had taken Jose's place and he smiled as he filled a glass with Especial beer, then he tensed. Mikki had asked a question, and mentioned a name. Was it Constantine? Boyd had never heard the last name before. He glanced in the mirror and saw shadows cross the faces of father and son. The bartender moved away.

"You'll want a prego. It's their specialty here – marinated thin slices of beef, fried, served on a poppaseca, the local bread," Mikki said, returning to his side after the Azevedos had gone back to the kitchen.

"I'll need another beer. How do you say that in Portuguese?" Boyd asked.

"*Dos giraffe, por favor,*" she said, still standing behind Boyd, looking at the menu, then added, "*Un prego, uh, sardinhos, grelhado.*"

The two draft beers arrived in gigantic frosted mugs, at least 30 ounces of beer each. They dwarfed the smaller 8-ounce draft Boyd had gotten from the bartender. Mikki sat and hefted hers with both hands, smiling as they silently enjoyed the cold local brew.

The shadow told Boyd someone had entered behind him. The furtive glance from the bartender told him it was the person Mikki had asked about. He turned to see a barrel-chested, fair-skinned man dressed in khaki shirt and pants standing there, glaring at him, then breaking into a faint grin when he saw Mikki.

"*Constantine! Senti tanto a sua falta!*" She rose to meet him and threw her arms around his neck, but then stiffened ever so slightly.

Constantine's towering presence dwarfed the waiter and caused Boyd to stand. Constantine was taller by an inch.

"Boyd, this is my old friend Constantine Coelho. Constantine, Boyd is a banker from America who has agreed to work in my bank. It is his first Atlantic crossing," Mikki said gaily.

Nothing that she said seemed to be welcome news to Constantine, who made a wooden attempt at a smile, ordered a giraffe, and sat across from Boyd at their table. He was soon engaged in conversation in Portuguese with Mikki. She seemed to be filling him in on events since their last meeting, not too long ago it seemed to Boyd.

Though a small bar, Peter's has two doors a dozen feet apart. As Constantine had entered one, two Portuguese came in the other. Their eyes on Boyd made him wary. Now another fair skinned man entered, staring at Boyd and Mikki, he took a seat alone.

"Constantine is my business contact in the Portuguese colonies in Africa," Mikki said.

"Former Portuguese colonies," Constantine added darkly in heavily accented English. "Angola and Mozambique have gone their own way."

Mikki took a sip of her beer, then leaned back into her chair. As she did so, her shoulder brushed against Boyd's. A moment later there was another touch, and he felt the warmth of her closeness. Constantine was older than Wolf, and larger, though not as completely developed. His large hands made his arms appear smallish, though not in any sense weak. His voice was loud and grating. He finished the beer in half a dozen gulps and ordered another.

Another shadow caused Boyd to turn to see another Portuguese enter and take a seat behind him. The man was small and swarthy like the fishermen having their lunch at a nearby table. Though he didn't look at Boyd, just his presence behind him made Boyd uneasy.

Jose the younger returned with a picture he'd taken years before of a huge wave hitting the barrier cliff at the mouth of the harbor and splashing 180 feet into the air. He pointed out that the splash made a perfect face of Neptune, god of the sea. Mikki stood next to Boyd, arm draped casually across his shoulders as they looked at the picture. Hair bristled on the back of his neck. He knew this game. When he sat, he moved a bit around the table, getting his back away from the Portuguese along the wall.

"Boyd saved my life," Mikki said to Jose as he gathered up his picture. "A wave nearly this big washed me into the sea. I don't know how I can repay him."

She held Boyd's arm, her breast against him. Her leg brushed the length of his.

Constantine's face grew red, he finished the second giraffe and ordered a third. He fidgeted in his chair.

Boyd excused himself for the men's room. He noted an exit through the kitchen. Returning, Mikki pulled away from a close conversation with Constantine and smiled at Boyd.

"So, you will work for Mikki?" Constantine said to Boyd, leaning into the table as Mikki headed for the john.

"We've talked about that. I don't really know what she wants me to do."

"You are a bodyguard?"

"No. I'm a banker from Oklahoma," Boyd lied. It didn't sound convincing even to him.

"Humph! You are no banker. With Carlos behind you," he said, nodding to the Portuguese who came in later to sit behind Boyd, "you grew restless. You moved your back to see him. Who are you?"

"Who are you?" Boyd asked, trying to be as belligerent as possible.

Jealous lover was the only role here. He couldn't be seen as a threat to whatever it was they were planning.

"I am Mikki's lover and business partner," Constantine said, standing up.

This move was designed to strut his stuff and probably had stopped innumerable disagreements on this island. He was a big, big, man.

Jose Azevedo was scurrying out the rear, for the police Boyd hoped. Several locals made a hasty exit out the front. Constantine's men were still seated.

"Mikki has many lovers!" Boyd said loudly, glancing toward the rear. He wondered why Mikki had set this up and seemed to be riding it out in the pisser.

Constantine picked up his beer mug just as Mikki opened the door. He stood there, eyes blazing, brandishing the mug.

Boyd feinted with his left. Constantine made a clumsy blocking move with the right arm that held the giraffe, and beer spilled out over the now empty tables. Boyd came in with a full force right cross that hit Constantine square on the chin, and the big man went down backward across a table laden with lunch for the group of fishermen who had just exited out the front.

Boyd paused over the dazed Portuguese, lying on the broken tabletop, surrounded by broken beer glasses and spilled plates of fried sardines. Boyd rubbed his newly broken right hand, adrenalin high just now kicking in. He swung around, grabbed his nearly full beer and hurled it at the two surprised Portuguese just rising from their seats. They ducked and Boyd turned and headed for the back door.

Mikki's eyes were wide and bright.

"I'm not stayin' to see the inside of a Portuguese jail. If you're comin', come on," he said as he ran out the back into the alley, Mikki right behind.

"Why did you do that?" She was yelling from behind, running as fast as she could in her calfskin boots, wobbling along a rough cobblestone alley.

"He came for me," Boyd said, already thinking of a way to explain it to the police.

They were all out full speed as they turned the corner at the end of the alley and sprinted down the center of the street, paved with larger, flat stones. The harbor was a hundred yards away. Whoever Constantine was, he'd just learned, painfully, the first lesson in bar fighting: Never bluff.

Someone was shouting up the street toward Peter's Bar as they took the steps down to the Zodiac. Boyd could hear several people running in his direction. He fumbled with the lock on the line, looking up to see Constantine, very much awake at this moment, trailed by two of his Portuguese companions. He had a pistol.

"Get in," Boyd said, turning to see Mikki already in the back, as the engine sprang to life.

"*Chica do calle!*" Constantine cried out as the Zodiac churned the bay and began to plane. He reached the bottom of the steps and ran along the bank, repeating his announcement, then stopped and brought up the gun.

Boyd took that statement, made several times, to be a sign of general disrespect, and lowered his profile.

The first shot was way high. The second hit beyond them in the water, throwing up a tall, thin splash. *Chardonnay's* diesel started. Boyd looked up to see Constantine running along the walk parallel to their course, gaining on them. He stopped again and braced the pistol with both hands. Boyd flattened again in the bottom of the Zodiac.

The burst of automatic weapon fire hit right in front of Constantine, and the half dozen pillars of spray caused him to drop to the ground, pistol forgotten. The second burst ricocheted off the rocks beneath the walkway he stood on, and he rolled back to be further from it. His companions jumped behind a dry-docked fishing boat.

Boyd turned toward *Chardonnay* to see Wolf standing on the rear, an AK-47 resting in the crook of his casted right arm, a big smile on his face. Neville was throwing off the mooring line.

CHAPTER THIRTY NINE
PIRATES

"Chardonnay! Return to Horta immediately or Portuguese authorities will board your ship on the high seas and detain the criminals you are harboring."

Mikki translated the message that had been repeated in Portuguese over their radio for the past half hour.

Neville had persuaded her to leave her stateroom to listen to the message.

She grabbed the microphone and answered with a question that included the name Ponta Delgada.

There was a pause of more than a minute. No doubt her proposal was causing some discussion at the other end. During this time, Mikki glared alternately at Boyd and Wolf. They glared at each other. The radio came back to life with a long message that included Ponta Delgada several times.

"They won't send the navy after us if we stop at Ponta Delgada and drop these two off," she said, looking at Neville. "When will we be there?"

"By dawn."

Mikki turned back down the stairs and stalked toward her room. As she passed Donn and Pamela, she paused.

"The American Consulate is on Ponta Delgada, at San Miguel. Wolf can go to the German Consulate. The consuls can make an apology and negotiate a fine. Constantine is well known in these islands, his reputation has been damaged. He fired the first shot, that will help. I will pay for Wolf to fly back to Geneva. You must leave, too. We will find another crew in Ponta Delgada."

Pam looked stunned. Donn was mute. Mikki waited for an answer and, receiving none, continued to her room and slammed the door.

Disengagement was an important skill if you played games the way Mikki did, Boyd thought, listening from the top of the stairs near the radio. That's what consuls are for, to sort out who did what to whom and to figure out what it was going to cost.

This was perfect. Boyd was sure Ferguson would have notified the Portuguese by now, and their navy was his best chance to get this boat stopped and properly searched. What better place to get his hands on Ebola that in a Portuguese port? He could get the Portuguese to quarantine it there and get Joe Smith and his boys in to do the dirty work in their hazard suits. That'd be job done, then back to Shaw and the Poinsett range … and that waitress. He was tired of this chase. He walked back toward the wheel and Neville. Their eyes met, but nothing was said.

****

Boyd awoke when the engine went to idle and forward motion stopped. *Chardonnay* rocked gently in a mild sea. In the pitch dark of the guest stateroom, his watch showed 0336 hours. Pamela, head at the other end of the same bed, was still asleep. He sat up, head clearing. He'd manned the helm from dark until after midnight so Neville, up since before dawn, could get some sleep. Now Neville was at the helm with Donn as crew.

There was a shout from the deck, and he quickly pulled on his jeans and felt for the door. The saloon was well lighted, and his pulse quickened as he climbed the steps. There was another diesel alongside, bigger, also idle.

A spotlight blinded Boyd as he stepped from the doghouse. He shaded his eyes and saw the fishing boat from which it came. It was large by Azorean standards, but no larger than a small tugboat, with the same high bow and deep draft. Though much shorter than *Chardonnay,* the fishing boat's bridge was higher, and the deep gurgling of its engine at idle indicated substantially more power and speed. Shouts were coming from several crew members along its deck. Donn was forward, adjusting fenders between the two ships, which were rising and falling in unison with the swells.

"Is this the Portuguese Navy?" Boyd asked Neville as he strode back to the wheel, curious that there was no flag or insignia.

"No," Neville said simply, then nodded back toward the fishing boat where a crewman stood with an automatic assault rifle pointed at them.

Realizing the danger now, Boyd looked back along the deck to see the large figure of Constantine Coelho approaching with a boarding ramp. He wore a leather pistol belt with a large revolver covered by a leather flap. Crew from the fishing boat jumped across and attached lines to cleats on *Chardonnay's* deck. The ramp spanned the space between the two vessels, and Constantine came aboard, eyes locked on Boyd.

"So, you want to fight, but only for one blow? We can finish now." He walked quickly up to Boyd as he spoke, and a roundhouse right caught Boyd on the chin.

Boyd went down easily and sat on the deck, dazedly rubbing his jaw. Quickly he took in the scene, looking for an opening. There was none. One seaman stood forward of the doghouse with his weapon covering them all. Another was on the starboard side, his back to the fishing boat, right behind Constantine. A third manned the spotlight, keeping *Chardonnay's* crew squinting and shading their eyes.

"What is this?" Mikki demanded as she emerged from the doghouse, wearing jeans and a wool sweater. Her rapid strides aft slowed as she squinted, shading her eyes, trying to see the ship alongside. When she saw it wasn't the Portuguese authorities, the pace slowed. She stopped when she saw Constantine.

He stepped toward her, impatient to close the gap she left when she stopped. The blow was open palm but no less determined than the one that had floored Boyd. The slap hit her face, and the follow-through lifted her off her feet as it propelled her forward toward the doghouse hatchway. She landed flat and quickly rolled into a ball, whimpering, cowering. She crawled, not toward the hatch and momentary escape, but toward Constantine, supplicating.

The tirade was in Portuguese, with Constantine pointing at Boyd and then himself. In seconds, she transformed from the arrogant mistress of the sea to a little girl trying to avoid another spanking. Constantine bent and grabbed her by the arm and jerked her to her feet. The scolding continued. She responded, beginning to regain composure and giving an explanation. She pointed to Boyd, Neville and then below.

Wolf appeared in the hatchway door, one arm in a sling, the other a cast. He was followed by Pam, just zipping a jacket over the T-shirt she'd slept in.

Constantine stopped, seeing Wolf and Palm, and asked a question. Mikki shook her head. He gave a command in Portuguese, and the seaman from the front went below, rifle at the ready. He called out from below. Constantine looked at Mikki, shook her arm. She responded, and he repeated it loudly to the seaman below. Five minutes passed before the seaman came up the steps, rifle slung over his back, carrying two aluminum cases, each about the size of a small suitcase. They were padlocked.

This was Ebola. Boyd wondered at how its strategy seemed to find just what it needed at the right moment. Greed had opened its cage. Perversity had refined it. Malevolence now reached for the lever of its power. The seaman nimbly leaped across the gap between the vessels and disappeared into the wheelhouse of Constantine's fishing boat. He returned holding a case of dynamite. Just as nimbly as before, he hopped back onto *Chardonnay* and descended the stair.

"Wait! This is piracy," Neville cried out. "You'll all hang for this!"

Constantine laughed. He shoved Mikki toward the ramp joining the two vessels. She tripped, falling to her knees.

With a grunt, Constantine's boot lifted her thin butt waist high, and her high-pitched yelp of pain distracted the seaman behind Constantine.

Boyd leaped forward, covering the six feet between them before the man realized his mistake. The gun barrel turned back in Boyd's direction just as he reached it with his hand. He grabbed the gun and shoved it down, momentum carrying him into the seaman. His left hand delivered a body blow with all he could muster.

The muzzle of the big pistol in Constantine's hand exploded, and flame shot across the deck toward Boyd. In that instant, the flash illuminated Constantine's face. Beelzebub stood there, fire blazing in his eyes, death in his hand.

Boyd was hit in the right chest, the impact straightening him up and slamming him backward. His buttocks hit the safety railing. Powerless against the force of the huge bullet that carried pieces of his sixth rib and scapula many yards behind him, Boyd's body flattened backward and sailed out over the rail.

Peace settled over Boyd as, silently, slowly, he dropped the eight feet to the water below. He felt like an autumn leaf falling from the top of a great oak, languidly drifting down. The impact with the water was like settling into a feather bed, and the Atlantic closed over him, warm and kind.

CHAPTER FORTY
PONTA DELGADA, PORTUGAL

ACORIANO ORIENTAL NEWSPAPER
September 18
(translation from Portuguese)
YACHT EXPLODES, ALL HANDS LOST!

<u>Ponta Delgada, San Miguel, Azores, Portugal.</u> The luxury yacht *Chardonnay* exploded and sank with all hands early this morning just hours after an armed confrontation in front of Peter's Café Sport in Horta, Faial. The vessel pulled out of Horta without Port Authority permission, and the Portuguese Navy frigate at Ponta Delgada was put on alert. The captain of *Chardonnay* had agreed to stop at Ponta Delgada for a customs inspection and to release into custody those responsible for the exchange of gunfire. In addition, communication with the government of the United States had warned that this vessel was smuggling contraband material and should be detained and searched. The explosion, 25

miles off the southeastern corner of Sao George Island, came without warning or distress call at 3:45 AM and rattled windows as far away as Ponta Delgada. *Chardonnay*, owned by the Meilland family of Luxembourg, has been a frequent visitor to the Azores for many years. There is speculation that piracy might be involved. An investigation is pending.

CHAPTER FORTY ONE
THE ATLANTIC OCEAN

The veneer was gone. Donn Wilde had been hiding inside big stories, fancy cars and expensive clothes for 20 years. He'd always known he was a lie, and he assumed everyone else was, too. Now he was coughing seawater out of his lungs and treading water, clad only in his boxer shorts, in the middle of the Atlantic Ocean. The only man he'd ever known who'd been real everywhere Donn tested – more than real, bedrock – had just jumped in front of certain death to give him a chance to swim 25 miles to the nearest island, and he wasn't man enough to even try.

Chardonnay blew up with a concussion that kicked him in the nuts and stopped his breath. He cringed as the mainmast tumbled a full turn and lanced down into the fireball like a toothpick into a canapé, and the whole thing sucked down into the black, leaving only some scattered debris on the surface. Donn was ready to quit, slide beneath the waves and be gone.

Donn saw a head bobbing in the water, visible only because of the dying glow of the debris reflected on the surface. He swam toward it.

Boyd Chailland was there, barely alive. Only his eyes and nose were out of the water.

"Boyd," Donn said, cradling the head just as it was about to sink

There was no answer, the eyes were fixed on infinity, staring out at the glowing remains of *Chardonnay.* The limbs had stopped moving.

Donn had been this close to death, teetering on the railing, with Wolf towering over him and unleashing a fury that in itself was incapacitating to a lifelong coward. Boyd Chailland had stepped in and stopped the big German with his first blow. The savagery that followed was the stuff of myth.

Those had not been mortals on the deck that night. Backlit by the spotlight on the mizzenmast, gods fought there, as bone splintered and blood sprayed. Good and evil had had a showdown, and Donn had laid there, a slave to the winner.

"Boyd, are you alive?" Donn asked, his own plight forgotten for the moment.

There was breath.

The extra weight caused Donn to have to speed up his legs. He pulled Boyd across his chest, face near his own, and kicked toward the wreck. There would be something floating there.

A swell lifted them and Donn rolled sideways to see debris floating down in front of them. The two men dropped into a trough and blackness was all around. He kicked steadily.

First it was a piece of railing that he draped his left arm over to help hold him up, kicking still, but able to catch some breath now. Then a cushion from the cockpit came into view, and he stuffed it beneath to float Boyd's chest. He saw the blood smear over his own bare chest, and kept kicking.

The life raft was in a white plastic case that was supposed to deploy a beacon if it got wet. There was no beacon. Donn traversed the debris field, then rolled from under Boyd to kick himself out of the water as far as possible to see further on the next swell. The case was fifty yards back the way he had come. He started kicking again.

Nearly exhausted when he reached it, Donn held on to the side, barely able to maintain his hold on Boyd. Vaguely, the brief Neville had given on their first day out returned. He deployed the raft, and inside were life vests, flares, food, water and a radio. He crawled in and hauled Boyd over the side. That's when he saw the hole in Boyd's back. He could put his fist into the place where a shoulder blade should have been, and blood and bubbles oozed out all over the bottom of the raft.

"Anybody!" A faint call came from the direction of the wreck.

Donn found a flashlight and turned it toward the call. Like a wet dog, Pamela was paddling steadily toward him.

CHAPTER FORTY TWO
TERCEIRA ISLAND

Serenely, he floated in the hot tub in Narvel Rhoades' backyard. Narvel, mayor of Kennett, Mo., Boyd's hometown, talked about rendezvous and beacons. Narvel's wife, Betsy, floated next to Boyd in the hot tub, her soft breasts periodically covering his face, her thighs entwined with his. A cold wind came, and Boyd was chilled. He and Betsy sank beneath the warm water while Narvel droned on.

Narvel – the lanky Lothario of the Missouri Bootheel who had found ways to beat Walmart at the small-town drugstore game – and Betsy – bleached, tucked, augmented, psychoanalyzed and saved – had been his best friends since grade school. They'd stayed home and made excitement in their own fashion while Boyd saw the world. His visits were always a major reunion. They'd been in the tub a few times but never with Betsy rolling around on him and Narvel expounding, oblivious. Still, it felt good. He dozed.

****

Whack, whack, whack. The beating had a powerful background-engine sound.

Boyd awoke to a strange face strapping a belt around his middle. He was lying, wet and cold, in the bottom of an inflatable, seven-man life raft. Pam and Donn's faces peered over the shoulder of his new acquaintance. A Puma helicopter hovered 50 feet above them. It was morning.

Confusion reigned. Where were Narvel and Betsy? Who was this guy? Where was *Chardonnay*? Why did he feel so bad? Where was all that blood coming from?

"Boyd!" Donn shouted. "You crazy son of a bitch! You're still alive, and the Portuguese Air Force is here to rescue you!"

The sea was picking up, and whitecaps were at the top of some swells. They rose and dropped in that rhythm he had become accustomed to in these last three weeks.

He was on a board, in a wire basket that started to move upward. The movement shot fire into his shoulder and chest. He coughed, and the pain was excruciating. He moaned and felt the winch begin to pull him away from the raft and his friends. The cable twisted as he ascended and he got a revealing 360-degree view of the open Atlantic with the sun just above the horizon and just below a bank of low clouds. Dawn would be brief today, he thought. Then the basket turned, and he could see a pink glow as a brief moment of sunlight hit the mountain Pico far to their rear, then another island behind Pico that he'd not seen, and then as he turned, another ahead of the Puma, green and terraced with fields.

The rotors pushed the waves into the sea, blowing off the crests and sending spray out in all directions. In spite of the perfectly timed moment of maximum sunlight on a dull day, the sea appeared gray and foreboding.

"*Bon dia,*" a Portuguese with a bushy mustache called out as Boyd neared the open side of the Puma.

He was dressed in a flight suit with one hand casually held onto the inside top of the door, while the other was on the winch control just inside it. He smiled as he crouched and grabbed the cable, pulling Boyd toward the door. Another man behind him stood ready to help.

"Good morning, Capt. Chailland," a clearly American voice came from a middle-age man, also in a flight suit, who helped slide the basket into the helicopter. "I'm Dr. Abbott from the Air Force hospital at Lajes Field, Azores."

Warm hands stripped away his bloody wet shirt, a cold stethoscope probed front and back. A prick at his arm drew his attention for a moment as a needle probed for a vein. He shivered as voices talked about shock and hypothermia, and warming the saline.

****

Sunlight was streaming in through lace curtains tied open when Boyd awoke. Something had touched his side, and he felt it all the way through to his back. He looked toward the bubbling sound on his right and saw the top of a girl's head, bent, hands working on that something that was sticking out from his side.

"Oh, I'm sorry. Did I hurt you?" She looked up.

Wide hazel eyes caused him to focus close, and her smile made the pain disappear. She was dressed in a green scrub suit, and around her neck was a pink plastic stethoscope.

Pain shot through his chest again when he inhaled to speak, and he just winced instead.

"You have a tube in your chest, see?"

She stepped back, holding up a tube the diameter of Boyd's index finger and filled with blood. His? Bubbles coursed through the tube toward a glass bottle, also filled with blood.

Donn Wilde had been dozing in a chair at the end of the bed. Turning to look out the window of a hospital room and beyond, Boyd could see the ocean, azure under a blue sky, with fluffy white cumulus clouds moving sedately past. The events of the day before were as a dream, misty, vague and unreal.

The nurse efficiently gathered up the gauze and tape from the dressing change and deposited it in a large red container labeled Biological Hazard.

Boyd was offended that fluids from his body might be labeled as hazardous.

"I'm Lt. Kelly. If you need anything, I'll be right outside the door," she said with a bright smile as she picked up her dressing tray and left.

"Ah, you're awake," Donn said, stretching. "You've been out for 24 hours. The doctor tells us you didn't lose much lung. You were lucky."

"Didn't lose much lung?" Boyd pinched his face into a look of disgust.

"You do remember getting shot?"

"Yeah. Constantine."

"That was a .357 magnum. It blew you over the side like you'd grabbed a handle on a southbound freight."

Boyd nodded.

"We assumed you were dead, and that we'd be, too. When the shooting started and Pam and I jumped, there you were, treading water and bleeding into that great black ocean."

Donn perched at the edge of his seat, imitating Boyd treading water and slowly looking about, dazed.

"Don't remember," Boyd responded darkly.

"The rest of the story is bad. People died yesterday, Boyd. Our friends."

Donn stood, walked to the window and turned back to face him.

"Pam?" Boyd asked.

"No. She's fine. She's sacked out in the next room. We're quarantined here. More about that later. When you jumped the Portuguese seaman, Wolf pulled a pistol out of his sling and started shooting. He yelled for us to jump, and we did. Neville came up with that AK-47 Wolf used in the afternoon. He had it hidden under the cushions in the cockpit. Pam and I were port and aft, no place to go but overboard."

"Did somebody shoot that son-of-a-bitch Constantine?" Boyd asked, remembering the fire in the big Portuguese's eyes as he had discharged his hand cannon.

"They shot somebody, but we don't know if it was Constantine. We drifted away. Then they shot Wolf. He cried out and fell in not far from us. Neville kept shooting, hunkered down in the cockpit, for several minutes, and then it was quiet. Constantine's boat cranked up and left. *Chardonnay* blew up about five minutes later. It was a big ball of fire with pieces flying all around. Afterward, I swam over there and looked around. There was stuff floating in the water, including the life raft, but no Neville, and no Wolf."

Donn continued, tears glistening in his eyes.

"Wolf casually opened the latch on the life raft while Constantine was beating Mikki. He looked at me and motioned with his head toward the side. I'll never forget him standing there, behind the doghouse. Bullets were zinging everywhere, glass breaking, splinters flying off the teak, and him firing left handed, the sling still flapping from his arm, right arm in a cast, yelling for us to jump. Wolf saved our lives, Boyd. We'd all be dead if not for him and Neville."

"He nearly killed you himself last week," Boyd reminded, painfully moving himself higher in the bed.

"We got over that. He apologized. Mikki had led him to believe they were going to be together, then she assigns him the watch, and when he comes up there a little early, as is his habit … You know, he was always early for everything."

Tears were streaming down Donn's face.

"Yeah." Boyd remembered Wolf, totally Germanic in habit and mannerism. He was always early, prepared, his stateroom neat as a military school.

After Boyd busted him up and he was nearly helpless in cast and sling, he cheerfully assumed a support role. He pitched in wherever he could, joked and talked with Donn and Pam and the crew, even did some cooking. For a moment, Boyd chuckled as he remembered Wolf flipping pancakes in the galley by working a spatula under them with his casted right arm and then jumping into the air.

"You must be used to this life. I've never done anything like this, Boyd. It's too much."

Donn broke down completely. He was sobbing, chest heaving uncontrollably.

"Wolf and Neville, and that beautiful ship, all gone."

"What about Mikki?"

Donn shrugged, drying his face, regaining control.

"Donn, I'm no different from you. Small-town guy, played some ball, got into the Academy on a football scholarship, went to flight school. Last year, the Air Force decommissioned my squadron, and I was without a job. I stumbled onto some guys jinking with the system, and the Air Force sent me under cover. Some people got killed. It turned out all right, so now, apparently, they think I'm some kind of fixer they can send in when the shit gets deep."

"The shit *is* deep," Donn answered soberly.

"Take the long view on this thing," Boyd said, painfully rolling back to his back and scooting up in the bed again. "This is an important job. We didn't pick you at random, just like they didn't pick me at random. You had something we needed, and you still do. We've got to figure out where that virus went and what they plan to do with it. It's like any other military mission. You do it or go down trying. Later, you sort out how it felt."

"Well, we don't know where it went," Donn said, turning as the door opened and the nurse entered.

"Capt. Chailland, you have a telephone call. It's a general."

The young nurse was all business as she picked up the phone from the bedside and put it within his reach. As she stepped around the electric cord to the suction machine pulling blood out of Boyd's chest, she bent close to Boyd and he could smell her fragrance, faint, simple, pleasant.

"Ferguson," Boyd said heartily, feeling better in an instant.

Maybe it was the nurse, a reminder that a sane and safe world back in the States still had fresh, young, normal women. Women who could blush if they came near a handsome man whom they were nursing back from a gunshot wound taken in the prosecution of some mission so secret that she'd been forbidden to mention him away from the hospital. He looked up into her eyes, and the blush spread from her cheeks to her ears and down her neck. She backed up against the suction machine, nearly stumbling.

Boyd answered the phone as Lt. Kelly hurriedly left the room. Donn had missed the entire exchange and sat, face lined with fatigue, eyes on the horizon out the window. He needed a haircut.

"Boyd, I heard you were shot. Are you OK?" Ferguson's voice was surprisingly clear, considering the call was patched through two operators, a satellite and the ancient telephone at the nurse's station.

"They tell me I'll recover. Donn was just telling me what happened after I fell overboard. Is this line secure?"

"No. Consider this a social call. We'll set up a secure line later. When will you be well enough to talk? We've got problems."

Looking at Donn, Boyd felt tired. The momentary improvement he'd felt when Lt. Kelly entered had passed. He looked at his watch and realized it was just 24 hours since he'd been pulled from the ocean, and he'd been in surgery for part of that time. "Give me until tomorrow. I've got to get some sleep."

"That's good. I've talked to the wing commander there, told him to treat you guys like kings."

"They've done that already. We're in good shape."

Ferguson wished him well and broke the line. Boyd was alone with a sleeping Donn Wilde. In moments, the oblivion of sleep closed around him, too.

****

Smoke curled up from a cigarette as Pamela Prescott read a magazine, seated in the big chair in the corner. She wore faded pink cotton hospital pajamas with a drawstring at the waist. The window was open by her side. It was dark. She looked up as she blew smoke toward the window and saw Boyd watching her.

"Welcome back from the land of the damned and the dead."

"Thanks. You're looking buff today. Donn asleep?" He rolled partially to his right side, coughing, looking down at the blood draining out.

"Yeah, he's in the other room. They won't let us leave here. I told them you were a smoker and would want one when you woke up, so they'd let me smoke in here. Want one?"

"Not the thing to do with one lung," Boyd said with a little laugh that made him cough. "Actually, I don't feel too bad, considering."

"I guess Donn told you about Wolf and Neville?" She shifted, sitting up straight and taking another deep draw before stubbing out the cigarette in the ash tray on her lap.

"Yeah. Are you sure they're dead?"

"I'm sure Wolf is. I heard the bullets hit him, and he fell over the side like you did. He must have gone straight down. We looked but there was no sign. We even took a quick circle after they picked us all up in the helicopter. Nothing."

Boyd shook his head. He'd not been friends with Wolf, but his passing seemed sad. He'd felt a kinship with the big bodyguard. They were a lot alike. Neville's face appeared in his mind, creased face squinting into the horizon, smoke trailing off from his pipe.

"How come they won't let you guys leave?" Boyd asked, shaking off the melancholy.

"Ferguson called from the states right after we got here. It seems someone in South Carolina has Ebola. The whole East Coast is in an uproar. The doc said the base is going to get us a house tomorrow and keep us away from the rest of the populace here until they're sure we don't have it."

"So Constantine, if he isn't dead, loaded the virus and vaccine up into his fishing boat and took off, presumably with Mikki, though maybe not."

"She jumped over to his boat while we were jumping into the water."

"So, even if they did get Constantine, she still has the virus."

"Yes."

"Was that just jealousy that motivated Constantine to go out there with his crew and a case of dynamite? Was he planning to kill all of us and blow up *Chardonnay* just because I punched him in the nose and took off with his woman?"

"No. There's more to the story. Something you don't know."

Pam got up and took the straight-back chair next to the bed.

"Now listen, I'm going to tell you this because it's part of my job, sort of. But, it's got to be just between us. And here's why. Though it may sound a little strange to you just now, considering Donn's behavior with our recent hostess, bunking with her and all, we'd made some plans. There's a bank in Wewoka, Okla., for sale."

"Ha! You jumped his bones before you put him in the pen. I know you did," Boyd said, laughing, coughing and wincing with the pain it caused.

"Quiet! Dammit, you adolescent boys are all alike. You think your little dicks are at the center of the universe. He's just in the next room, and that stupid nurse may still be awake down the hall. This is important, and I'm not gonna tell you if anyone comes in here."

She spoke in a loud whisper.

"OK, I'm listening."

"Mikki paid $5 million, in gold, for Ebola. She used *Chardonnay* for the Atlantic crossing to circumvent the laws on carrying that much cash and to get it back across the Atlantic without having to explain what was in those funny cases. She's known Constantine since they were kids, and she's hired him to smuggle the virus into Africa."

"Wow! How did you find that out, and what makes you think it's the truth?"

Pam leaned into Boyd's face, hers just inches from his.

"Mikki plays girl games," Pam whispered, eyes flicking toward the door. "It's a completely different scene than the one you guys are so familiar with. She sees something she wants, and asks for it. She expects a negotiation."

Boyd turned on his side to see her better. Her face was flushed, eyes moist.

"She asked the first day out. I said I wasn't interested, didn't do that sort of thing. She took Donn, thinking the price could be to give him back. I ignored her offer to send him back and began asking banker questions about her business dealings with Planter's National Bank and Lymon Byxbe. She gave vague answers. She thought I wanted a job and offered me one. I turned her down but gave a little sample of what she wanted."

"When was that?" Boyd asked.

"Before Bermuda."

"Sample?"

"None of your business," Pam said sternly. "I flirted with her is all. She had already seen the merchandise."

"OK."

"I asked her what her business was with Lymon Byxbe. She began giving me bits and pieces of it. She thought she had given me enough and was going to get her reward the night after you threw Wolf overboard."

"Did she?"

"No. The bitch was lying." Pam's face grew hard, her jaw tightened.

"Oh," Boyd said, not really understanding.

"She'd cashed in all her fun tokens by the time the storm was over, and she was looking at a week to the Azores without anything."

"Fun tokens?"

"Sure. Each game is set up, plays to a climax, and is over. You noticed that, surely," she said impatiently.

"Well, I admit I expected our little … thing, would, ah, go on longer than it did," Boyd said, embarrassed that Pamela saw his wrenching emotional pinnacle as just the climax of a game.

Pam shook her head, frowning in disbelief.

"She really was nearly dead," Boyd retorted defensively.

"True."

"So, what happened?"

"It came down to a show-and-tell in her room, the night after you slept with her. She pulled out the suitcases and offered to show me what was inside. I agreed to consider her offer. She opened the cases. In one there were small vials of yellow powder. She said that was a vaccine for a tropical disease she'd never heard of and said it was only enough to vaccinate a few hundred people, but that more could be made from that. The other one had larger vials of white powder and she said that was the freeze dried virus itself. I asked her who it was for, and she said she couldn't say. I was sure we had enough to make a federal case for conspiracy to commit murder, currency violations, customs, enough to keep her in jail until she was old and gray."

"Sounds like enough."

"Then it got weird. I still don't believe what she told me. It's all about the diamond cartel and the price of diamonds in equatorial Africa."

"Diamonds in the Congo? That's where the virus came from initially."

"It seems alluvial diggers keep the price low."

"Alluvial diggers?"

"Poor dumb fucks who muck around in the mud along the Congo and its tributaries, looking for diamonds. The small operators sluice along the rivers just like the gold miners in the Rocky Mountains did a hundred years ago. Those diamonds find their way to India and Pakistan or China to be cut, and it undermines the diamond cartel. Mikki's grandfather has been working with some fool who wants to spread Ebola around Africa to scare off or kill alluvial diggers just to raise the price of diamonds."

"That's sick," Boyd said, disgusted. "They don't have enough money, they need more? You sure she wasn't lying, stringing you along to get what she wanted?"

"I kept my end of the bargain. We cozied up. She wasn't in a hurry. She opened a bottle of champagne, and then brought out a bottle of vodka."

"Uh oh."

"Yeah. With a couple of drinks the bartering seemed to be over. She admitted the whole virus thing was a hare-brained scheme and that her grandfather is probably senile and shouldn't be trusted to run a trillion dollar bank. She took the lead and got what she wanted. I had another couple drinks, just to unwind. Then, she turned the tables on me. She said she planned to get rid of the virus at the next stop. I told her that would be the smart thing to do. She stood up, blond and tall and proud, with a wicked grin on her face, and said we weren't through."

Pam sobbed.

"You don't' need to tell me what you did."

"I know. Round 2 was very different, and included her asking me a bunch of questions. It was over! We had what we needed."

"And more."

"Yeah. Then I told her I was an FBI agent."

CHAPTER FORTY THREE
SAVANNAH, GEORGIA

Mysterious Illness Kills Savannah Man
The Associated Press

SAVANNAH, Ga. — Memorial University Medical Center here reports that a 47-year-old man from Savannah died today after a brief illness. The man's name has been withheld pending notification of family. Physicians at University Hospital say he was seen in the emergency room early in the morning of Sept. 14 with high fever and flulike symptoms and was admitted to an isolation ward. Later in the day, he developed unexplained hemorrhages and died before a diagnosis could be made. His medical records are being requested to see whether he was taking any blood-thinning medications. A team from the Centers for Disease Control and Prevention has arrived from Atlanta but has not released a statement.

CHAPTER FORTY FOUR
RED EYES

Two red eyes glared from the blackness of the other bedroom. Lymon Byxbe had heard it breathing for some time now but had been unable to move, much less try to escape. The eyes were at least two feet apart. No wonder the breathing seemed to take the air from his room and return it hot and fetid – the thing was enormous. Is this how death came, to sit by its victim, watching? Would it squeeze through that door and, what, just grab him and it would be over? He was ready.

He'd lost 20 pounds in a week. He hadn't eaten or taken water in four days and, in the past 24, hours he'd shit blood until he couldn't make it to the bathroom anymore. His nose dripped blood constantly onto the pillow, and the wheezing, racking cough brought up thick clots of black, metallic-tasting blood.

The wind rustled the branches of the old cypress in the yard, heavy with Spanish moss, and he remembered why he had bought this house. Sugar Landing had been a smuggler's rendezvous for years. The creek behind the house was deep enough for a cabin cruiser or blue water fishing boat and fed into the Ashley River by Charleston and the Intracoastal Waterway. He had liked the thought that if isolation in the swamp south of Charleston failed him, he could slip away into the maze of creeks and saw grass at his back, and they'd lose him again.

Was that really death in the other room, waiting? With the next gust of wind, a floorboard creaked. Maybe that was something else in there.

The $5 million dollars in gold, stacked now in neat uniform rows on the dresser, had seemed a burden from the first. Charles Meilland had insisted on his taking gold, said it was safer to transport because it didn't take up the smell of drugs like paper money did. He'd taken his boat out 50 miles into the Atlantic to meet Michelle Meilland to exchange the money for the virus and vaccine. Five million bucks worth of gold turned out to weigh nearly exactly what he, Lymon Byxbe weighed: 185 pounds. Well, had weighed. He was down to nearly 160 now.

Money had never been the attraction for him that it had been for others, like Cooper Jordan. Yet, here he was, dying a rich man. He'd wanted fame and the thrill of discovering something no man had ever known, which had made him change his mind and lie low, buying groceries from a small mom-and-pop country grocery on the Savannah highway instead of running with his money. He wanted one more grab at the brass ring. He already had a half a dozen pigtail Macaques in a monkey house. He'd set that up when he bought this property two years before. The temptation to play with death one more time had seemed to pay off. He'd vaccinated the monkeys three weeks before he delivered the vaccine and virus to Michelle Meilland. He'd exposed them, being careful in his hazard suit, and none died, though several were pretty sick for awhile. He'd had two weeks of robust health to enjoy the triumph of creating a vaccine for an evil disease. Then, only six days ago, he'd noticed in the mirror that his eyes were red.

It slid over the floor, and boards creaked. Byxbe strained to raise his head to see it as it squeezed through the door. A gasp escaped his parched lips as it came into the moonlight and was, for the first time, clearly visible. Nothing in science, or myth, or his religion had prepared him for this. The red eyes were wise and knowing.

Insight, as clear as any knowledge he had ever gained, flooded him in the last moments of his life. He didn't get Ebola from a monkey or from carelessness in handling the virus. Lymon Byxbe got Ebola from a mosquito.

CHAPTER FORTY FIVE
LUXEMBOURG CITY

Flinging white spray across blue water, the swordfish leaped, and the ecstasy of his strength and determination to be free thrilled Charles Meilland. Line sang out of the reel as the tan young man leaned back with the rod, testing his mettle against that of a magnificent fish. Two hours they had fought, and quit had not occurred to either.

"Grande espada!" the swarthy Azorean crewman cried out as he brought some water from the pilot house of the stubby fishing boat. Its undersize diesel putted relentlessly, pulling the fish through the pristine waters of the Princess Alice Banks.

Charles heaved again, holding the rod high above his head and, for the first time, felt the fish weaken and slide sideways momentarily before regaining composure and pulling back.

"I've got him!" Charles shouted. "He's coming in."

A glass slipped from his grip and fell to the floor, breaking with a loud tinkle. The scene of the North Atlantic blurred, and the fish, cut into steaks and fried for a festival 50 years before, was gone again. Long dead, too, were the Portuguese crewmen who witnessed the battle and took the prize home in pieces at the end of the day.

Only a rheumy old man remained, drool dripping from his chin as he returned to the present and the broken glass, and his library, grown cold and dark at the end of the day. Brandy soaked into the pale green wool of the Chinese rug, a simple geometric design cut carefully into the pile.

Meilland rose and brushed aside the broken glass with a slippered foot. He turned on the reading lamp by his head and shuffled to the sideboard and selected another crystal brandy snifter, holding it to the light to be sure it was clean. He poured 2 ounces of Cognac into it and returned to his chair. The fish wouldn't come back. Instead, a little girl, blond and blue-eyed, ran across that same rug to jump into his lap. He sipped the Cognac, and the memory flowed over him. The first tears in three-quarters of a century slithered down his flaking, age-speckled cheeks and fell onto his smoking jacket.

A sob escaped as his head dropped to his chest and his shoulders shook. His misery was made complete by the knowledge that the loss of his granddaughter was entirely the result of his own greed and the abandonment of the values and teachings that had been the foundation of a family business, prosperous since the time of King David.

Candido Mendes' telegram had come after a week of calling the bank trying to reach Meilland. The language barrier, and the assumption by his middle managers that nothing of interest could come from a Portuguese fisherman, had insulated him from the news that his beloved *Chardonnay* had blown up and sank with his only granddaughter.

He that exacted punishment from the generation of the Flood, and the generation of the dispersion will exact punishment from him who does not abide by the spoken word.

Charles had not read the Talmud since his early 20s, yet now that quotation would not leave his conscious mind. Honor, without the need for written contracts, had been the basis of commerce in precious stones. Where Jews were welcomed, the diamond trade had flourished, and the Jewish bankers who served the brokers, judges, artisans and smugglers had prospered. His father had left him a prosperous bank that had catered to the diamond trade. Under his leadership, it had become something entirely different.

CHAPTER FORTY SIX
QUARANTINE

The waves marched in to the island from the northwest in half-mile-long rows, cresting as they crossed some unseen ledge out from the shore, and crashed into a carpet of foam and spray before the swells rode a dozen feet up the 100-foot-high cliff. The spray became mist, and the wind carried it up and across the pastures, brilliant green in the sunlight and surrounded by carefully built rock walls. Black-and-white Holstein cattle grazed peacefully.

Sheltered from the breeze by a rock wall of volleyball-size black lava stones, Boyd was comfortable in shorts and no shirt. An empty longneck lay in the grass beside his lawn chair, and Donn and Pamela played Frisbee below him in the yard. They'd been given a vacant Air Force housing unit in which to live out their quarantine. It had three bed-rooms, a full kitchen and the best view of the ocean on the whole base. Food and beer had been dutifully delivered daily, making their stay as pleasant as possible.

"Who said you could drink beer?"

Boyd turned to see Angela, the nurse from the hospital, who had volunteered to come out each day to change Boyd's dressing.

"Who said I couldn't?" Boyd retorted, rolling from the lawn chair to his knees and standing with some difficulty. He'd been out of the hospital for only one day, and three days ago still had the chest tube. It hurt like hell to move quickly, but he tried to make it look effortless.

"Dr. Abbot was very clear about keeping that dressing on your back in place," Angela said. "If that comes off, your lung might collapse again. Come inside and I'll change it."

She wore jeans and a white sweatshirt with "Lajes, Crossroads of the Atlantic" printed on the front.

"Agent Prescott, could you help me?"

Boyd was amused at this situation, where Angela was so careful about any appearance of impropriety when she came to change his dressing. Being alone with him in his bedroom seemed so innocent, especially in light of the routine on *Chardonnay*. Gamely, Pamela broke off her game with Donn and followed.

"There, you see that hole? That's bone at the bottom of it."

Angela was absorbed in changing the dressing and kept pointing out anatomical points of interest in Boyd's back. Boyd was prone on his bed in the downstairs bedroom.

"I'm going back outside if you show me any more internal parts," Pam said, holding a basin of warm soapy water while Angela washed off the accumulated blood and drainage.

"Who shot him?" Angela asked innocently.

Curiosity could be dangerous in this game, Boyd thought, and he stiffened for a moment, and then relaxed. Angela was read into their mission and had the security clearance, so keeping her in the dark wasn't necessary.

"Constantine Coelho," Pam said simply, reading Boyd's body language.

"Dr. Abbot said most men would have died. You were … uh … stronger, I guess."

Boyd knew she was blushing; he didn't need to turn over to see it.

"He kept bleeding all night, but it was mostly from the muscle around that hole," Pam said. "Just before dawn, we thought we'd lost him."

Pam had seated herself beside Angela on the bed and was pointing at the exit wound in Boyd's back.

"Shock?" Angela was fascinated now, no longer playing the role of expert.

"He'd been shivering and moving. He got blue and cold and just … laid there. He had a pulse, but it was slow."

"What did you do?" asked Angela, who had been slowly washing the same spot during the conversation.

"We had this silvery plastic bag. It's supposed to conserve heat. We stripped off his wet clothes and put him in there. When he didn't warm up, I stripped off and got in there with him. We zipped it up and gradually he warmed back up and started moving again."

"Oh. All your clothes?" Angela asked her voice very small. The washing continued in the same spot.

"Angela, you're even more naïve than he is," Pam said. "This man jumped in front of that gun and saved my life. Getting naked isn't even interest on what I owe him."

Pam laughed to break the tension of her suddenly passionate answer. "Besides, we didn't have any secrets, did we big boy?"

"That explains my dream," Boyd said quickly. "I dreamed I was in a hot tub with Betsy Rhoades, my best friend's wife. She kept wrapping her legs around me and covering my face with her boobs."

"Worked, didn't it?" Pam laughed.

"Angela, some people were killed out there, and this mission is still hot. Get too close to us, you may have to join us for the next phase. Remember security," Boyd said, sounding like Ferguson again.

"Oh, of course. I mean, if you need anything, please, anything. I could go if you need me."

"Is that hole back there clean yet? I think I can feel wind blowing through it all the way to the front."

"Oh, yes. Here, I'll put some gauze back on it."

Angela busied herself with Vaseline, gauze and paper tape.

Boyd rolled over, raised his right arm as far as he could and the left one over his head and stretched.

"What about this one?" he asked, pointing to the entrance wound over his right nipple, now pretty much healed.

Angela looked at the wound and then, unavoidably, into his eyes. The closeness was too intense, her blushing deepened and she stood.

"Well, that one looks good. I mean, better. I won't need … uh … well, to put anything there," she stammered, backing up.

"We'd better clean up this mess," Pam broke in. "We got blood on his sheets there. If you'll help me, Angela, we can change this bed."

"Sure, I can do that."

"As long as you're here, why not stay for dinner?" Pam said, winking at Boyd as she bent to pull the corner of the sheet out. "We don't get many guests. You know, isolation and all. We have some spaghetti on."

****

"The shit has really hit the fan back here, Boyd," Joe Smith said a week later during a daily phone update. "We've got cases of Ebola springing up in Charleston and south toward Savannah."

"Joe! Good to hear from you. Ferguson's getting a little hard to take," Boyd replied good naturedly, pulling the phone cord of his secure phone line into the bedroom and closing the door.

Angela had just returned from a shopping expedition and was spreading lace and linen over the kitchen table. She and Pamela were comparing pieces and trying to explain to Boyd and Donn the importance of such handmade items.

"Don't tell me about hard to take," Joe said. "Ferguson's holding us – that is, me and you – responsible for this thing getting out. He said we've dropped the ball and let Ebola get away."

"Oh," Boyd responded. A vision of Ferguson scowling made his mind focus on the issue more clearly.

"The Centers for Disease Control is in charge now. They've got Charleston and Savannah closed down tighter than Aunt Tillie's knickers. The airports, interstates, harbor, nothing's getting out of there. The Global Surveillance Response Team, at least the military part of it, is no longer in charge. That takes the heat off me for a while."

"Sounds serious," Boyd said, looking out the window at the ocean and counting off the days until his quarantine would be over.

"It is. The CDC has been working round the clock. We've gone back to basic epidemiology on this, sticking pins in a map to figure out how it spreads. It's all centered on the swamp south of Charleston, and it looks like it's being spread by a mosquito vector."

"Uh oh."

"It's always been spread by contact before, and it was bad enough then to be the most feared disease in the world. Either it always had the capability, or it developed the capability to live in the acid environment of a mosquito's stomach. That's horrific unless we can find some way to vaccinate or stop it."

"Well, Jacques thought he created a vaccine."

"Yes, and we wish we had some of it. CDC is trying to duplicate what Jacques did. I've got some ideas, too. I'm leaving for China tonight."

"China?"

"Yeah. Hubai Pharmaceuticals has been working on an antibiotic for viruses. It's similar to ribaviron, one that's already been used a lot, and it might work on Ebola."

"So, how'd it get into mosquitoes along the South Carolina coast?"

"Latest theory is that there were two customers for the virus, Meilland and someone else. They're working off of a terrorist scenario, expecting to get a ransom demand."

"That doesn't make sense," Boyd retorted.

"You got any better ideas, from your vantage point there at vacation central?" Joe asked, frustration and anxiety revealed by a hostile tone.

"Hey, lighten up. Three days, and I'm out of here, back in the saddle."

CHAPTER FORTY SEVEN
FERREIRA

A cigarette dangling from his lips, his gray eyes scanned the inside quickly when Boyd opened the door. A leather jacket was draped over Ferreira's shoulders.

"Boa tarde. I am Ferreira. My English is not so good." He offered his hand. He made no effort to enter. "We go."

Ferreira turned and nodded toward his car, an old Toyota, still running at the gate. His face was long and more heavily lined from sun and cigarettes than one might have thought for a military officer in his mid-40s. He was taller than most Azoreans, but only average by American standards. Turning to the street, he showed a bulging belly in an otherwise trim physique.

Glad to dispense with formalities and get out of quarantine after three weeks, Boyd grabbed his jacket and followed.

"You're gonna like this guy," Gen. Ferguson had said less than an hour before. He'd called to officially call off their quarantine and put Boyd back on the case. "Col. Ferreira is the chief of security at the base there. Everyone says he's the guy to help you with the local picture."

"You sure we want some worn out old fart? How about someone younger, with a bit of fire?"

"Ferreira's not some worn out old fart. He's the toughest guy on that island. He's been fighting the wars for 20 years."

"What wars?"

"You need to study some history, Boyd. The Portuguese colonies of Angola and Mozambique, in southern Africa, broke away from Portugal in the '60s, but the Portuguese Army has been stuck there fighting guerrillas ever since – Cubans, South Africans, mercenaries and communists of various stripes. They've had no help from the UN or anyone else. It's been a nasty, lethal, crippling war. Ferreira knows how to keep his eyes open and his head down."

Boyd rushed to catch up as Ferreira strode through the gate to his car and got in, waiting only until Boyd's door closed to gun the battered machine to life and make a U-turn in the middle of the street. They careened down the hill toward the main base. Boyd scanned the flight line, counting a couple of transient aircraft, two Puma helicopters and a Casa 212. He figured the usual flight-line tour would take about half an hour.

Ferreira flew past the flight line road heading for the main gate. A sign ahead said each passenger should produce ID for inspection by the uniformed Portuguese Army guards. Boyd was reaching for his wallet as Ferreira slowed with the traffic and then downshifted into second gear and pulled out around them to pass on the right. When the blue Toyota cleared the gate, all three guards were rigid at attention, saluting.

"My men," Ferreira said, returning their salute.

The Toyota sailed through the traffic circle and turned onto the road that crossed the end of the runway, headed toward the mountains.

Boyd was delighted to be off the base so quickly. He'd been limited to what he could see from his quarters.

The four-lane blacktop whisked them up from the coast into the mist blowing over the island from the Atlantic as Ferreira pushed the old blue Toyota flat out. There was little traffic and apparently no enforced speed limit. Soon they were passed by a BMW and a Chevrolet. Cow manure on the highway suggested that it might not be as limited in access as people in the States are accustomed to enjoying. A small three-wheel cart, more a garden tiller than highway vehicle, toiled up the hill on the shoulder. They passed two donkey carts, likewise toiling in the now bright sun. They stopped to allow a farmer to move his herd of two dozen cows from a field on one side of the road to a field on the other side. The farmer yelled and whistled to speed the process, looking anxiously up the hill in anticipation of a Mercedes topping the rise at full speed. Ferreira remained silent while the cows passed, then gunned the Toyota up the hill. Just before the crest, he turned onto a cobblestone road and entered a small town. The whitewashed stone houses sported red tile roofs.

Galanta's was the least appealing of the half dozen buildings in the village, with a back section of the roof near collapse. The sign had just the name and a picture of a black and white cow, nothing to identify it as an establishment of a social nature. Ferreira parked across the road, and they entered a dark, tiny, low-ceilinged bar with hats, pictures and souvenirs of all description hanging from the ceiling and walls. The mix of U.S. license plates and pictures of Azorean festivals and bullfights indicated this was a place of cultural interface, like Peter's in Horta, but with much less class.

"Ferreira!" the proprietor called out, midway into pouring a shot of some clear spirit out of an unmarked bottle. He stopped and stepped around the bar.

They embraced and spoke rapidly in Portuguese. There were only two small tables and eight chairs in the bar, which didn't occupy all of a fairly small building. There was room enough for only one to stand behind the bar, and a curtain covered the back door to a tiny kitchen. Three swarthy customers were watching a soccer match flickering on an old black and white television, oblivious to the newcomers.

"This is Chailland, my friend from the base."

"I'm Leo. Welcome. Are you new to Terceira?" Leo spoke better English than Ferreira. In fact, it was very good English. With his round features and bald head, Leo looked more like an American than an Azorean.

"Just a few days," Boyd said.

Leo was already reaching for the Whitehorse scotch when Ferreira said something, irritable. He poured several ounces into a plastic tumbler and added an ounce of water from a pitcher and quickly handed it to Ferreira.

"Cerveja," Boyd responded when Leo looked at him.

Leo opened a bottle of Sagres and handed it to Boyd. He reached beneath the bar and brought up a plate of fried chorizo and another of large flat beans. Ferreira turned abruptly and walked back out the door. Confused, Boyd followed. Leo was right behind with the two plates.

A small stone patio on the side of the building had a stunning view back down the hill. The base was visible, like a miniature village perched in a green pasture on the edge of the vast blue Atlantic. Ferreira had finished his scotch by the time Boyd found a seat. Leo was right behind him with a refill.

"These are fava beans," Leo said to Boyd, picking one of the large beans from the plate. "Squeeze it from the skin, like this."

He squirted the bean from the skin into his mouth and dropped the skin onto a small plate on the table, then returned to the bar.

"The Brigadiero, our commander, has assigned me to work on your problem. I am not Azorean. My home is Lisboa, but I know the people here. It will be very hard. Constantine Coehlo is Azorean. His family lives on all the islands. He is well known."

Boyd turned his chair so he could see the side of the bar. Leo came around the side with the Whitehorse bottle again.

"Does he know who we're talking about?" Boyd asked after Leo had disappeared into the bar again.

Ferreira frowned and shook his head, as if the question maligned his integrity and then started in on his third scotch.

"The man's a smuggler?"

"Smuggler to you, businessman to them," Ferreira said, nodding toward the bar.

"What did they tell you about Constantine?"

"He kidnapped a French banker and blew up her boat. Two sailors died. It was an international incident," Ferreira replied, with pointed nonchalance.

"That's not really what happened," Boyd said. "What did they tell you about me?"

"A policeman, incognito."

Ferreira was not Boyd's buddy. This was a job he had to do. He was annoyed, and it showed. He'd been treated as an insignificant functionary by the American Consulate's political officer by being given limited and faulty information.

"The story is much better than that," Boyd said, and began to relate the tale. After five minutes it was clear Ferreira's English wasn't up to the task.

"Stop," Ferreira said, clearly not following the story. He stood, looking down the mountain along the highway. "Angeja is coming. His English is better."

Boyd picked up a piece of chorizo on a toothpick and put the whole piece into his mouth. It had a spicy, meaty taste, but chewing didn't seem to diminish it at all. It seemed to grow larger, and then tasted more like gristle soaked in hot sauce. Boyd couldn't swallow it, and it would be rude to spit out their local delicacy. He could see Ferreira watching him. Then he thought of toenails.

"Excuse me, I need to get my hat," he said and rushed around the side of the building. Safely in front he spit the chorizo out and watched it bounce along the sidewalk and down the hill. He retrieved his baseball cap advertising a chain of building supply stores owned by an old friend. He'd worn it to bars, pig roasts, bluegrass concerts and an ass-kicking or two. It belonged at Galanta's.

Capt. Angeja pulled up in a base pickup, dressed in a flight suit. A decade older than Boyd, he wore aviator's wings. Leo appeared silently with a Coke as Angeja joined Boyd and Ferreira on the patio. Like Ferreira, he did not look happy to be there.

"You fly the Puma?" Boyd asked casually as Leo retreated.

"Yes. We have search and rescue responsibility for the middle Atlantic. I'm on alert until 1800 hrs."

"You the one who picked me up?"

"When?" Angeja didn't recognize him and hadn't made the connection.

"Three weeks ago. There were three of us. I was the one with the bullet hole," Boyd said, opening his shirt.

Everything changed in an instant. Angeja spoke rapidly, in hushed tones, to Ferreira. This went on for several minutes, during which he repeatedly pointed to the southwest, and they both looked back at the healing bullet hole.

"We were told you went out on the air evac rotator the next day," Angeja said, returning to English and still incredulous.

"We've been here, quarantined the whole time," Boyd said.

As Boyd related his mission over the next hour, Ferreira and Angeja remained spellbound by the story. By the time Boyd took a gunshot in the chest and *Chardonnay* went up in a fiery blast, they were speaking in whispers, faces just inches apart.

Boyd was exhausted by the end of his story. He'd been in bed for most of the past three weeks, and the hole in his back still had Vaseline gauze covering it while scar tissue built up to cover the missing piece of scapula and rib. His face must have shown his fatigue.

"I know Constantine Coelho," Ferreira said. "He lives in San Miguel, in a villa. He owns three tuna boats." He then reverted to Portuguese, with Angeja translating.

"The Azores' only exportable product is milk and cheese, but the European Community won't allow any of it into mainland Europe because the pasteurization process isn't up to their standards. Constantine smuggles cheese into Africa and sells it."

"He couldn't pay for three tuna boats selling cheese in Africa," Boyd retorted, angry at what seemed a lie.

"He brings back hashish," Angeja replied simply, not waiting for Ferreira.

"Oh." Boyd nodded.

"For the tourists," Ferreira responded quickly.

"There aren't any tourists here," Boyd said.

His companions squirmed a bit.

"There are tourists on San Miguel and at Horta. Some Azoreans smoke hashish. It is illegal, of course, and the police have attempted to arrest him, but, like in your country, it is not always possible to prove what everyone knows. Many people live by Constantine selling cheese in Africa."

"We have people who make illegal whiskey. Moonshiners, they're called. Their neighbors protect them," Boyd said, eager to get beyond this part. He couldn't care less about cheese or hashish, and he was so exhausted he was worried about making it back to the car.

"Azoreans feel left out of mainland politics, and resent any intrusion into their affairs," Angeja said, "Constantine has played to that emotion very effectively. It will be hard to find him."

"You said he has a house in San Miguel."

"He isn't there," Ferreira broke in. "I called the police chief yesterday."

"You have that Casa aircraft. Could we scout the islands in that?"

Angeja squirmed a bit, and Ferreira looked out at the sea. Boyd thought back to the rows of abandoned houses, built to house officers no longer needed, that they'd passed as they drove through the Portuguese section of the base. He'd seen cracks in the asphalt parking lot of the Portuguese Officer's Club, cracks through which weeds grew because there was no longer enough traffic to keep the asphalt packed down. He recalled also how flying hours had been cut at his own base in South Carolina as the result of a shrinking military budget.

"My agency will pay for the flights, of course."

"We can leave in the morning," Angeja said in a rush.

CHAPTER FORTY EIGHT
RENK, SOUTH SUDAN

They should have fed the monkeys first. A hungry monkey is an angry monkey, and things got out of hand when Abdul-Haqq opened the first cage. The plan was for him to grab a monkey and let Hassan inject it with a small portion of liquid they'd been given in Khartoum, and they were to then release it on the outskirts of Renk, the first town on the White Nile inside the boundary of South Sudan. The monkey had other plans.

Bypassing the leather glove Abdul-Haqq wore to protect his hands, the vervet monkey chomped down on his forearm with impressive canine teeth. Abdul-Haqq screamed, fell backward and tripped Hassan, who dropped the syringe of liquid. They fell to the ground, and the monkey escaped. Getting up, Abdul-Haqq found the broken glass syringe stuck in his buttock.

Abdul-Haqq wasn't worried. The night before, when he'd been selected for this glorious mission because he knew how to operate an outboard motor, he'd been vaccinated with the vaccine to protect him from the "Wind of Allah" that would soon sweep the infidel out of the upper reaches of the White Nile.

"Allah will guide them," Hassan said as he opened the other three monkey cages and stood back as the little band of four vervet monkeys ran into the swamp. He and Abdul-Haqq fired up the outboard and backed into the Nile, the current sweeping them rapidly downstream past the still sleeping guards at the border.

CHAPTER FORTY NINE
A RED WACO

"The National Security Council met last night. Sources from Doha to Cairo have picked up talk of a vaccine of some kind, and a new secret weapon," Gen. Ferguson said on the secure line in the command post at Lajes.

Ferguson was in his element, Boyd knew. He could visualize him in the DTRA Command Center, barking into the phone, surrounded by scurrying staff officers, an air of urgency and purpose in every move.

"We don't know anything more specific, but we're taking it very seriously," Ferguson said. "The Navy has P-3's patrolling the Atlantic between the Azores and the mainland, and all along the coast of Africa and the Mediterranean, looking for a 90-foot tuna boat. We're watching for anyone buying a quantity of the reagents for the polymerase chain reaction, and if anyone in the world tries to pass through an airport with a large aluminum suitcase, they'll be stopped."

"Is there really a vaccine?" Boyd asked, standing in the secure command post wearing a new flight suit in preparation for a flight to search the islands with Angeja and Ferreira.

"There's a lot of skepticism about that here. Joe Smith's position all along has been that a vaccine makes the disease a very powerful threat as a bio-warfare agent. But, we don't have any of what Jacques made on that island to test. We have only his brief description of stripping the protein coat and using that as a vaccine, not enough to do anything with."

"Jacques and his buddy out there on the island sure didn't have a vaccine," Boyd responded. "At least, not one that worked."

"The CDC has isolated all the mutations that took place when Jacques heated the virus too hot, and they're convinced that the ability to withstand the acidity in a mosquito's stomach is somehow there."

"Still got an epidemic back in South Carolina?"

"No! They had a hard freeze last week and we haven't seen a new case in three days."

"Any ransom notes?"

"Nothing."

"How about the people who got sick?"

"Just like the wild virus; 80% have died so far."

****

"Whoa. What's that?" Boyd stopped in his tracks as he and Ferreira crossed between two hangars walking from Base Operations to the flight line after his call from Ferguson. Through an open hangar door, Boyd could see a red biplane.

"Our aero club owns that. It is being repaired," Ferreira said.

Memories of Boyd's childhood kept him rooted to the tarmac. Peering into the darkened hangar, he remembered souped up Stearman crop dusters swooping low over the cotton fields of his rural Southeast Missouri home. Later, he had flown his friend Ben Culpepper's King Cat, a modern biplane, in the high plains of Colorado, 1,200 horses in a big radial engine whose deep-throated growl stirred something in Boyd's soul.

"Wow. That's a Waco," Boyd said, walking into the hangar without waiting for permission.

Smaller than the Stearman or the Ag Cat, this Waco had been introduced as an all-purpose trainer in the '40s. Its two open cockpits lined up behind the aerodynamic cowling that housed a large-for-the-time 220-horsepower radial engine. The Waco had two wide stubby wings covered with

cloth and braced for aerobatics. The bullet-shape aerodynamic wheel covers were a signature feature.

"Does it fly?" Boyd asked, walking to the front of the
aircraft, savoring the aroma of high-octane aviation gasoline mixed with the unmistakable smell of the dope used to
paint over the cloth on the wings.

"Sometimes," was Ferreira's reply, still standing in the
door, smiling. "Angeja flies it. Ask him."

****

Banking over the island after their takeoff in the Portuguese
Casa 212, Boyd wondered at the primal beauty of the place.
The green volcanic mountains in the center were cloaked
in cloud, and the verdant periphery contrasted with the
deep blue of the Atlantic. By the time they had leveled off
at 5,000 feet, Boyd had spotted three other islands.

"Hey, they're all right here together," he commented to
Ferreira over the intercom, pointing to the two nearest.

"Sao George, Pico," Ferreira said, pointing in the direction they were headed. "Graciosa," as he pointed out the
right window. "There are nine."

Capt. Angeja, the pilot, lit a cigarette, Ferreira followed.
Boyd left the cockpit to walk to the back of the twin-engine
turboprop. It was a small transport the Portuguese use to

patrol the vast mid-Atlantic area for which they have search and rescue responsibility. Using binoculars, Boyd searched the sea on both sides, looking for any larger fishing boats. They descended to 1,000 feet and circled the coasts of Sao George, Pico, Faial and Graciosa, and returned to Terceira. At the end of the day, he'd seen hundreds of little fishing boats moored in scores of villages, a few sailboats, thousands of white stucco houses with red tile roofs, 10,000 black and white cattle, forbidding black lava cliffs smashed by waves, but no tuna boats hidden in any coves.

"Tomorrow, San Miguel and Santa Maria," Angeja said as they shut down the engines back at Lajes.

Boyd had the feeling they would fly him around all he wanted, but they didn't expect to find anything.

****

The giant aircraft appeared to float around the island on its downwind leg. Boyd and Angela had driven up the hill at the end of the runway and set up a picnic by the small block building that housed the radio navigation beacon for Lajes. Waves crashed into the island a hundred feet below; a C-5 was on final.

"Look at the wheels. Can you believe the thing has 20 tires?"

The C-5 flew past, at their level, and descended to hit the runway at the end. Smoke from the tires swirled in the eddy currents as the behemoth settled sedately down. It taxied to the end of the runway and then followed a blue pickup truck toward the parking ramp. When the C-5's four gigantic engines shut down, there was no noise but the wind and a few birds trying to find a roost for the night. Boyd drained the first bottle of beer and opened the cooler for another.

"I've seen a few people who've been shot," Angela said, taking bottled water. "I worked the surgery ward at D.C. General in nursing school."

"I don't recommend it," he said, opening a second Sagres.

"You've recovered faster than anyone I've ever seen."

"Healthy guy," he said, brushing it off.

"No." Her eyes probed his.

Boyd broke eye contact, turned and sat on the blanket.

"I'm not over it. I still can't raise my hand above my head," he demonstrated, wincing as his shoulder painfully stopped with his hand still in front of his face.

"You'll be stiff for awhile. It doesn't really bother you, does it?"

"No." He might as well tell her so she could get on with whatever her point was.

The sun touched the horizon, and the outline of Graciosa, not visible until now, was clearly visible, like a bite out of the bottom of the great red ball. Turning to look along the coast, they saw the spray from the waves hitting the rocks for five miles to the southwest turn pink as the sun's crimson deepened just before it disappeared. The magic light changed the island from the ordinary to a land where anything might be possible, and lasted for several minutes before dusk settled in.

"Do you believe in God?" she asked.

"Yes." He'd known this would come.

Watching the sun set, he remembered a night long ago, sitting on the porch with his father. He was 9. His father, not a churchgoing man, had told him sunset was a time to think about God. Tonight, he'd been thinking about both of them.

"You should talk about it." She was looking again.

"It won't work, Angela. You think I'm this bundle of neuroses because I got shot, and if I talk about it I'll be better, and you'll know me."

He was annoyed.

"Yes, I thought I was going to die. It didn't bother me. I still do. When it happens, it happens."

She looked down.

"Getting shot is not the problem. That's a passive thing. It can happen to anyone."

He was angry. She'd wanted to know him, and now she was going to.

"There's something worse than getting shot. On my first combat mission, in Iraq, I felt a mixture of fear and excitement. It was an energy I'd never felt before. I liked it. Then, last year, I had to kill two men, and that energy helped me to do it. It made the difference. Then, after, sitting there with the bodies, I ..."

He finished the beer. She was watching.

"I was different after. Later that same day I had to kill another man. He came this close ..."

He held up his thumb and index finger, nearly touching, trembling.

"It could have gone either way, but it was me still up at the end. After that, I wasn't one of the boys anymore. They had wives, families. I had Eight Ball, my dog, and something I don't understand."

She approached him, eyes glistening to put her arm around his shoulder. He stepped away.

"No. Hear it all." He reached into the cooler for another beer. "Anger opens the door to Hell. I enjoyed the strength, used it to win. It took something in return."

"You can learn to ..."

"No," he said, taking a long pull on the beer. "They're everywhere, guys like me. I went to a VFW and saw three sitting at the bar at one time. We never spoke. We all knew. I recognized Wolf Goebel as one of us before I heard him speak. A month ago, I nearly killed him when he pulled a knife while I was pulling him off Donn. I lost control and threw him overboard. I saw something in his eyes I didn't understand. That bothered me more than anything that happened that night. Then, when it was me going overboard, I understood."

"Boyd, please, I ..."

"It's OK to die!" He turned suddenly and hurled the beer bottle toward the now dark Atlantic. It arced high, whistling, then descended over the cliff into silent oblivion.

CHAPTER FIFTY
ANGELA

Wind roared by Boyd's ears as he looked down at the base from 5,000 feet. Angeja had put the Waco into a vertical dive, and they were screaming down at the antique trainer's top airspeed of 125 knots. In spite of the leather helmet he wore, Boyd was deafened by the noise, both wind and engine. In his F-16, he'd already be pulling out, going four times as fast, looking up to see where he'd be making his first turn if he were on the range, his escape if it were for real, and grunting against six G's. Angeja let the plane slowly spiral as it plummeted down, giving a changing panorama of base, blue ocean, foamy coastline or green hills.

With only muscle to pull the Waco's nose up and make it ride on the wind instead of hurdle down through it, their pullout was more gradual than dramatic.

"Whoo, yeah!" Boyd yelled, raising an arm in triumph and looking back at Angeja.

The smile and the 360 degree roll told Boyd his sentiment was shared. There was no intercom in the old aircraft, and the only radio was in the rear. By arrangement, Angeja turned over the aircraft controls after wagging the wings. Boyd was to try a few turns, a roll, and then head into the downwind leg and land. He found the controls easier than he remembered the Ag Cat in Colorado, but sluggish compared to his Falcon. The little trainer stayed trim and practically flew itself on the downwind leg. The landing was smooth.

****

"Wouldn't it be easier to lug up the hill if you drank beer in cans? You know we have to bring the bottles back down tomorrow," Angela asked innocently, eyeing the cooler filled with ice and beer.

They'd unloaded a small tent and sleeping bags they'd checked out from the base and were preparing to walk up to a campsite Boyd had seen from the air. It appeared to be a perfectly formed miniature volcano, only 200 feet high. He thought he'd recovered enough to make it that far.

"I could drink it from cans, but it wouldn't be as good. It's got to slide out of that longneck," Boyd shot back, smiling, then turned toward the hill they were preparing to climb. "You can tell from the air that this whole plain is the crater of the main volcano that formed the island. Those hills over there are one side of the rim and over there is the other side. This is a vent, a smaller opening that spewed out ash and lava after the main crater had cooled and filled."

It's an island tradition to allow free access to any part of the island, as long as cattle and fences are minded. Boyd lifted the cooler and tent over the fence, and they both slipped through the barbed wire and headed up the hill.

Rich, black volcanic soil covered the sides of the cone, and grass grew long and verdant. They followed a faint trail through the growth, indicating scant interest in the place. Boyd stopped to catch his breath halfway up. Looking around, he could see several other vents, but none as perfectly symmetrical as this one.

"Wow! It has a crater just like the big volcano," Angela said, reaching the top 20 paces ahead of the already winded Boyd. The crater inside the vent was 50 feet across and 30 feet down. Steep walls were covered by ferns and small shrubs with a few small trees at the bottom. The grass was even thicker inside than the walk up.

"I could tell from the air that the inside would be flat and protected from the wind," he said, panting as he set down his load. "It should be a great place to watch the stars. Hope it doesn't rain."

Later, after pitching their tent, building a fire in a ring of stones, cooking a hobo stew over the coals, and placing their sleeping bags side by side in the open, they walked to the rim to watch the sun set.

"I hope you didn't ask me along on this adventure with expectations that we'd have sex," Angela said, midway through the sunset.

"Of course I did," he said.

He'd been pretty sure that wouldn't happen.

"Poor Boyd. Have you ever been turned down before?" she asked with mock sympathy.

"Once, when I was 12."

"Seriously, I like men, and I like you. But, I've had this old fashioned idea that ..."

"Not a problem," he interrupted.

The half moon rose high in the sky, but it and the stars were periodically blocked by banks of low clouds scudding across the opening of the crater. Lying together on their sleeping bags at the bottom looking up, they felt like they were streaking across the earth beneath stationary clouds. The sense of movement was so intense, Angela became nauseated and had to stop watching. They embraced.

"In Culpepper, Virginia, we all went to the Baptist Church. Even today, if I watch television and a movie comes on and it's Sunday, I feel guilty," she said, breaking away after several minutes.

"Dancing is out of the question, then."

"Oh, yes, all those hot-blooded teens on that gym floor, pressing their loins together?"

They laughed.

"We never went to church," Boyd said. "Dad just handed me the Bible and told me to read it to him."

"Did you?"

"Sure."

"You understand then, how I feel?"

"I don't understand why you keep talking about it."

"Because I've never felt this way about a man before," she said, quietly.

"What's in that case?" Boyd asked, pointing toward the leather instrument case she'd brought along.

"Oh, I forgot. I brought my banjo." She jumped up and retrieved the case.

"A banjo? I never heard of a girl playing the banjo."

"Well, you have now. I don't get to practice as much as I'd like. The other girls in the Bachelor Officer's Quarters aren't music lovers."

She slipped the strap over her head and deftly began tuning it.

"Daddy plays in a bluegrass band. He wanted me to play fiddle, but I wanted to play what he played."

Her fingers rehearsed a riff before strumming two more times to test the tune.

"You'd probably go for train songs," she said gaily and jumped right into a spirited, complex arrangement of "Fireball Mail."

The grass and brush-covered walls of the crater dampened the sound of Angela's soprano just a bit before the rock returned an echo, while tinkling crystal sounds of the banjo seemed to radiate unchanged out into the cosmos. The intensity of her face as her flying fingers worked through variations on the original riff showed she was a serious student of her instrument, but the smile and purity of her voice on the chorus was what captivated Boyd.

"That's great," Boyd applauded as she finished.

"I don't play much here. I found out in nursing school most people think you're a hick if you even listen to banjo music. If you liked the last one, you'll love this one – 'The Wreck of the Old '97.' "

Boyd retrieved a fresh longneck from the cooler as she got to the familiar "she was going down the grade doin' 90 miles an hour," and tossed another log on the fire. The flame danced in her eyes, already bright with the music.

"That's a professional skill. You must have joined your father's band."

"The Clear Creek Boys became the Clear Creek Boys and Angela Kelly."

"I'll bet it was Angela Kelly and the Clear Creek Boys."

"Sometimes it was, but I had college and nursing school. How about a gambling song? Old Stewball was a racehorse ..."

Boyd's beer grew flat as he sat, riveted by the familiar tunes, played with a flair he'd seldom heard, and that beautiful, clear, laughing voice.

"Come on," she said, patting the ground beside her. "I'll teach you a song."

Boyd stood readily and sat, cross-legged, beside her.

"This is a gospel song that was our signature when we sang in the churches around Culpepper. Sing along with me on the chorus until you learn it, then I'll harmonize the next time."

"I'm game, but I make no claims to musical talent."

With no introduction, Angela belted out the introduction and first stanza, then nodded at Boyd for the chorus: "Better get in that number, that no man can number." She repeated that three times, then, "Comin' down, comin' down from God."

Boyd picked up the simple tune, and they started again. He could hear his own baritone echo from the walls. The third time he began to improvise on the harmony, with mixed results. Their laughter and music passed the evening.

"Let's neck, my fingers are tired," she said, taking the strap from around her neck and replacing the banjo in its case. She kissed him fully on the lips and pulled him back onto their sleeping bags.

"Was that lust or love?" Boyd asked, pausing.

"Do it again. I'm not sure yet." She rolled onto him, hands digging under his shoulders to pull him closer.

Minutes passed. Breathing heavily, Angela rolled onto her side and sat up, lifting her sweatshirt over her head. She quickly removed her bra and turned triumphantly to Boyd. The clouds parted and the half moon lit the crater with a white light that made her pale, pointed breasts glow against the dark background of the grass.

"I think this is lust," Boyd said, bending his face toward her.

"This is too good to be lust," she said, panting, drawing his face up to kiss him again.

Boyd's arms surrounded her and she fell back onto the sleeping bags. After a few seconds she struggled to sit back up.

"I've gone as far as I go, what do you have to show?" she asked with a breathless laugh.

Boyd removed his shirt. There was still a bandage on his back.

"Not good enough. More."

Shrugging, Boyd rolled onto his back and pointed to his jeans.

"May I?" She asked, reaching for his fly.

"You may."

With some difficulty she unbuttoned the fly and when he lifted his hips, she pulled his jeans and boxers down.

"Oh, my. You didn't look like that when we prepped you for surgery back at the hospital."

"You naughty lady. You're not supposed to have a prurient interest in such things when you work in a hospital."

"I was entirely clinical. But, we're not at the hospital now."

They fell back on the sleeping bags.

Boyd's cell phone rang.

"Ferguson," he said. "That's the command post's number. It's like he knows what I'm doing and can't stand it if he doesn't call to interrupt."

They broke camp, packed up and returned to the base to take Ferguson's call on the scrambled line in the command post. Driving back to the base, which was only a few miles away, Boyd realized it would be 0300 hrs in D.C. Something must be up to have Ferguson at the command post.

****

"Sorry to bother you at night, Boyd, twice in one week," Ferguson said. "Hope I didn't drag you away from anything."

Boyd suspected the duty officer might have told Ferguson that Boyd was camping with one of the nurses.

"Bible study group. We were on Revelation," Boyd said, deadpan straight.

"Hum, well, sorry to call you away from it," Ferguson said, then shifted into his more businesslike general-officer tone. "They've got the Wrath of God in Khartoum."

"There's a lot of that in Revelation," Boyd responded.

"Yes, well, it couldn't be in a better place. Khartoum is in the middle of the desert in Sudan, and their borders have been sealed."

"Looks like Constantine made the delivery in spite of all our efforts to stop him."

"He was probably in Africa by the time we started looking for him."

"What an odd place to try to use a bio-weapon."

"Raybon and Davann broke that story for us. Good thing, too. It's given us a real jump on this."

"I thought they told us the ragheads were planning to use it in South Sudan."

"The outbreak started in a jihadist camp just outside of Khartoum. Then when the first cases got to the hospital, it took out the hospital staff. Then people started getting sick all over town. It's a ghost town now. All the roads out are filled with cars, trucks, camels, donkeys, people walking."

"Bad guys must've gotten careless, like Jacques."

"Joe Smith said that's why nobody wants to work with Ebola. It's too dangerous. Also, Joe thinks this is just a trial and that the main thrust will be somewhere else."

"You'd have to think that if someone could come up with the millions of dollars they spent on this, they'd have a better plan than just dumping it out."

"The way this has spread, Joe said, pretty much confirms that it's spreading by vector now. We were pretty sure of that in South Carolina, but there was still the possibility someone was infecting each of those people. Now with a whole town getting sick, it's the only explanation."

"We've had some developments on this end. Mikki knew we were federal agents," Boyd said ominously.

"Someone talked?"

"She put it together from several of us. The point is, she knew. Constantine catching us on the open sea and wiping out all of us makes a lot more sense now, because it essentially seals off her trail."

"Cold-hearted bitch," Ferguson said quietly.

"Yeah. Neville practically raised her," Boyd said, thinking about Neville again. Neville had told him they were a fierce clan, unwilling to say anything against Mikki, but wanting to warn Boyd. "She has a grandfather. He's the principal of Meilland Frere's in Luxembourg City.

I'd assumed he was a brain dead old fart, he'd be in his late 80's, but now that it looks like she could have planned the explosion and the murders, we need to see if he knows where she might be. Could you see what you can find out about Charles Meilland? Also, better put a tap on his phone, cell phone, and a filter on his Internet."

"Principal? Boyd, you've been hanging around those bankers too long," Ferguson laughed, then added, "I'll get back to you in the morning on Meilland. Now, what about Pam and Donn. Do you still need them?"

"I think they can go home. The whole banker thing is done now. They're just on vacation waiting for something to happen. But I'd be a dead man if they hadn't found me in the water. I think a grateful government should give them something for that."

"We'll take care of them. The way travel to the Azores is, they're liable to be waiting for transportation for a week."

Going back to the truck to take Angela home Boyd thought about the telephone call. Ferguson had sounded too comfortable to have been called into the command post in the middle of the night. He was probably at home in bed, patched through to the DTRA command center on a scrambled land line.

CHAPTER FIFTY ONE
LUXEMBOURG CITY

Boyd found Bancque de Meilland Frere's on a radial street just off the Victory Plaza in the heart of Luxembourg City. The tasteful, understated brass sign beside marble stairs leading to the two heavy glass doors with thick brass handles was just what he'd expected after discussing the banking business with Mikki. Inside, he went through a small lobby and around a corner to a large interior room with tellers and a courtesy desk. Boyd had come here first just to get a feel for the place.

"I would like to see Charles Meilland."

The clerk, a young man, had a pleasant expression on his face as Boyd approached. Now, his eyes focused behind Boyd. His expression went blank, but he said nothing.

"I don't have an appointment," Boyd said, letting the guy off the hook.

"Monsieur Meilland has been ill. He does not take visitors. Perhaps one of the officers could accommodate you," he said, at his officious best now.

"Mademoiselle Meilland, then."

Shock transformed the face of the nice young man. He flushed, and eyes scanned Boyd, as if trying now to know him.

"Mademoiselle Meilland was killed in a tragic …" he stuttered. English was not his native language. "… maritime accident. The bank was closed last week in her honor. She was …our inspiration."

The French accent reminded Boyd of Mikki. In spite of the fact she'd been responsible for his gunshot wound and the death of two friends, he saw, for a moment, her face, with a smile. It was the face he remembered from when they sat contemplating Sand Island, with its ancient magnolia and long sandy beach.

"I'm terribly sorry. I didn't know," Boyd said, backing away.

He turned and left the young man standing there with moist eyes. He walked briskly back toward the plaza, checking once before he turned to see whether he was followed. He then went a block down and walked that street two blocks and turned back toward the bank and to Charles Meilland's home address, less than a block from Bancque de Meilland Frere's.

A butler answered the door. The embassy had called and he was expected.

Heavy draperies were drawn tightly against the daylight and traffic sounds from the street outside. Boyd felt that the rich oriental carpet, 19th century antique furniture and large oil paintings of pastoral scenes gave the room an oppressive feel. He sat in the chair indicated by the butler and looked up at the 12-foot ceiling with floral designs in plaster embellishing the margins. After 10 minutes, he got up to walk around the room and get a better look at the art. There was no sound but the ticking of a clock.

A faint sound in the marble entryway caught his attention just as the two walnut doors opened slightly and a very thin man entered. He wore a red velvet smoking jacket, slacks and slippers. The doors closed silently behind him as he smiled and extended a bony hand.

"I am Charles Meilland. Thank you for coming," he said in unaccented English.

His hand was warm, the grip firm.

"Please sit down. Lawrence will open some wine. I try to hold brandy for later, but you needn't."

"Wine would be fine, thank you." Boyd hadn't expected such a warm welcome or to like the guy.

"Your embassy said you were with Michelle and may be able to tell me about the accident. My only information has come from Candido, one of our seamen."

He sat in an overstuffed chair in front of the fireplace and directed Boyd to a straight-back chair nearby.

"Yes," Boyd said. "I sailed from Charleston. The three of us met her at a bank meeting there. She invited us for the crossing. We were the only survivors."

"Three survivors of the accident? Candido said there were none." The old man sounded incredulous.

He stopped at a faint knock. "Yes, Lawrence, come in."

Lawrence, the middle-age French butler, entered with a tray, balancing two glasses and an open bottle of Vouvray, the same chateau Mikki had served on their first trip up the coast of South Carolina. Pear and apple slices were arranged alternately in a circle on a simple white china plate. Meilland's eyes searched Boyd's the entire time. The butler poured wine into the two glasses, set them on the table between the two men and was gone in a moment.

"Yes, sir. What did Candido tell you?"

"He said someone from the boat got into a brawl in Peter's bar, and that shots were fired. Neville took *Chardonnay* out of the harbor to avoid any problems with the Portuguese. They may have been intercepted by another boat. I have the paper from Horta here."

He pulled a newspaper clipping from his jacket and showed it to Boyd. It was in Portuguese.

"All that is correct," Boyd said, bending to look at the paper.

Charles roughly translated the article, which was front page, but short. It said all hands had gone down with the ship and speculated that American drug dealers might have been trying to steal *Chardonnay* for illegal purposes. It was defensive about any speculation of wrongdoing by Azoreans.

"I'm an American federal agent. We were rescued by the Portuguese Air Force the morning after the explosion. Our government was able to prevent release of the fact that there were survivors," Boyd said apologetically.

Tears filled the eyes of the old man.

"She was my only remaining family," he said. "My wife died in childbirth. My son drowned in a diving accident, and Michelle's mother was a suicide. My brother died five years ago, and his profligate son, a morphine addict, whom I haven't seen in years, is heir to the bank my grandfather founded. I am alone."

He bent his head almost into his lap and sobbed, the tears flowing onto his expensive slacks.

Boyd said nothing.

"Did she drown?" He looked up expectantly, like maybe that was better than some other way of dying.

"Sir, before I tell you what I know, I need to know what you know about Mikki's trip to the United States."

As he said this, Boyd imagined himself as a streetwise cop on TV.

"It was a holiday. She wanted to make a crossing by herself."

The old man was obviously lying.

"It wasn't a holiday. It was business. You sent Wolf Goebel with her as a bodyguard," Boyd said sternly.

The old man seemed to sink back into the chair, the adversarial nature of their talk accepted.

"Did you send her on *Chardonnay* with $5 million dollars to buy something from Lymon Byxbe?" Boyd leaned toward the old man, but spoke softly. Sun Tsu and Clausewitz both teach that when an adversary retreats, keep the pressure on.

"Who?" A feeble response, as Meilland sank further into the chair.

"Lymon Byxbe," Boyd said loudly.

The old man looked up blankly. The red, rheumy eyes, the tears, the nearly hairless scalp and the quivering lips were all real, but he was still lying.

"Sir, did you pay Lymon Byxbe to send someone to Africa to capture the Ebola virus, purify it, sneak it into the United States, make a vaccine for it, and then smuggle it out of the United States?"

Boyd was leaning right in Meilland's face.

Fear turned to terror in Meilland's eyes.

"Sir, did you plan to infect alluvial diggers in the Democratic Republic of the Congo to manipulate the diamond market? Did you plan to kill a million people to make some more money?"

Boyd was genuinely angry now. He'd only known half a dozen bankers in his life, and so far they were all crooked.

"Sir, did you lose your granddaughter because you sent her on a venture to make money you don't even need?"

That did it. Meilland's face turned straight toward Boyd and, with tears filling his eyes, said, "Oh, don't say that again. No, I didn't." He came out of his chair a bit, and wiped his eyes. "I'll tell you what I know."

Boyd moved his chair closer to Meilland and squared it right in front of him, between the big chair and the fireplace. He leaned forward so that their heads were only two feet apart.

"My grandfather and uncle were minor partners when the diamond cartel consolidated control in the 1920's. Our family had been in the diamond business for hundreds of years. We changed our name and moved here from Paris before the turn of the last century. Our bank, with its proper French name, handled the bribes and smuggling to get diamonds out of the dozen countries in Africa where they are found. Others did the sales and promotion to the retail jewelry industry."

Meilland was freely telling his story now, and he began to regain the mannerisms of the banker, with hand gestures and emphasis.

"Gradually, the cartel consolidated and became more of a corporate entity, and minor partners were pushed out. We began to compete with the cartel, and our customers were independent diamond cutters in Israel, Antwerp and New York. We also sold to cutters in Lebanon, Pakistan, Qatar and China.

"Until recently, almost all of the world's diamonds have come from Africa. I worked with the Portuguese traders in Angola and Mozambique, the Belgians in Rhodesia and the Belgian Congo, the Afrikaners in South Africa, and the French along the coast of West Africa. Others brought out the legal diamonds, facilitated by bribery of government officials. I bought the diamonds their employees stole, or the ones found by illegal miners. I started right after World War II, as a young man of only 22. In Nairobi, I bought the best pink stones stolen by the miners at the Williamson Mine in Tanganyika, then Swakopmund, on the coast of what is now Namibia, buying alluvial diamonds found along the Atlantic beach."

The old man was beginning to enjoy his story. He looked beyond Boyd into the fire, eyes on the long lost adventure.

"Leopoldville was best. I would check into the Intercontinental. Before the porters could take my trunk to the room, there would be miners gathering in the lobby. I bought diamonds from noon until dark, every day. I always had the best room, the best food, the shiny black girls; always the best."

He smiled.

"So you competed with the cartel?" Boyd asked.

"Yes. They have the industrial diamond market tied up, because they own the mines at the very source of diamonds. The pipe, it's called. The jewelry market is based on the larger, perfect stones, the ones that are large enough to be noticed along a river bank. The ones fine enough to make a man risk his life for them in the mines or along a remote stretch of river. A man waits 20 years for just the stone. If he gets it out, he can retire. The cartel makes it very hard to steal diamonds from them in the mines, but it happens. If a large stone does get out, they want to prevent anyone else from bringing it to market, it would depress the price. No, the cartel wants to be the only source for the stones that men die for."

"So what happened to make you come up with this scheme?"

"The cartel bribed the governments to stop independent buyers, giving them a monopoly on alluvial diamonds, too. Michelle got the story wrong. We weren't going to set Ebola out to stop the alluvial miners. They're our source.

We were going to infect some monkeys around the diamond mines. All it would take is a few miners to get sick in those dirty, crowded camps where the miners live for a few months before going back home. We could stop the mining of diamonds in Africa."

The old man looked down. The smile from the shiny black girls was as gone as they, no doubt, now were. Old, wrinkled, used up, starved out and dead, the sweaty embrace they had provided in the vigor of their youth to a young Jewish diamond merchant long, long ago forgotten.

"Was it your idea?"

"No. The Arab traders came up with the idea. They've been in the diamond business for a thousand years. Much of Africa is Muslim, so they already have an advantage. They wanted to try to push the cartel out."

"Why you?"

"Most of my business is now with the Arabs."

"What about your Jewish contacts?"

"Not so much. Mostly the Arabs."

"So you've been helping Arabs compete with Jews in a traditionally Jewish business."

"We broke the monopoly of a few Jews who took advantage of other Jews in the diamond business. Now many diamond cutters have access to the world's supply of diamonds that were limited to the few before."

"So you moved gradually from Jewish clients to Arab clients?"

The air began to go out of Meilland again and he sank back into the chair, but the story wasn't over yet.

"Our reputation suffered. When we started competing with the cartel, we had to smuggle our diamonds out of Africa. We helped people move wealth around the world. We became known as smugglers more than just bankers."

"When was that?"

"My father started before the war. I was at university. Families were moving away from Hitler. They had diamonds to sell. Then in the '50s, there were hard times, too. I was always ready to buy."

"So you profited from Jews leaving Germany during the war?"

"Many did. Yes, I did, too. I admit it."

"So, your reputation suffered because of what you and your father did during the war?"

"The spoken word is sacred to us. We took advantage."

"But that wasn't the worst thing you did," Boyd said, aggressively now, still not understanding where this was going.

"I'm a Jew. All I have, I got because I'm a Jew. My family have been honorable Jews for 4,000 years. My punishment for dishonorable dealings was the loss of my granddaughter." He seemed frantic now, needing to be understood, as if his confession to Boyd would absolve him.

"So, it's OK to cheat the Arabs, but not a fellow Jew."

"I didn't cheat the Arabs, I didn't need to. Just letting them into the cutting and distribution was enough to alienate the other Jews."

"This is all way too complicated. How did Mikki get involved?"

"Michelle became almost possessed. She had no interest in banking or diamonds. She travelled. I worried, so I sent bodyguards."

"That was before the Ebola idea."

"Yes. I hired Byxbe three years ago. When Byxbe called me and said he'd found the virus and could isolate it and make a vaccine, I told her the plan. She was excited. It was like the days when she was a little girl and everything I did interested her. She stayed here, in Luxembourg City, and worked at the bank, preparing for the time when the cartel would be broken and our status as the alternative would be enhanced. It was a happy time for me."

"And now?"

"Now, there is nothing. I deserve it. I am not a Jew. I am not a grandfather. I am nothing."

"So, if there were even a chance Mikki is still alive, you would do anything to get her back?"

The old man froze. He didn't even blink.

"There is a chance?"

"Yes."

"Anything. I have a great deal of money. I could pay a ransom," Meilland said quickly.

"No, it won't be about money. It'll be something you know."

"Anything."

"OK. First, who bought Ebola?"

"I don't know. My contact was Hamid Tamim, a diamond trader in Doha."

"He came to you with the plan?"

"Yes."

"So, he was just an intermediary?"

"Probably."

"So they had the plan and you were their agent in execution," Boyd asked as he wrote furiously in a notebook.

"That is accurate."

"And how were you to deliver the virus?"

"Michelle was to meet an Arab trader from Senegal east of the Cape Verde Islands and make the transfer at sea."

Boyd shook his head. It was turning out to be so mechanical.

"What was she to deliver? All of what you got from Byxbe?"

"No. Just two vials of virus and two of vaccine."

"Were there any other customers?"

"No."

"Did it occur to you that they might have some other plan for the virus, something that had nothing to do with diamonds?"

"No."

Boyd was sure he was lying.

"OK, now to the pirate. Wolf Goebel and Neville St. James died trying to save Mikki and *Chardonnay*. They were loyal friends and employees. Constantine Coelho was the pirate who stopped us that night."

"Constantine?"

"You know him?"

"He learned to sail on *Chardonnay*. His father was a sea-man. I loaned him the money to buy his first fishing boat, I taught him how to smuggle and loaned him the money for his first big boat."

"So, you created the pirate?"

"Pirate?"

"He shot me, Wolf and Neville, and his men planted the dynamite that blew up *Chardonnay*. That's piracy."

"He wouldn't hurt Michelle. They were children together. We spent summers in Horta."

"Mikki may not be as endearing to all as you think."

"Did he take Michelle with him?"

"He could have. We didn't see her body. We didn't see Neville's either."

Now Meilland was thinking fast. His face a mask, he was in high negotiation mode.

"Listen, Meilland, this game is over. You think you know where he is, you'd better tell me now. They found your buddy Byxbe yesterday morning south of Charleston. Ebola got him. That virus has gotten out everywhere it's been. It's in South Carolina, Khartoum, and it's gonna be wherever Constantine Coelho is. There's no sign that vaccine has helped anyone. In fact, that may be what killed Byxbe. It's a long shot, but we're flying in a new antibiotic that might work if someone gets Ebola. If you want Mikki, you'd better hope I get to her before Ebola does."

The logic in that seemed to sink right in.

"Constantine owns an island," Meilland said, face sagging in defeat.

"Where?"

"He owns Corvo."

CHAPTER FIFTY TWO
NEW YORK

"This is Lester Holt with NBC News interrupting afternoon programming. We have breaking news from Africa. The outbreak of hemorrhagic fever in Khartoum, Sudan, reported on the Nightly News last night, has been identified by the World Health Organization as the deadly Ebola virus. That nation has been isolated in the world's first national quarantine, but enforcement of the quarantine is proving difficult. With the latest, we will go right to NBC chief foreign affairs correspondent Richard Engel in Cairo. Richard, what do you have for us on this shocking development?"

"Thank you Lester. The Egyptian Army has set up hospitals inside Sudan to treat thousands of refugees fleeing that nation. Tanks and infantry are arrayed along the entire border preventing those refugees' passage into Egypt. This film, taken from an aircraft this afternoon, shows Wadi Halfa, the first town inside Sudan along the Nile River. You can see the stream of vehicles, camels and people streaming north from Khartoum, some 300 miles to the south.

"The outbreak of the dread Ebola virus in Khartoum is widely believed to have come from monkeys carried by jihadists camped in the desert just outside town. Jihadists were drawn there by the promise of returning the nation of South Sudan back into the realm of the New Caliphate, as it is being called. The government of Sudan strongly denies having anything to do with this outbreak and disavows any connection with the several hundred jihadists.

"Reports are coming in that the outbreak began in the jihadist camp and that many of them are among the sick and the dead. However, in a development first reported by Al Jazeera, many of those jihadists seem to have been spared and remain in their camp at Khartoum, claiming that true believers are immune to 'The Wind of Allah,' which has devastated the population of Khartoum. Lester …"

"Richard, how is the quarantine going?"
"Lester, it seems strange, but look at these pictures we took this afternoon. You can see the

refugees streaming along the road there into Wadi Halfa, and you can see the roadblock there with people milling about. Now, as we pull back, look outside of town in the desert at the trail of trucks and vehicles bypassing the roadblock and headed into Sudan."

"Headed into the outbreak?"

"Yes, Lester. It seems that thousands of jihadists are rushing into this trouble spot to have their faith tested by the 'Wind of Allah.' And, I'm told that the roads from Cairo to Wadi Halfa are packed with vehicles of all types, rushing to jihad."

"Thank you, Richard. We'll be back with Richard Engel later in the broadcast, but now for the report from the World Health Organization on what they know about this outbreak of Ebola."

****

When Boyd walked into the American Embassy at 1800 hours local, the embassy staff was still there. It was early evening, and the staff should have been gone for the day, but they were clustered around the big screen in the staff conference room watching the satellite feed of world news. He stopped to watch.

"What's up?"

"That virus outbreak in Africa, it has something to do with jihad," a staffer said, popping the top on a can of American beer. "The fucking Arabs are going nuts."

A clip from Al Jazeera showed an Imam praising the jihadists for carrying the fight to the infidel and praying that many of them would pass the test of faith and survive the "Wind of Allah" to finally, after eight centuries restore the "Empire of the Faithful, the New Caliphate."

"Are you Chailland?" a staffer called out from the communications room.

"Yeah," Boyd said, feeling the long arm of Ferguson on his shoulder.

"You've got a call."

"Is this secure?" he asked, taking the phone from the staffer."

"Yeah, scrambled, satellite," he said, closing the door.

"Holy Christ, Chailland, we've got a shit storm of the first magnitude here. You better know where that pirate is with the Ebola or have that goddamned French banker's nuts in your pocket."

"Both."

"Only good news I've had all day. The news media wants to know if we're going to send the Global Response Team into Khartoum, Congress wants a full report of what we know and when we knew it, the president sent his national security adviser over here, and the CDC is saying we botched this thing from the get-go and should have let them handle it. The CIA is getting reports from a half a dozen places that there's a lot of interest in Ebola, and the price is now $10 million. I've got a blue flame under my butt to find this guy and shut him down."

"Sucks to be you, sir."

"Where is he?"

"Corvo. It's one of the Azores. I flew over it last week, didn't see anything."

"Does he have the virus?"

"Don't know. Meilland seemed truly surprised that Constantine was involved, but he's such a good liar I can't be sure."

"So he was in the Azores the whole time."

"They were to deliver the virus to a rendezvous east of the Cape Verde Islands. That's about a thousand miles from the Azores. He could do that in about a day and a half with that souped up tuna boat he has. So he probably delivered the virus before I was even out of surgery the day after *Chardonnay* blew up. He could have gotten back just as quick or gone somewhere else."

"Good work! How'd you find out?"

"Some Arabs cooked this up to try to put the diamond cartel out of business. They came to Meilland as their agent. An old man, he was willing to kill a million people to get the feeling of power again. He lied the whole time I was with him, always holding something back in hopes of keeping what he had, and getting what I had. It was just like Cooper Jordan, Lymon Byxbe and Mikki Meilland. You have to take what they say and comb through it to find the truth."

"It sounds like we've got some solid leads now."

"Meilland didn't intend for the Arabs to get all the virus and vaccine he had, so Constantine almost surely has more," Boyd said. "Sir, I've been on this trail now since June. The closer I get to Ebola, the worse the people are. Constantine Coelho got his start from Charles Meilland, picked up some additional pointers on interpersonal relationships from Mikki, and is now on the leading edge of badass. We need to get that island sealed off, quick.

"But, Constantine has three tuna boats, meaning he'd have about 30 sailors, maybe more. If they were all on the island at once, that would be a significant force. In addition, he got the final payment for the Ebola, a million in gold. You can buy a lot of firepower on the black market with that, and he's had three weeks to get it there."

Ferguson said, "OK, we've got some Marines just out of Norfolk, but they're at least a week away. It looks like Corvo is about 200 miles from our base at Lajes, that about right?"

"Yes, sir. We flew out there in a Casa 212. It was right at 200."

"We could alert the 82nd Airborne and get some infantry into Lajes in 48 hours."

"It'd be tricky to parachute onto an island that's only a couple of miles wide, and part of it is steep as hell," Boyd said. "There is a runway there that the Casa lands on, but I don't know if a C-130 could land on it."

"They don't want to put a C-130 filled with airborne soldiers down on a contested landing strip."

"Maybe I can put together an advance party from the Portuguese here to at least hold the runway."

"See what you can do."

"OK, we'll need the State Department to lead on this. That's Portuguese territory there, and they're real touchy about their space. The first guy on the beach is going to have to be Portuguese. The other issue is their navy. We're going to need their frigate to block Constantine from jumping into one of his tuna boats and slipping out the back door with Ebola. They have other demands on their resources here. Someone needs to blow in their ear."

"We have no Navy in the area that can be there that quick," Ferguson said. "We have State already here at the command post, so I'll task them with this right now. I'll get our Joint Staff member moving now to get permission for the insertion. That has to go all the way to the White House. Shouldn't be a problem, they're the ones turning up that blue flame under my butt. Now, who did Meilland sell the virus to?"

"An Arab in Doha, Qatar, named Hamid Tamim."

"Always tricky dealing with Arabs. We'll get the State Department on this, too. I doubt the Qatari Emir wants Ebola breaking out in his oceanfront neighborhood."

"I've got a flight back to Lisbon in a couple of hours, then the next flight back to the Azores gets me in there noon tomorrow."

CHAPTER FIFTY THREE
MARZANABAD, IRAN

The vervet monkey peered through the double layers of glass with a plaintive look on his face. Mahmoud Nashtarudi, his handler, knew this monkey well; they were friends. Mahmoud could tell he wasn't feeling well. He was supposed to be well. He'd been vaccinated with a new vaccine and then, just three days before, exposed to some virus they were studying.

"Get Dr. Namazi," he said, rushing out of the viewing port into the Level 3 containment facility buried 40 feet underground and hidden in the mountains north of Tehran.

The director came immediately, worry on his face as he rushed into the safe control room of the containment facility, his long white lab coat flapping behind him.

"See, his eyes, sir. He is sick," Nashtarudi said, concern in his voice.

Nashtarudi needed this job, and any adverse effect on a monkey in his care reflected on him personally. He'd been working in a veterinarian's office in the Caspian Sea coast town of Chalus when a civilian administrator from the prestigious Revolutionary Guard approached him about a job at a secret laboratory in the nearby mountains.

"Hummph," Namazi said. "You are right. How about the others?"

They opened the door to another viewing room and approached the other window. Two other vervet monkeys were playing happily in their cages. They were joined in the viewing room by two young Ph.D. candidates working with Namazi.

"It's OK, Mahmoud," Namazi said, breezing back out the door and heading out of the control room, the two Ph.D.s right behind him.

"Odd," Namazi said to them as the door closed behind them. We know from the Protein Data Bank that the crystal structure of the C-terminal domain of the Ebola virus has a pocket for a small molecule inhibitor that can prevent virus propagation. That crude protein coat strip of mRNA attached to a plasmid we replicated last month fits perfectly, and the inhibitor we manufactured didn't."

The three of them walked quickly down a long hall and into another corridor where Namazi's office was located.

"Our fermenters aren't big enough to make any quantity of vaccine with such a crude structure. We need to find out why that simpler molecule didn't work. Get the 3-D kiosk viewer up and put in the Ebola C-terminal image and I'll be there in a minute," Namazi said, dismissing his students and closing the door.

He rummaged in his desk for a piece of paper and logged on to his computer. He went to a secure Internet connection, logged in to a webmail account and called up a draft message. He added a sentence to the draft message and then logged out.

In Doha, Qatar, Kahlid logged into that same webmail account and went to the same draft message. He read Namazi's message, logged out and pulled a cell phone out of his robe. He called a man in Egypt.

CHAPTER FIFTY FOUR
CHARLES MEILLAND

Can a man negotiate with God?

Charles Meilland hoped so. He'd learned banking, the diamond trade and smuggling as a young man. It was a family business conducted at the margins of legality, and often outside those margins, for hundreds of years. The Meillands had changed their name from Oppenheim when they moved from Alsace to Luxembourg and opened the bank, and they'd always specialized in moving wealth about Europe and the world, hence the design, building and utilization of *Chardonnay* had been all about business and not for pleasure.

Halakhah is the Hebrew word for Jewish law. Its more literal translation would be "the path that one walks." Charles Meilland had strayed far from that path. He knew his sins, and he knew the law. He had some explaining to do in the afterlife, which for him was fast approaching.

When Hamid came to him with a crazy scheme to release sick monkeys around the diamond mines to scare away the miners and close the mines, Charles was wary. He knew Arabs. He'd competed with Arabs buying diamonds as a young man, and he'd come to represent them in all manner of transactions, legal and not legal. He had moved the wealth of emirs, crown princes, dictators, officials and bureaucrats out of Arabia and into his and other banks for years. *Chardonnay* had been in the Persian Gulf many times.

Arabs are not detail people. There are no Bedouin plumbers or carpenters or electricians. They're above all that. Consequently, Arabs depend on others to manage their infrastructure. Many times in his dealings with them, Charles had recalled the scene in *"Lawrence of Arabia"* in which Peter O'Toole delivers the line to Anthony Quinn that Arabs will always remain an insignificant people because they are "ignorant, and petty, and cruel." So, when an Arab came to him with a plan that required fastidious attention to highly technical detail, he was pretty sure they would somehow screw it up. He was counting on it, in fact.

Charles Meilland had taken an incredible risk with the lives of people around the world in order to have a chance at saving his own immortal soul. He'd recognized an impatience in Byxbe, a tendency to cut corners. All the better, because Meilland was pretty sure the Arabs were going to try to do this caper on their own, and they'd probably let Ebola get out. Meilland's deal to God was to save the Jewish people, because he knew from the start it wasn't about diamonds in Africa. It was about Tel Aviv.

CHAPTER FIFTY FIVE
PIRATES

The sword flashed in the bright sunlight, and Boyd ducked, hearing the swish as it passed over his head. Constantine towered over him, the pirate's chest covered only by crossed bandoliers of .50 caliber bullets and an oil-tanned leather vest. His bulging biceps strained against serpentine silver bracelets, and a thick leather belt held up baggy, blood-soaked canvas breeches. He roared in frustration as Boyd ducked away, his own sword heavy in his hand, slowing him down.

Constantine's massive hobnail boots shook the wooden deck as he pursued Boyd, scurrying beneath the barrels of cannon, still hot from the just-ended sea battle. Men in pitched combat shouted and cried out all around them as they hacked, stabbed and died. The wounded ran to the rail, slipping in pools of blood as they threw themselves over the side, preferring a 20-foot drop and sharks below to death at the hands of Portuguese pirates.

Coming to the bow, Boyd turned to make his stand. He swung the heavy sword in an arc, and Constantine stepped nimbly back, then in and, with a backhand motion, knocked the sword from Boyd's hands. Empty-handed now, Boyd lunged, hoping for a leg hold to take down the man who seemed to be even larger than a moment before. A blow from the butt of the big man's sword stunned him, and he fell to the deck. He rolled quickly over, expecting the blade. Strong arms grabbed him, pulled him fully upright and swung him back toward the forward mast, pinning him to it, feet off the deck.

"Not so fast little man. It wants you," Constantine said, his voice like distant thunder.

The clamor around them subsided, and only pirates stood, watching.

"Who?" Boyd wheezed.

"It." Constantine laughed again, and stood aside, pointing with his sword toward the open passageway. Stairs descended into the dark ...

****

Only the seat belt kept Boyd from leaping over the seat in front of him and landing in the lap of a plump Portuguese

schoolteacher returning to the islands from a music symposium in Lisbon.

"Por favor, senhor!" The stewardess ran back to Boyd
and touched his shoulder.

Looking around with wild eyes and panic, Boyd slowly
realized where he was. He'd not slept the night before in
Lisbon and had finally dropped off on the plane to the
Azores. "It" and the pirates and Constantine faded, but his
heart still raced.

"Obrigata, senhora. Un cerveza, por favor," he mumbled, sitting back down.

Wars are won and lost in battles, and battles come down
to skirmishes, and skirmishes are won and lost by individual
men, eye-to-eye with their enemy, hot and tired and scared.
Men who have trained a lifetime, then travel, march, run,
climb and fight until only sheer will is left. Two men, each
peering into the face of death an arm's length away, decide
it all.

Boyd's hand shook as the stewardess handed him a beer,
wrapped neatly in a damp napkin.

CHAPTER FIFTY SIX
PORTO MARTINS, AZORES

"They are boys, here for basic training. They are not men for a fight," Ferreira said. He was somber, speaking of the Portuguese Army recruits training on the island.

They were sitting in a low-ceilinged, dark bar with thick volcanic stone walls and small windows overlooking a tiny bay with a dozen dories pulled up on the concrete landing. Rain fell steadily without wind and splashed into the street from a broken downspout, right in front of the open door.

Angeja nodded, drinking a Coke and stubbing out a cigarette, and said, "One frigate is with the tuna boats nearly to Iceland. The other, at Ponta Delgada, will go to Corvo in the morning. Constantine's boat will not escape, but we cannot send men onto the island yet."

"No airfield there?" Boyd asked.

"There is an airfield there. The runway is only 800 meters. We land the Casa there every two weeks in the winter, or if they call an emergency. People go to Flores by ferry the rest of the year. It is for the people who live on the island to visit the other islands. We begin the flights in November," Angeja said, earnestly, explaining why they couldn't rush Corvo with what they had.

"I suppose if we went in there early, they'd know something was up?" Boyd asked, knowing the answer already. "It sure would be nice to know what's on that island."

"There is no hurry,' Ferreira said. "In a week, we will have two frigates, two U.S. destroyers, a company of airborne troops from Lisbon, and your Marines. Nothing Constantine can do would help him then."

"OK. I'll wait," Boyd said, finishing his beer and still uneasy but resigned to waiting. "You guys gonna eat here?"

"No, I must go home. My wife ..." Angeja took the opportunity to bow out. He pulled some bills out to cover his tab.

"Yes, eat with me. We will have a good meal," Ferreira said, motioning for another Scotch.

"Not any of that *chourico*?" Boyd asked suspiciously, remembering the fried red sausage that tasted like toenails.

"No. *Polvo guisado*, it is very good. A man is going to meet us here tonight. He is a fisherman who is home from the tuna fleet. He knows Constantine and his island."

Boyd and Ferreira wished Angeja a pleasant meal with his wife, then stood in the door with their drinks and watched him sprint to his car across the road. The low clouds had darkened the early evening an hour before sunset, and the sea was a dull gray, with sullen swells grudgingly breaking at the last minute to roll into the rocks not 40 yards from the little fisherman's bar that sheltered them.

A half-smoked cigarette dangled from Ferreira's mouth, and his graying hair ruffed up in back with the breeze now beginning to come off the water, as he stood looking over the boats and the water running across the road and down the concrete ramp. He looked very much like he belonged here, though Boyd knew he was from the teeming slums of Lisbon and had spent his youth killing Africans and Cubans in Angola and Mozambique. They stepped back across the heavily beamed threshold and re-entered the simple restaurant.

Their table had been transformed. A fresh red tablecloth had been laid and set with traditional brown glazed pottery dishes with a ring of tiny red flowers around the rim. The bowl in the center of the table was filled with a steaming, purple dark stew, and a pottery pitcher held wine. Two bottles of Luso, the local mineral water, were open, and each plate had a few shreds of lettuce and carrot. A loaf of heavy Azorean bread was cut into odd-size chunks and piled in a napkin-lined basket. Butter and fresh cheese, only days from being milk from the local black-and-white cows, were in matching bowls. A side dish of piri, the local hot pepper sauce, awaited application to the bread and cheese.

"How did we come to know about this fisherman coming here tonight?" Boyd asked, sitting down, nodding at the owner, smiling to hide the uncertainty the sight of the stew was causing to his normally robust appetite.

"The island people know what is going on here," Ferreira said, thickly buttering a piece of bread and pouring them each a healthy large glass of the heavy red wine. "They trust me, and they trust you Americans. If he has broken international law, they will not shield him. Also, Constantine has made enemies."

The owner, standing in the door to the kitchen with an apron around his middle, beamed with pleasure at this opportunity to serve his renowned *polvo guisado* to such distinguished guests.

"So, what is this?" Boyd asked again, peering down at round bits of purple meat in a dark stew with onions and spices and a heavy sheen of oil on the top.

"I don't know the name in English," Ferreira said, digging in to his with a large spoon. "They have eight arms."

"Octopus?" Boyd asked, looking again at the stew. He could see suction cups on some of the pieces.

"Yes, better taste it. Augusto will be offended."

Boyd took a tentative bite. The octopus was rubbery, with an oily, garlicky taste. He smiled at Augusto and took a big bite. It went well with the heavy red wine and crusty bread.

"*Vinho de cheiro,*" Ferreira said, holding up the wine. "It is a local wine. The vines grow on the ground along the black lava soil."

He finished his, and the heavy dark red wine stained even the empty glass.

The pitcher was refilled, and they finished the stew, made purple from the liberal addition of wine during the cooking process. They lingered over the rest of the bread. Ferreira was loosened considerably by the several double Scotches before dinner and the two liters of wine they had consumed.

He spoke of the local bullfights. Wild bulls are brought into the streets where they run free, while young men of the island sprint up to touch them, then leap over fences and through windows to escape. The old people watch and remember when it was they who sailed over the same wall, fleeing the grandfather of that same bull. Then Ferreira told tales of storms that had swept away fishing boats with their entire crews, never to be seen again.

A larger wave crashed against the rocks, and the wind picked up, blowing water onto the concrete floor. Boyd looked up to see a figure pass the window in front and stop in the door. Underneath the worn yellow slicker, he wore faded jeans and a plaid flannel shirt. Boyd noticed cow manure and mud on his nearly knee-high rubber boots as he stepped from the now dark road into the light.

The man paused a moment, shaking rain from his slicker, eyes adjusting, checking out the corners and the kitchen through the partially drawn curtain. His face was furrowed by the sun, and his tanned hands looked too large for the sleeves of his faded shirt. He walked to the bar and scraped the bar stool as he sat. Augusto, surprised at another customer on such a night, entered from the kitchen where he had been eating his own meal.

"Boa tarde," Augusto said, laying down a small paper napkin.

Boyd recognized only the greeting. The rest of their conversation was beyond his superficial grasp of the language. Ferreira ignored the man completely.

A car slowed in front of the bar, pulled off the road and parked behind Ferreira's Toyota. A small man rushed across the street, protected from the now gusting wind by a thin leather jacket and gray slacks. He, too, paused at the door before entering and joining the first man at the bar. He ignored Boyd and Ferreira but spoke to Augusto and the other man.

When Augusto returned to the kitchen, Ferreira scooted his chair around to make room for another, and then leaned over to pull two more chairs to their table. The two men brought their beers to the table and sat down.

Another large wave crashed outside, and the rain was producing a puddle in the middle of the floor. Augusto walked quickly from the kitchen as if the water was a new event and closed the front door. The crash of water from the broken downspout was only muffled, and the room seemed smaller. The smell of cooked octopus was stronger.

"Don't use the name of the man we are here to talk about," Ferreira said as they all leaned into the center of the table and spoke in Portuguese. "Our friends are afraid of retribution from his family."

After 10 minutes he turned to Boyd.

"They are very angry. He has taken control of the island by moving his fishing boats and crews there. They have forced out or intimidated the people who lived there before. This has all happened in the past year. The young were only too happy to work for him, and the old ones content to watch the television brought to them by the big new satellite antenna he built. They get all the channels from the big European satellite we can't get here."

"Do these guys work for him?"

"Mauricio did, but was fired because he didn't want to go to Africa anymore. It's a rough crossing. The older one is his uncle, who worked on the boats before the new business."

"What's that?"

"They've been smuggling guns."

"What happened to the cheese?"

"They don't do that anymore. Freighters stop at Corvo at night and unload. They run the guns into Liberia and Mauritania. They bring back hashish and wild animals."

"What kind of animals?" Boyd asked quickly.

"Monkeys."

"Shit. Guns and monkeys, couldn't be any worse than that," Boyd said, shaking his head and looking out the window.

"Oh, yeah, it could," Ferreira said. "When Mauricio came home from Corvo, he told his uncle he was on the last trip to Africa. They traded a metal suitcase for a wooden box about the size of a case of wine, and it took two men to carry. They're gassing up to do it again."

The waves now were cresting at the entrance to the bay, and the rain splashed at the window, and the wind was a constant low howl. Winter in the North Atlantic was beginning.

CHAPTER FIFTY SEVEN
CAIRO

"This is Lester Holt with NBC News interrupting 'The Tonight Show With Jay Leno.' We have breaking news from Africa. The outbreak of the deadly Ebola virus in Sudan has spread to Egypt. We are going live to our chief foreign affairs correspondent, Richard Engel, in Cairo. Richard, what do you have there?"

"Thank you Lester. Behind me is the main highway from Cairo south, toward Sudan. Units of the Egyptian Army are streaming by, headed into the desolate Sudan border area where the Ebola quarantine line has been breached. Thousands of jihadists, bent on testing their faith against what they are calling 'The Wind of Allah,' flanked the quarantine barrier at Wadi Halfa and drove to the jihadist camp at Khartoum. Many died there, and hundreds, now sick with Ebola, streamed back across the border making a mad dash for hospitals in Cairo. They have been stopped at Aswan, 400 miles to our south. Film taken this afternoon as we flew over the Khartoum area shows the dead are littering the desert. Though they brought tanker trucks filled with fuel on their journey, hundreds are now stranded in the desert without fuel. Others have plunged into the swamp along the Nile toward South Sudan, where the South Sudan Army has set up a quarantine line at Malakal. Lester …"

"Richard, is this a general uprising of Islamic warriors?"

"It seemed so yesterday, Lester, but today we have footage from Al Jazeera of Sheikh Ali Gomaa, the Grand Mufti of Egypt, contradicting the Imam that has been broadcasting encouragement for the faithful to join jihad. The Muslim Brotherhood, the main political power in Egypt right now, is taking a hard stand against jihad and has instructed the army to arrest anyone caught approaching the new quarantine line. Lester …"

"Richard, any estimate of the number of dead so far?"

"Lester, the government of Egypt is not talking about fatalities, but the World Health Organization estimates 10,000 dead so far. That includes citi-zens from Khartoum, the jihadists initially pres-ent, and the early arrivals of jihadists from Cairo. All roads out of Cairo are jammed, the airports and ferry terminals are packed, and anything that will float is headed into the Mediterranean and across the Red Sea filled with people. Lester …"

"Thank you, Richard. This has been Lester Holt with NBC News with breaking news from Egypt. We now return you to 'The Tonight Show.'"

CHAPTER FIFTY EIGHT
CORVO, AZORES

"From what I hear about the weather out there, I wouldn't worry too much that your pirate will get away," Ferguson said over the scrambled phone line in the command post at Lajes.

Mimicking the hurricane that had chased *Chardonnay* to Horta, a giant low-pressure area had stalled in the central Atlantic, sending 30-foot swells east to smash into the rocks of the Azores, and 80-knot winds to close the runway at Lajes for three days. Now the Atlantic was placid and the morning bright.

"The storm passed and the runway is open," Boyd responded, still winded from running up the hill from his quarters after the duty officer called. "The Portuguese Navy sent their frigate that was watching Corvo back to Horta to wait out the storm. He could have slipped out last night or early today in one of his tuna boats."

"See if you can talk your hosts into sending over their Casa 212 to check out the island. The cavalry is on the way. In addition to two destroyers, we have a Special Operations Unit loading at Fort Bragg right now."

"Loading into what?"

"C-130s, three of them."

"That's a 2,400-foot runway, sir," Boyd said, not calmed in the least.

"They practice that stuff. They can do it." Ferguson seemed sublimely confident. "What's this about a new customer?"

"Now that word is getting out about what a bad actor Constantine is, every sailor who's ever had a beef with him is coming forward. These islands are like a small town. Everyone knows everyone else's business. A guy came over on the ferry this morning from Sao Jorge, said he was on Corvo before the storm. Constantine knows the jig is up and is planning to cash out with one last score."

"We're doing all we can. He won't get away."

"Yes, sir," Boyd said, shaking his head, remaining silent while Ferguson closed out their conversation. He slammed the door shut as he left the command post, the long-suffering officer who'd called him a half a dozen times for secret messages frowned as he passed, no doubt hoping that whatever this was would soon be gone and leave him in peace.

****

"A fishing boat capsized near San Miguel," Angeja said over the whine of the turboprops of the first Casa as he walked across the tarmac to the second, natty in his tight-fitting flight suit and carefully shined boots. "Our first responsibility is to the search-and-rescue mission. We must use the Casa to find the fishermen. Perhaps this afternoon we can send one of them to Corvo."

"Damn, Felipe, this is important," Boyd shouted over the engines.

"Fishermen are important, to their families, and to our country," Angeja said, patiently, swinging quickly into the open door of his aircraft. "Want to come along?"

"No, thanks," Boyd said, slowing, then making a salute as Angeja appeared in the cockpit. He turned and walked dejectedly back toward the Portuguese Operations building as the engines in the second Casa began to crank.

Ferreira stood in the door, smoking as usual. He watch dispassionately as Boyd traversed the ramp. He was dressed in his jungle fatigues, unusual for him.

"I guess that slippery bastard Constantine gets away, and I'll have to catch him someplace else," Boyd said, kicking the side of the building. "No one here seems to give a damn about him."

"We could fly over in the Waco," Ferreira said, smiling and pointing toward the hangar. "I have permission from the Brigadiero."

****

The thrill of lifting off the island and seeing the white foam at the edge of the rocks give way to blue Atlantic, and then the other islands appearing to the west, only masked the uneasiness. This was a mission that bordered on the fool-hardy. Enjoying the cold wind in his face, Boyd laughed to himself as he saw Ferreira in the front cockpit looking down and about through the old aviator's goggles they both wore.

The Brigadiero, a Portuguese Air Force two-star general and a pilot himself, had come down to the operations area to be sure they knew exactly how to plan this mission. He had checked the calculations of fuel and distance and given advice and reassurance that the air traffic net had been alerted to the Waco's journey. While he talked, he paced and chain-smoked.

The Waco was only a trainer and was 60 years old at least. It carried no navigation instruments. Corvo is an island 5 miles across and nearly 200 miles from Lajes. It could be reached without losing sight of land if one hopped across Sao Jorge, Pico and Faial headed out 310 degrees, and turned around if Flores didn't show up before Faial was no longer visible behind. Corvo is 12 miles from Flores.

Slowly, the antique fabric-and-wood biplane climbed to 5,000 feet, and Boyd throttled back to save fuel. Stuffed into the seat beside Ferreira was a satchel with pistols, ammunition, a radio capable of getting back to Lajes, lunch and some mail for the local schoolmaster, made to look like a Federal Express shipment. It might fool somebody, the Brigadiero had said, helpful to the point of betraying his own desire to be along on such an odd adventure.

Fishing boats fanned out from Terceira, the island that Lajes is on. After three days of stormy weather, the indomitable Azorean fishermen were eager to get back at the fish. As the old Waco rattled and roared toward Sao Jorge, Boyd could see boats setting out there, too. The dories were visible only by their modest wakes.

Boyd's mind slipped back to the height of the storm, when Pamela, Donn and Angela had stayed indoors for three days straight, eating, drinking and playing Monopoly. Angela had stayed close. She was acting like part of a couple.

"It won't work," he'd said. Best to have this out now, so she wouldn't start feeling something for him that would have to come undone.

"Oh?" She'd said.

"I told you before. I'm different."

"Yes, you are."

"It's like there are a few of us who don't mix with the flock. We stay out here and watch."

He'd made a circle with one hand, while the other hand remained motionless, poised above.

Angela had dropped it there, and it remained an unsettled issue.

Back in the present, Sao Jorge approached. Less populated than Terceira, with fewer roads and more level land, Velas is the only community of size. As they flew over it, Ferreira stretched at his shoulder harness trying to lean out and look down. He made some hand signals Boyd didn't understand, but they might have indicated Ferreira knew a woman who lived at Velas.

Ahead across the Sao Jorge Channel and 20 degrees left of their course toward Horta on Faial, loomed the volcano Pico. *Chardonnay* lay in her watery grave beneath 2,000 feet of Atlantic Ocean on the other side of that island, with Wolf and Neville. Boyd thought of them and then saw Constantine's face, eyes ablaze with rage and hatred, the huge pistol in his hand.

Boyd snapped out of his reverie when he noticed a white executive jet parked at the end of the runway at the Pico Island Airport, just around the northern coast of Pico from

Madalena. It was tucked into the side of the volcanic cliff and barely visible. He checked the map again. This small municipal airport has a 4,000-foot runway, long enough for small airliners. He strained to see well enough to identify the aircraft. Similar to a Gulfstream, Boyd finally decided it was a Daussault Mystere Falcon, a hot new executive jet, easily capable of intercontinental travel.

Boyd wagged the wings to get Ferreira's attention and then pointed down. Ferreira had the binoculars and used them. He looked back and shrugged. In a couple minutes they were over the narrow straight between Pico and Faial, and the runway at Pico disappeared behind the volcano's shoulder.

Fuel was adequate, and over the tower at Horta, Boyd changed course to compass heading 310. He checked in with the tower at Horta and began to climb. He wanted to be sure he could see Flores.

The day was clear and bright, with no clouds except a ring around the volcano Pico. Boyd saw Flores 10 minutes out from Faial, with Faial and Pico still very much in evidence behind them. He relaxed, and soon Corvo popped up, too. They landed at Flores for fuel; no sense getting to Corvo and into some conflict and being out of gas.

"Bon dia?" An attendant approached the plane as Boyd shut down the engine and got down. He waved but let Ferreira do the talking. This was just another aero club flight.

Looking around the field, he saw a small hangar, and in it was a Cessna 172, the same one he'd seen at Lajes a few weeks before.

"We'll circle the island a couple times,: Boyd said as they stood watching the chubby Azorean attendant fill the Waco. "If it looks like we might meet a hostile reception, we can head back and let the Special Ops boys do the job tonight. At least we can give them some idea of what to expect."

"The private jet at Pico," Ferreira mused, looking back in that direction. "That is very unusual. International flights are not allowed to land there. There is no customs or immigration."

"Whose Cessna is that?" Boyd asked.

Ferreira stopped the attendant as he was securing his hose and they spoke briefly. Boyd thought the man's eyes looked shifty when he replied.

"He says it belongs to one of the fishing fleets. They use it for spotting tuna," Ferreira said, climbing back into the front seat.

Soon they were roaring and bouncing along the runway. Corvo rose dark and misty 12 miles before them as they rose over the open ocean. Boyd could see a short runway and a cluster of houses on a teardrop of island that pointed out toward Flores and sloped into the sea. They even had a small beach. The rest of the island was a dark green rim around a volcanic crater, which, upon drawing closer, was mostly marsh and lake. A new house, built of the island's volcanic stone, had been erected on the rim of the volcano, hundreds of feet above the town, thrusting itself into the raw Atlantic wind like a challenge to nature. It was freshly whitewashed and had a large satellite dish next to it. There were no tuna boats in the small harbor.

They crossed the runway and flew across the island at 1,500 feet. A road snaked up the hill from town to the large house, then down into the crater and around it to the other side of the island. A large tuna boat was anchored on the northern side of the island, protected from the pounding surf by a cleverly designed cove dynamited out of the rocks at the base of the cliff. This mooring might not withstand a full bore storm, but looked adequate for a routine storm if the winds came from the south, which they usually did. It was certainly handy if someone decided they needed to leave in a hurry. Circling the uninhabited bulk of the island, they came back over the town, Vila Nova Do Corvo. There was one red pickup truck and a few donkeys in the whole town.

Boyd wagged the wings, and when Ferreira turned around he pointed down. Slowly, Ferreira nodded in the affirmative. They circled into a downwind leg and Boyd announced his intention to land over the radio. This was for other traffic that might be in the area; there was no tower at Corvo.

On final approach, the Waco floated over Vila Nova Do Corvo, and the townsfolk seemed to be staring dumbly up, standing in the street watching this unexpected event. There were only a couple of dozen of them, and they all appeared to be female, or old, or both. The Waco used up only half the runway in landing and taxied back toward the town.

Boyd had decided to risk a landing because, he reasoned, those townspeople wouldn't be standing around watching if they knew an ambush was about to occur, and because of the Falcon he'd seen at Pico. If this were the new customer for Ebola, come to the nearest runway to pick it up, he couldn't wait for the navy or special ops troops. The pattern continued; whoever this customer was would be smarter and more dangerous than the last one and was certainly better financed. Someone had sent a $10 million plane to pick up the virus, and it could be anywhere in the world in a day. This wasn't about alluvial diggers in Africa anymore.

The Waco rattled to a stop at the lone gas pump at the side of the runway. Nobody came to meet them. Boyd and Ferreira dismounted and scanned the town. In addition to the couple dozen houses was one modern school building, identical to the one Boyd had seen at Lajes. There were schoolchildren playing in the yard.

"How do you want to do this?" Boyd asked, holding open the satchel with the guns and looking at Ferreira.

"I feel like the sheriff in one of your Western movies," Ferreira said, taking the satchel and pulling out a 9 millimeter pistol with holster.

"Keep yours handy," he said, as he pulled the web belt around his waist and cinched it tight, his belly hanging over. He checked the clip, chambered a round and turned toward the village.

Boyd, in civilian clothes, walked beside Ferreira as they traversed a grassy field and then a cobblestone street to the center of town.

An old man sprawled asleep in a chair in the front yard of the first house they passed, a skinny black dog at his feet. The dog awoke and gave them a perfunctory bark, and the old man stirred, but did not rise. A few doors down, a woman was bringing in her laundry from the clothesline in her yard. Ferreira stopped and talked with her. She answered, but her eyes darted up the road toward town, and her answers were brief. She was afraid.

"The boats left this morning," Ferreira said, resuming their walk up the hill.

The village was so small that after they went by a few more houses, they were on their way out of it.

"Antonio Borges Da Silva is the constable here. I think he lives over there," Ferreira said, stopping to light a cigarette. He nodded to a two-story house at the edge of town.

The multifamily dwelling had four front doors, each with flanking windows and two windows above. Children were playing in the yard, but when Boyd and Ferreira approached, they were called inside. Ferreira walked up to the closest door, which was open, and looked in

"Boa tarde, senhor," he said with a jolly tilt Boyd knew he didn't feel.

An older man descended the interior stairs, tucking in a shirt. He was pretending to be happy to see Ferreira and invited them in. The small room had some religious artifacts on the walls and some old photographs. There were two wooden chairs and a couch covered by a faded red fabric. Two children from across the street appeared in the yard and looked into the still open door. Ferreira talked earnestly with the constable, and then turned to Boyd.

"It sounds like there's been a mutiny," Ferreira said. "Someone in the big house up there got sick last week, and died. Antonio says they heard it was something terrible, and the fishermen were afraid, so as soon as the weather cleared, they left. The phone system is disabled, and these people have been unable to call the other islands for more than a week."

"He still here?" Boyd asked, looking back toward the airfield.

Ferreira nodded as he took the satchel from Boyd and pulled out the other pistol and handed it to Boyd, then said something to the constable. As they walked back across the front yard the building behind them came alive as the constable began instructing his neighbors to spread the word through town, then he set out toward the school, his ample belly juggling to and fro as he glanced anxiously down the hill.

"Constantine is at his warehouse on the waterfront. Antonio said he's been carrying stuff up the hill all morning. He's got one guy with him."

"Even fight," Boyd said, strapping the holster to his waist. He pulled the pistol and removed the clip to be sure it contained bullets.

Ferreira looked at Boyd, brows furrowed, but said nothing.

The red truck appeared in front of them as it rounded the corner, wheels spinning. For a moment they stopped, motionless in the middle of the road as the truck approached, picking up speed. Boyd could see Constantine's bulk in the driver's seat, and the big pistol came out the driver's side window and pointed his way. He and Ferreira moved simultaneously, running to opposite sides of the road and leaping over the ever present stone fences that bordered the yards there. A shot ricocheted off the fence as Boyd's body dropped behind it.

Automatic fire from the passenger side raised dust in the yard of the house on Ferreira's side of the street as he rolled back into the wall as close as he could. The truck flashed past.

Boyd popped up his head, weapon at the ready. A bullet smashed into the trunk of a stubby tree in the yard, and Boyd dived back into the dandelions. Constantine fired blindly back at them two more times as the truck fishtailed up the steep hill toward the house. Another burst from the passenger side, better aimed, kept Ferreira pressed against the wall. In a few seconds, it was out of sight.

"He'll get out the back way," Boyd said, standing, holstering his weapon.

"The frigate will catch him," Ferreira said, dusting himself off.

Boyd turned and looked into the open ocean toward the east and Faial, from which the frigate should be coming. No sign of it yet.

"How fast is one of those tuna boats?"

"Twenty knots."

"How fast is the frigate?"

"Twenty-five knots."

"Can you get word to the frigate not to let anyone come aboard? We don't want Ebola off this island. If it gets on your frigate, and back to San Miguel, we've got another outbreak to cope with."

Boyd vaulted over the fence and stood in the road, legs spread, hands on hips.

Ferreira, looking older, walked to the gate and opened it, pulling it shut behind him and taking care to close the latch. His eyes flicked up at the house on the hill, then back to the road in front of him, but not toward Boyd.

"I can call Lajes only."

"They could call the navy at San Miguel," Boyd opened the satchel and handed the radio to Ferreira.

Boyd paced the street looking up at the house and down toward the waterfront while Ferreira made the call.

"Let's go down to his warehouse," Boyd said, trying to sound positive. "If he's been running guns ,we should be able to get some heavier firepower."

"What for?" Ferreira asked suspiciously. "The navy will be here in two hours, he is finished."

"What if he comes back down that hill?" Boyd asked, nodding up toward the house.

"OK." Ferreira turned toward the waterfront, a crease of a smile on his face. "Good idea."

Armed with Kalashnikovs and plenty of ammunition, Ferreira seemed to feel better. He laughed and joked as they walked to the corner where they'd first seen the truck and leaned against the side of the building, trapping Constantine from returning to the town. They could see the house, and whoever was there could see them. Ten minutes passed.

Boyd heard distant sounds, so faint at first he thought it was coming from up the hill. That sound made his hair stand; it was the drums again, warning. Ferreira was calmly finishing his cigarette. Boyd's unease grew.

Ebola was up there, and the pattern was not true if capture was this easy. How could Ferreira know how fast Constantine's boat was? How come they couldn't see the frigate? Why had Constantine been content to leave them armed in the town?

"We've got to go up that hill," Boyd said, stepping out into the street.

"Why?"

"This doesn't add up. Something's not right. Look, just back me up. We'll stay off the road, go around the side over there."

Boyd started walking up the street, parallel with the waterfront, shielded from the view above by buildings in town.

To the east, the most direct route, they quickly were blocked by a cliff that could only be scaled by a technical climb. They retreated through the town and around the airfield. The gradual, grassy approach seemed easy, until an hour had passed, and they were still only half way up. It grew steeper.

Ferreira stopped for a cigarette, winded. Boyd retrieved the binoculars and scanned the horizon to the southeast. The frigate was a tiny dot on the horizon.

"There's your navy," he handed the binoculars to Ferreira.

Boyd wondered why Constantine was waiting for the frigate. An answer occurred to him that made him reach for the binoculars.

"How much do you know about tuna boats?" Boyd asked.

"Not much. I have never been on one."

"His boat has two diesel engines. What if he's faster than your frigate? It comes out here,he heads back to the rest of the islands. If he can get to Pico 10 minutes ahead of the frigate, he's gone."

They started climbing again, passing the carcass of a dead mule drawing flies on the side of the hill.

The red pickup was still at the house when they dragged themselves up the last few yards of the hill at midafternoon and peeked over the top. It was 10 degrees cooler at the top, and the wind was brisk. The Atlantic was a 360-degree panorama that caused them to pause in appreciation of Constantine's view. They crouched and moved toward the house. The compound was a fortress, the walls and out-buildings arranged to protect from any incursion along the road. Two satellite dishes and some other antennas indicated a sophisticated communications link.

Behind the house, the crater dropped steeply 300 feet to a bog at the bottom, the sides covered with brush. They slid a few yards down into the crater, hanging on to the sides to traverse the open area around the pool, and came back up behind a small pool house. The main house was built right on the rim of the volcano and was balanced on the only hundred feet of level ground before the hill dropped off at the front. The water in the swimming pool was pristine, its surface ruffled by the wind.

Ferreira covered the upstairs windows with his AK-47 as Boyd climbed onto the patio. He covered as Ferreira followed. They traversed a covered walkway and entered the open kitchen door.

Boyd stopped to take in the kitchen. Though Constantine might be a pirate, snubbing his nose at the world and its rules, in his home he was a traditionalist. There was a brick, built-in, open hearth oven for baking bread, like Boyd had seen in the restaurants he'd visited with Ferreira, and a wood-burning as well as gas stove, with copper and clay pots in all sizes. They walked into the dining room and passed a wrought iron gate, locked, leading to a wine cellar. The dining room table seated 12, and the adjacent living room was huge, looking out at the village below and the Atlantic beyond through large windows. A large stone fireplace with stone mantle carried the traditional motif from the ornate dining room. Religious symbols adorned the walls.

Radio static and the sound of someone talking could be heard up the stairs. Boyd pointed out the front window. The frigate was in sight, a puff of black smoke behind it serving as an accent and indicating flank speed. Moving into the room, Boyd could see two sentries manning the front of the house, watching the road from town. They had Kalashnikovs at the ready.

A door slammed in the back, and Boyd and Ferreira retreated into the dining room. A Portuguese seaman walked in from the other side of the stairs and ascended in a hurry. He began talking as he went up. Moments later, he came back down, bearing the two metal suitcases. He returned out the other side of the house in back.

Boyd heard a faint metallic zing and turned towards Ferreira. No longer hesitant, his eyes were alight, and he held a black commando knife from the sheath on his webbed pistol belt. He moved quickly to the side of the stairs just as the back door slammed again.

The seaman returned through the back door and turned the corner to climb the stairs. Like a spider grabbing a fly, Ferreira was behind him. One hand clamped across the seaman's mouth and yanked the man's head back, the other slashed the throat and caused a cascade of blood down his chest and onto the tile. The second slash nearly severed the head, and a dying gurgle was muffled as the head dropped down onto the chest as Ferreira let him slump backward to drag him into the darkened dining room from which he had just sprung.

Boyd gaped at the blood covered tile. Even the walls were sprayed. Ferreira reappeared, alone now, and looked up the stairs, then waved his arm upstairs while pointing his weapon at the front door.

Taking care not to slip in the already congealing blood, Boyd gingerly walked up the tile stairs. He was relieved when the smell of blood gave way to the smell of new masonry higher up. The barrel of the Kalashnikov was right behind his nose as he crouched and looked around the corner at the top of the stairs.

Mikki was chained to the wall in the master bedroom, nude, bruised, beautiful.

She saw him and stood; the chains rattled. Boyd's head reeled. The iron collar and oversize chain attached to a large iron ring buried in the thick stone wall was right out of a dungeon scene, but the perfectly coiffed hair, thick hand-woven Portuguese rug and ornately carved king-size bed fit into a palatial estate. In the moment they stood facing each other, her nipples puckered. She took a breath, and seemed to grow taller. Her eyes flashed.

That could only mean someone was about to die. Boyd had begun to turn before he heard the swish and ducked instead. The sword hit the masonry just above his head with a metallic clank. Boyd rolled away from the stair, dropping his rifle. Constantine's bulk blocked the light from the other end of the hall, where he'd been sitting in a combination office and radio room. He wore a Kevlar vest with the big pistol strapped to his thigh.

Boyd aimed a kick at the nearest knee and Constantine shifted weight to deflect it. Boyd scooted toward the bedroom, regained his feet and fled headlong toward Mikki, who stood against the wall, lips curled back in an ecstatic grin.

Boyd fumbled with the snap on the holster of the 9 millimeter automatic. Constantine entered the room and raised the sword above his head. It was a curved Turkish sword, usually seen hanging over mantles for decoration, but this one was sharp, and the similarity to the dream he'd had caused Boyd to freeze in terror. Two steps and the big man was upon him, and death was about to descend.

There was a burst of automatic weapon fire from the stairs below, and they were all distracted for a moment. Boyd regained some composure, realizing that at least Ferreira had his back. He grabbed a wooden chair from a make-up table to deflect the blow, and when it came the sword whacked out a great sliver from the leg, but the chair held it from Boyd. Constantine dropped the sword and grabbed for Boyd. He still had the pistol but apparently felt this killing should be done bare-handed. They fell backward over a fainting couch into a corner of the bedroom. Constantine was on top, meaty hands around Boyd's throat. His dark eyes bored into Boyd, his breath was hard and reeking of fish and garlic as his thumbs found Boyd's windpipe.

"Ungghuh!" Boyd grunted as he shifted his weight to free his right hand and draw his pistol. Then he remembered that the safety was on and there was no round in the chamber. With one hand, it was useless. Constantine didn't know that, though.

Boyd brought it quickly up toward the big Azorean's head, and just as the periphery of his vision darkened, Constantine let go and grabbed the gun. Boyd struggled as if to fire it, buying time, gasping in precious breath. He glanced over Constantine's shoulder and saw Mikki at the end of her chain, crouched, straining to get closer, to see him die.

"Argghh!" The pistol was now the weapon, and Constantine let out a guttural roar as he raised it above his head with both hands to bash Boyd's brains out on the tile floor.

Boyd flexed his knee, and his left hand grabbed a knife from an ankle sheath. He'd learned one thing from Wolf: Always have a little something to fall back on in tough times. His arm was still pinned to the floor, but as the pistol descended, he twisted just enough to take the blow on the side of his head and deflect it, and jab the knife into Constantine's calf.

"Yeoohh!" Constantine cried out in pain and extended his leg, pulling his calf away from the knife.

Boyd stabbed him in the thigh.

Constantine rolled off and pointed the pistol at Boyd, pulling the trigger. There was no round in the chamber. Boyd flicked out a right cross, his best punch this close. The gunshot from a month before had taken the strength and flexibility from the arm, and the punch was slow and ineffectual. Constantine chambered a round. Boyd rotated to the left and kicked Constantine in the chest. Constantine went down backward on his butt but bought up the gun, cocked and ready to fire. Boyd kicked it out of his hands and across the room.

Several single shots rang out downstairs, then a long burst of automatic fire. Bullets ricocheted off the tile of the stairs and into the plaster wall at the top.

Constantine stood, grabbing for his big pistol, but the sheer size of it slowed him down long enough for Boyd to come up from the floor with a full force body punch. A month before, that is what had taken the steam out of Wolf, a smaller but more heavily muscled man. This time, it was nothing. The pain in Boyd's shoulder returned as if he'd been shot again. He stepped back and gave Constantine a left jab to the face.

Constantine staggered back. The gun came up. Boyd grabbed it with both hands and pushed forward. Constantine fell back on the bed, and Mikki was on Boyd's back, arms around his neck. No question now where her loyalties were.

The gun exploded and plaster fell from the ceiling. Mikki's arms slipped from around his neck, and she stepped back. Constantine's free left hand began to bash Boyd on the side of his face, while both of Boyd's wrestled with the right hand, pushing the gun down into the pillows. Two more shots thundered out, filling the room with smoke and feathers.

"I'm shot," Mikki moaned from behind.

Boyd found the trigger and squeezed off three more rounds, then let go of the gun and jumped back, he was gasping for breath and, in spite of the adrenalin, his limbs felt heavy. Constantine jumped up, his eyes diverted to

Mikki. Boyd flicked another right. It turned Constantine's head but didn't stop him.

Mikki moaned, clutching her side. Blood ran down her thigh.

Boyd stepped back and ducked a roundhouse right but rose too late to counter and caught a following left. It pushed him back to the door.

For the first time in his life, Boyd was whipped. He was exhausted from the gunshot a month before, the climb up from Vila Nova da Corvo and now the fight. It was worse than the dream. If he'd had a sword, he wouldn't have had the strength to drag it, much less swing it. Constantine paused, catching his breath, circling. Now Boyd noticed something else.

Constantine's eyes were red, very red. Mikki's too. She stood, looking at the wound on her left side. It was just at the top of her hip, and appeared to be just a nick. The bruises on her body weren't from blows. They were blotches like he'd seen on Jacques, irregular at the edges and pur-plish in the center. He wasn't just up against a Portuguese pirate and his whore. This was Ebola.

The breeze blew gauze curtains billowing into the room from French doors that opened to a small balcony overlook-ing the pristine desolation of the crater and the Atlantic beyond. The swimming pool was off to the side. Boyd took two steps to the window and vaulted over the balcony. Sailing out over the back of the house, he scanned down, looking for a landing site. He'd remembered the brush and the drop-off into the crater, and that's where he was headed.

The first bush snapped off and whipped by his face. He couldn't see anything beyond that as he crashed down the steep hillside. The slope was gradual enough that he hit the ground every few feet, eventually slowing down. He kept his legs crossed and his arms across his face as he was whipped and jabbed and scraped down the hill. Stopped, he slithered under a bush, exhausted, panting, terrified but alive.

Shots rang out from above as Constantine found his gun and emptied the clip at nothing in particular in the crater. Moments later an explosion rocked the house. Boyd was too tired to move. From beneath his bush, he looked up the hill. He heard the back door slam, and the red truck started up and roared down the back road into the crater. Boyd didn't have the steam to run, and his hiding place wasn't that good. He pulled himself up the hill to keep the bush between him and the truck, but Constantine had lost interest in Boyd. He spun around the curves, traversed the crater and spun up the road on the other side. In the truck bed were the two aluminum suitcases.

CHAPTER FIFTY NINE
MALAKAL, SOUTH SUDAN

"It's got the turbine nozzle from a GE T700 turboshaft engine off that busted Blackhawk over there, and it's run by a spare boost pump from a C-130. Jury-rigged, I know, but it'll pump 10 gallons a minute and spray it into a fine cloud."

Ace Digby wiped the grease off his hands onto his coveralls and threw a hose clamp into his tool kit.

"Flip that switch over there, and it'll pull out of your auxiliary fuel tank," he added. "So you don't get confused and try to run the engines out of the auxiliary tank, I've disconnected it from your fuel system. You're gonna need some help mixing that stuff up in the cramped space here. I should probably rig up another pump so you can just pump the bug spray out of the barrels."

"You want to go along on the ride?" Raybon Clive asked hopefully. They stood in the back of the Grumman Albatross in the shade of a hangar in Malakal, South Sudan.

"Not me," Digby replied. "I fix 'em, not fly in 'em."

"Your country is amazing," Gen. Oyay Ajak said, stepping off the ramp at the back of the Albatross, agile for his size. "Whenever something must be done, someone who can do it just appears."

"I didn't just appear, general. I've been here repairing your Blackhawks for six months," Digby said, following out of the stifling heat in the back of the Albatross.

"My country appreciates you Americans and all you can do. I didn't understand why we needed helicopters, but now here they are, and our pilots have been having a fine time shooting Arabs along the river."

"Yes, sir, a Blackhawk is a handy thing to have," Digby said with a laugh, his gnarled hands holding to the side of the aircraft as he gingerly stepped down. "I've been working on helicopters since Vietnam. The army retired me 20 years ago and still, there's always somebody needing a good mechanic to keep their rotors up."

"And we are grateful for Davann and Raybon, two fine American patriots who have decided to help us," Ajak said, slapping Davann Goodman on the back.

The four of them walked to the open hangar door and stood watching the activity at this once sleepy backwater airport. It was now transformed into the major front-line airfield for the South Sudan defense holding off the assault of hundreds of sick and dying jihadists from dozens of Arab countries trying to fight their way south, up the White Nile from Sudan. Five Blackhawk helicopters were in various stages of refueling and re-arming, their Kenyan pilots lounging in the shade of the terminal. Fifty laborers were busy unloading barrels of Malathion from the back of an unmarked C-130, which had just landed.

At that moment, three large trucks pulled up towing 105 mm howitzers. They were followed by a dozen trucks filled with men in uniform.

"Ah, my artillery is here, I must go," Gen. Ajak said, stepping back into the hangar to a map on the wall. "We will set up five miles from the river, here. Just at dusk, we will lay down a brief barrage of artillery. That will keep their heads down. The mosquitoes will just be coming out. You run down the river at 100 feet and spray the Malathion."

"Sounds like a party," Davann said, looking at the map.

"We'll have about 20 minutes of spray, and I'm hoping it will spread a quarter mile on either side of the plane. Once up and once back, and we should cover five miles of river," Rabon said, not feeling as confident as Davann.

Flying down the Nile at a hundred feet with a hose hanging out the back of his aircraft and hundreds of crazed Arabs below with automatic weapons didn't sound like a party to him. Still, Uncle Sam owned the aircraft, and this new adventure had been an occasion for a contract renegotiation. He and Davann were planning to open a Tiki bar and restaurant in Juba. Mariam Ajak, Davann's fiancé, was now part of the team.

"Good, we'll do it again at dawn," Ajak said. "We'll start the barrage when you take off."

Ajak strode out into the sun and climbed into his Humvee and pointed up the road to the north. The trucks rumbled after him, stirring up a great cloud of dust.

CHAPTER SIXTY
CORVO, AZORES

"Chailland! Chailland!" Ferreira's face appeared at the top of the hill.

"Here," Boyd said weakly and struggled to stand. He emerged from beneath the bush and brushed himself off, conscious of every scrape and bruise on a thoroughly scraped and bruised body. He pulled at the bush above and began to work toward the top.

"I thought you were dead," Boyd said, accepting Ferreira's hand for the last pull over the ledge. "What was that explosion?"

"He threw a hand grenade down the stairs, just to clear out the first floor. Didn't matter to him if one of his men or I was still standing," Ferreira said with a grin.

"It must have been you still standing."

Boyd felt around his back to see if something was sticking out of him there. It felt like it.

"Yes, in the front yard. I know that trick well. I have used it myself."

Ferreira was obviously very happy.

"Did you get 'em all?" Boyd asked, looking up at the window he'd just leaped out of.

"There were three."

"Been upstairs?"

"No."

"Don't go." Boyd felt nothing protruding from his body and started toward the kitchen. "I need some water."

"I hear her crying."

"Don't go up there." They re-entered the kitchen, and Boyd found a liter bottle of water, draining it as fast as it would flow. Ferreira did the same. He opened another and took a drink, carrying it into the living room.

"Grenades are hard on houses," Boyd said, surveying the damage.

The wall across the foyer from where the grenade had detonated was splattered with shrapnel, the front window was blown out and the walls near the foyer were blackened from smoke. He took another drink of water as he walked to the window.

"Our navy," Ferreira said proudly. The frigate was still at flank speed circling to the west of the island to cut off an escape into the North Atlantic.

Boyd stepped out into the front yard through the window, stepped over the bodies of two Azorean sailors and walked to the edge of the yard. He looked to the east.

"And there's Constantine."

The tuna boat, throwing spray 30 feet out from its bow, was booking around the east side of the island headed back into the archipelago.

"Call Lajes on the radio," Boyd said. "Tell them to load up some police or whatever they have and get over to Pico. Even at 35 knots, it'll take him three and a half hours to get there. At least now we know where he's going."

Ferreira hurried inside through the door, which was hanging from one hinge, and retrieved his radio. They stood together on the hill watching Constantine's boat crash through the 4-foot swells while Ferreira made the call.

"We'll get that son of a bitch," Boyd said, turning back to the two dead sailors in the front yard.

He walked over and turned one over. It was a man in his late teens or early 20s. His shirttail was out and, without bending down, Boyd hooked his boot under it and ripped open the front. There were three bullet holes in the chest and two more in the abdomen. There was also a fine red rash, visible even in death, and several blotches.

"See that?" He pointed with his boot. "That's Ebola. I saw it on the guy who first captured this beast, and it's gotten everyone who's touched it so far, including Mikki up there," he said, nodded toward the second floor.

"That's what we want to keep here, on this island till we can kill it," Boyd said, the emotion rising in his voice as he got mad.

Ferreira looked somberly down, then made another call on his radio. He talked for several minutes and got heated himself.

"They understand now," he said. "We will have men with guns on the shore at Pico in two hours. Your Special Operations C-130 is in radio range, three hours out."

"Not close enough," Boyd replied, disinterested as he watched Constantine's boat.

The breeze was pleasant, and they stood looking at the view, then walked over to the back and watched the frigate finally get the message and turn back toward the islands.

"Look, the sheep are out," Ferreira said, pointing to the ocean.

"Sheep?"

"The waves are capped with the wind. Azoreans say the sheep are out when they see that, because it looks like sheep grazing in the sea."

The whitecaps did scatter about the darkening Atlantic like sheep in a field. It meant the swells were up, too.

"I thought you said there were three more sailors?" Boyd asked after finishing his second water bottle.

"The third one didn't have a gun, or it would have been him standing in the hallway when the grenade exploded."

They walked back into the house and Ferreira led the way into the darkened parlor. They switched on the light.

"Her," Boyd corrected as he turned over the body sprawled on the hand woven rug, staining it crimson with blood from a dozen stab wounds in the front and a gaping slit throat. A long stiletto knife was by her open hand. A slender young black woman, she was clad in an expensive silk blouse and jeans snug on her long legs.

"She came from behind me, in the dark," Ferreira pulled up his shirt to show a stab wound on his back, and another on his right hand. "We fought for several minutes, she was very strong. It was the hardest fight I ever had to kill a man … a person."

His hands shook as he lit another cigarette.

"She looks tough," Boyd said, having another look. She was tall, athletic. Blood dribbled from her nose.

"Let's get out of here," Boyd said suddenly and walked out the front door, looking up to find Constantine's boat.

"Whoa! Where's that slippery son of a bitch going?"

Constantine's boat wasn't headed southeast, but south-west, toward Flores.

"The plane," Ferreira said softly.

Boyd's mind raced, calculating speeds and distances. He turned toward the house.

"Give me your 9 millimeter, and one of those long guns. Got any more clips?" He took the web belt from Ferreira and picked up a Kalashnikov. "He'll get there before me, but maybe he'll take a long downwind leg."

Boyd sprinted for the gate and the road down the hill. Just outside was a bicycle leaning against the fence. He leaped on it and careened down the hill.

Bouncing across the grass, still at breakneck speed from the hill, Boyd was upon a small group gathered around the Waco before they knew of his approach. The sight of the tall American with the pistol belt around his middle and the Kalashnikov over his shoulder was enough to scatter them. He jumped into the back seat of the Waco, where the radio was located, donned the leather cap and goggles, and cranked the engine. It started right up, and he turned into the 20-knot breeze from the southwest and was airborne before he even got to the asphalt runway.

The bicycle was a lucky break. It had given him a jump, and he was airborne before Constantine. He climbed to a thousand feet and pulled out the binoculars to watch for the Cessna. It climbed out from takeoff and headed southeast, toward Pico. Boyd followed it up to 5,000 feet. The Cessna pulled slowly away from the Waco, which was shaking loudly at its maximum speed of 115 knots. Boyd knew the Cessna was rated around 120 knots, so he couldn't catch it, and he had half an hour to figure out how to stop it from landing.

Pico popped out of the ocean after 20 minutes. The late afternoon air wasn't as clear as the morning had been, with whitecaps dotting the area before him. Soon, Faial and Sao Jorge were also visible, the volcano appearing to be in the middle of the group from this direction. Constantine didn't appear to be in any hurry as he descended toward the runway on the island Pico, he crossed the runway at the departure end, just over the waiting Falcon and turned east, descending on a downwind leg. Constantine was turning back into the wind for final descent two miles from the end of the runway as Boyd arrived over the center of the runway. He put the old Waco into a dive right over the Falcon and, hurtling down at 120 knots, the rattles and wind turbulence louder than the engine, stowed the Kalashnikov as too unwieldy and chambered a round in the 9 millimeter.

At the end of the runway and only 50 feet off the ground, Constantine was confronted with the Waco pulling out of a dive and headed right at him, only closer to the ground. Instinctively he pulled up, aborting his landing. The Waco howled beneath him.

Maintaining level flight with his left hand, Boyd turned and fired three shots into the Cessna as it passed. That was for the shock value of having bullets actually hitting the Cessna so Constantine wouldn't have sense enough to just cut the engine and land on the remainder of the runway. It worked. Constantine powered up and was ascending from the departure end of the runway as Boyd turned into the mountain, still with some speed from the dive, and climbed out after him.

Constantine headed out across the 5-mile-wide straight between Pico and Faial. Boyd wasn't fooled. With a slower aircraft, his only hope of preventing the handoff of Ebola to whoever was there in the Falcon was to stay between them. He climbed but circled back toward the runway. Constantine turned to circle around the south side of the island.

Boyd cut inside his circle and intercepted the Cessna halfway up the side of the volcano Pico on the south side. This time, Constantine shot first, and his plane veered as he turned rearward with one hand to fire a volley from his Kalashnikov out the door. Boyd passed over him and rolled upside down, pushing the nose down to give him time to empty a full clip at the Cessna, which maintained a course around Pico.

Boyd flashed back toward the mountain beneath Constantine and replaced the empty clip with a fresh one, then cut beneath Constantine quickly to avoid another chance for him to shoot, rolled inverted above and outside the circle and emptied that clip into the Cessna. It blew out part of the windshield. Falling behind again, Boyd pulled into the mountain again to catch up. The Cessna's door opened wider this time, and Constantine gave him a full clip with both hands, shots hitting the engine and wings. He'd put the Cessna on autopilot so its course was away from the mountain. Boyd scooted quickly behind the Cessna, and when Constantine returned to hands on control, Boyd cut inside and caught up again. Now they were close to the dirt.

Pico is 7,053 feet high and composed of ash, settled back from a long-smoking volcano that cooled over millennia to produce a smooth, symmetrical, picturesque peak. The two planes raced around it 1,500 feet below the top. Boyd's wing tip was at times only feet from the surface, black as asphalt, hard as a cinder block. Constantine wouldn't get that close, his inexperience forcing a wider circle, thus, Boyd pulled ahead with a slower craft. They were nearing the eastern side of the mountain, and the point at which Constantine could pull away from the mountain and glide down to land, leaving the Waco behind.

Just as Constantine came to the eastern edge of Pico, Boyd dropped beneath him and, from the outside, rolled up over the Cessna, the two aircraft now straight and level.

Boyd pushed the Waco down on top of the Cessna, carefully locking his landing gear in front of the Cessna's wing. Then he cut the throttle and pushed the nose down. The sudden drag slowed both aircraft and pushed the Cessna's nose down. No amount of strength from Constantine could overcome the control surface of the Waco's two huge wings as their noses pointed down and their airspeed dropped. The Cessna reached stall speed first, lost lift and control from its wings and began to fall. Boyd pushed the throttle forward just as the Waco reached stall and felt his landing gear release from the Cessna's wing. He dropped his right wing and fell off down the mountain, gaining speed. He pulled the nose up and looked back.

"Practice stall recovery much?" Boyd called out as the Cessna spiraled down the face of Pico and crashed into its side. A moment later the wreckage exploded in a ball of flame.

Boyd rolled away from the fireball out toward the sea. His chest thudded as he looked back to make sure Constantine didn't rise again. The fire burned brightly, sending black smoke up from the side of the old volcano. He throttled back and coasted down the side of the mountain toward the airport. The Falcon was moving already, and by the time he crossed the runway it was airborne, accelerating quickly out of sight.

CHAPTER SIXTY ONE
"Orion is with us"

Boyd pointed the Waco back toward Corvo. He hoped he had enough gas to make the trip. The whole purpose of this mission was to stop Ebola, and if he brought it to another island by stopping for gas, he'd have failed.

Mikki's blood was on his back and smeared around the cuts and abrasions he'd gotten jumping into the crater. He'd been nose to nose with Constantine during the fight and breathed his adversary's breath while still hot and moist. If Ebola was contagious, he would have it.

The engine drone and rush of the wind faded out for a moment, and Boyd looked down into the sea at the whitecaps, now topping every swell, and remembered Ferreira's description of the sheep. Faces appeared as he looked down: Wolf; Neville; Constantine, looking strangely benign now; and then finally, Ferreira. Was there a special section in eternity for warriors? After death, did you, your compatriots and your enemies spend eternity together, away from the rest of humanity, or were you just alone?

Shaking his head to recover concentration, Boyd used the radio to call the tower at Horta and report Constantine's crash. He asked them to call the command post at Lajes and asked them to track the Falcon on radar, at least far enough to see which continent it was headed for. In 10 minutes, he was out of radio range and still out of sight of Corvo. The sun's rim touched the western horizon, and the late afternoon haze made the ocean and the sky merge ahead of him. He kept a careful eye on the compass and attitude indicator, because missing the island entirely in the haze would have him drone on into the empty North Atlantic, exhaust fuel and fall silently into the ocean. The thought was appealing, but then he saw the beacon at Flores, then Corvo.

In the gathering gloom, Boyd landed the Waco, though there were no runway lights. He didn't see the C-130 until he was safely on the ground. Troops walked in groups around the airport, and a flashlight beckoned for him to follow to a parking spot. He shut down the engine and removed his goggles and leather helmet.

"Hands up, Pancho!"

Boyd's head snapped around to see a U.S. soldier, in full battle regalia, hand grenades attached to his Kevlar vest, face blackened, rifle pointed at him. He raised his hands. He was too tired to be annoyed.

"I'm American!" Boyd shouted, climbing down to the wing.

"Could be," the man said, not impressed. "Keep 'em up anyway."

"I'm Capt. Chailland," Boyd said, turning when he reached the ground.

"Face down! Now!"

"It's over! There's no threat here. I hope you guys haven't shot anybody," Boyd said, dropping to the ground to lie face down.

"It's over when Capt. Peabody says it's over, and he ain't," the man said, showing no sign of letting up.

"Look, I'm tired and thirsty. If you'll just call Gen. Ferguson at the STRATCOM Command Post ..." Boyd was nauseated now, with fatigue, thirst and hunger.

"I'm just a sergeant, sir. I don't know no generals. I take my orders from Capt. Peabody," the man said, accentuating his Southern drawl.

A Humvee approached from behind him.

"Let him up, Sanders," a voice from the Humvee said as it stopped behind the soldier, its lights blinding Boyd in the darkness. "Who are you?"

"I'm Capt. Boyd Chailland, U.S. Air Force."

"What are you doing in that funny old airplane? You flyboys gonna try to take this island with a crop duster?"

"This island doesn't need taking," Boyd said, regaining his stature, still in front of the lights. "The show is over, and for God's sake, keep your men out of that house on the hill."

The captain looked up the hill momentarily, then back at Boyd.

"We found some dead people up there, buddy. You involved in that?"

"Yes." Boyd cautiously approached the vehicle. Peabody seemed more amused than threatening.

"How about El Capitan up there?" Peabody asked. "The guy in the funny green jungle fatigues. Do you know him?"

"That would be Col. Ferreira of the Portuguese Air Force, and senior officer on this island. I hope you have shown him proper respect, or your next promotion won't be in this decade," Boyd said, beginning to have enough energy to be annoyed.

All lights were out as they passed through the deserted town and ground up the hill toward Constantine's house. Boyd determined that Peabody and a lieutenant were the only officers and that the C-130 had landed with a Humvee and 30 heavily armed airborne troops. They had radio communication with the Command Post at Lajes and through to the STRATCOM Command Post. Boyd was soon in charge.

"Ferreira, old friend," Boyd said, dismounting, seeing Ferreira unhurt and talking with troops in the yard as they watched the last of the sunset. "Did they have you slated for the firing squad?"

"Chailland!" He opened his arms and embraced Boyd. "Did you catch that son of the devil?"

"He bit the big one on Pico and burned up with his tiny friends," Boyd responded, feeling better. "Suppose they got any beer on this island? I'll tell you all about it."

****

"Orion is with us," Boyd said, stretched out on his back by the swimming pool, all lights off, watching stars.

"And Scorpios," Ferreira answered from nearby, speech slurred slightly.

"Where?" Boyd sat up to see Ferreira point.

Constantine's wine cellar contained 10 cases of Super Bock, and Boyd and Ferreira had made a pact to finish it before either of them died of Ebola. Three days had passed, and they were more than halfway through the beer.

"Look in the Milky Way. See that orange star, the bright one? That's Antares. Now, do you see the scorpion?"

"Yes. What else?" Boyd asked, sitting back down.

From the hilltop, with no lights on and scarcely a light in the town, this was one of the darkest places on Earth to watch stars. The depth of the night sky was thrilling and put one in the mood to contemplate eternity.

There was no morgue on Corvo. Boyd had made the decision to bury the two sailors and the black woman, with Mikki, on the mountain.

"Pleiades, over there ..."

"That's just a cluster, yeah, I see it."

They'd selected a burial site behind the house on the edge of the crater and put all four in a line. There was a better place, two dozen yards toward the Atlantic edge, overlooking the village and the black cliffs that dropped to the waves below. It could be used for any additional burials that might become necessary.

"You ever see the Southern Cross?" Boyd asked, pitching an empty bottle toward an empty case they'd set out to collect spent rounds. He rolled clumsily off the lawn chair and lifted the lid to the cooler filled with ice. Constantine had equipped his hideaway with an institutional ice machine.

"Many times, in Mozambique," Ferreira said, belching loudly.

Mikki had died horribly. Steeled against what he might find, Boyd went back up the stairs after explaining to the army that the fewer of them involved with the dead and dying, the more of them could leave the island in a day or two. He and Ferreira would clean up the mess. Mikki's bullet wound was superficial, but her Ebola was much worse.

"What are you?" she'd screamed in French, wide-eyed and terrified, as she sat on the bed with the lights on, looking out the window into the total black of the crater. She was oblivious to Boyd. In the hours since he'd last seen her, the blotches had become larger and more numerous, and there were red spots now. Boyd brought up food and water, but she ignored them. She brushed away his attempt to bandage her wound. Boyd slept in the extra bedroom upstairs.

"Don't come in here!" she screamed during the night, all attention on the window, burning with fever but refusing all that was offered.

At dawn, Boyd was awakened again by the rattling of her chains. Warily, he got up from the bed and walked to her room. Mikki rolled and choked on the floor, her chains thrashing against the tile. Her nude body, once stately and elegant, had wasted during the night, and she looked middle age. She punched the air and swatted at some unseen threat, rolling away, and tried to get under the bed.

"Don't touch me!" she screamed and, as Boyd entered the room, her eyes fixed, she stiffened with her arms at her

443

sides, flexed violently with her legs and convulsed rhythmically for more than a minute before relaxing and going to sleep, panting from the exertion. Mikki's body was twisted repeatedly by convulsions through the morning. At noon the day after Constantine died on Pico, she vomited bright red blood, and by 2 she was dead. Blood covered the bed and was splattered on the walls. She looked old.

"Cassiopeia. It looks like a W," Boyd said, rising unsteadily again and making his way to the edge of the crater behind the pool to stand and send a long arc of beer piss down into the blackness, hearing it splatter on the lava below.

Ferreira's cigarette glowed in the dark. He said nothing.

The Emerging Infections Surveillance and Response team from Fort Detrick had arrived just after the burials the afternoon Mikki died. They'd flown by C-17 to Lajes and been ferried to Corvo by the Portuguese Casa 212. They disembarked in their biohazard suits and scurried officiously over the island, irate that Boyd had buried the four victims already. That night, there was talk of digging them up for autopsies and to collect specimens of the virus. Boyd distanced himself from that discussion. The prospect of himself being the next to be taken apart, peered into and preserved in little bottles made him nauseous, and he and Ferreira started in on the beer right after breakfast.

CHAPTER SIXTY TWO
CAIRO

"Good evening, this is the NBC Nightly News with Brian Williams, coming to you live from Rockefeller Center in New York.

"There is breaking news from Africa. We have Richard Engel, our chief foreign affairs correspondent, standing by live in Cairo. Richard, what can you tell us?"

"Thank you, Brian. The outbreak of the deadly Ebola virus has spread to Cairo. Egyptian authorities tell me they have quarantined several dozen men who fled here from Sudan, caring for them in a makeshift acute hospital on the outskirts of Cairo. They insist no refugees from that outbreak in Khartoum have made their way into the city proper. Still, people continue to flee Cairo by any means at their disposal, and the city streets are deserted. In a related development, the quarantine line established at Aswan seems to be holding, with all traffic headed south stopped and turned back. That traffic has slowed to a trickle after Sheikh Ali Gomaa, the Grand Mufti of Egypt, issued a fatwa declaring any jihad directed against the nation of South Sudan as being contrary to the teachings of the Prophet Muhammad.

"In a related development, Brian, the battle lines around the South Sudan city of Kalafal seem to have held, and the jihadists attacking from Khartoum have turned back or died in battle. We have been in communication with Gen. Oyay Ajak, commander of the Army of South Sudan, who says the situation is stable. They have taken action to ensure that no infected mosquitoes make it to any populated areas along the Nile in South Sudan. Brian, back to you."

CHAPTER SIXTY THREE
RED EYES ON CORVO

"Congratulations, Boyd! Your second Air Force Cross has been approved. A grateful country awaits your return," Ferguson said, his voice crystal clear through the satellite links now set up on the hill by the villa.

Boyd was sitting in Constantine's office, feet on the desk, looking out over the Atlantic.

"Now?" Boyd responded, speech slurred from the half dozen beers he'd downed to ward off melancholy brought on by seeing Ferreira arise that morning with red eyes and go into a hospital room that the response team had rigged up in the villa.

"Well, no. When your quarantine period is over."

"Joe Smith showed up with new viral antibiotic?" Boyd asked, trying to sound nonchalant.

"He's still in China, supervising the manufacturing process. We should have something any day now."

Ferguson sounded evasive.

"Who was in that Dassault Falcon at Pico?"

"They headed toward Europe, then turned off their transponder and disappeared," Ferguson said. "We're looking at the registration of all the Falcons. It was a private charter. It's a new plane, there are only a few dozen in service. We should be able to find out where each one was on that day. Once we identify the plane, we'll know who it was."

"Sir, this game isn't over until we know."

"Why is that, Boyd? They don't have the virus. You saw to that," Ferguson said blandly.

"I don't think it's just about the virus."

"What do you mean?"

"The virus was locked up safely in those aluminum suitcases, yet something came across the Atlantic with *Chardonnay* that hasn't been stopped yet."

"You've lost me now, Boyd. As soon as we get by three weeks with no cases of Ebola there in the Azores, and the same time in Cairo and Sudan, we've got this genie back in the bottle."

Boyd could hear Ferguson shuffling papers on his desk, already working on something else.

****

The thick, rich broth covered chunks of meat and bone, and the beefy garlic scent filled the room as Boyd climbed the stairs with the latest food brought up the hill by the grateful villagers.

"Ah, alcatra," Ferreira said, looking better since the nurse had given him 3 liters of intravenous fluids. They were beginning to hope that the symptoms had been a hangover from the strong Portuguese beer and not Ebola at all.

Boyd entered the isolation room in a hospital gown and mask, as the biohazard suits were reserved for the team from Fort Detrick. The terra cotta pot had been in a wood-fired oven all day, and its outside was blackened by the smoke and from the evaporation of the wine and cooking liquid. He dished out two large bowls and broke some heavy crusted bread.

"Well, old friend, it looks like the beer has held off the virus," Boyd said, raising a wine glass filled with the heavy red wine the locals had provided in quantity since they had learned that Ferreira preferred it to the mainland wines Constantine's cellar held.

"Maybe not," Ferreira replied, and pulled up his shirt to reveal a small blotch on his chest.

****

The soft red light of the setting sun illuminated the six graves as the cold winter wind blew steadily from the north.

Grass had grown to cover the break in the earth, and the soil had settled back from many months of rain to leave depressions. Weeds grew around the simple marble headstones. The town below sprinkled with a few lights. The villa was vacant, windows broken, roof partially collapsed, returning the hilltop to the mercy of the North Atlantic wind.

Now there were fish to be caught, cattle to be tended and children to be taught in the ways of the Azores. The world had new conflicts and concerns, and these graves were from a chapter passed and forgotten.

Boyd rolled to his side and opened his eyes, coming back from the cold hillside. The loneliness remained. Fighter pilots are supposed to die in a ball of fire and live on in legend and memories from a grateful nation. Though the grateful nation had provided a team to tend to his every need, they stayed in those damn suits that made them look like alien space invaders, and he couldn't tell one from another because their voices all sounded alike. He'd talked daily with Angela since he'd gotten sick, and her attempts to cheer him only made their futility more obvious.

Ferreira, sharing the isolation room with Boyd now, had had a bad night. Delirious with fever the night before, he'd pulled out his intravenous lines when he leaped from the bed and tried to run down the hall. The nurses had to strap him down and give him morphine. He'd slept all day, and now it was night again and he was getting restless. Boyd had not talked to him in two days.

The red eyes were in the room across the hall from Boyd's bed. They were distant at first, and he thought they might be navigation lights on a ship coming over from Flores, which could be seen through the windows on that side of the villa. But now they were large and closer. They were eyes. There was pain, too, in his joints, especially the large ones, and in his head a pounding worse than any hangover. The Corvo islanders brought him food for every meal, and the alcatra pots and pottery bowls covered the bedside table, untouched. He couldn't eat.

The drip of the IV was a heartbeat, and the green glow from the cardiac monitor was the only illumination on a dark night. The North Atlantic howled just on the other side of the window behind him, trying to claw off the roof and get inside. Something moved across the hall, and the floor creaked. The other bed was vacant, and Boyd was alone.

****

"You have a visitor, Capt. Chailland."

One of the faceless aliens stood in the door. It was daylight. There was an oxygen mask on his face. He couldn't raise his head.

"Boyd, it took a presidential order to get them to let me come here," Angela said as she entered. She was wearing her white nurse's dress as she stepped into a surgical gown.

"Come in," he rasped. He'd intended to cover his ecstasy at seeing her with a polite greeting. His heart pounded. She was beautiful, and the sight of her face before she covered it with a surgical mask made him feel stronger. Claws scraped against the tile out in the hall as something large that had been sitting in the door retreated to the other bedroom.

"I'm so happy to see you." She rushed over and, hands clad in surgical gloves, grabbed his.

He was overcome. He couldn't speak. He grasped her with both hands. She sat, and the aliens left the room.

"Do you need anything?" she asked, bending over to look into his eyes.

"It's bad," he said, no longer able to hide the fear, which was not of the pain or the death. He'd take on that thing in the other room but, then what?

"Death is here," she said "I can feel it."

"You got that right. It's been looking through that door all morning."

"It's not for you."

"I'm afraid."

"Boyd, don't you see?" She leaned in closer, peering into his face. He could see the little flecks of brown in her hazel eyes, and the tears running down her face.

"There's something else in here," she said. "Something good. Something strong. Can't you feel it? Boyd, don't you know?"

"Know?"

"You were never alone."

CHAPTER SIXTY FOUR
PENTAGON CITY

"Silent night, holy night, shepherds quake at the sight …"

The children's choir sent their angelic innocence reverberating off the glass and steel that held a cold December rain from the food court at the Pentagon City Mall.

Boyd decided to take the train. He didn't have the 500-yard sprint across the Pentagon south parking lot left in him. He took the escalator to the Metro Station.

He hadn't died of Ebola, and he wasn't the last to have it. Donn Wilde had driven him up from Culpepper, Va., the night before. At the funeral, he sat next to Angela's mother, and listened as the chief nurse of the Air Force gave the eulogy in the small Baptist Church.

Angela had brushed his lips as she turned to leave him that morning when the red eyes were at the door. The Emerging Infections Response Force had dutifully collected specimens from all who'd been ill, and the reports were in. It had been the wild Kikwit strain, the same one Boyd had

had, the one with the 80 percent mortality, not the South Carolina strain with the 100 percent mortality and the ability to spread by a mosquito vector.

He put a five in the automated ticket machine rather than look up the exact fare and rushed through the turnstile to get on the train while the reporter following him fumbled for change. He'd be through security at the Pentagon before the next train came by.

Boyd could see Ferguson's eyes scanning the crowd as he came up the escalator. They looked right through Boyd.

"Do I look that bad?" Boyd asked when he got beside the general.

"Oh, damn. Boyd, you've gotten quite a tan, and maybe a little thinner." Ferguson said, recovering.

They turned and passed security and headed through the mall on the first floor. It isn't often one gets escorted through security by a major general. They walked quickly down the corridor.

"We've got the tank in 20 minutes. A lot's happened in the last week. This thing was way bigger than we ever thought. You'll hear all the details. The Joint Chiefs want to meet you, but you needn't speak."

"Whatever you say, sir."

They made their way through a maze of corridors, once coming to the A-ring windows that look out into the garden in the center of the Pentagon with the mature magnolias planted there when the building was built in 1943. They stopped at an unmarked door. Ferguson pecked in a code, and they entered. A guard lounged on the other side behind a glass. He scrutinized Ferguson's pass and Boyd's military ID. They went down a narrow hall to the waiting lounge for those about to brief the chairman and the Joint Chiefs of Staff.

"Boyd! God, you look like shit," Joe Smith rushed over and brushed away Boyd's outstretched hand to throw his arms around Boyd in a bear hug.

"Thanks for letting me know," Boyd said, a little embarrassed by the attention. "I kept notes on what it feels like to have your favorite infection. It's a bitch."

"You have no idea how glad I am to see you," Joe said soberly. "Ebola did something so sinister, so clever, so unexpected ..."

His voice quivered and he turned away.

"We sent some guys in biohazard suits up to see if those suitcases were intact, but it was like someone dropped a canister of napalm on the site to cook it."

"Why would you want that stuff?" Boyd asked suspiciously.

"We didn't. Gen. Ferguson just wanted to be sure someone else didn't go up there and get exposed."

"So, you went in with flame throwers?"

"Well, no. They had some specimen containers. Just in case there was something viable," Joe said defensively.

Ferguson was looking at his notes.

"What about that antibiotic? I kept hoping that would come in like the cavalry and save somebody," Boyd said, trying to ignore a cold nagging spot in his consciousness.

"Didn't work out. We were trying it on monkeys in China, and it didn't do a thing. I almost brought it along anyway when I heard you were sick. But if it doesn't help, it doesn't help."

Joe looked away, tears brimming suddenly in his eyes, and said, "I'm sorry, Boyd."

The telephone buzzed and an aide answered. "You're on," he said, and they filed into the small meeting room.

"We have Maj. Gen. Ferguson with Col. Smith from USAMRIID and Capt. Chailland with the latest on Ebola."

Boyd was directed to a seat and took it. When he looked up, all eyes were on him. A screen descended silently behind the lectern. The electron micrograph of Ebola was already on it. Ferguson began speaking.

"Capt. Chailland led the team that found and finally stopped Ebola. He's just recovered from having it himself. I've asked him to come today, but he's not prepared to answer questions just now. I hope you'll understand."

There were a few nods, and then Ferguson continued.

"Since our brief two weeks ago that Ebola was contained, a lot of information has been gathered about who wanted it and why. Nothing has stirred up the dark forces in the world like Ebola. It's sobering. To recap, a European merchant banker, Charles Meilland, contracted with Lymon Byxbe, owner of BioVet Tech in South Carolina, to capture Ebola, replicate it and develop a vaccine for it. That was a tall order, but Byxbe pulled it off. He delivered viable virus and a vaccine to Michelle Meilland at Charleston in September. In spite of our best efforts, she delivered some virus and vaccine to couriers for an Arab jihadist group, and they deployed it in an unconventional attack on South Sudan.

"The vaccine worked initially, but they ran out, and the virus quickly spread to the unvaccinated. That is, combatants, health care workers, and noncombatants. Fortunately, we were forewarned by members of Capt. Chailland's team in Mombasa and advised the Egyptians to move quickly to close their border. The loss of life in Sudan was staggering, approaching 20,000 this week. But it could have been much worse. There were only a few dozen cases in Egypt, and they were from combatants who fled back from Sudan and got through the border checkpoints. Let me break from the recap to let Col. Smith fill you in on what we've learned about the virus."

He sat, and Smith took the podium.

"Byxbe's plan was a sound one," Joe said as he pointed at a picture of chromosomes from Ebola on the screen. "He had his technician set up with a lab in the Seychelles to break the Ebola's gene sequence here, attach it to a plasmid, which is a fragment of RNA that will take the sequence into a host's cells and incorporate it into the function of the cell. Once a part of the cell, that sequence would then use the cell's resources to produce the outer protein coat of Ebola in some quantity. This is how most of our genetically engineered pharmaceuticals, like insulin, are manufactured. When released into the bloodstream, that protein would be recognized as foreign and the host would produce antibodies against it. That's how immunity is created. This next slide shows a monkey lymphocyte with some fragments of RNA in its cellular structure. We got this from the Seychelles."

"From where in the Seychelles?" one of the Joint Chiefs asked.

"It's from one of the dead monkeys at the lab. That proves they were working with plasmids and gene sequences. The process of breaking the chromosome, attaching it to the plasmid and reproducing it in quantity involves heating to precise temperatures, repeated centrifuging and exposure to some chemicals. Jacques, the technician had all the equipment to do that on the island. His letter about the virus mutating was correct, but it didn't mutate in a monkey, it mutated in his lab. He overheated the virus while he was replicating it and created the South Carolina strain. That got mixed back in with the wild Kikwit strain, and when he infected monkeys after they were vaccinated they got sick and were bitten by mosquitoes. The vaccine worked, most of the monkeys survived.

"Jacques sent some of that vaccine to Byxbe, who replicated it in his lab in South Carolina. Then, when Jacques brought fresh monkeys in for another round, they got sick right away, and he did, too. They got sick from mosquitoes that were living on the island and had blood in them from biting the first group of monkeys while they were sick."

Some of the flag officers looked confused.

"Here's the new strain," Joe said as the picture changed and the little red dot from his laser pointer danced about. "There are two changes in the gene sequence. This one changes the Ph of the outer protein coat to allow Ebola to live in the digestive tract of a mosquito. It couldn't do that before. The other one, here, increases its virulence. It has become 100 percent lethal."

"Why do you call it South Carolina?"

"We name them after the location where we first isolate them. Instead of fleeing the country with his $5 million worth of gold bullion, Lymon Byxbe laid low at a house in the swamp south of Charleston and tested the vaccine again on some monkeys he had there. It got out the same way it did in the Seychelles. Mosquitoes bit the monkeys while they had active infection and then bit some people nearby. Fortunately, there was a hard freeze right after that and that stopped the spread. If it had broken out in June, it would have gone across the nation in two weeks."

"The vaccine works?" The chairman asked.

"It does, but it's not as simple as Jacques thought. It took us weeks of working with it to perfect the technique. The good news is, yes it works for both strains."

"How'd you find Byxbe?" someone asked.

"The smell," Joe said derisively. "He was in bed, surrounded by stacks of gold coins, a perfectly good Boston Whaler tied up at his dock."

Then Joe went into a discussion of random mutations and how overheating the virus resulted in just another random mutation.

The hair on the back of Boyd's neck stood straight up. It was the same pattern he'd followed from the beginning. It was like Ebola was a living, thinking, scheming thing. He remembered the red eyes in the dark, Mikki's terror and Ferreira's scramble down the hall. In the past six months, he'd encountered the extremes of good and evil, and they were not random.

"Khartoum was a close call," Joe began another stage of the presentation. "The first wave of jihadists had some vaccine that did work on a few dozen people when the virus got out, giving them the false sense of security that drew thousands in to be infected and die. Fortunately, there are 400 miles of the world's worst desert between there and Wadi Halfa and another couple hundred to Aswan. The Egyptians, to their credit, were quick to move and apparently have stopped the spread. There hasn't been a death or a new case in Egypt in two weeks."

That ended Joe's part of the presentation. He sat down, and Ferguson stood.

"We've learned valuable information about the worldwide jihadist movement," Fersuson said. "It's clear they aren't in any way unified. The jihadists that started this epidemic were freelancers from Qatar with big ideas. Khalid Adnani and Hamid Shah hatched the plan. They showed up dead in Doha last week, dumped on the street with their hands tied and their throats cut. That's a classic message of Arab revenge.

"But their twinkle of success by giving the virus a charismatic name attracted thousands of young men eager to prove themselves and be involved in jihad. That tells us jihad is a cultural phenomenon with widespread appeal and a hair trigger. Radical clerics jumped on the bandwagon and encouraged more young men to leave their homes and race into the desert. When the folly of their attack became evident, the Grand Mufti of Egypt issued a fatwa, or religious edict, to stop – and they did. He represents moderate Islam. Khalid and Hamid were working with Iran, and they gave some of their virus and vaccine to the Iranians."

"Might the Iranians carry on with the plan?" One of the Joint Chiefs asked.

"They might, but nobody wants a repeat of the Khartoum debacle," Ferguson said. "That set jihad back a generation. They'll be very careful."

"That brings us to the next shocker – the identity of the aircraft parked on the island Pico to receive the remainder of the virus and vaccine. We tracked it to Switzerland. One of the world's largest pharmaceutical companies was willing to pay $10 million in gold to acquire the vaccine on the black market and slap a patent on it. We gave them and several other pharmaceutical companies the material Col. Smith and Capt. Chailland got from the Seychelles, so now it's a race between free enterprise and the jihadist to see who can tame Ebola. I'm betting on free enterprise."

CHAPTER SIXTY FIVE

"I've got reporters camping out in the hall outside my room at the Ritz-Carlton, calling me on the phone, television cameras in the lobby," Boyd said as they packed up and left the conference area. "Any chance I could move over to Andrews or Fort Belvoir, stay on base, get out of the public eye a little? I need some rest."

"Really?" Ferguson asked, surprised. Joe had already left for a medical school lecture in Georgetown.

"I feel like a rock star, or a criminal. They just won't quit."

"OK," Ferguson said, thinking as they walked. "The Ritz-Carlton was the closest hotel. We wanted you there for this meeting. I'll send someone over for your clothes."

Ferguson took a ring of keys out of his pocket and pulled two off.

"Here, take this. Do you know where the Pentagon Athletic Club is, just out the back door by Corridor 8?"

Boyd nodded.

"Go out the back door, cross the road that goes along north parking, there's a footbridge to the Lyndon Johnson Grove, and there's a marina over there, the Capital Marina. This will get you into the dock area, and this one is for my boat, slip 76. She's a 43-foot Hatteras flying bridge sportfisher. She's all plugged in to water and electricity. There's food, a propane heater and a good bed. I'll come by later and we'll talk."

****

The rain had let up, but the wind hadn't. Not a steady gale like the Azores, this was a soul-numbing breeze off the Potomac that made its way through the light jacket and summer uniform Boyd wore. Pausing on the bridge, Boyd looked across the river. The Washington Monument seemed to be holding up the sky, as its peak was just into the low clouds.

Boyd looked at his watch. Pam and Donn would be closing on their bank in Wewoka, Okla. The exuberance of their plans had brightened the trip back from Culpepper the afternoon before.

"I'm gonna be a bank president," Pamela had confided to him. "Turns out Donn is a lot smarter than I thought.

465

He explained it to me. Me, the lawyer and CPA. He had 800,000 bucks in clean, taxes-paid money. It was legal compensation for work he did before he was arrested and, since it wasn't money from the savings and loan that went under, it is not recoverable by the Resolution Trust Fund."

"You sure?" Boyd had asked. It was Donn who'd taught him how dreams were the surest conduit for a scam.

"I'll have to test it, of course, but it's him putting up the money, not me. If he's trying to pull something, he's going to lose his pouncing privileges, and I don't think he wants to risk that," she said with a happy laugh.

In the weeks Boyd was in isolation on Corvo, they'd returned to Oklahoma and convinced the Bank Board they were legal, and their deal had been approved and should be closed by midafternoon. It made Boyd feel better. So much was gone, something, at least, should start. He crossed the bridge and found the marina.

It was past dark when Ferguson boarded his boat, the *Granite Mistress,* with Boyd's clothes, a pizza and a case of Bud longnecks. Curled up in a blanket, asleep, Boyd was disoriented and grumpy. He was still on Azores time, which is five hours later than D.C. He finished a beer and a piece of pizza listening to Ferguson go on about some Pentagon intrigue.

"Sir, I really appreciate your letting me stay here. I've grown rather fond of the feel of water under my bed," Boyd said, smiling blandly.

"I can see you're going to need some time off," Ferguson said. "We'll cut the debrief. I pretty much got the story as it happened. I'll write the final report for the Joint Staff. Tomorrow, you'll go to the White House for your Air Force Star. We have 10 minutes with the president. Be pleasant."

"Yes, sir." Boyd tried to smile.

Ferguson pulled a manila envelope out and laid it on the table between them. For a moment, Boyd thought it might be another mission. He fought back a wave of nausea.

"Two months convalescent leave. Here's the paperwork." Ferguson laid the paperwork down. "You're medically grounded, of course. I've leaned on the Surgeon General's Office. They've agreed to wait until the summer to do a full eval at the Aeromedical Consultation Service at Brooks City, Texas, before deciding about your flying. They've as much as agreed you could go back to flying, it's the high-performance stuff that'd be the problem – ejection seat aircraft.

"In the past 18 months, you've had a fractured skull, two collapsed vertebra, three broken ribs, a gunshot through the lung breaking another rib, and a near-death brush with Ebola. They wonder that you're still alive."

"Sir, flying fighters is all I ever wanted to do," Boyd said, looking down at the envelope. He wasn't angry, he knew the rules.

"How old are you," Ferguson asked, sternly.

"Twenty-eight."

"Two years below the zone for major, with two Air Force Crosses and a commendation letter from the Chief of Staff of the Air Force and two from the president of the United States. Buy some oak leaves. Second, how many majors over 30- do you know flying front line fighters?"

"A couple."

"Promoted below the zone and waiting for orders to Air Command and Staff College, or back from there and flying as the squadron ops officer and waiting for the Lt. Colonel Board," Ferguson said, softening his tone a bit. "The pyramid is getting steeper. We've got fewer high-performance aircraft and a steady stream of young jocks to fly them. Flying fighters isn't a career, it's a phase, and not a job for anyone over 30. Look ahead."

"Yes, sir," Boyd said, feeling worse.

"Boyd, I'd like to have you on my staff. I need you on my staff, but I know you want to fly. So, the Chief of Staff makes the final decision on return to flying. We'll keep you flying, don't worry."

"Yes, sir," still looking down.

"Now, I have a letter from Clyde Carlisle."

Boyd opened the letter and read the first paragraph.

"Eight Ball has lost some weight, but he can knock down brush for four hours straight chasing quail, without a rest. He's primed for the season."

Ferguson said, "Here's a South Carolina and a Georgia hunting license, and a letter from the commanders at Fort Jackson and Fort Stewart putting you on their lists – and they're very short lists – to hunt quail on the military reservations there."

"That sounds great," Boyd said, warmth flooding him as he thought about how excited the black lab got with an exploding covey of quail.

"Got some billeting reservations here for the quail trips for you and a guest at the DV suites at Fort Jackson and Fort Stewart."

"Well, uh …" Boyd struggled somewhat, his friend meter was nearly on empty. "I could use some of that."

His mind wandered. Maybe Clyde Carlisle could get some time to go hunting, or he could call Patsy Burke, the waitress he'd met in Sumter. Pulling himself soberly back to the moment, he said, "There's one more thing." He leaned elbows on the table and hesitated, looking at Ferguson.

Very slightly, the boat rocked, and water lapped at the dock.

Ferguson's eyes shifted, alert.

"You guys are gonna call me again," Boyd said. "We both know it. Some shit storm is gonna come along, and you're gonna call. I can't work this way if you hold back. You owe me the whole story."

"Sure," Ferguson said, looking right at him, but he said nothing else.

"Charles Meilland."

He wasn't afraid; Ferreira was there to back him up, and Wolf, and Neville, and Angela. They all wanted to hear it, deserved to hear it. Were going, by God, to hear it.

"OK," Ferguson said and let out a sigh. He leaned into the table.

"We didn't tell the Joint Chiefs, because they have no need to know," Ferguson said. "This is Top Secret, Sensitive Compartmented Information. You'll have to be read into it tomorrow, so when you come by the office, that's another bunch of papers for you to sign. When we put a filter on Meilland's computer, we found out he was sending emails to Israeli Intelligence. The CIA confronted them. He's been a Mossad agent since 1962. Charles Meilland conned the Arabs into sending their hothead jihadists into a death trap in Sudan."

"Why didn't you interrogate him?"

"Oh, I didn't tell you? He died in his sleep two weeks ago."